Dangerous to Know

Also by Tasha Alexander

And Only to Deceive

A Poisoned Season

Elizabeth: The Golden Age

A Fatal Waltz

Tears of Pearl

Dangerous to Know

Tasha Alexander

Minotaur Books ≋ New York

DANGEROUS TO KNOW. Copyright © 2010 by Tasha Alexander. All rights reserved. Printed in the United States of America. For information, address St. Martin's Press, 175 Fifth Avenue, New York, N.Y. 10010.

www.minotaurbooks.com

The Library of Congress has cataloged the hardcover edition as follows:

Alexander, Tasha, 1969–
    Dangerous to know / Tasha Alexander.—1st ed.
        p. cm.
    ISBN 978-0-312-38379-4
    1. Murder—Investigation—Fiction. 2. Aristocracy (Social class)—Fiction.
3. Normandy (France)—Fiction. 4. Rouen (France)—Fiction. I. Title.
    PS3601.L3565D36 2010
    813'.6—dc22

                                                              2010032506

ISBN 978-0-312-38381-7 (trade paperback)

D 10 9 8 7 6 5 4

For Andrew—
Everything, always

No excellent soul is exempt from a mixture of madness.

—Aristotle

Acknowledgments

Myriad thanks to . . .

Charlie Spicer and Allison Caplin, whose insightful comments made this a better book.

Andy Martin, Matthew Shear, Sarah Melnyk, Anne Hawkins, and Tom Robinson, whose tireless efforts never go unnoticed.

Mary-Springs and Stephane Couteaud, who kindly let me stay and write in their beautiful home while I explored the Norman countryside. Without them, this book would not have been possible.

Brett Battles, Robert Gregory Browne, and Bill Cameron, Joyclyn Ellison, Kristy Kiernan, Elizabeth Letts, and Renee Rosen, fabulous writers and even better friends.

Christina Chen, Nick Hawkins, Carrie Medders, and Missy Rightley, each of whom I could not do without.

Gary and Anastasia Gutting, for continuing to read piles of manuscript pages.

Xander, for begrudgingly accepting that Colin can't go around shooting people. Katie and Jessie for not thinking Colin should be shot.

Andrew Grant, for all the happiness in the world.

Dangerous to Know

Although a stranger to the Norman countryside, even I knew a dark pool of blood under a tree was not something a tourist should expect to see during an afternoon ride. Sliding down from the saddle, I put a calming hand on my horse's neck, then bent to investigate more closely. Had I been able to convince myself the congealing liquid was something less nefarious, the sight of a pale hand, blue fingertips extended, would have changed my mind at once. Without stopping to think, I rubbed my abdomen, the remnants of dull pain still present after my own encounter with violence, and took a step towards the body.

Only a few months ago, during what was meant to be a blissful honeymoon, I'd been trapped in a cavernous cistern deep below the city of Constantinople with the villain who shot me in an attempt to keep quiet my discovery that he was guilty of murder. His efforts were, of course, in vain. But although I succeeded in exposing the odious man and saving the life of the sultan's concubine whom he'd held as a hostage, I'd lost something more dear. I did not know when I stepped into the gloomy bowels of the city that I was with child. Now, instead of preparing for an heir, my husband and I were no longer sure we could ever have one.

Colin Hargreaves was not a man to be daunted, even in the face of such tragedy. He insisted that nothing mattered but my recovery and packed me off to France the moment I was well enough to travel. His intentions were the best. His choice of location, however, fell something short of perfection. Not Normandy itself—the lush countryside was stunning, the rich, cream-laden food magnificent—but our lodgings at his mother's house left something to be desired. Although that, too, is not entirely precise. There was nothing wrong with the manor, a sprawling, comfortable building constructed primarily in the seventeenth century by an aristocrat whose descendents did not fare well during the revolution. Rather, it was I who was the problem. At least so far as my new mother-in-law was concerned.

I'd heard nothing but complimentary words about Mrs. Hargreaves, who had fled England after the death of her husband some ten years before. Her own father had been left a widower early, and encouraged his daughter to remain at home—not to take care of him, but because he, not much fond of society, felt she should be allowed to lead whatever sort of life she liked. His fortune ensured she would never need a husband for support. Free from the restraints of matrimony, Anne Howard passed nearly twenty years traveling the world while her girlhood friends married and had children. It was only when she reached her thirty-sixth year that, halfway up the Great Pyramid at Giza, she met Nicholas Hargreaves. By the time they were standing again on terra firma, the couple were engaged. Three days later they married, and afterwards, never spent a single night apart.

I had hoped Mrs. Hargreaves would shower me with the warmth she showed her son—that she would rejoice to see him so happily matched. But after a fortnight of her cool detachment, I determined to spend as much time as possible away from the prickling discomfort of her disapproving stare, and it was this decision that led me to the unhappy resting place of the girl sprawled beneath a tree, her blood soaking the ground.

Bile burned my throat as I looked at her, my eyes drawn from her fingers to her face, framed by hair so similar in color and style to mine we might have been taken for twins. There was no question she was dead, no need to check for any sign of life. No one could have survived the brutal gashes on her throat. The bodice of her dress was black with blood and had been ripped at the abdomen, revealing what seemed to be an empty cavity.

I could look no further.

I wrapped my arms around my waist as my stomach clenched. I wasn't sick, but only because I was too horrified, too stunned even to breathe. Closing my eyes, I tried to focus, to move, to think, but was incapable of anything. I spun around at the sound of a sharp crack, like a branch breaking behind me, then turned back as my horse made a hideous shriek and reared. Realizing I'd neglected to tie him to the tree, I started towards him, but was too late. He'd already broken into a run.

Which left me six and a quarter miles from home, alone with the murdered girl.

Trees and grass and flowers spun around me as I tried to regain enough composure to take stock of the scene before me. I should have been better equipped to deal with this. In the past two years, I had become something of an investigator after solving the murder of my first husband, Philip, the Viscount Ashton, whom everyone had believed died of fever on a hunting trip in Africa. Since then, I'd thrice more been asked to assist in murder cases, the last time while on my wedding trip in Constantinople. Colin, my second husband (and Philip's best friend), worked for the Crown, assisting in matters that required, as he liked to say, more than a modicum of discretion. Because no man could gain entrance to the sultan's harem, he had asked me to work with him in an official capacity when a concubine, who turned out to be the daughter of a British diplomat, was murdered at the Ottoman Palace.

Successful though I'd been, none of my prior experience had prepared me for the sight before me now.

I squinted, blurring my vision so the field of poppies beyond the tree and the body melted into a wave of crimson buoyed by the wind. My boot slid on slick grass as I stepped forward and forced myself to look, memorizing every detail of the gruesome scene: the position of the girl's limbs, a description of her dress, the expression on her face. Simultaneously confident and sickened that I was capable of giving a thorough report of what I'd seen, I turned and started the long walk back to the house, my stomach lurching, my heart leaping at every sound that came from the surrounding fields, my legs shaking.

For the briefest moment, I wanted to pretend that I'd seen nothing, wanted to abandon myself to fear. Tears, ready to spill, flashed hot in my eyes, and I dug my fingernails into my palms. Which was when I heard a twig snap. I stopped long enough to see a rabbit scurrying across the path in front of me. And all at once, my fear turned to anger—anger that I no longer felt safe in this place that was supposed to offer respite. Pulling myself up straight, I marched back to the house, ready to tell Colin we had work to do.

It had taken me more than two hours to reach Mrs. Hargreaves's manor, nestled in a tree-filled grove deep in the Norman countryside northwest of Rouen, but as long rides had become my daily habit, I had not thought my absence would strike anyone as unusual. Hence my surprise when my husband rushed to greet me almost as soon as I'd opened the door. Overcome with relief at the sight of him, I collapsed into his arms, hardly pausing to breathe as the story tumbled from my lips.

"You're not hurt?" he asked, patting my arms and taking a step back to inspect me.

"No," I said. He looked me over again and then, seemingly satis-fied, took me inside, sent the nearest servant to get the police post-haste, and sat me down on an overstuffed settee in the front sitting room. His mother, who had been reading, set aside her book and rose with a look of horror on her face.

"What has happened?" she asked.

"Emily has found a body," Colin said, pacing the perimeter of the room. Mrs. Hargreaves remained perfectly still, her face serious, as he recounted for her all that had transpired.

"The police?" she asked.

"Are already on their way," he said and directed his attention back to me. "You're quite certain of the location?"

"I'll have to show you. I don't know that I could explain how to get there," I said. "I hadn't followed a specific route."

"I was frantic when your horse came into the garden without you," he said. "I wanted to look for you but had no idea what direction you'd gone."

"I can't imagine you frantic. You're beyond calm—infuriatingly calm—in the face of danger."

"Not, my dear, when it comes to you. Not anymore." He sat next to me and took my hand, rubbing it with both of his.

"I will not stand for you going all protective," I said. "Next thing I know you'll be sending me to bed early and censoring the books I read."

"I know better than to try to influence your choice of reading ma-terial."

"You do have excellent taste," I said. "I might consider taking your advice."

His mother sighed loudly and all but rolled her eyes. "I wish you would let me send for my physician to look her over, Colin," she said. "Do you think, Lady Emily"—she insisted on addressing me for-mally, her voice full of sharp scorn, to remind me of her disapproval of the use of the courtesy title to which I, the daughter of an earl, was entitled—"that you'll be quite able to bear the sight of the body again? I can't help but worry about the constitution of such a delicate and sheltered girl."

"I'll be perfectly all right," I said, feeling my cheeks blush unpleasantly hot. "Anyone would be upset by what I've seen, but that doesn't mean I'm incapable of doing the work necessary to ensure justice for the victim of this unspeakable crime."

"And am I to believe you are better capable of achieving such a thing than the police?" she asked. I had no time to reply as the butler announced Inspector Gaudet, a towering man, tall and broad, with a beard and handlebar mustache that made his face resemble George, newly created Duke of York, younger son of the Prince of Wales. His size, however, would have dwarfed the duke.

"I assume," he said, crossing to me, "that you are Madame Hargreaves, who found the body."

"*I* am Madame Hargreaves," Colin's mother said, stepping forward. "I believe you want Lady Emily."

"I'm afraid my own lack of a title puts me beneath my wife in rank," Colin said, shaking the policeman's hand. "Hence the confusion. But I must say, there's no other lady I'd rather have precede me."

"Yes, of course," Mrs. Hargreaves said. "At any rate, Lady Emily is the one who found the murdered girl."

"Investigation will determine the cause of death," Inspector Gaudet said.

"There can't be much of a question," I said. "She was brutalized." Before I could stop them, tears sprang from my eyes. I pressed a handkerchief to my face and tried to compose myself.

"I do not need you to describe for me what had been done to her. I've already summoned a doctor to analyze the state of her body. He can't be more than ten minutes behind me. What I need is for you to show me the precise location of the scene. Do you feel able to do that?

I understand how difficult all this is." His voice was full of sincere worry.

"I appreciate your concern," I said. "But I'm prepared to do whatever is necessary."

Within a quarter of an hour the doctor and another policeman had arrived, and we were all mounted on horseback, Colin keeping close to my side. Mrs. Hargreaves had debated joining the party, but in the end was persuaded by her son to stay behind. We set off, and it quickly became apparent retracing my route was not quite so easy as I thought it would be. I had followed a path from the house beyond the road that led to the village, but then diverted through fields on whims in search of flowers, or to follow the sound of a particularly fetching birdsong, or hoping to find the peace that had eluded me since the day of my injuries in Constantinople.

"I know it wasn't much farther," I said, frowning. I'd made a habit of timing the length it took me to reach the beginning of the village road—exactly half a mile from the house—and I knew how long I'd been riding at approximately the same speed. Six miles in any direction was not so easy to find, and I made enough missteps—mistaking one field of poppies or flax or wheat for another—that the others began to doubt I would be of any use to them. In the end, I managed to recognize from afar the twisted limbs of the tree that stood over the body.

My horse reared as we approached, sensing, I suppose, my own tension as much as it did the smell of blood that hung in the air. We all slowed, then stopped, no one moving for several minutes. I could not bring myself to look again at the hideous sight.

"I can't believe it," Colin said, dismounting, his voice gruff. "I never expected to see something like this again."

"Again?" Inspector Gaudet stood next to him.

"It's as brutal as the murders in Whitechapel," he said. The collective terror that had descended on all of London when Jack the Ripper stalked women in the East End was something no English man or woman would soon forget. Chills crawled up my arms at the mere thought of his horrible handiwork. "Emily, did you hear anything at all when you found her? Sounds that suggested someone was close by?"

"Only the crack of a branch," I said, hesitating. "But I can't say I was aware of much beyond her."

"She hasn't been dead long." The physician was kneeling beside her. "You're lucky not to have arrived any earlier than you did, Lady Emily."

My eyes lost all focus. I came off the horse and tried to walk towards Colin, but my knees buckled. He stepped back and moved to catch me, but I pushed him away, knowing there was no stopping the inevitable. I ran as far as I could from the tree, then doubled over and was sick.

Gaudet turned to the other police officer. "Organize a search. We must comb the entire countryside. Hargreaves, take your wife home and look after her. She's done all we need of her and ought not trouble herself with this matter any longer."

2

From the beginning of our marriage, I had taken much pleasure from sharing daily routines with Colin. Dressing for dinner, for example, had become a time during which, once we'd shooed away our servants, we could discuss, quietly and in private, the events of the day. Often my husband dismissed my maid, Meg, before I was quite done with her, so he could help me finish fastening laces or buttons or jewelry. The only area into which he would not stray was the taming of my hair. Tonight, our rituals were the same, but I could not stop my hands from shaking long enough to put on the dazzling diamond earrings he had given me for a belated wedding present.

"It's possible you've reached your physical limits, Emily. Now is not the time to be pushing yourself." He took the dangling jewels from me and pulled me up from my seat in front of the vanity.

"Don't be ridiculous," I said. "My only problem is that I'm embarrassed and disappointed in myself." With gentle hands he turned my face to him and carefully snapped each earring into place, then kissed my forehead.

"I've seen men with greater experience and stronger stomachs than yours have more violent reactions than you did today. But I do worry, my dear."

"And you worry me. You promised you wouldn't try to keep me from working when opportunity presented itself." I leaned towards the dressing room's mirror, biting my lips to give them color. I'd chosen a gown of shell-pink satin with a delicate moiré in a darker shade, hoping the hue might enhance my complexion, which looked unnaturally drawn and faded.

"I wouldn't dream of stopping you. But now is not the time—"

"How can you say that?" I asked, pulling one of my hairs from the sleeve of his perfectly cut cashmere jacket.

"First, because you're still recovering from your injuries. Second, there's no reason to think Gaudet needs any assistance. He seems competent." He stood behind me, checking his appearance in the mirror.

"How can you say so? He hardly even interviewed me."

"He didn't want to push a lady in your condition."

"I'm not in a condition anymore."

Silence fell between us. Colin put his hands on my shoulders, bent down, and kissed me. "Forgive me. I didn't mean—"

I reached up and squeezed his hand, watching him in the mirror. "I know." We did not speak much of our loss. It was too depressing and filled me with guilt.

"We don't have to go down to dinner tonight," he said. "I can have a tray sent up to us here."

"No, your mother would never forgive me for ruining her plan to introduce us to the neighbors."

"Given the circumstances, she would understand," he said.

"She would take it as further proof of my inadequate constitution."

"She doesn't mean to be hard on you."

"Of course not." I sighed, the damp air that had crept into the ancient house chilling me to the bone. "But she's certain I'm not nearly good enough for you."

"My dear girl, in her mind, no one could be good enough for me." He kissed me again. "Thankfully, I've never been one to give the slightest heed to other people's opinions. I think you're absolute perfection."

"I shall have to content myself with that. Your mother is a force nearly as unmovable as my own."

"Give her time, my dear, she'll come around. As I was the only bachelor brother, she's come to depend on me since my father died."

"I don't want that to stop," I said. "She should be able to depend on you."

"And she will, but she'll have to get accustomed to sharing me. She's used to having me all to herself much of the time. I admit I thought she'd adjust more readily and am sorry her reaction to you has caused you grief."

"It's not your fault," I said. "Come, though. If we don't head down now, we'll be late, and that will only serve to put her off me all the more."

He took me by the hand and led me to greet his mother's guests. The oldest parts of her house dated from the fourteenth century. Built in traditional style, the low ceilings and beam construction on the ground floor made for cozier surroundings than those to which I was accustomed. The space was warm and welcoming. Long rows of leaded glass windows lined the walls, letting in the bright summer sun. The surrounding gardens were spectacular, bursting with blooms in myriad colors, and enormous pink, purple, and blue hydrangea popped against the estate's velvety green lawns.

Halfway down the narrow, wooden staircase, Colin stopped and gave me a kiss. "I suppose it is for the best that you decided not to take dinner upstairs," he said. "As I do have a surprise for you. Coming, I think you'll agree, at a most opportune time. She's likely not only to cheer you immensely, but also to terrorize my mother into accepting you."

"Cécile!"

"Mais oui," he said.

I'd met Cécile du Lac in Paris, where I'd traveled while in the last stages of mourning for my first husband. An iconoclast of the highest level, she was a patron of the arts who'd embraced Impressionism when the critics wouldn't. She'd had a series of extremely discreet lovers, including Gustav Klimt, whom she'd met when we were in Vienna together the previous winter, and considered champagne the only acceptable libation. Although she was nearer my mother's age than my own, we'd become the closest of friends almost at once, brought together by the bond of common experience. Like mine, her husband had died soon after the wedding, and like me, she had not been devastated to find herself a young widow. Of all my acquaintances, she alone understood what it was to spend years pretending to mourn someone. And even when our histories diverged, it did not drive a wedge between us. When, at last, I came to see Philip's true character, and found my grief genuine, she accepted that as well, even if it was due to empathy rather than sympathy.

Had Colin not informed me of her arrival in Normandy, I would have guessed in short order, as the yipping barks of her two tiny dogs, Brutus and Caesar, greeted us at the bottom of the stairs. Cécile patently refused to travel without them. I rushed down—realizing full well the hem of my dress was about to be the victim of a brutal attack—and reached for my friend.

"Chérie!" She embraced me and kissed my cheeks three times. "It is unconscionable that you have made me miss you so much and for so long. Paris has been crying for your return."

"I'm beyond delighted to see you," I said, squeezing her hand and then tugging at my skirt in a vain attempt to remove the two sets of teeth bent on destroying it.

"They are terrible creatures, are they not?" She picked them up, one in each hand, and scolded them, Caesar, as always, receiving the lighter end of her wrath. Cécile viewed preferential treatment of his namesake the only justice she could give the murdered emperor. "Ah, Monsieur Hargreaves, is it possible you have become even more handsome?" She returned the dogs to the floor so Colin could kiss her hand while she glowed over him.

"Highly unlikely, madame," he said. "Unless you can see your own beauty reflected in my face."

She sighed. "Such a delicious man. I should have never encouraged Kallista to marry you without first trying to catch you for myself." Soon after we'd met, Cécile had adopted the nickname bestowed on me by my first husband, making her the only person who'd called me Kallista to my face. Philip had used it only in his journals, and I'd not known of the endearment until after his death.

"You flatter me," he said. "But truly, your timing could not be more flawless. I can't think when we've needed you more."

"I've been waiting for the invitation." We had not seen Cécile since our arrival in France. When the *Orient Express* dropped us in Paris, my health was not so good as it was now, and I'd been in too much pain for even a short stay at her house on the Rue Saint Germain. "You are pale, Kallista, but that's to be expected after what Madame Hargreaves tells me you've seen today."

My mother-in-law entered the corridor, a bemused look on her face. "Are you planning to stand out here all night? Do come sit, Madame du Lac," she said. "I'm longing to improve our acquaintance." She looped her arm through Cécile's and led her into a large sitting room, where the rest of the party waited for us. The furniture reminded me of that in Colin's house in Park Lane—functional yet comfortable, elegant in its simplicity. The silk upholstery on slim chairs and a wide settee was the darkest forest green, blending beautifully with the walnut wood of the pieces.

Mrs. Hargreaves made brief introductions—her neighbors, the Markhams, a handsome couple, had already arrived—and dove into eager conversation with Cécile. As they were of an age, it did not surprise me to see them quickly find common ground. I hoped their new friendship might distract her from criticizing me. Colin pressed a glass of champagne into my hand then crossed the room to bring one to Cécile and his mother. I took a sip, but could hardly taste it, still feeling more than a little disjointed, off-balance, after the events of the day. Mr. Markham came to my side.

"Do you find this all quite nonsensical?" He was English, but looked like a Viking—broad shoulders, blond hair, pale blue eyes. "Someone was murdered today and we're all to stand about acting as if nothing's happened? Drinking champagne?"

"It's beyond astonishing," I said, relieved to have the subject addressed directly.

"And you're the one who stumbled upon the body, aren't you?" he asked. "Forgive me. Have I made you uncomfortable? I've a terrible habit of being too blunt."

"There's no need to apologize. Nothing you could say now would make the experience worse." My stomach churned as I remembered the brutal scene.

"What are the bloody police doing?" he asked. "Will the inveterate Inspector Gaudet be joining us for dinner? Will he regale us with tales of his investigation?"

"George, are you tormenting this poor woman?" His wife, slender and rosy, appeared at his side and laid a graceful hand on his arm. He beamed down at her.

"You are unkind, my darling," he said. "I wouldn't dream of tormenting anyone, let alone such a beauty. Lady Emily and I were merely discussing the way everyone is avoiding the topic much on all our minds."

"I can't imagine the tumult of emotions throttling you at the moment," she said. Her English was flawless, but made exotic by her thick

French accent. "But I must admit I'm desperate to ask you all sorts of completely inappropriate questions."

"I shan't allow that," her husband said. "You, Madeline, don't need any fuel for bad dreams."

"He's beyond protective." She beamed up at him. "But so handsome I'm likely to forgive him anything."

"She requires protection," he said. "Anyone would, living where we do."

"Are you afraid the murderer will strike in the neighborhood again?" I asked.

"No, one murder does not make me believe the area's entirely dangerous—not, mind you, because I have any faith in Gaudet's bound-to-be-infamous manhunt. Protection is necessary because the condition of the château in which we live would give Morpheus himself nightmares. Half the time I expect to wake up in the moat and find the entire building collapsed. The one remaining tower has grown so rickety I'm afraid we'll have to tear it down—it's unsafe."

"My love, it's not all that bad," she said. "Structurally you have nothing to fear. Aside from the tower, that is. But that hardly matters. What concerns me is our recent visitor."

"Visitor?" I asked.

"Intruder, more like. We've received a rather unusual gift," he said. "A painting."

"And how is that unusual, Mr. Markham? Are you known to despise art?"

"Quite the contrary," he said. "And you must call me George. There's no use in adopting airs of formality this far in the middle of the country. We're all stuck together and may as well declare ourselves fast friends at once."

"A lovely sentiment," I said. "Do please call me Emily. But why do

15

you disparage Normandy? I can't remember when I've been to such a charming place."

"It is too far from civilization," he said.

"Which is why, perhaps, a kind friend thinks you need art brought to you," I said. "After all, there are no galleries nearby." This drew laughter from them both, and their happiness was unexpectedly contagious.

"What makes it strange, though, is that it was more like a theft than a gift," Madeline said.

"A reverse theft," her husband corrected.

"How so?" I asked, intrigued.

"The painting was delivered in the middle of the night and its bearer left evidence of neither his entry nor exit. He set it on an easel— which he'd also brought—in the middle of a sitting room."

"With a note," Madeline continued. "That read: 'This should belong to someone who will adequately appreciate it.'"

"And this, you see, is why I have no confidence in Gaudet," George said. "He's been utterly useless in getting to the bottom of the matter."

"What sort of painting is it?" I asked.

"A building, some cathedral. Signed by Monet."

"And what has the industrious inspector done on your behalf?"

"He questioned my servants, none of whom could afford to buy a pencil sketch from a schoolgirl, after which he declared himself sympathetic to my lack of enthusiasm for the canvas."

"You do not like Impressionism?"

"No, Gaudet is simply incapable of reading a chap correctly. I adore Impressionism," he said. "We have seventeen works in that style. I bought two of Monet's haystack series last year."

"So the thief knows your taste?" I asked.

"Evidently."

"We've no objection to the painting," Madeline said. "But how am I to sleep when an intruder has made such easy entry into our home?"

"You've every right to be unsettled," I said. "What is the inspector's plan?"

"He's concluded that there's no harm done and no point in looking for the culprit."

"Madame du Lac is great friends with Monet. She could perhaps find out from him who previously owned the work. You may find you've been the victim of nothing more than a practical joke at the hands of well-meaning friends." We called her over at once and relayed the story to her.

"Mon dieu!" she said. "I know this painting well. It was stolen from Monet's studio at Giverny not three days ago—he wired to tell me as soon as it happened. He'd only just finished with the canvas. The paint was barely dry and the police have no leads."

I would not have believed, a quarter of an hour ago, that anything could have distracted me from the memory of the brutalized body beneath the tree, but suddenly my mind was racing. "Was there anything else in the note?" I asked.

"Some odd letters," Madeline said. "They made no sense."

"It was Greek, my darling. But I didn't pay enough attention in school to be able to read it."

My heartbeat quickened with a combination of anxiety and unworthy delight. It could only be Sebastian.

"Your imagination is running away with you entirely," Colin said as he untied his cravat and pulled it from his starched collar. The Markhams hadn't stayed late, and Colin and I had retired to our room soon after their departure, while his mother and Cécile opened another bottle of champagne. "Although that's not a bad thing in the current circumstances."

"How can you not see something so obvious?" I asked, brushing my hair, a nightly ritual in which I'd found much comfort from the time I was a little girl. "This screams Sebastian!"

The previous year, during the season, an infamous and clever burglar who called himself Sebastian Capet had plagued London and never been caught by the police. He moved in and out of house after house in search of a most specific bounty: objects previously owned by Marie Antoinette. When he broke into my former home in Berkeley Square, he liberated from Cécile's jewelry case a pair of diamond earrings worn by the ill-fated queen when she was arrested during the revolution. But he left untouched Cécile's hoard of even more valuable pieces. The following morning I had received a note, written in Greek, from the thief. Later, swathed in the robes of a Bedouin, the devious man imposed upon me at a fancy dress ball to confess he'd been taken with me from the moment he climbed in my window and saw me asleep with a copy of Homer's *Odyssey* in my hand. Correctly determining that I was studying Greek (the volume I held was not an English translation), he had delivered to me, over the following weeks, a series of romantic notes written in the ancient language.

"Capet is not the only person in Europe capable of quoting Greek," Colin said.

"Of course not," I said. "But you must agree the manner of the theft sounds just like him. Stealing a painting to give it to someone who would appreciate it?" I slipped a lacy dressing gown over my shoulders and pulled it close.

"How does that bear any similarity to a man who was obsessed with owning things that belonged to Marie Antoinette?"

"It's the spirit of it! They both reveal . . ." I paused, looking for the right word. "There's a sense of humor there, a clever focus."

"Heaven help me. You're taken with another burglar." He splashed water on his face and scrubbed it clean.

"There is no other burglar. I recognize Sebastian's tone."

"And you remain on a first-name basis with the charming man. Admit it—for you, my dear, there will never be another burglar."

"You're jealous!" I said.

"Hardly," Colin said. "In fact, I don't object in the least to you investigating the matter further. It might prove an excellent distraction."

"Did you really have the impression that Inspector Gaudet is competent?"

"He seemed perfectly adequate." He drew his eyebrows together. "Has he done something to lose your confidence?"

"George wasn't pleased with the way he handled the issue of their intruder."

"Which is why I suggest you spend as much time as you'd like investigating the matter," he said.

"And the murdered girl?"

"Sadly, Emily, she is none of our concern."

5 July 1892

I'm trying my best to tolerate my son's child bride, but the effort would be taxing for a woman of twice my stamina. I realize she's not so young as I imply, but youth, I've always believed, is less about age than experience, and this unfortunate girl has a dearth of it. She's been sadly sheltered for most of her years and perhaps it is unfair of me to expect—or hope for—more from her. Still, given the way Colin had spoken of her, I'd imagined another sort of lady entirely. I thought he'd be bringing me someone who might prove an interesting sort of companion. Instead, I should perhaps have paid more attention to what her first husband fixated on: her appearance. There may be a reason he went no deeper.

She, of course, views things differently altogether, and is quite proud of her accomplishments—imagines herself an independent woman of the world, despite the fact she's the pampered daughter of some useless aristocrat. I don't mean, of course, to insult her father, whom I'm told is a decent man. But I have no use for a social hierarchy that places accidents of birth above merit and achievement. It was my own dear Nicholas's cause, and I've taken it on as mine since his death. Unoriginal, I suppose, to do such a thing. Colin tells me his wife did the same after Ashton died—says that she learned Greek and reads Homer and has a propensity for the study of ancient art. Such endeavors must require a certain aptitude and intelligence, but I've yet to see her demonstrate much ability to accomplish anything beyond reading a seemingly endless supply of sensational fiction.

She is taller than I'd expected.

I woke up early the next morning, the first day since we'd arrived in Normandy that I'd come downstairs before luncheon. The combination of my injuries and my mother-in-law's scorn did little to inspire me to action. But today Cécile and I were to visit George and Madeline and examine the note left by their mysterious visitor, and the prospect filled me with excitement. We rode to their château accompanied by a protective footman, following winding roads that meandered through golden fields and into a small, dense wood opening onto a moat whose water was so clear I could see the rocks settled on its bottom. Branches hung heavy from weeping willows along the bank, and on the far side of the water stood a round stone tower with a pointed roof. It could, I suppose, be described as crumbling.

To say the same about the rest of the château wouldn't be entirely correct; George, it seemed, was prone to exaggeration. This was not the refined type of building found in the Loire Valley or at Versailles. It was more fortress than Palace, a true Norman castle, with an imposing keep. We looped around the water and over a rough bridge, then followed the drive along a tall gatehouse fashioned from blocks of stone and golden red bricks, its windows long and narrow. Defensive walls had once enclosed the perimeter, but now all that remained of them were bits and pieces of varying heights, few much taller even than I, most of them covered with a thick growth of ivy or dwarfed by hydrangea bushes. Long rows of boxwoods lined gravel paths in the formal garden, and the flowers, organized neatly in pristine beds, must have been chosen for their scents, as the air was sweet and fragrant.

"The garden is much nicer than the house," George said, rising from a stone bench and coming towards us, a gentleman with a large, dark moustache at his side. "You'd be wise to stay outside. I can have tea sent to us here."

"You're doing nothing, sir, but increasing my curiosity about the interior," I said. "The exterior is lovely."

"Very medieval," Cécile said, tipping her black straw hat forward to better shade her eyes from the sun.

"If only I had a catapult," George said. "We might have some real fun. May I present my friend, Maurice Leblanc from Étretat?"

The other man bowed gracefully. "It is a pleasure," he said as George introduced us.

"Maurice is a writer—does stories for every magazine you can think of. Excellent bloke."

"If you can overlook my failure to complete law school," Monsieur Leblanc said.

"What sort of things do you write?" I asked.

"I've just finished a piece on France's favorite ghost," he said.

"Ghost?" I asked.

"I'd hardly be inclined to call any ghost a favorite," George said.

"But this one isn't full of menace," Monsieur Leblanc said. "She's sad, lonely, searching for a better mother than the one she had."

"Do tell," I said.

"Years ago, early in the century, there lived, in the small port of Grandcamp-les-Bains here in Normandy, a young mother notorious for neglecting her daughter. She let the girl wander through the village at all hours of day and night, didn't send her to school, could hardly be bothered to take care of her."

"I have heard this story, Monsieur Leblanc," Cécile said. "And find it hard to believe any woman would treat her own daughter in such a manner."

"It wasn't always that way," he said. "But after the woman's husband, a sailor, died in a shipwreck not far from the coast, she could hardly stand the sight of the child. She looked too much like her father, you see, and the grieving mother could not cope. One day, when the girl had begged and begged to be taken on a picnic, they went to Pointe du Hoc, a promontory with spectacular views high above the sea."

"And of course the mother wasn't watching the girl," George said.

"Correct," Monsieur Leblanc said. "And while she was playing, too close to the edge of the cliffs, she slipped and fell to her death. And ever after, there have been stories of people—women—all through France seeing her. She wanders the country in search of a better mother, one who would look after her properly."

"Ridiculous," Cécile said.

George laughed. "Madeline thought she saw her once. Beware, Emily, she may come for you next."

"I'll keep up my guard," I said. "But why does she limit her search to France? Are there no decent mothers to be found elsewhere?"

"There might be, but the food wouldn't be nearly so good," Monsieur Leblanc said, and we all laughed.

A groom appeared from the direction of the barns standing on the opposite side of the grounds from the central building, close to a heavy dovecote built in the style of the nearby tower, all stone, no brick. He took our horses from us as our host led us inside, where Madeline greeted us at the thick, wooden door.

"It's so good of you to come," she said, kissing us both on the cheeks. "I've asked Cook to make a special fish course. We've mussels, as well, and I—"

"They've not come for dinner, darling," George said, stepping forward and taking his wife's hand. "Just tea, remember? And you asked for *douillons*."

"Of course," she said. She spoke with steady resolve, but looked confused.

"No one makes pastry finer than your cook," Monsieur Leblanc said, his voice firm. "I am full of eager anticipation."

"Let's go to the library before we eat." George's words tumbled rapidly from his mouth, as if to redirect the conversation away from his wife's blunder as quickly as possible. "I want to show you the note left by that dreadful man."

"You are confident it's from a man?" Cécile asked. "Do you not believe a woman might be equally devious?"

"I'd like to believe a woman wouldn't be able to climb into my locked house with a painting on her back. Not, mind you, because I consider the fairer sex incompetent or lacking a propensity for crime. But surely a lady with the strength to accomplish such a thing would look awful in evening dress, don't you think?"

"Not at all," I said. "I think she'd be elegant beyond measure, and deceive you completely in the ballroom."

"And would make a most excellent villain. Perhaps I should write about her." Monsieur Leblanc tilted his head and looked into the distance, as if deep in thought. "Only think of the adventures on which she might embark."

"I shall not argue with any of you," George said, leading us through the door into the keep's cavernous hall, its arched ceiling supported by wide columns. The room was overfull of furniture. Around a sturdy table that might have comfortably seated a dozen, eighteen chairs had been set, too close together. Six suits of armor were on display, three separate sitting areas contained settees and more chairs, and on the walls hung a series of tapestries, finely embroidered with scenes of a hunt, the work as fine as that displayed on *The Lady and the Unicorn* set I'd seen in the Cluny museum in Paris.

"How beautiful," I said, standing close to the first panel.

"They've been in the château since the fifteenth century," Madeline said. "We think some long-ago grandmother of mine worked on them."

"This was the center of the original castle," George said. "Twelfth century. And as you can see, no owner has parted with even a shred of furnishing in the ensuing seven hundred years. The room above this serves as our library, but other than that, we don't use the space for much but storage. A manor house was built later, and I've constructed a passage to connect the two buildings. Will you follow me upstairs?

He led us up a flight of hard stone steps to a much smaller room lined with bookcases. The windows were nearly nonexistent, better suited for shooting a crossbow than looking at the view of the garden below.

"It's a horrible space, I know," he said. "Terrible light. But then, there are those who say books should be protected from the sun."

"*Magnifique*," Cécile said. "Functional rather than beautiful. And impenetrable by enemies, I imagine."

"Which was, no doubt, significant to the original builders. Perhaps I flatter myself, but I myself don't feel in imminent danger of being under siege," George said. Madeline laughed and kissed him, blushing when she realized we had all seen her.

"You must forgive me," she said. "I do adore my husband."

"Something for which you should never apologize," I said.

Monsieur Leblanc blinked rapidly and shifted his feet in awkward embarrassment. "This would make an excellent writing space. Few distractions."

"You're welcome to use it any time." Our host riffled through the drawers of an imposing desk fashioned from heavy ebony, pulled out a note, and handed it to me. "For your reading pleasure."

I recognized the handwriting in an instant. There could be no doubt Sebastian had penned it. My Greek, which I'd been studying for nearly three years, was much better now than it had been when I last encountered the clever thief, and I translated the brief phrase at the bottom of the paper:

Ἐχθααίρω τὸ ποίημα τὸ χυ, χλι χόν, οὐδὲ χελεύῳ χαίρω, τίς πολλοὺς ὧδε χαὶ ὧδε φέρει· Μισῶ χαὶ περίφοιτου ἐρώμευου, οὔτ᾽ ἀπὸ χρΰης πίνωω· σιΧχαίνω πάντα τὰ δημόσια.

"*. . . I drink not from the fountain; I loathe everything popular.*"

The passage had to be from the *Greek Anthology*, a collection of ancient epigrams. Sebastian quoted from it frequently in the earlier missives he'd sent me.

"I have missed Monsieur Capet," Cécile said with a sigh. "He's such a rare breed of gentleman. Refined and focused, clever, but with the sort of dry wit I admire so much. Although after the success of the haystacks, he really ought to consider Monet popular."

"You know this man who is causing our troubles?" Madeline asked. "Is he dangerous?"

"Dangerous? No, not at all," I said. "Sebastian might steal everything valuable you own, but he'd never harm you."

"He'd be more discerning than that," Cécile said. "He'd only take a selection of your best items."

This drew a deep laugh from George. "I've half a mind to invite him back, if only I knew how to contact him. We've far too much crammed in most of these rooms, and the attics are a complete disaster. Would he be interested in furniture, do you think?"

"Darling, you know we can't get rid of anything while *Maman* is still alive," Madeline said. "It would disturb her too much."

"You shouldn't talk about me as if I'm not here." All of us but

Madeline started at the sound of the voice. An elderly woman stood near the doorway, leaning against the wall. I had no idea where she'd come from or how long she'd been standing there. Her gown was of a rich burgundy silk, beautifully designed, an odd contrast to her coiffure—her white hair hung long and wild down her back—and the strained expression on her face.

"Are you the one they've sent to stop her? She's come again, you know. My daughter's seen her, too," she said, crossing to George. "We should, I suppose, be introduced."

Not hesitating in the slightest, George kissed her hand. "George Markham, Madame Breton. I'm Madeline's husband."

A shadow darkened her face for an instant. *"Bien sûr."* Her eyelids fluttered. "It's this dark room. Impossible to see anyone until you're directly in front of them. Who is Madeline? Should I be introduced to her?"

"Madeline is your daughter," George said.

"It's all right, *Maman*," Madeline said, taking the old woman's hand. "Would you like to have tea with us?"

"Tea?"

George put an arm firmly around her shoulders. "It's time for something to eat. We've *douillons,* and I know how you love pears. Come sit with us. I can read to you after we're done."

"She doesn't like the books," she said. "She's crying again and won't stop."

"Who's crying?" I asked.

George caught my eye and subtly shook his head before leaning in close to her. "We'll go for a little walk and you'll feel better. Then we'll have tea."

"I can't stand the crying," she said. "Someone has to make it stop."

"I'm so sorry," Madeline said, turning to us as her husband led the old woman from the room. "My mother's not been well for some time. It's nerves—they plagued my *grand-mère,* too. The doctor tells us there's nothing to be done, and George agrees. He trained as a physician in London, you know, but hasn't had much occasion or need to work. He's the only one able to help her when she has a spell."

"She's fortunate to have him," I said. "But how dreadful for her to suffer so."

"I don't think she has any awareness at all of her condition," Madeline said. "Sometimes she's lucid, and when she is, she has no idea that she's ever not. Eventually she'll remember nothing. By the time my grandmother died, she didn't recognize any of us. But, come, now, I don't want you all to feel awkward. Let's start our tea."

Monsieur Leblanc offered her his arm, and we followed them into a narrow corridor lined with tall windows that ran from the keep to a seventeenth-century manor. Stepping into this newer section of the structure was like entering a contemporary Parisian house. Bright yellow silk covered the walls on which stunning paintings hung at regular intervals. There could be no question of the Markhams' love for art—their collection ranged from Old Masters to Impressionists, grouped by color rather than style. It was a fascinating method of organization, unlike any I'd before seen. A Fragonard beside a Manet, the two Monet haystacks across from a Vermeer portrait.

"Where have you put Sebastian's bounty?" I asked.

"It's just across the corridor," Madeline said. "We'll show you when George returns."

Sitting on a tall, rigid chair, I accepted a cup from Madeline. She must have poured it before we'd arrived—there was no teapot in sight, and the drink had gone cold. Cécile raised an eyebrow as she tasted hers, but said nothing and abandoned the beverage for the *douillon* on her plate. Flaky, butter-filled pastry surrounded a whole pear sweet with cinnamon and sugar, all drowning in crème fraîche. It more than made up for the inadequate tea.

"Have you heard anything further about the murdered girl?" Madeline asked. "Does anyone know who she is?"

"We've been told nothing," I said. "But I would imagine they've identified her by now."

"It is horrifying. Here I am worried about someone breaking in to give us a painting and some poor girl was killed not two miles from me," she said. "It doesn't seem possible. And it's made our intruder all the more frightening. No one in this neighborhood could have done such an awful thing, so this stranger must be the guilty party. And what if he'd gone into a murderous rage while he was in our house?"

"I'm confident Sebastian would never do such a thing—" I began, only to be interrupted.

"I'm so sorry, Adèle," Madeline said, addressing me directly, her eyes open so wide they looked strained, an odd, unfocused expression coming over her as she began to speak. "I did try to contact you about our change of plans, but I'm afraid you didn't receive my note. Would you very much mind if our excursion is only to Yvetot, not Rouen? I've not yet had the pleasure of meeting your friend, Sebastian, but he's more than welcome to join our party."

"I—I'm afraid I don't understand," I said, confused and a bit frightened, unsure what to say or do.

"You know how it is when you're having trouble with household staff. I shall make sure Marie is disciplined firmly," she continued. "She must have neglected to send my note."

Cécile and I exchanged baffled glances while Monsieur Leblanc stared at his plate.

"You must, however, give me the name of your newfound dress-maker," Madeline continued, her voice light and happy. "You did promise and I can't have you keeping secrets from me."

George entered the room, his mother-in-law conspicuously absent, and the moment Madeline saw him, her manner changed. But it wasn't simply her manner—the light in her eyes altered conspicuously. "Apologies," he said. "In the end I thought it best Madame Breton not join us."

"Should I go to her?" Madeline asked, her pretty lips pressed together, her face pale. The transformation unnerved me. She looked entirely different than she had just moments ago and showed no sign of being aware of what had happened.

"She's settled, but I'm sure would enjoy some company," George said. "I was afraid talk of an intruder might upset her."

"Of course," Madeline said. "You're so considerate, my dear. Will you excuse me? I'll go sit with her."

When she'd gone, George took her untouched *douillon* and scooped up an enormous bite. "It's terrible, this trouble with her mother. She's been ill for as long as I've known her, but it's got much worse in the past few years. It used to be she was just a bit batty, but her forgetfulness was almost entertaining. Now, though, it's as if the charming, refined woman she used to be is disappearing entirely."

"How dreadful," I said, wondering if it would be appropriate to mention his wife's apparent lapse in sanity. "And there's nothing to be done?"

"Apparently not." He swallowed another bite of pastry. "I've researched the matter thoroughly. It's wrenching to watch her. Would break the heart of the strongest man."

"Je suis desolée," Cécile said.

"You're very kind," he said. "We did not, however, bring you here to earn your pity. *Maman*'s condition is something we must bear, but expending too much focus on it will serve to do nothing but depress us. Have you finished your tea? I want to show you the painting."

"Monsieur," Cécile said. "Unless I am drinking champagne, I am always finished."

"An admirable policy. I think I should adopt it myself." He ushered us out of the room and down a long corridor. "As you can see, this part of the château is much more livable than the rest. It's almost modern." We entered a grand hall, this one done in shades of green, from the darkest forest to pale lime. In the center, standing on an easel, was Monet's painting.

"Rouen," Cécile said. "One of my favorite cathedrals." Golden tan hues dominated the canvas, the building seeming to soar from the street, the brushstrokes easy and loose.

"I'm afraid I couldn't tell whether it was Notre Dame de Paris or Notre Dame de Rouen. Churches aren't my specialty," George said, continuing forward, a curious look on his face. "This was not here before." He picked up an envelope resting against the canvas, glanced at it, frowned, and handed it to me. My name was scrawled across the front. With shaking hands, I opened it and pulled out the note it contained:

It is good of you to come back to me.

4

Sebastian's arrival excited me more than a little. He amused me, and I rejoiced at having something other than all things tragic to think about. Colin's response, on the other hand, might be less than rhapsodically enthusiastic, and this caused me no small measure of concern. As soon as Cécile and I had returned to his mother's house, I gave the envelope to him. His dark eyes danced when he read Sebastian's missive. "I knew it," he said. "Am I to have a rival, Emily?"

"Far from it," I said, taking the note back from him. The afternoon had turned chill as a bracing rain began, and we gathered in a timbered sitting room in front of a hulking stone chimneypiece to take champagne tea, a concept introduced by Cécile and embraced at once by my husband. He had opened for us a bottle of Moët, and Cécile was inspecting the bubbles in her glass.

"You know, Monsieur Hargreaves, that I much admire our clever thief," Cécile said. "But his every quality pales in comparison to you."

"I do appreciate the vote of confidence, Cécile," my husband said, inspecting an array of hors d'oeuvres on the table before him. *Oignons blancs farcis*, stuffed with herbed roast pork and Gruyère cheese, poached truffles, and a spectacular pâté de campagne. "I'm not surprised in the least, now that we know your old friend is behind this, Emily, that he should have found you. No doubt when he learned you were in France he set about manufacturing a circumstance to bring himself back to your attention. He could have easily determined that my mother is friends with George Markham—it's reasonable to assume two expats living in such close proximity would keep company."

"So he stole a painting to get my attention?"

"I think he stole it to ward off ennui," Cécile said. "His life has undoubtedly become tedious since he's stopped following Emily."

"An excellent point," Colin said. "But now that he—"

"Who is following Lady Emily?" Mrs. Hargreaves asked, entering the room and sitting next to her son.

"An old nemesis, mother," Colin said. "And the man who put the painting in the Markhams' house."

"Sebastian is far from a nemesis," I said. "If you remember, he turned out to be quite good."

My mother-in-law coughed. "Sebastian? You are on a first-name basis with a thief?"

"He's not simply a thief. In the end, he agreed to protect—" I began.

She raised a hand to silence me. "I'm afraid we haven't time for it now, Lady Emily. I've come with business. Are you well enough to speak to Inspector Gaudet? I worried that perhaps this gallivanting about the countryside might have set your recovery back, so I've left him waiting in the corridor while I inquire."

"I'm much better, thank you," I said. "But I do very much appreciate your touching concern for my health." Now it was Cécile's turn to cough, and I caught a wicked glint in Colin's eyes at my ironic tone. His mother disappeared only for a moment, returning with the inspector.

Gaudet nodded sharply at us as he entered the room. "I under-stand you believe you've identified our thief?"

"He's someone familiar to me, yes," I said.

"Has this man a history of violence?"

"No," I said. "None at all. He's more likely to protect someone than harm him."

"My dear," Mrs. Hargreaves said. "I do hope you're not operating under the misapprehension that your limited experience has rendered you capable of judging the criminal mind."

"Emily is more than capable," Colin said. "She knows this man—Sebastian Capet, he calls himself—as well as anyone."

"Do you consider him dangerous, Monsieur Hargreaves?" the inspector asked.

"I would hesitate to consider him in any way until I learn where he was at the time of the murder."

"We are searching for him now," Gaudet said. "Although it seems a hopeless business. He's left no clue as to his whereabouts."

"Have you identified the murdered girl?" I asked.

"*Oui*," he said. "Edith Prier. An inmate who'd escaped from an asylum outside Rouen nearly six months ago. Her family lives in the city and her father identified the body."

Nausea swept through me at the thought. To have found the body of a stranger in such a condition was bad enough. Seeing a loved one so brutally slain would be beyond anything I could tolerate. Plagued with thoughts of the baby I'd lost, my senses all began to swim.

"Have you any leads in the case?" Colin asked.

"None. We've found no evidence, no suspects, no witnesses. But that's why I'm here, Lady Emily. I need you to think carefully about finding the body. I want you to describe for me everything you can remember."

"I've gone over it all more times than I can count, Inspector," I said. "Truly, I noticed nothing out of the ordinary beyond the body itself. I'm more sorry than I can say."

"Surely you weren't wholly unaware of your surroundings?" my mother-in-law asked.

"I'm afraid I was, Mrs. Hargreaves," I said, tears springing to my eyes. "I've rather a lot on my mind, and had not the slightest idea I was about to stumble upon a murder. I do hope you can find it in your heart to forgive me."

Without another word, I rushed from the room and tore out of the house. My chest bursting with anger and grief and regret, I ran towards the tall stone gate, unsure where I planned to go, pausing only when I heard Cécile call out to me.

"*Chérie!* Do not make me run. It will anger me and force me to sic Caesar and Brutus on you, a situation from which no one would benefit, particularly Caesar. The food here does not much agree with him and I fear a few bites of lace would do him in entirely."

This made me laugh, despite myself. "I'm so sorry."

"I had to stop your husband from following you as I wanted a word on my own. But you must know he's terribly upset and giving his mother a good scolding. Madame Hargreaves is being deliberately difficult," Cécile said. "This was not, I fear, a good place for you to seek respite after your loss."

Tears smarted. "So far as she's concerned my losing the baby is just further proof of my inadequacies."

"That unfortunate event may not have endeared you to her, but she can hardly blame you for it."

"Of course she can," I said, sobs coming close together now. "If I'd not been so reckless—if I'd behaved like a lady, as my own mother so politely put it—it never would have happened."

"You saved an innocent girl from a brutal death and rushed into the face of danger without the benefit of knowing the condition in which you were."

"I suspected it," I said. I'd spent much of my honeymoon worried that I might be with child. And, rational or not, I could not help but think my ambivalence towards the subject led me to a disastrous end. Cécile stared at me, standing close.

"You did not cause this. The dreadful man who shot you did. I shall let you torment yourself for precisely three minutes, but thereafter you will lay the blame on him and him alone."

She gave me closer to twenty minutes before she marched me to a secluded spot in the garden and sat beside me on the grassy bank of a sparkling pond. "I'm so sorry . . ." I began.

"Stop at once," Cécile said. "We'll have no more of it. I'll not have you driving yourself mad like poor Madeline."

"It was distressing, wasn't it, when she changed so radically as we spoke to her? But she was lucid nearly all the rest of the time. Do you really think she's mad?"

"She's on her way. There were small things as well as the screeching insanity of that conversation. That tea was undrinkable, and she thought we'd come round for dinner."

"I noticed that as well," I said. "Will she turn out like her mother?"

"I'm afraid so. You, Kallista, have a husband who loves you and friends who would do anything for you. You've suffered a terrible loss, and we're all here for you while you grieve. But do not deliberately make it worse than it is. What married woman do you know who hasn't lost a child? You've got the terrible occasion out of the way early."

"I—"

"And don't act horrified that I'd speak so openly about such things. We both know it's true."

She was right, but it brought me no comfort. I had to let myself feel the responsibility for my actions. Given the same circumstances, given what I knew at the time, I'd make the same decisions again.

Regret was not precisely what I felt. Instead, I was struggling to accept and understand that in some ways I was less capable than my peers. I might be able to read Greek and converse on any number of cultural topics, but I had neither the inclination nor the ability to do what was expected of every woman. And it was this lack of inclination that troubled me the most.

"My mother sent this up for you," Colin said, handing me a book. "If nothing else, it should amuse you." After Cécile and I had come inside, I'd retired early, not staying downstairs long after dinner, preferring the comfort of our curtained, four-poster bed to having to further contend with my mother-in-law. Cécile promised to try to tame her on my behalf, but I had no desire to watch her attempt.

I sat up, took the volume from him, and tried to choke back my laughter. "*Madame Bovary*?"

"She knows it's one of my favorites," he said. "And Flaubert did, after all, live in Normandy."

"Perhaps she hopes it will inspire me to behave as badly as its heroine so that you might be left alone."

"I believe she meant it as a peace offering. And I can think of something better to inspire you." He kissed me. First on the lips, then on the neck. "I can't risk having you sitting around being unremittingly grim all the time."

"You think *Madame Bovary* might make me grim?"

"More like make me grim." He kissed me again, and I knew when his hand deftly unfastened the pearl button at the top of my nightgown it would be a long time before I slept. Even then, although he'd sent me off to sleep in the most pleasant fashion, I tossed fitfully, tormented by my dreams, hideous scenes of the cistern in Constantinople haunting

me, each more terrifying than the reality through which I'd lived. I'd
be trapped underwater, feeling my lungs fill, or I'd be clawing at the
wooden door, unable to open it before rough hands gripped my neck.
I struggled, tangling myself in the sheets, and then screamed when the
sensations became too real—something had pricked my neck and
drawn blood.

And then Colin's arms were firm around me, his voice calm and
soothing as he covered my face with gentle kisses.

"It's all right, my love. You're awake now," he said.

"It's more than a dream," I said, tilting my head back and feeling
for what I was certain was an actual wound. I took his hand and
placed it on the torn skin.

"That's no small scratch," he said, lighting the lamp on our bedside table. "What have you done to yourself?"

I reached for the floor to collect a pillow I must have flung from
the bed while I was dreaming, but instead of picking it up I gasped,
my heart pounding and my eyes throbbing as I looked at something
just out of my reach: a single rose with a small piece of paper wrapped
around its stem. I touched the scrape on my neck and knew the in-
strument of the injury was a thorn. Colin, reaching from behind me,
scooped up the offending flower.

"This best not be from your admirer."

"Sebastian? Who else do you suspect would creep into my bedroom? He does have a history of doing just that."

"*Our* bedroom." He handed me the paper without looking at it.
"What does it say?"

I read aloud:

Κε χροπὶ ῥαῖνε πολύδροσον ἱ χμάδα Βά χχου, ῥαῖνε,
δροσιζέαθω συμβολι χὴ πρόποσις· Σιγάσθω Ζήνων ὁ σοφός,
χύ χνος, ἅ τε Κλεάνθους μοῦσα· μέλοι δ' ἡμῖν ὁ γλυ χύπι χρος
Ἔρως.

"Jar of Athens, drip the dewy juice of wine, drip, let the feast to which all bring their share be wetted as with dew; be silenced the swan, sage Zeno, and the Muse of Cleanthes, and let bitter-sweet Love be our concern."

I've missed you.

My husband leapt out of bed with inhuman speed. In a few steps he was at the window, which I'd watched him shut before we'd retired. It was still closed and the shutters locked.

"Bloody hell!" He spun around and started for the dressing room. "Light the lamps, Emily. I want to make sure he's not hiding somewhere." Once he left our chamber, he crept as quietly as our intrepid intruder must have, not wanting to scare him off should he still be inside. Colin's talent for stealth was extraordinary—neither his mother nor Cécile woke when he entered their rooms. But his search was to no avail. There was no sign of Sebastian in our room, nor anywhere else in the house. Confident no one was lurking nearby, Colin tucked me into bed, but did not crawl in next to me. Instead, he perched on a chair near the window. The shadows under his eyes the next morning told me he'd not let himself sleep.

We had the sunny breakfast room to ourselves, having come down at a ridiculous hour. Not, however, too early for the excellent cook, whose warm, buttery brioche tempted me the instant I sat down. I took one from the large basket looming in the center of the table, broke it apart, and slathered more creamy butter seasoned with flakes of sea salt on the steaming halves.

"So your mother knows nothing yet?" I asked.

"No," Colin said. "I saw no need to disturb her. There will be plenty of time for upset once she wakes. I'll take care of everything with her— you need not trouble yourself about it."

"At least you can assure her Sebastian is harmless."

"We don't know that, Emily. We've no idea what he's been up to since we last encountered him."

"Surely you don't think he's capable of murder?"

"You know me well enough to expect I would categorically refuse ruling out viable options until they're proven impossible."

Colin, who did discreet work for Buckingham Palace, was one of the best agents in the empire. He handled difficult cases, often involving matters that needed to be kept quiet, and was more spy than detective. We'd become close while I was investigating the death of my first husband, and in the subsequent years had worked together to solve three further murders. But it was only on our last case, in Constantinople, that I'd been allowed to act in an official capacity. Queen Victoria, the Palace had informed me, was pleased I'd caught the man who'd killed the daughter of an English diplomat, but horrified to learn I'd been injured in the process. She did not think it appropriate for me to place myself in the line of danger again.

Her position, no doubt, was a direct result of the influence of my own mother, who had, in her youth, served as a lady-in-waiting to Her Majesty. They remained close, and neither hid her irritation when Colin and I had eloped on the Greek island of Santorini rather than taking advantage of the queen's generous offer of the chapel at Windsor Castle for the wedding. My mother made a habit of being dissatisfied with me. She had no tolerance for any of my intellectual pursuits. She found my interest in Greek antiquities and ancient literature inappropriate for a lady, abhorred the idea that I had begun to think about the issue of women's suffrage, and exhibited visible pain at my skills as a detective.

The detecting was, to her mind, the most offensive of my many sins. She objected in principle to anything that might be perceived as a useful occupation. A lady should lead a life of leisure, as should her husband. She did not much like Colin's work, but the fact it was a bit mysterious and had twice led to the queen wanting to knight him (he'd refused both times) vindicated it. Nothing, however, could justify my own involvement in such things.

Colin's mother swept into the room. "You're looking something of a disaster today," she said, glowering at me. She was a striking woman—tall, her hair still more dark than gray, thick and wavy like her son's. Her taste in clothing was impeccable, every item she wore personally designed by Charles Frederick Worth, the father of haute couture and the finest dressmaker in the world. I admired her gown—the waist impossibly tiny, the skirt, a cascade of rich maroon silk, flared and full below her hips.

"I'm afraid we didn't get much sleep," I said.

"If it won't pain you too much, Lady Emily, I could do without impertinence so early in the day," she said, waving away a footman who appeared behind her with a silver dish of poached eggs and reaching instead for a plate of sliced melon.

"I meant nothing of the sort—" I began, looking to Colin for assistance. I was in no humor to apologize when I felt she ought to.

"We had a visitor last night," my husband said.

"A visitor?" she asked.

"I'll leave the two of you to discuss it," I said, excusing myself as he began to recount the story. I preferred not to hear Mrs. Hargreaves's reaction to the violation of her home. Cécile, who felt it indecent to make a habit of rising before noon, was not yet awake, so I decided to call on the Markhams, a spare footman accompanying me just in case the murderer was still in the neighborhood. I decided to walk, not wanting the clopping of a horse's hooves to mask other, more nefarious sounds. Instead of making my way through the woods, I kept to the road, but even so I started at every snapping twig and dog's bark. The servant was twice as nervous as I, and insisted on walking behind me, thinking it was a better position from which to offer protection. But his footsteps caused nothing but more unease. Listening to them made me wonder if Edith Prier had heard something similar as her attacker approached her.

Our pace, fueled by nerves, had increased almost to a run by the time we approached the bridge over the moat at the Markhams'. The footman did not like my French, and refused to reply to any of my attempts at conversation, and I was all too glad to part company with him when we reached the château. He ducked around to the servants' entrance, while the butler pointed me to the garden, telling me I could find his master in the direction of the maze. Thanking him, I made my way around the house to the dovecote, where I slowed as I felt a prickly sensation moving down the back of my neck. I was being watched.

I turned on my heel, but there was no one behind me. I strained to hear anything unusual, but there was only silence. No one lurked in the willows, no one jumped from the shadow of a hedge. Still, the unnerving feeling did not go away. Instead it grew stronger. Stepping closer to the dovecote, I peered with more intensity, but saw nothing. Nothing, that is, until I looked up to a small window on the top floor. A pale face watched me from above, its wide eyes lacking any warmth. It was a child—a girl—who couldn't have yet been five years old. A blue bow peeked out from her blonde hair, and her white dress hung too big from her narrow shoulders. I stopped and stared back, our eyes locked until I jumped when a bumblebee, too interested in the flowers on my hat, flew into my face. When I looked back, she was gone.

"Hello?" I pulled open the building's door. The interior was dark and musty, full of dust and cobwebs, broken pieces of furniture scattered across the floor. My sole response was the rustling and squeaks that could only have been caused by some sort of unwelcome creature. A tightly curving, steep staircase rose across before me, and I started for it, stepping cautiously through the debris. "Is anyone here?"

No reply came. The flap of wings announced the arrival upstairs of what might have been the descendents of the dovecote's original occupants. Moving tentatively, I climbed the stairs, only to find an empty, dirty room. Three pigeons roosted, taking no notice of me, but I heard more scampering from below. Not eager to make the acquaintance of a pack of rodents—if it was packs in which they traveled—I clattered down the steps and pushed through the door, bursting back out into bright sunlight. Above me, the window was still vacant. I saw nothing behind its wavy old panes of glass.

I set off for the maze, my knees wobbling, my hands shaking, the image of the sad little girl—she must have been sad—seeming to hover over me. And try though I might, I could not stop from seeing her in my mind with every step I took. As I approached my destination, I saw George, dressed in a fine linen suit and studying a heavy gold pocket watch.

"That's fourteen minutes," he called to someone—I assumed Madeline, though I couldn't see her—his voice booming. He was standing on tiptoe as if he could somehow make himself tall enough to see over the yew and boxwood hedge that formed the outer wall of the maze. "You'd better hurry." He snapped the watch closed and strode in the direction of an elaborate cast-iron bench, a bright grin on his face. He hadn't spotted me.

"Am I disturbing you?" I asked, crossing to him, an unaccountable rush of relief flowing through me.

"Emily! What a delightful surprise!" He kissed my hand. "You've come at a perfect time. Madeline is in the maze—I'm timing her. I took twenty-three minutes to get through. She's bent on beating me. Would you like to try?"

"It's been a bit of an odd morning," I said. "I'm not sure that losing myself in a maze is quite what I need at the moment."

"Tell me the Norman Ripper isn't stalking you!"

"The Norman Ripper?"

"Have you a better idea of what to call him?" he asked. I felt deep creases digging into my brow. "Oh dear. I've caused you further distress. I've a terrible habit of turning to humor when I find myself upset. Do forgive me."

I wished I could have laughed with him, but found myself wholly unable to divert my emotions. Still frightened, I swayed on my feet. George ushered me to the bench. "It is I who should apologize," I said. "I'm a wretched visitor."

"Not at all. Tell me, though, has something new happened or are you suffering from the memory of that poor girl?"

"Girl?" I realized he meant the murder victim, not the apparition I'd just seen. "No, it's not that. Your thief has called on me," I said, and recounted for him what had transpired the night before.

He listened carefully and then paused, as if considering his reply. "And does Hargreaves think this Sebastian is our murderer?"

"He's not willing to reject any possibilities."

Laughter coming from the maze interrupted us. "You've no chance of winning." It was Madeline, her voice a singsong full of light. George reopened his watch.

"You're going to be disappointed," he called to her, then turned back to me. "Is there any assistance at all that I can provide?"

"Not at present," I said. "Inspector Gaudet plans to find Sebastian."

"And you think that buffoon can accomplish such a thing?"

"Only if he has my husband's help."

"Ah. Which leaves you alone to remember gruesome sights. I'm so terribly sorry, Emily," he said, and placed a light hand on my arm.

"We can't have you feeling morbid. I shall make it my mission to entertain and distract you."

"You're too kind."

"Not at all. I accept it as my moral duty. What English gentleman could do otherwise? I shall start by insisting you take tea with me. And Madeline, of course." His voice rose. "Who has now no chance at defeating me. Perhaps together the two of you can earn bragging rights."

Madeline appeared, stepping out from behind the tall, carefully manicured hedge. "I'm capable of timing things too, my dear," she said. "I bested you by three and a quarter minutes."

George laughed. "And so you have. I knew I shouldn't let you have a watch." He embraced her, kissed her on both cheeks, and took her hand. "Inside. We're all in dire need of tea."

"Have it sent out," Madeline said. "It's too beautiful a day to be indoors. And I'm desperate to catch up with Adèle."

George winced as she called me by the wrong name, but quickly pasted a smile on his face. "This is Emily, darling."

"Of course," she said, blinking the confusion out of her eyes.

"You'd like tea outside?" George asked. She nodded. "Your wish, madame, is, as always, my command." With a low bow, he took his leave from us, promising to return with the genial libation and generous portions of hot beignets.

Madeline, once again herself, looped her arm through mine and led me to a soft patch of lawn between the moat and a cluster of topiary pines. "My favorite spot for a picnic," she said, lowering herself onto a large blanket already spread on the ground, books and papers and a handful of freshly picked wildflowers happily scattered across it. I joined her, still feeling troubled, my mouth dry, my skin prickling. Disturbed though I was by the murder, at the moment, the image of the little girl was causing me more distress.

"Are there any children living on the estate?" I asked, suddenly conscious of the possibility of a simple explanation. "One of the servants', perhaps?"

"No," Madeline said, sighing. "George and I have faced a number of . . . disappointments. It might appear cold, I know, but I can't bear to have other people's children underfoot. After my fifth . . ." She stopped, bit her lip hard. "One of the under gardeners had a little girl. We gave him notice because it was too painful for me to come upon her playing on the grounds."

"I understand all too well," I said. She asked no questions, required no explanation, but took my hand and squeezed it. "How old was she?"

"The gardener's girl?" she asked. I nodded. "Three, maybe four."

"Where do they live now?"

"Oh, I don't know. We gave him an excellent reference. I've no doubt he easily found another position."

"How long ago was this?"

"Ages ago," she said. "At least six years."

Which meant, clearly, that the little girl in the window could not have been the gardener's daughter. I remembered what Monsieur Leblanc had told us about the ghostly child searching for a mother and shuddered, unsure why I wasn't able to immediately dismiss what I'd seen as a silly offshoot of a ridiculous tale. But something in me, deep and instinctual, screamed to me there was more to the story.

"Gaudet has officially asked me to help him find Capet." Colin's dark eyes flashed serious. It was late and we were snuggled in bed, both of us reading as rain pounded the glass beyond our shutters. I was finding *Madame Bovary* a different book than I remembered, and credited my happy marriage with the change in my opinion. Instead of sympathizing with Emma, I found myself despising her husband and caring nothing for her. I closed the book.

"Have you lost faith in him?" I asked.

"He was on the verge of declaring the search a failure."

"So soon?"

"He's interviewed everyone in the village and no one admits to seeing anything suspicious. Which means, in his mind, that your friend the thief has vanished—he assumes to Paris—never to be seen again."

"It wouldn't be the first time Sebastian has successfully eluded the authorities. Has Gaudet contacted his counterparts in Paris?"

"Only in the most perfunctory way. He's ready to write the whole matter off as unsolved."

"And what about you?" I asked.

"I want to interview Capet before I start throwing around accusations," he said. "I do hope your indefatigable friend can offer a reasonable alibi."

"Sebastian would never kill anyone."

"I hope you're right. But whoever did this is not to be trifled with. He's a brutal, twisted individual," he said. "This is not the first time there have been rumors of the Ripper striking in France. Until I'm confident Capet is not our man, I want you to be cautious in the extreme."

"You think there will be more murders?" I asked.

"I can't promise you there won't be," he said. His words scared me. I deposited my book on the bedside table and curled up next to my husband, grateful for the safety of his arms. I didn't believe for a second that Sebastian was capable of such brutality, but nonetheless was unsettled, and I didn't like the feeling in the least.

7 July 1892

I can't say I much like being scolded by my son. He was quite firm with me yesterday over this business with his wife. I ought to expect it—it's not fair of me to test his loyalty or push him to choose me over her. I'm well aware of that. But juvenile emotions do, on occasion, get the best of all of us. I sent him off with a copy of Madame Bovary *for her. As she's spent so much time traipsing about the countryside she's bound to recognize the setting of the book, and I hope that by choosing what might be considered a controversial title she'll recognize I'm attempting to consider her a woman of superior intellect and modern sensibilities. Whether she deserves such accolades remains to be seen. I long to be surprised by her.*

She does not eat sweetbreads.

6

The situation began to deteriorate from the moment we awoke the next morning. A gnawing feeling in my stomach disturbed me soon after the sun rose, far earlier than I would have liked. I pulled on a soft dressing gown, threw open the shutters covering our bedroom windows, and watched a fine mist begin to lose its struggle with the light making its way through rapidly thinning clouds. Colin, who'd got up before me, stalked out of his dressing room almost as soon as he'd entered it. He was holding a note, from Sebastian, of course. It had been placed on top of the shoes he'd worn the day before and contained a brief message:

> *So sorry we couldn't chat this evening.*
> *I understand you're looking for me.*

My husband, usually all calmness and composure, turned ever so slightly red as he pressed the paper into my hand. "He was here again last night."

I sighed. "It's so very Sebastian."

"He needs to stop." I started to speak but he did not allow it. "Not,

Emily, because I'm jealous or because I believe he's a murderer. But he's a person of interest in this investigation, and the sooner he presents himself with an alibi, the less chance he'll have of being guillotined for the crime."

I swallowed hard.

"I don't mean to be harsh, my dear, but Sebastian's games are not of use to anyone right now—particularly himself."

"What can we do?" I asked.

"Eventually we shall have to find him." He tucked a small notebook into his jacket packet, smoothed his lapels, and ran a hand through his thick hair. "He's unlikely to have gone far. He doesn't want to be away from you."

"How do we begin?"

"We don't. Not now anyway. I've got to meet Gaudet. Scotland Yard have asked for some details pertaining to the murder. If it's the Ripper, clues from this crime might be instrumental in catching him."

"What's your opinion?"

"I would have expected him to keep to cities, given his methods so far. If—and it's a big if—we're dealing with the perpetrator of the Whitechapel murders, I'd be stunned if he'd chosen to stake out new territory in the countryside."

"Is there anything at all I can do to help?" I asked.

"No. You've nothing to worry about today beyond amusing yourself." Kissing me hard on the mouth, he said good-bye and headed down the stairs. I followed and watched from the landing above. His mother was calling to him, but he didn't stop to reply; the front door thudded closed before the footman had time to realize he should have been there to open it in the first place.

Not wanting to draw my mother-in-law's attention, I slipped back into the bedroom and rang for Meg to help me into a riding habit. I had no intention of staying in the house on my own until Cécile had awoken. After my maid was finished, I adjusted the smart tie and smoothed the snug jacket—single-breasted and cut like a gentleman's—then tugged at my collar. I was nearly ready to go when Mrs. Hargreaves appeared in my dressing room without so much as knocking.

"Planning to escape, are you?" Her tone suggested a joke, but her eyes were severe. "A man purporting to be an acquaintance of yours is here. Maurice Leblanc? You'd best deal with him before you leave."

"Of course," I said, my voice low.

"He's an attractive man." Judgment dripped from her voice. "Extremely young. Can't be much older than you."

Anger bubbled in my chest and my face flushed hot. I bit my lip, holding back a sharp retort. But then I felt a calm come over me. I narrowed my eyes and returned her stare. "What are you suggesting, *Belle-mère*?" I'd still not found a comfortable way to address her directly. The French term for *mother-in-law* popped into my head and seemed, in my current state, an excellent, if ironic, choice.

For the first time, she met my gaze with an evenness, a look of respect. A look that disappeared almost as soon as her face started to relax into it. She closed her eyes, pulled her shoulders back, and drew herself to her full height. "I don't deign to make suggestions."

"Then I suppose all I can do is thank you for alerting me to Monsieur Leblanc's arrival." I swished past her, my heart pounding. I half expected her to eject me from the house. My eyes burned and my throat stung as I fought back tears, not wanting her to see the frailty of my straining emotions. And then, all at once, the calmness returned. "You're welcome to join us in the sitting room," I said, looking back to throw her a smooth smile. "He's quite a delightful gentleman."

She did not respond. I considered this a small victory in what was bound to be a most protracted battle. Which was unfortunate. It seemed, perhaps, that mothers and I simply did not get on. It took me several tries before I located the sitting room in which my friend waited. No servants stepped forward to assist me, and I wasn't about to ask for more details from my mother-in-law.

Monsieur Leblanc was on his feet the instant he saw me. I motioned for him to sit, and took a place across from him, a low, marble-topped table between his chair and my settee.

"I've become morbidly obsessed with this murder of yours," he said.

"Please don't call it mine."

"Edith Prier has a fascinating history. She wasn't some pauper left to rot in an asylum. She came from a well-respected and wealthy family."

"Should that make her more or less interesting to me?" I asked.

"More, I think. Given that her family had her committed and then all but forgot her."

"Is that unusual?"

"There are scores of odd rumors about her brother. Her *twin* brother." He frowned. "Something is rotten in all this."

I laughed. "You, monsieur, are obviously an excellent writer of fiction. Perhaps you could combine this crime with our gentleman thief and concoct a truly superb story."

"You're not interested at all?"

"On the contrary, I am. But I've promised my husband . . ." The words trailed.

"I do hope, monsieur, you are not setting up a romantic assignation." Cécile, looking radiant and extremely well rested, glided into the room, Caesar and Brutus trailing behind her. She stood in front of our guest, who had risen to kiss her hand.

"Far from it, I assure you." His eyes lingered on her just long enough to prove his statement true. "But if I may be so bold as to compliment your own beauty and grace—"

"You may not," she said, patting his arm and sitting next to me.

"I shall content myself to admiring you from a distance, then."

"*C'est bien,*" Cécile said. "I anticipate it with great pleasure. But do realize, sir, that I have firm policies, and am absolutely set in my belief that no man below the age of forty can be anything that even begins to approach fascinating."

"I wouldn't dare presume . . ." he began, but she waved him off.

"Enough," she said. "Tell me what you've been discussing." In a few sleek sentences, he described for her his interest in Edith Prier.

"Gaudet said her family is near here," I said. "Do you know them?"

Monsieur Leblanc shook his head. "Not personally, no. Their manor is one of the finest houses in Normandy, and their wealth is enormous. They've also a house in Rouen, and that's where they are now. Madame Prier was the toast of Paris before her husband brought her to the country, and she's done much to bring culture to what she calls *la nature sauvage*. Hires musicians and actors from Paris to perform for her."

"This sounds far too familiar. Is she called Dominique Prier? Née Moreau?" Cécile asked.

"The same."

"I remember her. We came into society at the same time and were fast friends in that fleeting way girls are before they're married. She was charming, if more than a little eccentric. I'd completely lost track of her. I shall have to call and offer condolences."

"I suppose that asking why the family didn't visit Edith in the asylum would not be appropriate on such an occasion?" Monsieur Leblanc asked.

"*Non*, monsieur, it would not be." Cécile shot him the firm sort of look she reserved for unsuitable suitors, but the glint in her eyes suggested she was not wholly uninterested. Encouraged, he pressed on, flirting with her shamelessly.

When Mrs. Hargreaves joined us a few minutes later, the conversation moved to a discussion of household staff, and I took the first opportunity to excuse myself and go off in search of my favorite horse. I didn't want to ride outside the bounds of the estate, so kept within the walls, but the exercise was nonetheless refreshing. The misty rain had stopped, but the air retained a heavy coolness, making it feel more like early spring than summer when I dipped beneath shady trees. I'd then emerge in sunlight again and bask in its warmth. I continued in this manner, tracing the circumference of the stone walls, until I spotted something out of place.

A bright red ribbon dangled from the limbs of a tall, narrow tree. Slowing my horse and then stopping her beneath it, I tugged to remove the envelope attached to its end. Sebastian was not, it seemed, ready to stop playing games.

> You're lovely when you ride, but your beauty has distracted me from my stated purpose, which was to follow your too-lucky husband. He'll never find me, you know. I'll appear when I'm ready.

With a sigh, I refolded the paper and tucked it into the pocket of my neatly tailored jacket. That he was trying to follow me came as no surprise. But I was not about to wait for him to appear. Colin had taught me surveillance techniques; he'd also taught me antisurveillance techniques. Given that we were on a limited property in the middle of the countryside, I knew it couldn't be too difficult to locate Sebastian. The trick would be keeping him from escaping. It wasn't as if I could sneak up from behind, leap on him, and bind him to the nearest obliging tree. Instead, I would have to rely on my wits—and his vulnerabilities.

To begin, I slid off the horse and stood perfectly still, listening for any sign of movement. He couldn't be on horseback—the animal would have been too obvious, and the groundskeepers would have spotted him. On foot, he'd be much slower than I, mounted, and I suspected he wasn't actively following me. He must be waiting, lurking nearby in order to watch me read his note.

Next, considering my options, I debated pretending to be hurt—Sebastian, hearing me cry out and finding me somehow immobilized, would scoop me up and deliver me to the house, where the servants could help me restrain him.

That, of course, would never work. He'd gingerly put me down within earshot of the house and disappear. My mind churning, I snapped the red ribbon out of the tree, regretting for a moment that knocking Sebastian over the head with a rock wasn't a viable option. I leaned against the tree, fingering the smooth satin ribbon, frustration consuming me. And as the feeling grew, it was compounded by everything else bothering me: the image of Edith Prier frozen in my brain, the coldness of Colin's mother, a confused muck of emotion surrounding the baby I'd lost. Just as I verged on being utterly overwhelmed, I saw the solution. If Sebastian admired me as much as he claimed, he would come to my assistance if I were upset. This required no manipulation, no game—only letting him see the honest truth of what I was suffering.

Or at least some of it.

For the first time in months, I stopped censoring my emotions, stopped trying to appear genteel and polite and strong. I sank down to the damp ground, my back against the tree, and I put my head in my hands.

I grieved my lost child.

I despised Colin's mother for her lack of support.

I remembered the hideous gash across Edith Prier's throat.

And I started to cry, heaving sobs that soaked my handkerchief and shook my body to its core. I don't know when Sebastian appeared. I never heard his footsteps nor felt his hand on my shoulder when he knelt beside me. At some point, however, I became aware I was holding a dry handkerchief and realized he'd handed it to me. His eyes were the bright sapphire blue I remembered them to be, and they were looking at me not with concern, but mischief.

"You're as bad as I am, *Mrs. Hargreaves*. Although I gather I'm not to call you that. It's *Lady Emily* now, isn't it? Correct address is so important."

"Don't torment me," I said.

"I'm merely applauding your performance. It was worthy of the Divine Sarah."

"You don't consider her a skilled actress?" I asked, wiping the rest of my tears.

"The finest. I saw her play Cleopatra not two years ago."

"Then you should not compare her to me," I said. "What you see before you is not acting."

"Come, now, you can't expect me—"

"Sometimes, Mr. Capet, all a lady has left is the truth." He was still resting his hand on my shoulder. I removed it and rose to my feet. "I feel a certain responsibility to you—I know not why, particularly as it seems you've abandoned your charge."

Sebastian had promised to look after Edward White, a young boy whom we had both encountered during Sebastian's quest for objects owned by Marie Antoinette. Only a handful of people knew the child's true identity—that he was the direct descendent of the last *dauphin* of France. The Capet family had protected Marie Antoinette's son, Louis Joseph, after his secret escape from the clutches of cruel guards during the revolution, and it was Sebastian's legacy to continue the tradition by looking after Edward. It was a role against which he'd rebelled, but eventually, after learning the boy had nearly been killed by a person with a vested interest in protecting the claims of a pretender to the French throne, he agreed to do his duty.

"I've done nothing of the sort!" he said. "He and his mother are on holiday at the seaside. They're perfectly safe."

"I'm not in a humor to argue with you."

"What's troubling you, my darling Kallista?"

"Don't call me that."

"You have no idea how you wound me." He sidled closer to me.

"You have to stop this, Mr. Capet."

"Darling, I know you call me Sebastian to everyone else. Why cling to formality when we're alone?"

"We shouldn't be alone. It's inappropriate. I want you to come back to the house with me."

"Absolutely not!" He brushed dust from his yellow waistcoat.

"Why must you make everything difficult?" I asked, tears pooling in my eyes. "I cannot take much more."

"Darling, please." He held out a hand; I pushed it away. "Gossip told me of your injuries, but I see that you're well recovered if you're able to ride. Although emotionally perhaps not quite so well as physically. What is troubling you?"

"More things than I care to recount. And if you've any of the qualities of a gentleman you won't press me."

"I shan't press you." His voice, low and gentle, had a rhythmic quality to it, almost musical. "Though it wounds me to think you believe I've any of the qualities of a gentleman."

"My husband feels strongly that you need to present yourself to the police and give an alibi for Edith Prier's murder."

"You don't think I killed her?"

"What is your alibi?"

He heaved a sigh. "When was she murdered?" he asked. "Surely you don't expect me to keep a catalog of morbid events in my head?"

"Sebastian!"

"First name. That's much better."

"Alibi."

"Right. Yes. Let's see . . . Thursday . . . Calais. I took a room at a remarkably dim tavern across from the hotel the Whites were in after a more than usually tedious channel crossing. Terrible weather."

"Can you prove it?"

"If I must. The owner would remember me. We had an infuriating discussion about continental politics."

"Do you have your ticket from the ferry?" I asked.

"I suppose I do somewhere."

"Will you please speak to Inspector Gaudet?"

"That fop?"

"You know him?"

"Only from watching you talk to him." He gave an overdramatic sigh. "If it will release you from even a small measure of stress, I can hardly refuse."

"It will also keep you from the guillotine," I said.

"A not unwelcome perk."

"There's one more thing I need from you." I untied my horse and started to walk. "Come with me."

"Very well. I may as well accept the inevitable. Is the dashing Mr. Hargreaves at home? I've been meaning to call on him for some time."

8 July 1892

An intruder in my house! I know not what alarms me more—his very presence or the fact that I slept so soundly and undisturbed during his visit. So far as any of us can tell, he's taken nothing beyond our sense of security, but I am most displeased. I dislike the violation, even more now that I'm aware he's no stranger to my incorrigible daughter-in-law. It is as if she has brought an unending supply of disturbance with her.

I can't believe I lent a book to a person of such dubious acquaintance.

I've had a letter from Lady Carlisle this morning, pleading with me to return to London. It seems the Women's Liberal Federation, a group in which I've been intimately involved (albeit from a distance) since its inception, is in the midst of heated controversy. They've decided to press forward with an agenda that includes actively pursuing the right of women to vote. All members of the fair sex throughout Britain ought to rejoice at such news. But instead, at least ten thousand of our members have renounced the organization in protest. Rumor has it they're starting a group of their own, one that will not support suffrage, and I'm afraid the Liberal Party leadership may prefer their priorities. What good is fighting for women's rights if those rights don't include being able to vote?

More ruckus beginning outside. I shall investigate and see what new inconvenience is to be heaped upon my household.

The walk back to the house was a short one, and after releasing the horse to a stable boy, I let Sebastian take my arm (only to keep him from trying to dash away) and led him into the drawing room, where Mrs. Hargreaves greeted us with raised eyebrows and an appropriate look of horror. I did detect in her eyes a slight glimmer of hope—perhaps she thought *Madame Bovary* had started to wear off on me. But it was Cécile's reaction that I most cherished.

"*Mon dieu!*" she cried, leaping to her feet and kissing Sebastian on both cheeks. "Those eyes . . . the color of sapphires. Stunning."

"Madame du Lac." He bowed low and kissed her hand with an affected reverence. "It is a delight to no longer be relegated to admiring you from afar."

"I am glad to see you," she said, looking him up and down. "I've always believed that it is a rare and magical thing to find a gentleman of such refined taste. Particularly one who will go to such unspeakably magnificent lengths to satisfy his every artistic whim."

"It is never whim, madame, I assure you. I am driven only by the most carefully orchestrated motivations."

"What a pity Monsieur Leblanc has already taken his leave from us," Cécile said. "I'm quite certain he would have been delighted to make your acquaintance. You might inspire his fiction."

"Fiction?" Sebastian asked. "Is this gentleman a writer?"

"Enough!" Mrs. Hargreaves found her tongue. "Who is this man?"

"Allow me to present Mr. Sebastian Capet," I said. "Mr. Capet, Madame Hargreaves, *ma belle-mère.*"

"*Enchanté,*" Sebastian said, turning his attentions to her. "I've much enjoyed your hospitality. Thanks are long overdue."

"What on earth can this mean? Emily, is this man not a thief? The man who has only just violated the privacy of my home?"

"Such harsh words, good lady." His smile revealed straight, fine teeth. "I assure you I've never taken anything of yours."

"I've asked the butler to send for Inspector Gaudet," I said. "Mr. Capet is here to give his alibi to the police."

"How are you acquainted with this man?" she asked, touching Cécile's arm.

"Primarily by reputation, and I can assure you he is a man to be much admired," Cécile said.

"He broke into my house."

"Now, Mrs. Hargreaves, you don't know that," Sebastian said. "The mere fact that notes from me were delivered to your son and his lovely bride does not prove I was actually here. You give me too much credit. It's entirely possible I paid a servant to do my bidding. Can you really think I would disrupt any part of your extremely comfortable abode?"

I didn't believe him for an instant, but Mrs. Hargreaves's features softened. It was hard not to be charmed by Sebastian's easy smile and affable manners, particularly when one first met him.

"But you just thanked me for my hospitality," she said.

"Which I obviously would have no need of doing had I invaded the seat of your domestic bliss."

"So I'm to forgive your other transgressions because you claim to have stolen nothing from me?"

"Transgressions?" He laughed. "My dear lady, someday I will regale you with tales of my adventures. If, after that, you still find me guilty I will repent and change my ways forever. But now I see our valiant inspector and your illustrious son coming up the path. Will you excuse me? I always like to get boring business out of the way without delay."

He raced outside, greeting Gaudet with an eager handshake. My husband, whose scowl was unmistakable, stood, arms crossed, two paces from Sebastian. I watched through the open window as they spoke, the inspector pulling out a notebook and writing in it furiously as Sebastian talked. I could hear nothing they were saying—the only thing audible to me was Cécile's efforts to convince Mrs. Hargreaves that our intrepid thief was something less than a complete reprobate—but in a short while Gaudet nodded. The pair shook hands again and the policeman walked away without so much as a glance towards the house.

Sebastian, grinning like a wicked child, returned to us, Colin following close behind, as if on guard.

"You're lucky to have had a ready alibi," my husband said to him as they entered the room.

"Did the inspector accept it?" I asked, crossing to Colin, whose lips barely grazed my hand as he kissed it.

"Kallista, darling, could you doubt he would? Your lack of faith slays me." Truly, Sebastian was infuriating! I could see Colin was about to reprimand him, but wanted to make the interjection myself. Otherwise, it would appear not only that my husband was being domineering, but, more importantly, that I myself did not object to the liberties being taken.

"Do not, Mr. Capet, take on tones of familiarity with me. And don't even consider making yourself comfortable," I said, my voice severe. "What did the inspector say about the stolen Monet?"

Sebastian laughed. "It was a trifle, really. No person of the venerable Inspector Gaudet's taste could really believe I'd take such a gauche painting. Besides, he can't prove a thing. My work here is finished."

"Not quite," I said. "We've one more errand ahead of us. I don't share the inspector's gullibility. You're going to apologize to the Markhams and return the painting to Monet."

Mrs. Hargreaves looked askance at me and drew Sebastian over to her. They stayed close, apparently deep in conversation for some time, and as we prepared to set off for the Markhams' château I wondered if she would express an interest in joining us, but she did not.

"I do hope, Lady Emily, that my household can return to a more normal state now that this business is finished," she said. "Added excitement is not what you need right now."

Sitting in the coach, I considered whether her comment suggested a warming towards me. Could she actually be concerned for my wellbeing? Or was I looking too hard to find signs of something simply not there?

The driver slowed as we clattered over the bridge leading to the château, the road cooled by the dark shade of tall willow trees. By the time we reached the house, Madeline had popped her head out a firstfloor window and waved.

"George is in the garden!" she cried. "It's so good of you to visit!"

Colin turned to me. "Could you find him? I don't want to let Capet out of my sight for an instant."

"Of course." I started down the gravel path. All but a few wispy clouds had vanished from the sky as the sun fought to eviscerate the last remnants of damp chill in the air. I turned away from the house, passed through a thick row of hedges, and emerged next to the circular dovecote, built in the same style, and undoubtedly the same time, as the tower. I felt a shiver of cold and rubbed my arms. But there was something else—something that filled me with an uneasy discomfort. My pace slowed, and I looked around. Nothing seemed out of the ordinary, but once again I could not shake the sensation of being watched.

I was afraid to look, filled with an inexplicable dread of what I felt certain I'd see. I stopped walking, breathed slow and deep. But I couldn't resist. Raising my eyes to the dovecote, I saw the small girl with blonde hair, a blue ribbon tied in it, one tiny, pale hand pressed against the window, the other clutching a worn-looking doll.

Rationality rushed from me. For an instant I froze, seized with fear. Another glance at the eerie figure, and I ran through the garden until, panting and sweaty, I found George on a bench by the maze.

"My dear girl, what on earth has happened to you?" he asked, standing to greet me. "Sit down and catch your breath. You look a fright."

"No, thank you, I'd rather stand," I said, trembling. "It's ridiculous, really. Mad." I wanted to blurt out what I'd seen, even though I knew there couldn't have been an actual girl in the dovecote. Last time I'd searched and found nothing. The shivers still running through me, I felt as if I'd seen a ghost.

"Ridiculous how?" He looked past me in the direction of the dovecote. "You're not seeing things, are you? Madeline does sometimes."

"No, no. Of course not." That Madeline saw things did not surprise me, but Madeline was not entirely sane. My mind was racing, spinning, trying to process what I'd seen. I'd lost a baby. My heart and my head were grieving and brought me an image of what? The child I might have had? A girl in search of a mother?

"She tries to convince me the château is haunted. You don't agree with her, do you?" I saw concern—real concern—in George's light eyes and forced a smile onto my face.

"Aren't all châteaux haunted?" I asked, slowing my breath and keeping my tone light. "I thought it was a requirement."

"I certainly hope not," he said. "I've enough to concern myself with trying to keep the roof from falling on my head, not to mention marauding art thieves milling about. The last thing I need is to worry about supernatural disturbances as well."

"It's the marauding thief who brings me to you today. Or, rather, I have brought him to you."

"You have brought him?" His eyes grew wide in disbelief.

"I caught him on Mrs. Hargreaves's estate this morning."

"How did you manage that?" he asked, the concern in his eyes replaced with a spark of astonishment.

"I, Mr. Markham, used myself as bait."

"Daring girl! I want to hear every detail. No wonder you're so flustered. I'd be overwrought."

Taking the arm he offered, I struggled to slow my racing mind. "I want to take him to Giverny, to let Monsieur Monet confront him."

"All the way to Giverny?" He bobbed his head back and forth, pensive. "That's more than fifty miles from here. And there really isn't any question of his guilt, is there?"

"No." I paused, my hands growing cold as we approached the dovecote. "But I confess to having something of a soft spot for Mr. Capet. I'm hoping Monet will perhaps forgive him and leave the police out of it."

"A soft spot for a criminal?" The slightest hint of amusement crept into his voice.

"It's not what it seems," I said. "It's just that when he's not liberating objects from their rightful owners, he pays an invaluable service to a friend of mine."

"Ah, now I begin to see. He is someone's lover."

"Heavens, no! He's offering protection to a child in an extremely vulnerable position."

"Is that so?" he asked. "Whose child?"

"A woman I know."

"This is all most mysterious, Emily. I'm intrigued. Do you have a checkered past?"

"Nothing of the sort." We had passed the dovecote, where the upper window was now empty. "The child's father is dead, so Mr. Capet looks out for him."

"And to ensure his continuing ability to do so, we must travel to Giverny?"

"Yes. We could telegraph Monsieur Monet, but a personal visit could make all the difference. Furthermore, he's a great friend of Cécile's and mine as well. We could picnic in his magnificent gardens."

"Now it's all clear to me—you're looking for an excuse to abandon the dreary halls of Chez Hargreaves. You ladies are not entirely impossible to decipher. Though I think you'd find things much more simple if you told us chaps what it is you actually want," he said.

"You're too clever," I said. I never made a habit of being deliberately opaque about my wishes. Picnicking was, in my mind, a secondary priority, but I saw no point in arguing his erroneous belief. At the moment, I was simply pleased to be away from the dovecote. As we approached the house, I saw Colin and Cécile standing, he placid, she bemused. Madeline, who'd joined them, was engaged in vigorous conversation with Sebastian and looked to be giving him a piece of her mind. When he saw us approaching he all but lunged at George.

"I must beg your forgiveness," Sebastian said, bowing low before him with excessive flourish. "Please accept my apologies. I never meant to disturb your household, only to provide what I believed would be an outstanding addition to your already spectacular art collection."

"I never object to a well-planned prank, sir, but your antics have deeply upset my wife," George said. "Which means I haven't had a decent night's sleep in longer than I care to remember."

"A tragedy, good man, but one that can be remedied." Sebastian turned back to Madeline. "My dear lady, I humbly beg your forgiveness and give you my word that I will never again disturb you."

"What good is the word of a scoundrel?" she asked, stepping toward him and meeting his eyes, smiling. "I couldn't possibly trust you. George, will you shoot him?"

"Not today, dear," her husband replied. "I never shoot on Wednesdays."

"You're a lucky man, Monsieur Capet," Madeline said. "I suppose I shall have to accept your apology."

"My gratefulness knows no bounds," Sebastian said, kissing her hand more slowly than necessary or decent. He knew exactly how to flatter and flirt and make his roguish self irresistible. George was, perhaps, not quite so impressed, but he laughed nonetheless.

"A consummate con man," Colin said, arms crossed, voice low, as he stood close to me. "I do hope you have the sense not to fall for his antics. He's not some romantic anti-hero."

I was not so naïve as to be completely duped by Sebastian. Still, I had to admit his charms did have a certain appeal. Whether Colin needed to know that was something I had not yet decided. "That may be," I said. "But we do need to keep him out of prison for Edward's sake."

"You give him far too much credit, my dear," my husband said. "I could ensure—"

But he wasn't given the opportunity to finish. Madame Breton, the skirts of her golden-colored gown swirling, stepped out of the house. Today her hair was well groomed, swept up in a flat twist, her face relaxed. She beamed when she saw Sebastian.

"Monsieur Vasseur! What a surprise! How we have missed you!"

Sebastian did not miss a beat. All elegance, he bowed, took Madame Breton's hand, and kissed it. "A delight to meet you. But I'm afraid you've mistaken me for someone else."

"*Impossible!*" Madame Breton said. "I could never forget those eyes."

"I should like to think you'd never have reason to," Sebastian said. "I can only wish, however, that I were the gentleman you have in mind."

"*Ce n'est pas possible,*" she said.

"*Maman,* you're confused," Madeline said. "This is Monsieur Capet. He's the one who brought us the painting."

"Painting?"

"Of the cathedral in Rouen." George took his mother-in-law's arm.

"*Oui,* I remember seeing it," she said, her voice strong and full of authority. "He captured the light perfectly. But then, Monet always does, doesn't he?"

"My mother used to paint," Madeline said. "She was an amazing talent. Exhibited with Berthe Morisot once and became quite close to her." Morisot was probably the most famous woman to paint in the Impressionist style, and Cécile was convinced her work had an influence on Manet's.

"I would love to see your canvases," Sebastian said.

"You've no time for anything right now but using your dubious powers of persuasion to convince Monet not to set the police on you," Colin said.

"Have you any idea how far Giverny is from here?" Sebastian said. "Surely you don't mean to leave now."

"We won't leave now," Colin said. "You shall be my guest this evening. We're long overdue for an extensive chat."

All this time I'd paid only half attention to the conversation. What I wanted to know was why Madame Breton called Sebastian "Monsieur Vasseur". So while Colin dragged our increasingly unruly thief into line, I pulled her aside.

"Do you recall where you met Monsieur Vasseur?" I asked, my voice hardly above a whisper.

"I've known him forever." She looked in Sebastian's direction. "Did you not hear me greet him? We're old friends."

Her eyes had taken on a cloudy look, surrounded by deep lines. I could see coherence slipping from her. "Of course," I said, not wanting to cause her further confusion or distress.

"You're a beautiful girl, Marie," she said, scrutinizing me. "But you shouldn't dress above your station. I know you can't possibly have afforded a dress like that on your wages, which can only mean you've an inappropriate gentleman friend. I can't keep you in the household given that kind of behavior. Especially with the child around."

"I—" How was I to respond to this?

"There's no use arguing. My mind is made up."

So I didn't argue, and left the Markhams' château utterly unsatisfied, though not disappointed my career as household staff hadn't amounted to anything.

The plan for our journey to Giverny materialized at a rapid pace. Cécile wired Monet, who replied at once inviting the four of us, even, *"le voleur audacieux,"* to stay with him overnight. But before we could set off, we would have to soldier through an evening that was likely to be interminable. I had not expected Colin would allow Sebastian the run of his mother's house, but didn't anticipate him wanting to lock our unwelcome visitor in a bedroom.

"He's not here to socialize," Colin said, smoothing his lapels as we prepared to go down for dinner.

"I realize that, of course," I said. "But there's no need to be uncivilized."

"My dear girl, how is it uncivilized to want to restrain a man who is a known thief?"

I sighed. "You know how good he's been to Edward."

"This isn't about Edward."

"Well I think it's a terrible mistake to lock him up." I snapped a wide gold bracelet around my wrist. "He's capable of picking any lock and getting in or out of any secured space. All you're doing is putting him in a situation that he will try to use to embarrass you. Don't you think he'd love to escape during your watch?"

"A valid point," he said, kissing me. "You've a brilliant mind, you know. But he's not going to escape. You should have more faith in me than you do in him."

"Have you any doubt that I do?"

"No, but I do like to be reminded now and again." With that, he pulled me to my feet, wrapped his arms around me, and kissed my lips.

"Why do I feel like *you're* reminding *me* of something more than the other way around?" I asked, delicious shivers running through me.

"There are several things of which I'd like to remind you, but I don't have adequate time for even one of them before dinner. You know how I value thoroughness."

"I've always admired your dedication to it," I said. "But now you've made me forget what I was supposed to remind you."

"Excellent. I've addled you. Not a simple thing to accomplish."

"You're the only one capable of doing it."

"Mmmmm . . ." He buried his head in my neck and started kissing it. The sensation was almost too much to bear. I was on the verge of begging him to send our apologies to his mother and tell her I'd come over ill and was unable to go down for dinner when a loud knock sounded through the room.

Muttering something under his breath, Colin opened the door. Giggling, I'd retreated into the dressing room to tame the stray curls that had escaped from my pompadour. My cheeks glowed so bright I feared no one at the table could mistake what had made them flushed. The beauty of being married was that no one would object.

No one save my mother-in-law, who was now standing in my bedroom, having a hushed conversation with my husband.

"You can't expect me to send a tray to his room," I heard her say.

"I certainly can."

"Surely he could dine with us and then you can keep him under watch overnight. Although I must say I don't like the idea of having a prisoner in the house."

"Would you prefer I take him to Gaudet and have him thrown in a cell? He's more likely to escape from him than me. And I know, Mother, that you do not want his escape on your hands." His voice was full of teasing.

"You can convince me to do anything, can't you?" she asked.

I walked into the room. "He's the most persuasive man alive," I said, regretting the words the instant they were out of my mouth.

"I've known that far longer than you, Lady Emily," she said, stiffening and not looking at me.

"Longer, yes," Colin said. "But no one comes close to knowing me so well as *my wife* does." I much appreciated his emphasis on the words.

She was nonplussed. "Am I allowed at least to send him a *nice* tray or do you have him on rations of bread and water?" Her voice changed entirely when she spoke to Colin.

"Feed him as well as you like. Give him cause to rave about your generosity. Serve him everything you're giving to us. In fact, the better fed he is, the more compliant I may find him after dinner. And you know, Mother, that I wouldn't have you embarrassed. This is your home. Treat him however you wish so long as you don't let him out of his room."

Satisfied, she patted his hand and left us to ourselves.

"She despises me," I said.

"It doesn't matter. I adore you."

I would have appreciated a grain of denial, but far preferred the attentions he bestowed upon me instead. We were exceedingly late to dinner.

Colin had spent no fewer than five hours with Sebastian before coming to bed the previous evening, and was surprisingly tight-lipped about the nature of their conversation. They met again in the morning, leaving me to breakfast with my mother-in-law, who was no happier to see me than she'd been the day before. Cécile, perfectly willing to rise early when she had a good reason, managed to converse with both of us, holding two separate conversations at once as we munched on what may have been the most perfect croissants I'd ever tasted.

We boarded the first train to the town of Vernon, which would put us nearly at Giverny. Monet and his longtime mistress, Alice Hoschedé, had bought the house some two years ago, after having spent nearly ten happy years there as renters. Their relationship had started oddly—Alice and her husband, together with her children, had lived with Monet and his first wife, Camille, and the couple's two sons. Ernest Hoschedé spent more time in Paris than with his family, and after Camille's death from tuberculosis, Monet and Alice soon fell in love. They lived together, with all the children, Monsieur Hoschedé more or less keeping his distance. Last year, however, he died, freeing Alice to do as she wished.

In all the time he'd lived in Giverny, whether as tenant or owner, Monet had dedicated himself to improving the gardens, where he spent countless hours painting canvases of exquisite beauty. Cécile had visited him there many times, but I did not know him so well as I did Renoir. She had introduced me to both of them, along with Alfred Sisley and a host of others, when I'd first met her in Paris, nearly two years after the death of my first husband. This new circle of friends, unlike anyone I'd known before, opened my eyes to a world of art and culture and a decidedly bohemian lifestyle, igniting my imagination and intellect.

I already adored the Paris studios in which I'd seen them work and I could not wait to be welcomed into a house about which I had heard so much. We made the short drive from the station through Vernon, crossing the Seine near the ruins of a twelfth-century bridge on which a half-timbered mill jutted into the river between two of the ancient piers. Moments later, we were approaching the village of Giverny, utterly charming, a jumble of stone and half-timbered houses against a backdrop of rolling hills. Cécile tugged on my sleeve and motioned to the back of a long, pink house, its green shutters peeking through a veritable wall of ivy.

"That is Monet's," she said.

He was waiting, leaning against the gate, a cigarette dangling from his mouth, his long white beard brushing against his chest. Alice, next to him, stepped into the narrow road and waved as our carriage approached. From here, there seemed nothing extraordinary about their home. We rushed through introductions and Colin nodded at Sebastian, who presented both himself and the painting, which Monet took from him at once.

"How did you get this?" he asked.

"Trade secret, I'm afraid," Sebastian said. "But I can assure you it wasn't simple, so you may rest easy. It's unlikely anyone with less artistic fervor than I would even attempt such a thing."

"This is meant to endear him to me?" Monet said, looking at me. "To persuade me to forgive him and not set the police on him?"

"Mr. Capet has more charm than sense, it would seem," I said, scowling in Sebastian's general direction.

"Forgive me, good sir. I'm a great admirer of your work," Sebastian said. "I object strenuously to the reaction you've had from certain critics and can assure you that all I wanted was to ensure the painting was in the collection of someone who would appreciate it."

Monet raised an eyebrow. "Is this your best strategy? To remind me of negative reviews and suggest that only a common criminal could find a person to like my work?"

"*Mon dieu, non!*" Sebastian's eyes went wide with horror. "I'm far from a common criminal, my good man. Let me assure you I have the finest taste. I offer Madame du Lac as a character reference."

"Cécile?" Monet's lip twitched and he tugged at his beard.

"His taste is excellent," Cécile said. "And though his methods are questionable, I do think he should be given credit for ingenuity and an admirable boldness."

"We will finish this discussion inside," Monet said. We followed a pavement perpendicular to the house and stepped into a garden magnificent beyond anything my imagination could have conjured. Perfect paths ran from the front of the building, dividing flower beds bursting with daisies, phlox, larkspurs, delphiniums, and asters. Benches placed at intervals were painted the same cheery green as both the house's shutters and the metal trellises straddling the paths. Above all of this, the sky, a crisp and clear blue, set off the bright colors on the ground.

With difficulty, I forced myself away from this vision of floral perfection and followed Monet and Alice up green, wooden steps into the house. We passed through a small corridor that opened into a modest-sized salon decorated entirely in shades of blue. The longcase clock standing in a corner and a cupboard holding gardening books on its upper shelves matched the walls perfectly, as did the upholstery on a charming settee. None of the artist's work hung in the room. Instead, he displayed exotic Japanese prints done, he explained, by well-known artists Hiroshige, Utamaro, and Hokusai. Their variety was spectacular: elegant women at their toilettes, scenes from nature—I particularly liked the crashing waves of the seascapes—animals, rain falling on a bridge, chrysanthemums and bees, peonies and butterflies.

Once we were all seated, Monet scowled at Sebastian. "I cannot have works disappearing from my studio. Your behavior is outrageous, regardless of whatever noble spin you may try to put on your motive."

Had I never before met Sebastian, I would have been taken in by the perfectly poignant look of remorse on his face. His eyes, half-closed and heavy-lidded, drooped. His lips pressed together. He wrung his hands. "Any amends I attempt to make would not be enough. Not even a decent beginning."

"You're right on that count," Colin said.

With a beautifully elegant and dramatic flair, Sebastian whisked a handkerchief out of his pocket and pressed it to his brow. "Motive may be irrelevant, but I assure you, Monsieur Monet, my heart, my soul, want nothing more than to see your work in the hands of those who appreciate it."

"Then perhaps you should change your line of work, Monsieur Capet," Monet said. "Become an art dealer instead of a thief."

"An excellent suggestion, in theory," Sebastian said. "And I've taken the first step towards following your advice."

Colin coughed and I rolled my eyes.

"Yes. Well." Sebastian waved us off with a flutter of his handkerchief.

"I have a note from Mr. Markham, the gentleman who received the painting," I said, handing a sealed letter to the artist, who opened it at once, read, and then laughed.

"The recipient of your so-called generosity is offering more than a fair price for the work," Monet said. Sebastian opened his mouth to speak, but the artist stopped him. "No, monsieur. Do not debase yourself by trying to convince me you negotiated the deal. It's obvious Kallista is behind this. I see her hand in it bright as the sun."

"Any admirer of Kallista's sees her hand in all good things." Sebastian stood and crossed the room to Monet. "Can you find it in yourself to forgive me?"

Alice wrinkled her nose. "You, Monsieur Capet, want to reach a resolution with far too much ease."

"Quite right, my dear," Monet said. "But I'm in a conciliatory sort of mood and inclined to accept his disingenuous apology. What man wouldn't do the same in the face of such happiness? Alice, you see, has at last agreed to be my wife."

"Champagne!" Cécile cried. "There must be champagne at once!"

"This is the best sort of news," Colin said. "When can we expect the wedding?"

"We were married three days ago," Monet said. "I couldn't risk giving her time to change her mind." We all erupted, cheering and embracing them.

"I could not be happier for you both, *mes amis*," Cécile said, kissing him on both cheeks.

"*Merci*," Monet said, moving close to Sebastian. "One more misstep, sir, and you will live to regret it. None of my paintings shall disappear from any location because of a scheme of yours."

"*Bien sûr*," Sebastian said. "I give you my word. If I could just—"

"I think you should not push your luck," I said.

"Some clarification, if I may," Sebastian continued. "I swear on whatever power, being, person, etcetera, means the most to you that I shall never again extract one of your works from its proper home."

"*Proper home* as defined by me, not you." Monet's voice was stern, but not without a hint of humor.

"Agreed," Sebastian said. "But I cannot tell you that I shall curtail all my . . . industry."

"You will not take any painting done by my fellow Impressionists."

Sebastian sighed. "Do you not want me to own anything pretty?"

"You might try buying as a manner of acquisition," I said.

"How pedestrian," Sebastian said. "Really, Kallista, you disappoint me."

Alice disappeared and then returned, carrying a tray laden with two bottles of champagne and six flutes. "Finish this negotiation, my darling husband, and let us turn our attention to celebration." She then opened the bottle and poured glasses for Cécile, herself, and me, leaving the other glasses empty. "You'll get none until you're done with this ridiculous haggling," she said.

I accepted a glass from her. "I wish you years of happiness," I said. We toasted, then left the men to a discussion of whether or not Manet, whose use of black deviated from the technique of the other Impressionists, should be included in Sebastian's forbidden group. Making our way through a bright yellow dining room, we stepped into the kitchen whose walls were lined with stunning blue and white Limoges tiles. Copper pans shone, hanging from their racks, and tall windows thrust open over the garden, a sweet, floral fragrance wafting in through them. Alice gave a series of instructions to the servants, then grabbed a platter laden with cheeses—Camembert and Neufchatel amongst others, along with a crusty baguette—and stepped through a door back outside.

"You have found heaven here, I think," Cécile said, taking a seat at a rough but welcoming table in a pleasantly shaded grove. The day could not have been more beautiful, a handful of puffy clouds dotting the cerulean sky. "Although I do not think I myself could be so far from Paris."

"Not you, Cécile," Alice said, breaking off a piece of the bread and cutting into the soft cheese. "But my dear Claude is miserable when he's not here. I do hope you can stay with us a few days, at least. There's so much on which we need to catch up."

"If I can convince Kallista and her dashing husband to remove poor Monsieur Capet without me, I could be persuaded," she said.

"That could be arranged." I grinned. "I can't thank you enough, Alice, for being so generous in your forgiveness of him."

"It is nothing," Alice said, waving her hand. "The painting is returned—and purchased—and all can be forgot. But I am interested in this friend of yours. He reminds me very much of a gentleman my husband painted years ago. Monsieur. . . . Vasseur, I believe was his name."

"Vasseur?" I asked, springing to attention.

"It's his eyes," Alice said, smiling at the serving girl who'd followed us outside with the rest of the champagne and was now refilling our glasses. "I've never seen any that color. Is it possible your intrepid acquaintance goes by more than one name? Perhaps to disguise his nefarious activities?"

"Surely Monet would have recognized him?" Cécile asked.

"Not necessarily," Alice said. "The portrait was done ages ago. Even before we'd come to Giverny. But we can ask him."

When the men joined us sometime later, I raised the issue at once.

"Him?" Monet was incredulous. "Absolutely not."

"You're quite sure?" I asked.

"My dear girl," Sebastian said. "I do think I'd remember having my portrait painted. Although now you mention it, it's not a bad idea. What do you say, Monet?"

The artist's reply was something akin to a growl, and I let the subject go. I had no reason to doubt Monet's sincerity (or his memory), but Sebastian's credentials were more than dubious. I wanted to talk to him privately, but was not to have the chance. Before we'd all retired for the night, he'd disappeared, slipping into the darkness, leaving no explanation, only a too-flowery note thanking Monet for the excellent wine and continuing to debate Manet's inclusion in the Impressionist movement.

My mood had lightened considerably by the time we left Giverny. It is difficult to be morose or to wallow when in the company of such friends, and their loving cheer was just the remedy for the ills I'd suffered since Constantinople. Fortified and feeling more like myself than I had in months, I was full of happy hope. Cécile had gone ahead with her plan to stay on a few more days, leaving Colin and me to set off on our own the next morning, aboard an early train.

"I can't say I feel keenly the loss of Capet," my husband said, snuggling close to me. "I do adore you on trains. Pity we don't have more privacy."

This brought to mind delicious memories of the time we'd spent on the *Orient Express* en route to Constantinople. "You do still owe me a proper honeymoon. Where shall we go? Egypt?"

"I'm thinking somewhere mundane and tedious, a place where intrigue cannot possibly find us."

"Sounds dreadful," I said, glowing. "Won't we be beside ourselves with boredom?"

"I have a number of ways in mind to keep you occupied."

"Do you?" I asked, scooting even closer to him. "Can we leave now? Please?"

"As soon as I've sorted out what Gaudet needs from me."

After the train arrived at the small station in Yvetot, the market town closest to his mother's house, we directed our waiting carriage to head for the Markhams' château so that we might redeliver Monet's painting to them. George beamed with pleasure when he saw us approach.

"You've caught us outside again. Madeline didn't want to squander weather this lovely," he said, striding across the lawn with his wife to greet us. "We know it can't last with those clouds on the horizon. Dare I hope Monet accepted my offer? The parcel you're carrying fills me with hope."

"No haggling necessary," Colin said, handing it to him.

"You're absolute geniuses," George said. "Will you come inside and help me hang it?"

"Must we right away, George?" Madeline asked. "It's too beautiful to be inside."

"You can stay out if you'd like, darling. I've a hankering for a decent cigar. Hargreaves, indulge with me? We can leave the ladies to whatever it is ladies do."

"I'd be loath to turn down such an attractive offer," Colin said. "If, Emily, you'll forgive me for abandoning you?"

"We're happy to see you go," Madeline said, her face shining. "Ladies need time for gossip as much as men do, and I can't stand the smell of tobacco."

I'd never supported the segregation of the sexes (it seemed, in my experience, the ladies always got the short end of the interesting conversation), and the thought of a decent cigar was more than a little tempting, but I had a feeling George would balk at giving me one. Resigned, I looped my arm through hers and we set off along the gravel path. The lushness of Normandy was a delight. As green as Ireland and rich with flowers in every bright shade: blue and vibrant purple, magenta and gold, orange and white. They grew wild on the sides of roads and paths, tamed only in carefully tended gardens. The formality of the Markhams' grounds was a stark contrast to Monet's, but both were stunning.

Thunder rolled far in the distance, but the sky remained bright. "I don't think we'll be driven indoors yet," Madeline said. "Do you mind if we keep walking? I do love it here, but admit to finding myself lonely sometimes. George is all I have, especially now that my mother's not herself, and his work keeps him busy much of the time."

"Art?"

"At the moment, that's what he's fixated on. Collecting, primarily, at least for the moment. He's always finding what he thinks will be his life's great passion, but it rarely lasts more than a few months, maybe a year."

"Focus can be a difficult thing," I said.

"I did think he'd stick with medicine. He was so happy with it for a while—years, not months. But that, too, lost its luster."

"What else has he pursued?"

"Egyptology," she said, her brow furrowed. "Let's see . . . there was cricket. That was before I met him. And Richard III. He was desperate to know if the king killed the little Princes in the Tower. He did a stint in the Foreign Legion—his adventure year—I missed him dreadfully. Collecting art has satisfied him for a while now, but he's also begun painting."

"Is he good?" I asked.

"He won't show anyone what he's done," she said. "And has made me swear that I won't disturb his studio."

"Is it in the house?"

"No." She shook her head. "One of the outbuildings near the dovecote. I don't like going there, so it's easy to respect his privacy."

"Why don't you like going there?"

"I had an accident in the dovecote a few years ago. I'd climbed up to the top—wanted to see the view. But coming down, I slipped. The stairs aren't as safe as they might be. I hadn't realized at the time that I was with child, but almost immediately after the fall it became apparent I was losing it."

"I'm so sorry," I said, a prickly feeling on the back of my neck.

She laughed, the sound tight and strained in her throat. "You must find it bizarre that I speak so openly about such things. But they consume me. I don't know how to begin to stop thinking about it."

"That's completely understandable," I said. "I know all too well how you feel."

"Sometimes, though, I find myself almost enjoying the grief. As if it's what defines me, and I don't know what I'd do without it." She tipped back her head, eyes lifted to the clouds now darkening the sky above us. "It's the only bit of my children I have."

This sent horrible chills running through me, and I found I had no desire to continue the conversation in such a vein. It cut too close to emotions of my own. "I had no idea about your accident," I said. "But I, too, have felt something strange each time I've passed the building."

"Did you hear anything?" she asked, coming to a sharp halt.

"Other than doves, no. Maybe some mice."

"I've heard the weeping of a child."

"When?" I asked, my blood feeling thick with sludge.

"Only a few days ago," she said.

"Was there anyone there?"

"I couldn't bring myself to go inside."

"What about the windows?" I asked. The wind kicked up, bathing us in quickly cooling air. "Could you see anyone standing in them?"

"I didn't even think to look," she said. "The only thing I could do was run. I nearly slammed into George when I reached the garden—and could see at once that he was worried. And I do hate being the source of so much concern to him. So I pretended to be jovial, and challenged him to race me through the maze. I think you came to see us shortly thereafter."

I had indeed. And there could be no doubt that the child I'd seen was the source of the crying Madeline had heard. I considered telling her, but hesitated. Her face, pale and drawn, looked so fragile. She was suffering a milder version—or earlier stage—of her mother's debilitating illness. How could I reveal to her something that would only upset her further? Particularly—and I hated to admit this—when I couldn't be sure that anyone had been standing in the dovecote.

Which made me begin, for the first time, to question the soundness of my own mind. Had grief made me, like Madeline, come unhinged? Had I not seen the ghostly girl—for I now thought of her as a ghost—I should never have considered such a thing. Yes, I had mourned. Yes, I was sad. But I had never thought the trauma I'd suffered could play tricks on my psyche. I glanced at my companion and wanted to tear straight to the dovecote, confronting these irrational thoughts, proving to myself once and for all that this was nothing more than stuff and nonsense.

"Let's go there, Madeline," I said, feeling at once reckless and brave. "Let's see that there's nothing there. That there's nothing to be afraid of."

"Now?"

"Yes, now." I turned on the path, ready to set off towards the hideous place. "We can't be daunted by things that aren't real."

"But what if they are real?" she asked.

"They're not," I said, my voice steady and firm, an illusion that bore no resemblance to the fears clouding my head. The wind blew harder, and the sky lost all its brightness to gray clouds heavy with rain. "You fell because the stairs are old and unsteady and worn. It was a terrible tragedy, but the location can hold nothing over you. There was no one left behind to weep."

Not believing my own words, I took her by the hand and we walked. Soon the dovecote loomed before us, its tall stone walls darker than I'd remembered. Our pace slowed as we approached. Madeline gripped my arm until it hurt, but I welcomed the pain. It kept me from picturing the sad face of the lonely child.

"Must we go inside?" Madeline asked. Her features were strained, her eyes wide and vacant, her hands shaking.

"Yes," I said, trying to muster confidence. "To confirm there's nothing there but an empty space." Three short steps and I was at the door. Just as I touched the handle, lightning cracked the sky and the clouds opened, pouring a sudden and apocalyptic rain on us.

Madeline shrieked, the most blood-curdling sound I'd ever heard. Thunder clapped and she cowered, shivering next to me. There was no need for us to speak. Without a word, I grabbed her and ran, top speed, all the way back to the house.

"You're beyond drenched," Colin said, standing close to me and whispering. "And you do know how fond I am of you drenched." The day we had eloped, we'd stood in the pouring rain on the cliff path high above the caldera on the Greek island of Santorini, a short walk from my villa. The memory warmed me at once, but couldn't send away entirely the fear that had filled me only moments ago. My hands were still shaking.

"I've been more than foolish," I said, leaning close so only he could hear. "Let's get home quickly, so I can confess my sins."

"Sins? I'm all curiosity," he said.

"You're not thinking of leaving." George came towards us, shaking his head as he put a tender arm around his wife. "I cannot allow it. Not when Emily is soaked to the bone. She'll fall ill."

"This is not *Sense and Sensibility*," I said. "Nor *Pride and Prejudice*.

There's an excellent literary tradition of catching the most dreadful diseases in the rain, but as I have need neither for Willoughby nor Bingley, I can assure you my health is perfectly safe."

"Emily, you're too amusing," Madeline said, her voice now light and full of laughter, as if nothing out of the ordinary had happened to us at the dovecote.

"I'm glad to see you're feeling better." I was not quite sure what to make of her sudden transformation. My knees were trembling, my voice unsteady.

"A little rain never hurt anyone," she said. "It was a grand adventure!"

"I don't doubt it," Colin said, shooting me a questioning glance. "But now I must get my wife home."

"You must at least accept a change of clothes," George said, turning to me. "Madeline can find you something to wear. You two couldn't be closer in size." The temperature had dropped radically when the rain started, and the damp cut straight through me. Standing in the cold hall of the château was not helping. I agreed to go upstairs with Madeline, who in short order found me a lovely dress. George had been right—it fit me perfectly, and we joked that we should share clothes more frequently.

I did not, however, feel entirely comfortable while we were changing. Madeline said nothing of substance, and when I tried to broach the subject of the dovecote, she laughed and told me she hadn't been there in months and wanted to keep it that way.

"It's not my favorite place on the estate, you see," she said. "It's silly, I suppose. But it's a ghastly building."

It was as if the conversation we'd had earlier never took place.

We made our way back to the sitting room and the gentlemen, and I watched as she sat, giggling and flirting with her husband. I was not, perhaps, being charitable, but I was horrified and wanted nothing more than to leave. Colin, excellent man that he is, recognized this with no prodding, and within five minutes, we were in our friends' carriage, bound for my mother-in-law's house.

"You know, my dear girl," he said, now that we were at last alone. "I've had enough of other people. If you don't object, I should like to have you all to myself for the rest of the afternoon and evening."

"Your mother won't like it."

"She's survived worse." He traced the line of my jaw with his finger. "I'm worried about you. You don't seem yourself."

"I'm not," I said, looking out the window. "Everything seems off to me. And I keep getting overcome with bad feelings."

"That's to be expected." He took my hand and rubbed it. "You're doing magnificently well considering all you've been through."

"One minute I'm fine, the next I'm in tears. And then there are times when . . ." I sighed. "It's too ludicrous."

"Nothing is too ludicrous to tell me."

"I've reconciled myself to what has happened. I couldn't have done that without you. Obviously your mother and I aren't becoming fast friends, which is disappointing, but not the end of the world. But then there was poor Edith and now . . ."

"Yes?"

"I—I think I saw a little girl in the dovecote at the Markhams'." I described for him exactly what had happened both times I faced the apparition, what Madeline had told me, and our aborted mission to enter the building.

"How odd," he said. "Madeline didn't seem shaken in the least."

"I nearly had to carry her back to the house. She recovered the instant she saw George."

"Do I have the same effect on you?"

"I hope not." I frowned. "I'd never want to have to hide my true emotions from you. She's protecting him by pretending to be happy. He's worried about her nerves, you know."

"He has every reason to be. I can't imagine the horror of watching the person you love above everything drift into a place you can't reach her. It would be worse than losing her entirely."

"You're right," I said. "But I'm tired of being morose."

"So am I." He kissed my palm. "I think, my dear, you need a distraction of some sort."

"Have you something in mind?" I asked.

"We need another bet."

"We're not investigating a crime."

"Perhaps that's the problem," he said. "There is one small thing in which you might be interested."

"You've been holding out on me." I sat forward, my blood feeling alive again. "What is it? Something about the murder?"

"No, my love. Don't get carried away. It's your friend, Sebastian." He drew the name out to too many syllables. "We've decided—"

"We?" I interrupted.

"The Palace and those I work with." He gave a wry smile. "The consensus is a man like Sebastian could be of use to us."

"That's why you wanted to talk to him on your own."

"Precisely."

"How did he react?" I asked.

"Not well, I'm afraid. He balked at the idea."

"And you want to involve me?"

"Who better to take on such a task? I must admit, begrudgingly, that you may be able to turn him quicker than I. And if you do, I shall personally travel to Épernay and collect for you a case of Moët's finest champagne."

"A fitting reward for a French adventure," I said. "And if I lose?"

"Then you collect the champagne."

"It's bound to be heavy. I might need assistance."

"I shall be watching from afar," he said. "I have every faith in your strength and can't imagine you ever calling for help."

He knew me far too well.

9 July 1892

Monsieur Leblanc, this friend of Colin's wife, appeared today while the others had gone to Giverny to visit Monet, who is, evidently, acquainted with Madame du Lac. She's a fascinating woman, Cécile, and one whom I would like very much to know better. The death of her husband certainly did not stop her, or even slow her down. It was not, perhaps, a love match, so our situations may be remarkably different, but I respect her greatly. She surrounds herself with interesting people—artists and scholars and anyone whom she fancies—and appears to constantly be expanding her horizons.

Just the sort of woman I admire. And I must admit the sort of woman it appears my daughter-in-law is trying to become. She does attract interesting friends. Things here will improve (one can only hope) once Cécile returns from Giverny.

At any rate, Leblanc called again, and I had tea with him. He's a struggling writer—publishing in any periodical that will take his work—but his imagination is boundless. I told him I'd always wanted to travel to Tahiti (whence, according to Cécile, her friend Paul Gauguin has fled to paint). For the next hour he spun magnificent tales of the place, inventing characters and intrigues that would amuse any audience. I could not help but notice, however, that one of his creations bore very close resemblance to that thieving friend of Emily's. He was also full of questions about the poor murdered girl. Too curious, one might even think.

But enough of that.

I have written a letter to Gladstone, urging him to throw his weight behind the cause of women's suffrage—to lead the Liberal Party in the direction it ought to be headed. His reply was a disappointment. Despite

DANGEROUS TO KNOW

the fact that his own daughter spearheads our group, he doesn't feel the midst of a general election is the right time to make such decisions. Lady Carlisle will be even less pleased than I.

Politics is a delicate business. I understand that well. But if a party is not willing to stand up for what is right, does it deserve to win back control of the government? The time is coming to take more radical action than we have in the past—and if that must wait until after the election, I suppose there's nothing else to be done. Of course if the Tories win, it will be more of a setback for us.

But afterwards, no matter which party emerges victorious, the Women's Liberal Federation needs to establish itself as its own political entity. And I'm afraid accomplishing such a thing will require nothing short of my personal intervention.

91

Mrs. Hargreaves had greeted me with no enthusiasm when Colin and I returned from Giverny, and I longed for Cécile to rejoin our party. When, two days later, she wired to say she was ready to leave, she asked if I would to meet her in Rouen, where she wanted to pay her respects to her old friend, Madame Prier. I welcomed the invitation, and planned the trip at once.

Cécile's train from Vernon had arrived before ours from Yvetot, and she greeted us on the platform, then ushered us into the Priers' carriage. Narrow medieval streets veered up and down steep hills and along the Seine, no obvious plan to their layout. We passed a square containing a market, fruits and vegetables, fish and cheese amongst the offerings, the noisy buzz of transaction masking the sound of our carriage. Many of the people dressed in the old costumes of the region—the men in full, baggy shirts, the women with tall hats fashioned from delicate lace, making those in modern dress look awkward and out of place amongst the city's medieval buildings. Colin tugged my sleeve, motioning out the window to the tower that imprisoned Joan of Arc during the Hundred Years War, and I shuddered at the thought of her ultimate fate, to be burnt alive in a space that now contained cheery shoppers.

"Frightening how shallow civility runs, isn't it?" Colin asked.

"Such a thing could never happen now," I said.

"I wouldn't be so confident." He leaned back against the seat. "And don't forget it was the English who killed her."

"You're a bloody race," Cécile said.

"Unlike you with the guillotine," Colin teased.

They continued to argue over which country had exhibited more brutal tendencies throughout history while I looked out the window at the Gothic towers and spire of the cathedral, ornate yet delicate spectacles rising to the clouds.

The Priers expected us at their town house, although to use such an English term did not quite fit in Rouen. Situated on a winding cobbled street not far from the *centre ville,* their residence took up nearly the whole block, the first floor of its half-timbered façade leaning forward like the buildings in York's Shambles. This was not a result of wood bending over the centuries. In Rouen, this sort of construction was deliberate, giving additional space on each floor above the ground. Boxes full of red geraniums hung from every window, a stark contrast to what must have been the mood of the home's inhabitants. A somber servant answered the door and showed us into a dark sitting room, its beamed ceiling low. Despite this, it was a pleasant space, cozy rather than dull, elegantly furnished in well-preserved renaissance furniture: heavy cabinets and narrow, elaborately carved chairs with red seat cushions.

"Cécile!" A door opened and in came a petite woman, swathed in black. "It is too many years since I've seen you."

"Dominique, *mon amie!*" Cécile embraced her. "It is a terrible occasion on which to call, but I could not leave you in your grief without offering my condolences."

"It means more than you can imagine to see someone from the old days. And these are your friends?" Introductions sped by—her husband, a lean, dour man, joined us as well—and soon we were all being plied with coffee. I found mine difficult to drink, not because I disliked it, but because a cold sweat had broken out over my body. I wondered if Edith's parents knew it was I who had discovered their daughter's body. Considering whether they did, whether they would ask me about it, contemplating what I would say brought the terror of the scene back to me, and seemed to drain all the oxygen from the room. I swallowed hard, steadied myself, and wished Colin was sitting near enough that I could grab his hand.

"The difficulties we have faced are enormous," Madame Prier said, dabbing conspicuously dry eyes with a black-edged handkerchief and glancing at her husband, who showed no sign of interest in the topic. "All I want now is comfort, not sadness. It's too much to bear. The situation, you see, is unusual. The loss of Edith surpassed any ordinary death."

I had opened my mouth to tell her I understood, that I, too, knew what it was to grieve a victim of murder, when the door cracked open and a girl who couldn't have been a day over eighteen popped into the room. Curvy and petite, she was built like her mother, with shiny black hair, wide-set eyes, and looking nothing like her unfortunate sister. She had eschewed imitating her mother's dress, however, and was clothed entirely in crimson.

"What a relief!" she said, in flawless English. "It's been too long since we've had new faces in the house. It's been unbearable, I tell you."

"Toinette, don't be horrible. We must break you to them gently," Madame Prier said, turning to us, her voice full of apology. "This is my youngest daughter, who is feeling much put-out by the requirements of mourning." Monsieur Prier glowered at his daughter and opened the book he'd been holding on his lap.

Despite her outrageous entrance, I felt a rash kinship to Toinette. Upon finding myself widowed, I'd initially felt relief followed quickly by resentment at being packed away to mourn—feelings that vanished as soon as I discovered the excellent character of the man who'd died only a handful of months after he'd made me his wife, before I'd come to know him at all. No doubt the enormity of the loss of her sister would soon find her, and sadness—real sadness—would come.

"I don't see why we're all pretending," Toinette continued, her crinkled brow at odds with the rest of her perfectly smooth face. "Edith went away ages ago and none of us has thought about her in years. This is a display of guilt, not grief."

"Toinette!" Her father's tone was severe, but he did not look up from his book.

Madame Prier froze, then straightened her back and flipped open a black fan, waving it vigorously in front of her face. "I do not think our guests are interested in your extremely superficial analysis of the subject." I caught Colin's eye and raised an eyebrow. He drew his lips firmly together and gave the slightest shrug.

"You've done an excellent job raising a daughter capable of thinking for herself," Cécile said, rescuing the conversation. "I would have expected nothing less."

"And I should have known you wouldn't be shocked by her," Madame Prier said. "She does, however, need to learn some manners or no one will have her for a wife."

"Which would be a terrible outcome. The threat, however, is not quite enough to make me mend my ways. Perhaps because I've not yet found a worthy suitor," Toinette said. Her eyes lingered on Colin. "You're very handsome. Pity you're already spoken for."

I expected he would have kindly, but firmly, brushed her off, as I'd seen him do a thousand times to awestruck females before. Challenges do present themselves when one is married to the most handsome man in England, but he never gave me cause for concern. This time, though, he sounded almost encouraging. "You are too generous with your compliments, mademoiselle."

"Not in the least, I assure you," she said, flashing a wholly inappropriate smile that revealed impossibly white teeth. "I'm frequently censured for being too hard on those around me." I waited for Colin to flash me a look of something—exasperation, or even apology. He grinned at me, but I was not reassured.

"That's quite enough, Toinette," her father said, his voice knife-sharp.

"Don't force me to send you away." Madame Prier frowned.

"You would devastate our guests if you did," Toinette said. "They'd be dead of boredom in a quarter of an hour. What would you have them do? Sit here quietly and pat your hand?"

"I shan't tolerate any more of this," Monsieur Prier said, slamming his book shut. "I will deal with you later, Toinette." He darted out of the room. Only a moment later the door swung open, this time with a bang, revealing a tall man, broad-shouldered, with close-cut hair and features that while not handsome, oozed all things exotic. His aquiline nose and regal bearing caught the instant attention of everyone in the room as his eyes, dark and liquid, the pupils rimmed with gold, surveyed the scene before him.

"Laurent!" Madame Prier stood and embraced him. "I've been beside myself. Where have you been?"

"Who are these people?" he asked, his words full of fury, with no suggestion of an interest in social niceties.

"Old friends from Paris," she said. "This is—"

"Society callers at such a moment?"

"Oh, really, Laurent, you're such a bore." Toinette's tone would have dismissed a lesser man at once. "They've come to pay their respects to dear *Maman* and poor Edith. Papa, of course, has fled. You can go elsewhere to brood."

"An excellent suggestion." He left without another word before we could be introduced to him.

"I'm afraid he has taken his sister's death badly," Madame Prier said. "They were extremely close as children."

"Twins, were they not?" Cécile asked.

"*Oui*. Like light and dark, the pair of them. Her a sunny day, all fair and bright, him inky midnight. It is all very difficult, you see. Edith fell ill and her sickness became unmanageable for us."

"She was a raving lunatic," Toinette said.

"Toinette, there's no need for that. Too much candor, *chérie*. You must restrain yourself."

"Laurent wanted us to bring her home," Toinette said, ignoring her mother. "But what does he know? He's never cared for anything but his own whims."

Toinette's words seemed to me an excellent description of herself. The initial sympathy I'd felt for her had vanished.

"It must have been a terrible time for all of you," Colin said.

"Far from it." Toinette's beauty would have shamed the brightest sun. "It was much easier to live without her than with her."

Her mother gave her a sharp tap on the wrist. "Enough."

"Are you staying for dinner?" Toinette asked, disregarding her mother entirely and looking at Colin.

"We wouldn't dream of imposing," he said, a rather too dashing grin escaping from his lips.

"It would be so helpful if you would," Madame Prier said. "But whatever you do, you must come back to hear the concert I've arranged for tomorrow evening."

A feeling not wholly unfamiliar—but utterly alarming—was creeping upon me. My thoughts sounded like those better suited to my mother. I raged against the idea of being a person who registered horror at the behavior of others when they veered out of society's norms, yet here I stood in disbelief that Madame Prier would host a concert so soon after her daughter's death. And Toinette now struck me as less a modern woman attempting to assert independence than a shameless flirt whose scandalous behavior could lead only to ruin and devastation.

A perhaps too-discreet voice of reason suggested to me my feelings might have differed if her attentions had met with direct and obvious resistance from my husband. Colin's gaze locked on mine, but I did not see in his eyes what I wanted and felt myself slipping into a sea of unpleasant emotions. Madame Prier reached towards me, concern on her face, her words revealing she'd incorrectly identified the source of my angst.

"Please don't judge us too harshly," she said. "When Edith was taken away, I mourned for longer than you can imagine. It was worse than death, knowing she was alive but inaccessible to reason. Toinette is correct even if her manner is . . . abrasive. Edith's passing is a relief—she's out of whatever strange hell trapped her all these years."

"It's outrageous that you would say such a thing." I hadn't heard Laurent return, but felt the weight of his hands on the back of my chair behind which he now stood, the fire of anger painting his olive complexion. "If you had let her come home, she'd still be alive."

"This is the sort of conversation that can lead to nothing but pain," Colin said, stepping around to hold out his hand to the other man. "Colin Hargreaves. I'm terribly sorry for your loss."

Laurent scowled but let Colin shake his hand. His mother introduced the rest of us, who were granted nothing beyond a stiff nod.

"Are you really going forth with this entertainment tomorrow, *Maman*?" he asked. "Your concert?"

"*Mais oui,*" Madame Prier said. "You know I have already grieved."

"Then stop drowning yourself in mourning clothes," he said. "The hypocrisy is outrageous. Or do you care more about the opinion of your acquaintances than in holding to your principles? You want to *look* as if you grieve."

"I shall not discuss this with you, Laurent," she said.

"And I shall not remain to hear any further nonsense." He turned to me, a look of ferocious intensity shooting from his eyes. "Lady Emily, it is you who found my sister, is it not?"

"I—I—yes," I said, cringing at the question and lowering my eyes to avoid his mother's gaze.

"I've returned to ask for a word with you in private." His voice held no note of query, only demand. He held out his arm, as if to guide me from the room. I did not rise from my chair. "Can you not move on your own? Must you seek permission? To whom do I apply to receive such a thing?"

Unaccustomed to being addressed in such a manner and para-lyzed at the thought of him questioning me about what I'd seen, I said nothing.

"It's perfectly fine, Emily," Colin said, coming close and helping me to my feet, his voice husky and quiet. "He's entitled to know, and it's best done away from his mother."

In principle, I agreed. Principles, however, are one thing in theory and another in practice, particularly when sticking to them means being sent off with an angry stranger to speak about a topic I'd have preferred to forget altogether. "May my husband accompany us?"

"No," he said and opened the door. "*Seulement vous.* This is not a garden party. You've no need for a chaperone."

Colin put a gentle hand on my arm. "Don't make him speak of these things in front of other people. It's too awful." I searched his eyes for sympathy to my plight. He touched my cheek.

"It's just that—"

"Go, Emily," he said. "It's the right thing to do."

Hardly aware of anything beyond the thumping of my heart, I

followed Laurent. Even before he'd closed the door behind us, Toinette's laughter filled the room.

Laurent balled his hand into a hard fist. "He should have taken her instead."

We walked along a small corridor and up three flights of a square turning staircase to a dim, wood-paneled room, whose wide windows afforded a glimpse of the top of the cathedral. In one corner stood a pianoforte, its case covered with haphazard stacks of paper similar to the ones scattered over a long table pushed against the wall. A glossy puddle of black had ruined the pile nearest an overturned inkwell, and the only chair in the room lay tipped on the floor.

"Did she suffer?"

"I—I—" How could I answer such a question? He grabbed my arms and shook me.

"Tell me what you saw. Did she suffer?"

"I didn't witness the crime," I said. My heart pounded and my stomach lurched, my breath catching in my throat.

"But you saw her. You saw what he did. I must know." His eyes, wild and fierce, scared me.

"Yes, she did suffer." Tears spilled from my eyes as I remembered her face and the unnatural angle of her head. "Unimaginable horrors."

"I must know everything."

"I don't know what to say."

"What did she look like?" he asked.

"Brutalized."

"She was strangled first?"

"I don't know!" I said, summoning the strength to push him away from me. "You will not force me to live it again."

"I have to know."

"Why?" I asked. "Do you wish to never sleep again? To be haunted by a ghastly and inhuman image?"

"No one possessed more humanity than she. Even in death she couldn't have lost that."

"You misunderstand," I said, my voice now firm. "I speak of the crime."

"Did you see her eyes?" he asked, clutching my arm in his strong hand.

"Her eyes?"

"Yes."

"I—" I closed my own and remembered hers. "They were vacant. Dark and empty."

He dropped my arm and turned away. "Then he did take her soul."

"No one's eyes look natural after death," Colin said. We'd returned from Rouen without Cécile, who had stayed behind to attend Madame Prier's concert. More, she assured us, out of a desire to observe the family's behavior than an interest in music. At the time of our departure, going home appeared a more appealing option, but after another painful evening with my mother-in-law, I was beginning to question the wisdom of the decision.

"There was something to the way he said it." I felt all knotted up inside. "The idea that the murderer took her very soul . . ."

"You're upsetting yourself unnecessarily."

"When, exactly, did I lose your sympathy?" I asked, pouring tea from the tray we'd had sent to our room.

"You haven't, my dear. But we cannot go on forever concerned with nothing but this business."

"Forgive me. I wasn't aware of a prescribed time for recovering after stumbling upon a ghastly murder scene."

"You know that's not what I'm suggesting. But—and do forgive me, Emily—you haven't seemed yourself for so long. I'm worried that you're . . ."

"That I'm what?"

"I don't know. That you're allowing these events—all of them—to consume you."

"All of them?" Shock did not begin to describe what I felt. It was as if the floor had crumbled beneath my feet. "Surely you don't include the baby?"

"I do," he said, not meeting my eyes. The sound of blood rushing loud in my ears, I took his face in my hands and turned it, roughly, forcing him to look at me.

"How dare you?"

"I don't want to lose you, too," he said. "What are you letting yourself become? You haven't looked at your Greek since we left Constantinople. You've made no mention of any of the myriad projects that used to matter to you. I can't even remember the last time you picked up a book to read without me prodding you first."

Studying Greek after the death of my first husband had catalyzed in me an intellectual awakening and transformed me from a typical society girl into a person I hoped was more interesting and open-minded. For months I'd dedicated myself to translating Homer's *Odyssey* into English, pausing only to focus on the task of cataloging the ancient art tucked away in country houses so scholars might know where to find significant pieces. The work was satisfying and challenging, and meant a great deal to me. It hadn't come as a surprise that I'd abandoned it during my honeymoon, but during the months thereafter, while I recovered from my injuries, I'd not returned to a state of productivity.

"I'm reading *Madame Bovary*," I said.

"Which my mother gave to you. You've not even browsed in the library here once."

"I don't feel welcome in this house."

"When has that ever stopped you before?"

"I've not had to deal with an unruly mother-in-law before."

"You surprised her, that's all," he said. "She expected to find you much different."

"How so?"

"She expected the lady I'd described in my letters. Someone independent and forward-thinking, someone in pursuit of an intellectual life."

"Forgive me if being shot, losing our child, and seeing the mutilated body of a girl who looked like me threw me into a state of agitation!"

"Of course I forgive you," he said. "I'm just asking that you come back, that you stop lingering in a sea of malaise."

"You *forgive* me?" Now outrage kicked in. "Forgive *me*?"

"Did you not just ask me to?"

"I was being facetious!" I shouted and turned on my heel to storm into the dressing room. The door slammed with a satisfactory thud. I sat in front of my vanity and waited for him to follow me. Ten minutes passed without a sound coming from the bedroom. Then a latch clicked.

But not the one to the dressing room. I heard his footsteps, faint, going down the stairs. Trembling, I dropped my head into my hands and wept.

Colin and I did not argue. Very few issues caused even a slight disagreement between us; he'd always been the most sympathetic and generous person I knew. How could the troubles we'd suffered alienate him so thoroughly? I thought of Toinette, petite and lovely, and wondered if he'd been much affected by her. Something about her—her confidence, perhaps—reminded me of Kristiana, the woman he'd loved long before he met me.

Kristiana was sophisticated and elegant, and in possession of a sharp intelligence. They'd met in Vienna, where she lived and worked as an undercover agent. Their relationship, deep and passionate, had gone on for years. Colin had even proposed to her, but she'd refused him, telling him she preferred to remain lovers and colleagues.

She was dedicated to her work, and someone on whom he could always depend. Although he'd never described the details, he had told me enough that I knew she'd faced a host of terrifying and dangerous situations without disappointing him.

And I knew—knew from what had disappeared from his eyes— that my inability to maintain calm and carry on in the face of trouble had disappointed him. I had not lived up to his expectations. Expectations formed by another woman, more strong and capable than myself. Kristiana had died in the line of duty. I'd survived, but only as a member of the walking wounded, a ghost of my former self. Colin had never wanted a weak, simpering wife.

Kristiana should have said yes all those years ago when he proposed to her.

When Meg appeared, ready to dress me for dinner, I refused, sending her downstairs for a tray. I'd hoped Colin would come with it, but he did not. Meg reported that he was sitting with his mother in the parlor. Too upset to touch my food, I asked her to help me get ready for bed. She unlaced my corset without her usual witty commentary on life below stairs. Her face was strained and she hardly spoke as she handed me a soft, cotton nightdress. I'm sure she had no idea what to say.

For the first time in our admittedly short marriage, I went not to the room Colin and I shared, but to the bedroom that connected to the other side of the dressing room. Four hours had passed since I'd stormed away from him, and in that time, he had sent no message, had not enquired as to my well-being, had not tried to persuade me to come downstairs. I crawled into bed before the sun had set, without even *Madame Bovary* to read. I'd left it in the other room. So I waited, my pillow wet from tears, until I heard my husband's footsteps in the dressing room. I held my breath, wondering if he would come to me, straining to listen as he readied himself for sleep: the rustle of his clothes, water splashing in the basin. My heart raced when he fell silent. I could feel his presence on the other side of the door and wanted more than anything for him to fling it open and take me in his arms.

Instead, I once again heard the click of a latch, this time followed by the creak of our bed in the other room as he lowered himself into it, alone. His parents had never spent a night apart after their marriage. Yet another way I'd fallen short of his mother.

I could not sleep, so I paced in front of the window, considering what Colin had said. I could not deny I'd lost all focus, virtually abandoning my intellectual pursuits since the tragedy that ended our honeymoon. I wanted to be the sort of person who rallied, who moved through adversity with grace and purpose, never daunted, always strong, but I'd failed.

I wished I'd stayed in Rouen with Cécile, wished I was back in London with my friends, wished I were anywhere but here. With a sigh, I leaned out the window, breathing in the cool night air. The moon hung heavy in the sky, silvery clouds blurring its edges, but not dulling the light it sent slicing through the night. The room Colin and I shared overlooked the back garden, but this one faced front, and I could see all the way down the drive to the gate. A rush of movement caught my eye in the lane beyond it—a flash of white fabric and a flicker of dark shadow. No sound accompanied what I saw, no crunch of gravel, no measured footstep. I leaned farther out, hoping to hear something, but my attention was met only by silence. Even the trees stood still and quiet, no wind rustling their leaves. Then, just as I started to pull my head back inside, a small cry cut through the night. It might have been an animal, the sound almost like a mew, until it changed to an obvious sob, gulping and hoarse, the voice thin and youthful.

My heart racing, I pulled on my dressing gown and slippers, cracked the door, and stepped into the corridor. My calves tightened as

I tiptoed down the stairs and sneaked to the front door, doing my best to avoid a spot on the floor I remembered to be creaky. Soon I was in the garden, moving carefully along the stone path slick with dew. The clouds had disappeared, but the increase in light did nothing to alleviate the eerie sensation swirling around me. Watching for shadows in the trees and beyond the end of the walk, I continued forward to the road. There, in front of me, only a few paces from the gate, rested a tangled blue ribbon, the color of a summer sky, identical to the one I'd seen tied in the hair of the little girl in the Markhams' dovecote.

I crouched down and stretched my arm through the balusters, but my fingers could not quite reach the dirt-stained satin. Even if they had, I wouldn't have been able to grab it given the force with which my limbs were shaking. I gripped the cold railing and pulled myself up, then swung around against the stone pillars connecting the gate to the wall. My breath coming hard and ragged, I closed my eyes and counted to ten in Greek. Then to twenty. I'd forgot how readily the ancient language soothed me. When I reached thirty I began to wonder if there had been some wisdom in what Colin had said. I needed to go back to my studies, needed to reclaim the things important to me.

This was not, however, the time for such contemplation. I surveyed the scene before me, looking for anything else out of place. The gate was firmly latched and locked, the garden quiet, yet something felt wrong. I stood completely still, my senses alert, my back pressed against the wall, so no one could creep up behind me. Ahead, the path to the house was clear. But on either side I faced mountainous hydrangea bushes and low-hanging willow trees. The distance to the door had grown enormous.

And the eerie cry again cut through the night.

Firmly in the grip of fear, grief and guilt lost their hold on me, and I did not miss them, my companions of these past months. The simple state of being scared was a pleasure in comparison—terror having buried in it a sort of thrill superior to hopeless sadness and a deadening sense of fault. Strengthened by this, I began to walk towards the house, planning to collect the key to the gate so that I might retrieve the ribbon.

I had taken no more than three steps when I heard a soft sound behind me and felt a firm grip around my waist, holding my arms tight, as a hand covered my mouth. I couldn't breathe, couldn't scream. All that was left to me was my legs, and I began thrashing at once, stomping down as hard as I could on my assailant's foot before I kicked backwards, smashing into his shin. Then, with a flash of inspiration, I dipped my head forward and crashed it back into his.

That is, it would have crashed into his had he not released me and stepped neatly aside at just the right moment. I spun around and stared into Sebastian's blue eyes.

"What are you doing?" I asked.

"Thought I'd pop in to remind you there's a killer on the loose, Kallista darling." His grin was maddening. "Where is that husband of yours? Surely he can't approve of you wandering about in the middle of the night in what I must say is a rather shocking state of dress?"

"How long have you been here?" I asked, pulling my dressing gown closer around my neck.

"Just passing by on an evening tour of the neighborhood." He brushed lint from his otherwise spotless tweed jacket. "Your friend Monet has thrown a spanner in too many of my plans. I've had to find other ways to amuse myself."

"How dreadful for you." I made no effort to disguise the sarcasm in my voice. "Is harassing ladies of your acquaintance the only other option you could conjure?"

"Not in the least, I assure you. Just this morning I called on your friend, Maurice Leblanc. Fascinating man," he said. "He ought to abandon journalism for something with more panache. Crime fiction, perhaps. It seems to me all he lacks is the necessary inspiration."

"And I suppose you think you could provide it?"

"I might."

"How did you get over the wall?" I asked.

He laughed. "I could scale that asleep and in chains. If you had any concern for my emotional well-being you'd at least make an effort at challenging me."

"Sebastian—" I began; he interrupted at once.

"How good it is to hear my name on your lips." He leaned close, as if he would kiss me, then pulled back. "If only I'd met you before that wretched Hargreaves got you in his clutches."

"You're not even a decent parody," I said. "But in all seriousness, I need your help. Did you see anyone else on the road?"

"At this time of night in the middle of the countryside? What would a person be doing? Pursuing some sort of nocturnal beast?"

I ignored his ridiculous question. "Did you hear anything?"

"Just you trying to sneak about," he said. "You really ought to work on your technique, Kallista. You're not completely without hope, but someone needs to guide you. There's much I could teach you, you know."

"Much though I appreciate what I'm sure is a remarkably generous offer, I'm afraid I must decline. There are others, however, who could benefit from your expertise."

His eyes widened and his mouth slipped into a crooked grin. "Who would that be?"

"Your queen and country," I said.

He sighed. "Don't bore me with such drivel."

"Wouldn't you like to work on the right side of the law for a change?"

"I know, my dear Kallista, that you must be sporting with me. And if you're not, pray don't tell me. It would shatter all my dreams. The subsequent suffering would be unbearable and could only lead to certain and painful death."

"You're impossible," I said.

"You noticed," he said, swooping into a low bow and kissing my hand. "I'd begun to think you'd lost sight of all my fine qualities."

"I wasn't aware you had any."

"You always were a tease."

"Let go of my hand and be serious, Sebastian. Did you hear anything? A child crying?"

"A child? It's after midnight. Don't be daft."

"I heard her from my window—it's why I came outside." I looked back at the ribbon, about to draw his attention to it.

"You must have been dreaming, Emily," he said. It was the first time I could remember him calling me by my proper name. "And hardly surprising after what you've been through. You're following the ghost of what you lost."

"How did you—"

He kissed my cheek and gripped the stone of the wall, neatly scaling it in a few deft moves. "*À bientôt,* my darling girl. I'll call again soon to make sure you don't require my services more than young Edward."

"Sebastian, wait!" I cried, running after him. He stopped. "What if I need you? What if . . ."

"What if what?" he asked, his voice suddenly tender.

"How can I contact you? What if I have nowhere else to turn?" I felt suddenly very alone.

His eyes softened, his lips parted. He slid back down to me and pulled the cravat from around his neck. "Hang this from your bedroom window and I will come to you at midnight that night, here in this spot."

"And if I'm not in this house?"

"I shall come and find you, somehow. You may depend upon it. Always."

With that he disappeared from sight. I heard the thud of his feet on the other side of the wall, but no footsteps followed. I peered through the gate to see where he must have landed, but he'd already vanished, disappearing into the shadowy night. Sebastian, however, wasn't all that had gone missing: the blue ribbon was nowhere in sight.

14 July 1892
Fête Nationale

I thought it might be amusing to plan some sort of observance of today's anniversary of the French Revolution. I thought, in fact, my ever-disappointing daughter-in-law might be persuaded to participate in planning the festivities—that it might help improve her state of mind.

I was unable to discuss the matter with her last night, however, as she kept to her bed all evening due to some sort of poorly explained ailment—the sort of thing that lies somewhere between general malaise and a desire to avoid one's social duties. I can't say I disapprove entirely of the latter. Colin was in something of a state—worried about her health, I suppose—but after what I witnessed this evening, my entire view of the girl needs to be reconsidered.

She skulked into the garden well past midnight, and I saw her talking to that inexplicably interesting thief, Mr. Capet. He came upon her from behind and grabbed her with a frightening force. She fought him off like a professional and had vanquished him before I could make it to the door to offer my assistance. I'd no idea she was so tenacious. Her normal movements are full of a delicate and easy sort of grace—not the affected elegance of so many society girls. I'm afraid I mistook it for weakness and a lack of sophistication, but I see it is nothing of the sort. She moves with a confident knowledge of herself, without feeling the need to walk or gesture in a certain way.

I wanted to cheer when she so thoroughly schooled that man.

But I do wonder what he wanted from her. They conversed for some time, and she didn't appear threatened, so I left them to their business.

Who taught her to defend herself so well?

12

I lingered in bed late the next day, having slept well past noon, the natural result of staying awake and fitful until nearly sunrise. Still upset about having argued with Colin, my emotions were reeling. Half angry, half hurt, I didn't know what to do. I felt sorry, too, knowing that I'd not reacted entirely fairly to what he'd said. I considered apologizing to him, but then found myself furious at the realization he'd not apologized to me. I was berating myself for being unreasonable when there was a sharp knock on my bedroom door. Expecting Meg with a fresh pot of tea, I called for her to come in. Instead, Colin peeked into the room, his eyes heavy and sheepish.

"Is the invitation to enter still offered now you know it's me?" he asked.

My eyes narrowed and I pressed my lips together. Much though I wanted to hold firm, the truth was I melted at the sight of him. "I can't say I much like being cross with you," I said. He opened the door the rest of the way.

"I don't think I've ever been in this room," he said. "Is it comfortable?"

"Exceedingly," I said, pulling the duvet up to my neck and snuggling against my pillows, feeling nervous as a schoolgirl. "I'm not sure I'll ever come downstairs again."

"I couldn't leave you to languish without company. It would be ungentlemanly. I do hope you wouldn't send me away in favor of other entertainment."

His smile as he flirted delighted every inch of me. "How do you think you could keep me amused?" I asked.

"I've several viable theories," he said, sitting on the edge of the bed and sliding close to me. "But we'd need to explore each thoroughly."

Relief and giddiness, tempered by a feeling of regret, flowed through me as we fell into our usual banter. "Colin," I said, my eyes fixed on the floor. "I'm so sorry."

He touched my face, his hand warm and gentle. "My dear girl. It is I who need beg forgiveness. I was a brute."

"You were, rather. But I was as well."

"You stormed out of the room with a remarkably elegant force."

"Don't be mean," I said, lowering my eyes.

"There's been too much pressure on us both," he said, holding my hands. "Coming here was not my most brilliant idea."

"We could go home."

"Soon, I hope, but not quite yet. I spoke to Gaudet this morning— I've heard back from Scotland Yard, and all signs suggest Edith Prier may have died at the hands of the Ripper. They want me to assist in the investigation. To make sure it's handled in the best possible fashion." He pressed his hands together. "But you're not happy here. My work needn't prevent you from returning to London if you wish."

"No," I said. "I'd rather stay with you."

"It might not be a bad plan. I just . . ." He stood and went to the window, beginning to pace, the way he always did when he worried.

"What?"

He leaned against the wall. "I'm worried, Emily, because Edith Prier looked so much like you."

"But in Whitechapel—"

"Yes, that was different. He may have altered his method of selecting victims, but he's not changed his manner of killing. And I cannot let you risk being hurt again."

"I'd feel safer with you."

"And I'd like nothing better than to protect you," he said. "But how can I see to it properly when I'm working? I've been too lackadaisical about taking care of you, Emily. I'll not make the same mistake again."

I sat on the window seat, contemplative. "This isn't like Constantinople."

"It could prove worse."

"I'm not involved in the investigation," I said. "And am putting myself in no danger."

"Have you considered he could come looking for you?"

"Is there a reason to think he might?"

He shook his head. "Instinct, maybe. I know I sound unreasonable, but all I want to do is pack you off to London."

"Surely this house is safe."

"We know how easy it is for an interested party to break in," he said.

"Sebastian was here again last night," I said.

"I know." He pulled a calling card out of his jacket pocket and handed it to me.

"'Sebastian Capet, A Thief of Refined Taste,'" I read.

"He's been leaving them for the people he burgles," Colin said.

I laughed. "He is amusing. You must grant him that."

"Amusing and on the verge of going to jail. He broke into Gaudet's house two nights ago."

"I shouldn't have thought the inspector in possession of anything Sebastian would want to steal."

"He wasn't," Colin said. "Read the note on the other side. He left it on a table near Gaudet's front door."

"'I shall return when you have something worth taking.'" I flipped the card back over. "You can't say you don't admire that just a little."

Colin's smile eased the tense creases around his eyes. "A bit, perhaps."

"So when did you see him?" I asked.

"We met after dinner last night."

"To discuss business?"

"Yes. And I admit freely to having made exactly no progress with the man. I'm beginning to think I'll never win one of our bets."

"I saw him last night as well," I said. "After midnight. I'd gone into the garden."

"The garden?" he asked, surprise coloring his face. "So late? Had you arranged to meet him and neglected to tell me? Or was it meant to be a secret? He didn't mention it when I spoke to him."

"No, nothing like that," I said. "His presence was entirely unexpected."

"I don't much like the idea of you wandering about alone in the middle of the night. It's not safe, Emily. Sebastian isn't the only one who could so easily scale the wall and stumble upon you."

"I had no reason to think I was in any danger. Nothing's happened to suggest our garden is unsafe. And you know how Sebastian likes to follow me. It was completely innocuous."

"This time, maybe. But how do we know someone else isn't looking for you as well?" He started to pace. "Did you speak to Capet about working for the Crown?"

"Not initially," I said. "But the subject did come up. He wasn't interested, but I'm certain I can work on him."

"Why had you gone into the garden so late?"

"I was looking for ghosts."

"Ghosts?" he asked.

"I couldn't sleep," I said, and described for him what had happened after I left the house, omitting the particulars of Sebastian's inhumane manner of sneaking up on me.

"You might have dreamed the ribbon," he said.

"It was real."

"You thought the girl in the dovecote was real, but no one was there."

"Not by the time I went inside, but that doesn't mean there hadn't been someone there."

"You're not suggesting—" He stopped. "Emily, there are no children at the Markhams' château."

"None they admit to."

"None full stop." He sat on the edge of the bed and pulled me onto his lap. "You've suffered a spectacular trauma. It's no surprise your mind would play tricks on you."

"The ribbon was in the road. I've never been more certain of anything in my life."

"You were half asleep and dreaming," he said. "And if I recall correctly, there's a painting in the Markhams' house—a little girl in a white dress, a blue ribbon tied in her hair. Degas, I think. You must have seen it and filed it away in your mind. Now the image has returned to you, combined with Monsieur Leblanc's silly ghost story, and is causing you to imagine things."

I didn't agree with him for a second. What I'd seen was eerie and sad, not like an odd version of a painting I had no memory of seeing. As for the ghost story, I was more inclined to think I'd been inspired by Madeline's accident than Monsieur Leblanc's fiction. Feeling ill at ease, I decided to change the subject. "So you made no ground with Sebastian?" I asked. "None at all?"

"None."

"Where precisely is the house of Moët?" I kissed him on the cheek. "I've a suspicion you'll be needing to make a trip there soon."

13

We passed the remainder of the day in a most pleasant fashion, making up for the time we'd lost the night before. There are few institutions with as much to recommend them as a good marriage, and the time alone with Colin made me long for the day we could return home to some real privacy, and I made the mistake of saying so out loud.

"You ought to go now, yourself," Colin said, tightening my corset with a strong tug.

"I don't want to be away from you." I slipped into my tea gown, fashioned from rich blue pompadour silk with Watteau pleats. Outrageously wide sleeves shot out at the shoulders, tapering thin at the elbows, tight at the wrists, and buttoning around a cascade of Venetian lace that covered my hands to the knuckles.

"And you know I've no interest in spending even a day away from you, my dear." He bent down, kissing the back of my neck. "But you're not going to torment me, are you?"

"Never." I turned to press my lips against his.

"Then you must agree to go home." His hands circled my waist.

"It's not fair of you to use your powers of persuasion this way," I said.

"Would you rather I stormed about the room and demanded that you go? That I book you on the ten-eighteen train to Paris without telling you?"

"It worries me that you know the schedule."

"I didn't get the ticket," he said. "Only investigated."

"You're very bad. Do you really believe this man is seeking out victims similar to me in appearance?"

"I don't know precisely what he's doing, but I'm convinced—and beginning to sound like you—we're missing something significant about him."

"He can't be the Ripper," I said.

"Why not?"

"None of it fits. The Ripper struck in a limited urban area and targeted prostitutes. Here we have one death in the middle of the countryside. Our murderer may be copying the method, but he's not the same man."

"I do love it when you recklessly speculate."

"You're only saying that to put me in an easy frame of mind so I'll agree to return to England."

"Am I that transparent?"

I sighed. "Is it so important to you?"

He took both of my hands in his. "It is. It may be ridiculous and irrational, but I need you to do it."

How could I deny him? I would want him to acquiesce should I have a similar sort of request; I considered it part of loving someone. You owed your partner the right to be unreasonable sometimes, when it mattered to him. I lifted his hand to my lips and kissed his palm. "Very well," I said. "I shall do as you wish."

He pulled back, his eyes wide, his mouth hanging open. "I cannot believe what I'm hearing."

"It all comes from adoring you," I said. "You leave me no other viable choice. But I must put you on notice: I have every intention of luring Sebastian to London with me. You'll have no chance of winning our bet."

"I'll gladly relinquish what would have been certain victory to keep you safe."

"Certain victory?" I blinked three times in rapid succession. "My dear boy, you are full of delusions."

"Am I?" he asked. "Sounds like you'd better kiss them away."

As I'd already started heeding his wishes, I saw no reason to stop now.

We agreed I would leave the following morning for Rouen, where I would stop for a few days to see Cécile, who was still with the Priers. I wanted to speak with her before departing for England, but wasn't keen on spending much time with her eccentric friends. Better them, though, than my mother-in-law. I would not mourn the loss of her company, but now that I was safe in the knowledge I had very few remaining hours with her, I could let myself feel the slightest guilt at my inability to get along with her.

Colin and I had dawdled so long upstairs that he couldn't join us for tea, instead heading out to meet Inspector Gaudet, while I went down on my own. Mrs. Hargreaves greeted me as she never had before, with what appeared to be genuine pleasure.

"I'm more sorry than I can say to lose you," she said, all chattiness as she passed me a steaming cup of tea. "You take milk, do you not?"

"Yes, thank you," I said, hoping my face did not register the astonishment I felt. "I can't thank you enough for sharing your house with us. It's a beautiful setting in which to recover." My words were not entirely disingenuous; the scenery did not disappoint. I loved the *bocage*, with its undulating hills and wide fields, apple orchards, and thick copses of trees. Few sights had delighted me like the seemingly endless expanses of flax, bright blue when in bloom, and the sky, heavy with moisture, loomed incomparable to any I'd seen elsewhere.

"I don't think you'll miss us much," she said, placing a delicate, buttery *palmier* on a plate for me. "But isn't this all somewhat outrageous? Whitechapel wasn't evacuated during the murders. Is my son overreacting? Or is this what you truly want?"

It was the first sentence she'd spoken to me void of irony, sarcasm, or condescension. "He's trying to protect me," I said.

"Do you need protection, Emily?"

"Would you?" I asked, shocked that she hadn't used my title.

She did not reply for a few moments. She stirred her tea, added more sugar, stirred again. "Probably," she said. "But I wouldn't admit it. There are times, I've found, when it's preferable to do what one can on one's own, without regard for the opinions of others."

I had not expected this sort of candor from her. "Why has your manner towards me changed so completely?" I asked. "Up to now you've had no interest in hiding your disdain from me."

"It is only now that I've begun to sympathize with you," she said. "You've begun to reveal some semblance of spirit."

"Because I'm being packed off to London?"

"No, because I saw how you fought off that dreadful man last night."

"You were watching?" The thought horrified me. What must she think?

"You're not so quiet as you'd like to think," she said. "I particularly liked the way you tried to smash his head. It was the first time I'd seen you show any sort of initiative. What did my son think?"

"I was a bit vague on the details when relaying the story to him."

"I might just come to like you, Emily. But you should never withhold details—no matter how small—from him. A marriage requires absolute honesty."

"I agree, of course. It's just that—"

"There can be no *just thats,*" she said. "Full disclosure on every subject or you'll mire yourselves in a web of deceit. What seems insignificant today may prove essential in the future."

I could not argue with her reasoning.

"It's sound advice and you know it," she continued. "So don't play Oscar Wilde. In this case, the only thing to do is *not* to pass it on."

I smiled, relieved as the tension between us dissipated. "Thank you," I said. "I shall heed your wise words."

"I expect you will. Now, onto the other matter much on my mind. Are you going to be able to give my son an heir?"

"I—I—" I sputtered, her words slicing through me.

"It's a simple enough question and I have a right to know."

She certainly did not have a right to know. "The doctor couldn't be certain," I said, disappointed I'd answered her at all. Too many years of social niceties had undermined me.

"Colin said as much. But what do you think? Do you feel capable of carrying a child?"

"I'm not sure I'm ready to contemplate it so soon after—"

"Don't be overly sensitive. It's desperately unattractive. A suitable period of mourning would have been necessary had the child actually been born. But in this case, you need do nothing but continue on. It's simple enough."

I did not want her to see me cry, and knew the tears forming would not be kept at bay long. "Of course," I said. "I was referring more to my own injuries and getting back my strength." I know not how, but I managed to keep my voice steady.

She nodded. "Excellent. I shall hope for good news from you before the end of the year."

"I'll do all I can," I said. "You must excuse me now, though. I can't leave Meg to pack my things wholly undirected." I held my composure until I'd closed the door behind me, and then ran up the stairs to my room, where I collapsed on the bed, sobbing. Did no one understand the pain of my loss? Was this grief so unusual?

No doubt it was. Because other women, like Madeline, who suffered disappointment after disappointment had no ethical ambiguities to torment them. They longed for children. I feared the ambivalence I'd felt made me different from them, as if my child had been taken because I hadn't wanted it enough. I felt myself falling into despair, an empty coldness in my chest, my hands clammy, my eyes blurred and swollen. Would it ever stop? Could a person ever be free from this sort of guilt?

I pulled myself to my feet and staggered to the window seat across the room. I could see Colin far off in the distance, speaking to one of the gardeners. The sight of him, with his easy, affable manners, brought a further round of tears, as I counted the ways I'd disappointed him. How would he feel in five years, or ten, if we still had no child? Would the way he looked at women like Toinette Prier change? Would he be filled with regret at his choice of a wife? Would he come to resent me? Was he already thinking back on the years he'd shared with Kristiana, wishing she were still alive?

Even worse, what would he be thinking now if she hadn't been killed? What if she were waiting in Vienna, biding her time, confident that eventually he'd become tired of me? Six months ago I wouldn't have thought it possible, but now it seemed nothing short of inevitable. I hated the fact that she'd been murdered while trying to assist Colin, but in a way hated even more that her killer had done me a despicable and unwanted favor.

14

Plagued with these thoughts, leaving my husband for England proved no easy task. My heart felt as if it were breaking when I reached the station in Yvetot and once on board the train, I didn't sit down until Colin's tall figure on the platform had faded from sight. I clung to a handle near the door and leaned out, waving frantically to him, the taste of his lips still on mine. As our speed increased, the conductor bundled me into the car, where I sank, miserable, onto my seat. Burying my face in a lace-trimmed linen handkerchief, I cried, leaning my head against the window.

"Lady Emily?"

I looked up at the sound of the unfamiliar voice, surprised to see Monsieur Leblanc. I wiped my tears and gave him my hand.

"May I join you?" he asked, motioning to the empty seat across from me.

"Of course," I murmured.

"You are not well?"

"Sad to be going away, that's all," I said.

"Ah. Is your husband afraid you might fall victim to the Norman Ripper should you remain here?"

"The Norman Ripper?" I asked. "I see you've spoken to George."

He shrugged. "It's not good, I know, but works better than anything I've come up with."

"I'm going to see Madame du Lac in Rouen," I said, not wanting to get into the details of why I was leaving.

"Ah," he said. "I'm off to Rouen as well. I've been commissioned to write a piece about Edith Prier's murder and want to see what I can learn about her."

"I'm staying with the Priers."

"Are you? I don't suppose . . ."

"I shall ask them if they'd be willing to speak with you, but can promise nothing."

"Merci bien," he said. "She had a lover you know, who wanted desperately to marry her. Jules Vasseur. Do you know him?"

"No." I paused at the name. Was it not that by which Madame Breton had addressed Sebastian?

"I only thought you might if you're a friend of the family. But then, I suppose they didn't want anyone to know about him."

"Why not?"

"Monsieur Prier is the sort of man who doesn't seem to understand aristocrats are no longer running the country. Didn't think a commoner like Vasseur was good enough for his daughter."

"What happened?" I asked, imagining Sebastian collecting lovers while assuming false identities. *More* fake identities, I should say, as I doubted I knew his real name.

"I'm still researching, of course, but it looks as if her involvement with Vasseur contributed in no small way to her committal."

"But she was ill, wasn't she?"

"Not anymore, according to her brother," he said.

"Laurent?"

"You know him?"

"A little, yes," I said.

"You can't believe much of what he says, but on some topics I'm inclined to listen to his opinions. This is one of them. He thought it was time she came home, but his parents refused. It seems as if he would have done anything to free her."

Piqued did not begin to describe my curiosity, and for the first time in months, I started to feel like myself. "So you're saying the family sent her away to avoid an embarrassing match?"

"Sent her away, yes," he said. "But did they also have her killed?"

"Why would they have done such a thing? She couldn't have given much trouble from the asylum."

Monsieur Leblanc looked at me, scrutinizing, and nodded. "I like that you do not balk at the idea they might have killed her."

"I'm no stranger to murders. I've solved four of them, you know."

"I had no idea you were so accomplished," he said. "I'm more used to ladies who brag about their linguistic skills or musical abilities."

"I'm afraid I'm painfully lacking on both counts. My German is appalling and I never even tried to be proficient in music. Pray that you never hear me sing."

"Your French is excellent," he said. "But tell me more about these murders."

"Should I start with my first husband?" I asked, enjoying the conversation.

"Killed him, did you?"

"No! But one of his closest friends did." The story of Philip's death brought us nearly to Rouen. Monsieur Leblanc was more interested, however, in Sebastian's role in the second crime I solved.

"This man fascinates me," he said.

"You'd like his latest venture," I said, and related to him the thief's visit to Inspector Gaudet.

Monsieur Leblanc laughed until tears streamed down his face. "I like this man more than I can tell you. But what do you make of his appearing here so close to the time of the murder? And what of the fact that the victim looked so much like you? Are you sure he's not targeting you?"

"Sebastian?" I asked. "Never." But as I leaned back against the seat, I considered the rough way he'd handled me the previous night. And I remembered the sound of the child's cry. No one but Sebastian could have collected her ribbon from the road. Had he dropped it there in the first place, just to scare me, so that he might find me in a vulnerable state? My imagination began to run wild as I racked my brain, trying to determine whether he could have overheard any conversation in which I'd made mention of the apparition in the dovecote and her hair style, but it was impossible. I caught hold of myself and nearly laughed at how ridiculous it all seemed. Colin was right—it was time I returned to my studies. Idle hands indeed proved the devil's tools.

"You are too quick to dismiss the notion," Monsieur Leblanc said. "Perhaps you admire him more than you want to admit?"

"I make no secret of admiring much about Sebastian, but can assure you it does not taint my evaluation of his character. He's a profligate and a thief, but he's not a murderer." I watched fields of barley flash past the window. "Have there been any other dramatic crimes in the neighborhood?"

"No," Monsieur Leblanc said. "We've had our share of tragic deaths and the gossip that follows, but nothing criminal."

"What sort of gossip?"

"I don't remember particulars. There was a young girl who died on the Markhams' estate—never did hear what killed her. But there was a general commotion on the property and all kinds of speculation about what happened and where she was buried."

"On the Markhams' estate? How dreadful," I said, wondering why Madeline hadn't shared this when confiding in me the day of our ill-fated visit to the dovecote.

"It was a terrible thing. I could never persuade Markham to tell me the details. I think Madeline insisted on nursing the girl instead of sending for the doctor when she fell ill. Most likely wouldn't have made the slightest difference, not with something that killed her so quickly. The poor woman was consumed with guilt, though. George has done his best to protect her—and done a good job of it, too. I've never heard anyone speculate regarding his wife's involvement. He worried, I imagine, that her . . . mental lapses could have spurred rumors."

"So what do the neighbors gossip about?"

"That the girl didn't receive a decent burial. Which, as you can well imagine, has led to her restless spirit haunting the countryside."

"Another ghost story?"

"*Mais oui,*" he said.

"Where was she buried?"

"I never did figure that out. Markham won't discuss it." He pulled out a notebook and scrawled in it. "But enough of this morose topic—it's a much more mundane story than the previous ghost we discussed. Too much reality here, I suppose. What was it you said Sebastian wrote on his calling card?"

Monsieur Leblanc and I parted amicably at the train station in Rouen, agreeing that he would call on me the following day at the Priers', after I'd had a chance to speak to them about him. The family had sent a carriage to collect me, but when I arrived, I found no one at home. Madame Prier had left a note, welcoming me to the house and telling me to treat it as my own. I followed a young maid to the bedroom I was to have, on the top floor across the corridor from Laurent's. Meg had unpacked the things I'd need for my short visit and then gone off in search of additional hairpins, convinced I didn't have an adequate supply. I knew her well enough to suspect this was an excuse to investigate the city's shops, and was glad to see her interested in our latest destination. It was hard to remember, sometimes, that she used to be a terrible traveler.

With the shutters and windows flung open, I had a spectacular view of the city as bright sunlight flooded around me. I dragged one of my cases from the dressing room and opened it, searching through papers and books until I'd found the copy of *The Odyssey* I'd begun translating from Greek more than a year ago. As I held the smooth, leather volume in my hand and flipped through its worn pages, I tried to remember why I'd abandoned the project.

Evil deeds do not prosper; the slow man catches up with the swift.

My eyes caught the sentence, and pleasure coursed through me as I found I could translate it so readily. Then I read it again, and felt as if the ancient poet was speaking the words directly to me. Some terrible man had murdered Edith Prier. I might have done nothing up to now to help solve the crime, but it wasn't too late to start. Slow and steady, I could catch the criminal. Monsieur Leblanc's conversation on the train inspired me, and I wanted to know more about the girl who'd lived in this house—and Jules Vasseur, the man she'd loved.

I opened a notebook and started to scratch questions on a sheet of paper, then paused at the realization I had only two days to find my answers. Gathering up a notebook and a sharp pencil, I clattered down the stairs, eager to discreetly speak to the servants about the romantic elements of Edith's life. Maids, I knew, were generally better informed and more observant than anyone in the families for whom they worked. Halfway down, I slammed into Laurent, who steadied himself with the banister. Not so fortunate, I tripped, my papers fluttering around me.

"Do forgive me," I said, picking myself up and straightening my dress before gathering my scattered belongings.

"What are you doing up here?" he asked.

"I'm to stay a few days. Your mother put me in the red room on the top floor."

"That was my sister's. Do you feel good sleeping in a dead woman's bed?" Without waiting for my answer, he continued up the stairs, stopping to pick up a piece of paper that had fallen out of my notebook. "What is this? What do you know about Vasseur?"

"Nothing yet," I said. "Is there something I should know?"

"Only that he's responsible for my sister's death." He turned back around and stormed up the steps.

"Wait!" I rushed to follow him. "You have reason to believe he killed her?"

"I am not discussing this with you." He kept walking, increasing his speed. I caught up to him quickly, but was stopped at his room when he slammed the door before I could come inside.

"I want to help you," I said, knocking on the door. "Please let me in."

He did not reply.

Moving as quietly as possible, I turned the knob. With a sharp jab he pushed open the door, nearly hitting me in the face.

"Do not consider, even for an instant, disturbing me." Again the door slammed. This time, I heard a latch click into place. I went back into my own room to sharpen my pencil, whose point had snapped on its trip down the stairs. As I fumbled through my bags in search of a penknife, I heard angry strains of music coming from what had to be Laurent's room, but it sounded as if it were next to me, not across the hall. I stepped back into the corridor. Two other doors stood between mine and the rear of the house, but they were both locked. I returned to my chamber and pressed my ear against the back wall. There was no question the music was louder here.

Curious, I moved along the wall, listening, the sound at its loudest near a heavy armoire, two-thirds of the way down its length. I strained trying to move it, but could not make it budge. Then, inspired by I know not what, I pulled it open. Inside I found three lovely but dated gowns—cut to be worn with a bustle—and a pair of satin dancing slippers. Chills ran through me as I gently touched them, trying to imagine the occasions on which Edith must have worn them. Images flashed through my head—visions first of a beautiful young girl at a ball and then of the mutilated body I'd found in the field. Terror consumed me and the room felt chilled, as if something unnatural had entered the space. I was about to close the wardrobe and run downstairs to beg for another room when I noticed a thin stream of light at the back of the cabinet. Now fear succumbed to intrigue, and I carefully slid the gowns to one side and lowered myself to my knees, coming level with a large panel, nearly half the height of the armoire, with a small leather strap attached to it.

I tugged at the strap and the panel started to move, gliding smoothly along a narrow track. As it opened, the music was louder, and I had a clear view into a room that had to be connected to Laurent's. It must have run the full length of the corridor we shared, but turned at the end, reaching all the way to mine. I stuck my head through the opening, craning my neck to see more. Stretching too far, I toppled over, landing with a crash on the floor.

In an instant, Laurent was standing above me, glowering.

"So sorry," I said, rising to my feet. "I had no idea your room came this far."

"*That* is what you're sorry for? Not for disturbing my privacy? Not for manhandling my sister's possessions?"

"There's no need for so much tension, Laurent," I said, hoping he couldn't discern how difficult it was for me to keep my voice from shaking. "I'm not trying to torment you."

"Leave my room."

"What's the piece you were playing?" I asked. "I loved the emotion of it. Is it Beethoven?"

"Are you simple-minded? Do you not understand the most basic commands?"

"I understand them perfectly well. But I've always had a problem following them." He did not respond. "My mother insists it's deliberate, but I think it's innate to my personality."

He stalked across the room, back to his piano. I followed him.

"I want to know more about Edith," I said. "I have a friend, a writer, who's just begun investigating her murder. He's convinced there's more to it than the police believe."

"And this is meant, what? To impress me?"

"I'm not sure I care what effect it has on you." He'd started playing again, the music crashing against the dark paneled walls of the room. "But I do want to know what happened to your sister."

"What interest can it be of yours?"

"I found her, Laurent. And doing so forged something between us. I didn't recognize it until today because I've been distracted with tragedy of my own. I—"

"I've no interest in your tragedy," he said.

"And I've no interest in sharing it with you. But I will find out why Edith died the way she did. You can choose to offer whatever meager assistance you can, or you can sit back and brood and help no one, yourself included. It's immaterial to me."

"If it makes no difference to you, why would I put myself out?"

"It might speed the process," I said. "I had the impression that you were close to your sister. That you might have some insight into her life." I watched him as he played. He did not look at the keys. His gaze, focused and intense, was fixed out the window, even as his head moved with his body, the music seeming to flow through him.

I walked back to the opening through which I'd tumbled. On Laurent's side, the door appeared to be part of the room's design, blending enough into the paneled wall so as to be hardly visible. Without a word, I stepped through and slid the cover back into place. I shuddered as I inadvertently brushed against Edith's clothes, and was happy to emerge in what had been her bedroom, a much brighter space than that of her brother's. I would not harass him. My work could commence without him, and when he realized I'd begun, he would want to know what I'd learned. And then I could make him first tell me what he knew.

A grating sound came from the back of the room as the hidden panel slid open.

"It was Beethoven," Laurent said, pushing the door to the armoire open. "You were right." He disappeared, closing the door.

Pleased, I set back down the stairs, ready to speak to the servants.

16 July 1892

In all the years I've stayed in France, I never felt lonely until now. Colin is the same gentleman he ever was—he already was a gentleman at five years old—and nothing could ever alter him. Not even his father was so assured in his character, or knew so early what he wanted from life. Much as I adore my William, this mother will admit to playing favorites amongst her sons, and Colin was always that.

It is not reasonable, of course, to think our relationship wouldn't change after his marriage. I would be displeased if it didn't—it would mean he didn't love his wife enough. And on that count he clearly does not fall short. What I didn't expect, however, was to lose him to someone whom I'd find disappointing. After meeting her, I decided the time I would most enjoy with my son in the future would be those moments when his wife was not with him. But her presence is immediate even when she's not here. He thinks of her all the time.

I'd had great hopes that our time together after she left for Rouen would be different. We've fallen into our usual habits, as I thought we would, but while we read together or discuss politics over coffee, she is always with us.

I wonder what she would think of our Gladstone—if she knows enough of the man to form an opinion. Would she be shocked by the work he and his dear wife did to save common prostitutes from poverty and despair? Is she capable of understanding the question of Irish Home Rule? What on earth does my son find to talk to her about?

Yet I can't believe that an unworthy lady would have so affected him. Which means, I'm afraid, I can only surmise there's a weakness on my own part. That I've not given the girl enough of a fair shot. That I should try better to see her as he does.

I have seen her wear riding dress to lunch.

15

"Have I heard right? Are you leaving for Paris in only two days?" Toinette asked, popping a piece of *pain au chocolate* into her rosy mouth as we all convened for breakfast the next day in a small but charming room in the back of the house. Bright tiles covered the floor, painted with a floral design, and a large bay window faced the garden.

"Yes," I said, spearing a bite of *oeufs pochés à la lyonnaise*—savory poached eggs with onions and a simple white sauce topped with browned Gruyère cheese. "On the morning train."

"It's so unfair!" she said. "I've just decided to head off to Yvetot tomorrow and had so wanted to call on you. I understand your *belle-mère* lives not too terribly far away."

"You can still visit Madame Hargreaves, darling," her mother said. I felt the beginnings of a headache, no doubt related to the thought of Toinette machinating an opportunity to flirt with my husband.

"I've a friend from school who lives nearby, you see," Toinette said. "I'm going to spend a whole week with her and we're bound to be bored out of our minds. I'm hoping she might host a dance. Apparently—" she paused for another bite, "her father opposes the idea, but I'm bound and determined to change his mind."

"You must invite Madame Hargreaves and her son," Madame Prier said.

"And the Markhams. May I have more chocolate, *Maman*?" She gulped from the cup the instant her mother had filled it. "I can't think of anyone else."

"Oh the Markhams. Yes, I suppose you must, although they're bound to be tedious."

"You don't like them?" I asked. "We found them pleasant company."

"George is all charm," Cécile said. "And Madeline as well. Eccentric in her way, but a very sweet girl."

"I never liked her mother when she was young," Madame Prier said. "And I'm quite certain she's beyond intolerable now."

"She's ill," I said.

Madame Prier nodded. "Precisely. Now, Toinette, what else do you need to prepare for your visit?"

I watched as she and her daughter prattled on about clothes and other details of the journey, surprised that she would dismiss Madame Breton with such contempt. Given the struggles with nerves faced by her own daughter, I should have thought she'd be more sympathetic.

But Edith's illness and death were topics garnering no interest in the household that day. Madame Prier snapped at me when I brought up the subject, and I feared my pursuit of further information might prove awkward, particularly as I felt uneasy at the thought of questioning the staff without the family's express permission. I asked Cécile's advice about addressing her friend on the subject.

"*Non*," came her response. "You will not ask first. If necessary, we will beg forgiveness, but we will not give her the opportunity to forbid us to carry out the task. And I am suddenly overcome with a suspicion that something might force us to go downstairs at any moment." Without pausing, she stepped into the corridor and opened the door that led down to the kitchen, deposited Brutus on the steps, waited until she heard his barks fade to almost nothing, and then took my hand and led me to the domain of the servants.

"*Mon dieu!*" she said, her face full of apology as she scooped the little dog into her arms. It had taken us fewer than three minutes to locate him in a dark corner of the butler's pantry. "The little cad is looking for beef, I think."

The cook, enamored at once by the small furry creature, insisted that we follow her to the kitchen, where the staff had just finished their luncheon. She fished a hearty bone from a soup pot and showed it to Brutus, who yelped thanks and panted at the sight of it. Cécile lowered him to the ground with his treat.

"No use trying to rush him," she said.

"None indeed." The cook nodded with pleasure at the dog's delight. "He's a sweet little thing."

Cécile shrugged. "When he wants to be. The rest of the time he's an absolute beast devoid of all good qualities."

"Too small to do much harm," the cook said. A willowy maid walked by, her arms full of freshly laundered sheets. Seeing the little dog, she paused.

"He doesn't belong to the house, does he?" she asked.

"No," the cook said, holding out her arms to take the laundry so the maid could bend over and pet Brutus.

"Miss Edith would've loved him," she said with a sigh.

"Your mistress told me Edith was excessively fond of dogs, that she liked them more than she did most people," Cécile said. "Do you agree?"

"Oh yes," the girl replied. "She loved them. Had three, you know. Two well-behaved, one a tyrant. Of course, she kept them in the country, not in the city."

"Did you know her well?" I asked.

"As well as anyone, I suppose."

"Jeanne was a lady's maid then," the cook said. "Took the best care of our young girl."

"Toinette?" I asked.

"No, no," Jeanne said, shaking her head. "She was too young for anything but a nurse. I was Mademoiselle Edith's maid."

"Would you tell us about her?" I asked.

"I don't know as we should be talking about her," Jeanne said, the cook nodding agreement behind her.

"It would help me ever so much," I said. I glanced up and down the corridor, hoping I looked nervous. "I found her body, you see, and the image has haunted me ever since." They all cringed when I mentioned the body, Jeanne covering her mouth with her hand. "I thought that perhaps if I knew more about her life, I could associate more pleasant memories with her name. Of course, I don't want to trouble Madame Prier—"

"She could use some trouble if you ask me," the cook said. "Come sit down. I suppose you'll be wanting a cup of tea?"

She went to put the kettle on while we followed Jeanne to a long, well-worn table lined with rustic chairs, mismatched, ten on each side, two each at the head and foot. She'd recovered the laundry from the cook and placed it in a large wicker basket, smoothing the sheets on top before she sat across from us.

"I miss her, you know," she said. "We was close. She was always kind to me."

"I'm so sorry," I said, reaching for her hand across the table, almost surprised she let me take it. Her skin was rough, but warm, her grip strong.

"They should never have sent her away."

"Why not?" Cécile asked. "She wasn't well and needed help."

"Maybe she did. But there was all that trouble with her brother."

"Weren't she and Laurent close?" I asked.

"Too close if you ask me." She leaned forward and dropped her voice to a whisper. "Wasn't natural."

"They were twins," I said. "And twins are frequently closer than ordinary siblings."

"Maybe," she said. "But he hated anyone else knowing her too well. He's a possessive one."

"Was someone courting her?"

"Well . . ." She squinted, as if measuring us up. "There was a gentleman, but once Monsieur Prier made it clear he wasn't suitable . . ."

"Did she go on seeing him?" I asked.

"Monsieur Laurent wouldn't have stood for it."

"It couldn't have been his decision," Cécile said. "His father's opinion would have been the one that mattered."

Jeanne snorted. "Some might think that."

"Do you know the gentleman's name?" I asked.

"Vasseur." Her voice softened, turned almost dreamy.

"Jules Vasseur?" I nodded, hoping she'd think I was more familiar with the man than I was. "Of course!"

"You know him?" she asked.

"Who has not heard his name?" Cécile spoke with a perfectly executed casual air.

Jeanne sighed. "I did not know him, of course. Not well. But I did, on occasion deliver messages to his house for my mistress. She loved him very much."

"You know where he lives?" I asked; she nodded. "Could you show me? I need to talk to him."

"He left Rouen as soon as Mademoiselle Edith was sent away," she said. "I couldn't tell you where he went."

"Did you ever hear from her after she left the house?" I asked.

"No, madame. We weren't to speak of her—it was too painful for Madame Prier. Only Laurent disregarded her wishes."

"He was upset," I said. "Yet you think it was he who did not approve of Monsieur Vasseur?"

"Monsieur Laurent's scheme did not work out as he hoped. He worked too hard at making his sister seem unhinged—and in the end drove her to madness. He'd wanted the doctor to prescribe rest so that he could take her to Nice to recuperate. Instead, he was too effective and she was bound for the asylum."

"You're not saying her brother deliberately drove her mad?" I asked.

"Oh he did, madame," she said. "I'm not the only one who knows it. But you're unlikely to get many of us to talk. We seen what he's done, you know, and don't want it done to us."

"How did he do it?" Cécile asked. "Surely such a thing would not be simple?"

"I can't rightly say," Jeanne said. "It was a gradual thing. First it all seemed small and unimportant. Until she started talking to the girl."

"The girl?" I asked.

"The girl." She looked away from us now. "The little dead girl."

A shiver ran through me. "What girl?"

"Don't know. It never made any sense," she said. "But it scared the devil out of me. She'd talk to her—at night especially—crying and moaning."

"Whose child was it?"

"I couldn't say. But she wept over it until she could hardly speak. And then she started sleepwalking—fell down the stairs more than once. With all of it, I don't see as how her father could've done anything but send her away."

"Tell me more about the girl," I said.

She nodded. "Monsieur Laurent, he told her some kind of ghost story, about a little girl who died in some sort of sad circumstance and was searching for a mother. My poor mistress, she took it to heart, she did. It ruined her."

"Did you ever see evidence of it?"

"The ghost?" She scrunched her forehead. "No. But I can tell you mademoiselle's bedchamber was always at least ten degrees colder when she said she saw it. I felt it myself more than once. Have you seen something funny in the room?"

"No," I said.

She shrugged. "I wouldn't want to spend much time up there. Even if there is no ghost."

Soon after Cécile and I emerged from below stairs, Monsieur Leblanc arrived to call on me as we'd planned. But rather than allow him to come inside and speak with the Priers, I intercepted him at the door and dragged him away from the house.

"Do ghosts travel?" I asked him.

"Ghosts? How on earth should I know?"

"You're a journalist. I expect you to have leads on any topic I throw at you," I said.

"You are a funny lady," he said. "I already told you my ghost story. And she does travel, the little ghost."

"Yes, but does she ever follow the same person to more than one place?"

"You're not serious?"

"I am."

"I can't say I've heard it said she's latched on to anyone in particular."

"I just wondered if she'd ever found a single person she thought might end her wandering," I said. He was looking at me as if I'd lost my mind. "How far away is the asylum where they sent Edith?"

"Ghosts, asylums, you're full of surprises today, Lady Emily." He adjusted his hat. "It's outside the city, perhaps fifteen miles or so. Lovely setting near the river."

"Can we go?"

"Now?" Surprise registered on his face, but a glimmer of excited delight crept into his eyes.

"Would it be possible?"

"I—" He paused, looked around. "We could hire a carriage." I set him to the task at once, and within a quarter of an hour we'd bundled ourselves into a comfortable hackney and were speeding along dusty country roads.

"Have you a plan for when we arrive?" Monsieur Leblanc asked.

"Fear not," I said. "I'll have hatched something by then."

The drive took longer than we'd anticipated due to the condition of the roads, which were dotted with potholes and washboarded from frequent rain. We passed through numerous small villages, the spires of stone churches rising from amongst thatched roofs; bright red, blue, and green market carts gathered in town squares; women sweeping their front steps with brooms fashioned from twigs. And then, the buildings would suddenly disappear, giving way to great expanses of fields— tall wheat and bending barley—their edges lined with crimson poppies. The occasional farm wagon, piled high with hay, slowed us further as it clattered along the way beneath the overstuffed white clouds dotting the sky.

We turned onto a smaller road and crossed the river. I leaned out my window, marveling at the ruins of a Norman abbey, its roofless chapel standing as if at guard near a much better preserved chapter house. Turning again to parallel the water, we drove on only a bit farther and then traversed another bridge, this one leading to a narrow island. The heavy foliage of old-growth trees hid all but glimpses of a reddish brick building buried in their midst, branches hanging so low they scraped the top of our carriage. The drive widened slightly as we approached the entrance.

The asylum had been built to mimic a castle—or perhaps it had once been a stately home. The reddish color and shape of the towers reminded me of a smaller Hampton Court Palace. The structure itself was well tended, with gleaming windows and pristine marble steps. After Monsieur Leblanc spoke to the driver, arranging for him to wait while we were inside, we went to the door and lifted a heavy brass knocker shaped as the head of a lion. In short order, a crisply uniformed nurse greeted us with a warm and welcoming tone in her soothing voice. She assumed we'd come to visit a patient, but showed no sign of surprise when Monsieur Leblanc asked to see Dr. Girard, the man whom, he'd told me on our way, had attended to Edith during her illness.

The nurse led us through wide corridors whose whitewashed walls stood bright and clean. The ceiling retained its ornate plaster moldings that must have been original to the building, and the parquet floors showed signs of the wear that comes from frequent, vigorous scrubbing. She tapped on a door at the back of the building and then, without waiting for a response, opened it. After motioning for us to enter the room, which was fitted up as a medical library and office, she disappeared, closing the door behind her.

"How may I help you?" A not unattractive man of average height and build rose from his chair at the large desk that commandeered the center of the room while bookcases filled with thick, well-worn volumes lined the walls. He was younger than I'd expected—in the prime of life—well-dressed, with an elegance to the way he moved. "I'm afraid we've not any openings for new patients at the moment, but—oh, do forgive me. I should have introduced myself."

"You require no introduction, Dr. Girard," Monsieur Leblanc said, offering the man his hand and giving him our names. "I know your reputation well. We have come to inquire on behalf of friends of the Prier family."

"A terrible tragedy," he said. "I did not think that many friends knew of the poor girl's plight."

"Not of her illness, perhaps," I said. "But the news of her death—"

"Of course. It horrified the entire region," the doctor interrupted. "Please, sit."

We did as he asked and he lowered himself onto his chair. The surface of his desk was clear except for two neat piles of papers and a copy of a medical journal carefully lined up on the upper left hand corner, an inkwell with two pens perfectly centered, and an ancient but polished clock to the right of the chair.

"I'm the one who found Mademoiselle Prier's body," I said. "And feel, as a result, a vested interest in her murder."

"I'm terribly sorry," Dr. Girard said. "I read the autopsy report and do not envy you what you saw. I understand, however, that the police have a suspect in mind?"

"They may," Monsieur Leblanc said. "But what concerns us is the victim. I am a writer, you see, and want to do a piece about her, so that her life is not forgotten."

"I can't imagine the family would welcome such a thing," the doctor said. "They're extremely private people. At least when it concerned the health of their daughter."

"Was she very ill?" I asked.

"Her condition deteriorated markedly in the time I treated her. When she arrived, her thoughts were scattered and she was consumed with anxiety. Her parents were concerned that she suffered from the same troubles that led to the death of her mother's second cousin. Madness running in the family can be terrifying."

"How long was Edith here?" I asked.

"Nearly five years. She disappeared—escaped, I should say, about six months ago."

"What was done to try to find her?" Monsieur Leblanc asked.

"Not much, truth be told," Dr. Girard said. "Her family, particularly her father, found her lack of progress frustrating."

"Did they expect her to be cured?" I asked.

"Initially, yes, they believed she would stay with us only temporarily."

"Despite the fact that they'd seen another relative die from a similar condition?" Monsieur Leblanc frowned.

"The symptoms of mental illness are not what kill those who suffer from it. The patient's inability to cope with her hallucinations and dementia can lead to despair, which often results in suicide. The Priers thought that a course of treatment might relieve Edith's symptoms. Unfortunately, however, her condition did not improve from anything I tried."

"Are your treatments successful?" Monsieur Leblanc asked.

"Sometimes. I consider my work more art than science. Some patients respond with remarkable results. Others . . . well, for them all I can do is offer comfortable surroundings. You'll see that we've cleared from this facility all the clutter and filth found in most asylums. The deranged mind is not aided by overstimulation, I think."

"What treatments did you prescribe for Mademoiselle Prier?" I asked.

"I agree with the principles of Philippe Pinel, who established the idea of moral treatment. No beatings, no shackles. Patients should be treated with respect. There are some medicines that can help restore a person's vital force, but I found they did little for Edith. I set her to work—having time strictly organized can help a troubled mind. She made clothing for dolls that we sent to church charities. I talked to her, tried to ease her pain. But she slipped further and further away from reality."

"Was she still able to work as her condition worsened?" I asked.

"Yes. Oddly enough, although she would forget where she was, forget those around her, her sewing grew more and more proficient. You could tell, however, that her mind was fixed in unusual ways. Every outfit she made included a blue satin ribbon. She was obsessed with them."

Swallowing hard, I pictured the ribbon in the road in front of Colin's mother's house, pictured it tied in the hair of the girl who stood in the window of the Markhams' dovecote, and wondered what, precisely, I'd seen. Trying to remain calm, I drew a deep breath. "Where do you think she went when she escaped?"

"The only member of her family who visited her was her brother. Initially, he was happy she was here, but eventually, he started pleading with me to release her. In the end, I think he came to realize that she could not live in an ordinary way. Her father asked for regular updates on her condition, but even when he came to speak to me in person refused to see her. Her mother never came at all, only sent letters at infrequent intervals."

"Did anyone else visit her?" I asked.

"One gentleman," the doctor said. "A family friend. Or so I thought. After she'd gone, I tried to get in touch with him and found it impossible to track him down. So far as I can tell the identity he'd presented to me—that of a Monsieur Myriel—was false."

"Do you know anything about him?"

"Only that he was extraordinarily kind to Edith, and that she enjoyed seeing him. I do hope someone's told him of her death. I was as thorough as possible in attempting to find him—I'm afraid he's disappeared."

16

"It's Vasseur, you know," I said. Monsieur Leblanc and I had returned to Rouen, but instead of going to the Priers', we'd settled into a café where we could discuss Edith's lover away from her family. Dr. Girard, though charming and pleasant, had refused to give us any further information about Edith's condition, and would not address the possibility that she thought she was seeing ghosts. "He had to be the one who was visiting her and calling himself Myriel. What do you know about him?"

"Very little despite extensive research," he said. "He's a career soldier, which wasn't a glamorous enough occupation for Monsieur Prier."

"He probably didn't want his daughter to marry a man who required an occupation."

"You aristocrats are an odd lot."

"Are the Priers aristocratic?" I asked.

"Not on his side, but his wife's family still retain their obsolete titles. Not the sort to want an undesirable son-in-law."

"Is Vasseur an officer?"

"He is. Spent some time in Indochina."

"And you've no idea where he is now?"

"I traced him to the Foreign Legion, and according to their records he was discharged eight months ago."

"It had to be earlier than that or he couldn't have been visiting her
regularly," I said.

"He could have had someone checking in on her on his behalf.
And then, when he was able to return to France—"

"He came for her," I said. "As soon as he could. So why, then, is she
dead?"

When I reached the Priers' house I went straight upstairs and pounded
on Laurent's door, which was locked. After being ignored (I could hear
him inside, his footsteps heavy on the old plank floors) I crawled through
the passage in my armoire.

"Don't you find this somewhat ridiculous?" I asked, smoothing
my skirts. "It would be so much easier to just let me in."

"Edith always liked making a game of it," he said.

"I'm not Edith."

"And I didn't invite you to speak to me."

"Monsieur Vasseur left the Foreign Legion not long before your
sister disappeared from the asylum."

"Is he back in France?" Laurent's face reddened and he clenched
his fists.

"I have no idea," I said. "Perhaps now would be a good time to tell
me what you know about him."

"He killed her because he couldn't have her."

"A romantic idea, to be sure," I said, incredulous. "But has it any
basis in fact?"

"My sister had a heart and soul unlike anyone's. She felt things
more deeply than ordinary people do. Vasseur fed her pretty lines and
poetry and seduced her with hardly any effort."

"Did she love him?"

"Desperately."

"Why do you despise him? Perhaps he loved her."

"There are things a gentleman doesn't do to a lady he loves."

"Such as?"

"I'm not discussing it."

"You frustrate me, Laurent," I said. "The police believe your sister was killed by a man who murdered prostitutes in London. If you have reason to believe someone else is guilty, you're obligated to come forward with whatever evidence you have."

"Do you like playing detective?"

"I do, in fact, and I'm good at it."

He laughed. "I suppose you always identify the killer before the end of Sherlock Holmes novels."

"Yes, but that's hardly the point. I caught the man who murdered my first husband; I cleared erroneous charges against a dear friend, and have solved two other crimes. I'm certainly more qualified than you to figure out what happened to your sister—although I can't vouch for you being capable of anything beyond brooding and playing Beethoven."

"I don't like you."

"I don't care. All that matters now is where your sister spent the last six months of her life."

He turned away from me and stomped across the room to a window, which he flung open. "Can you doubt he killed her?"

"Vasseur?" I asked. "I know nothing about him except that it appears he was romantically involved with Edith. The fact that you were jealous of their relationship is hardly cause to suspect him of murder. It's more likely to make me wonder about you."

"You accuse me?" He whirled around.

"No. But you give me nothing—not even the slimmest reason to doubt this man's feelings for your sister."

"He got her with child," he said, stepping towards me, his eyes full of menace. "And then left her to deal with the consequences on her own."

"But he wanted to marry her?"

"My father had forbidden his suit, but he continued to pursue her. Because they couldn't meet openly, he arranged clandestine meetings. And once he was able to be alone with her, away from all decent company, without any limits, he took advantage of her."

"She must have been devastated," I said.

"She wasn't." He sank onto his piano bench and dropped his head into his hands. "She was ecstatic. She wanted to marry him. Thought they would elope."

"Was he unwilling?"

"I wasn't about to leave her in the hands of a man who would behave so dishonorably."

"And the baby?"

"She lost it," he said. "Which was the best thing that could happen in such a situation."

"Did your parents know?"

"Of course not. Only Dr. Girard, who cared for her."

"So she'd already been sent away?"

"I was able to persuade her that she needed rest."

"I've heard stories that you drove her mad."

"It hurt her to hear the things I said. No one likes to be told her lover is a useless wretch. She was heartbroken, yes, but not mad."

"But she was with child when she went to the asylum?"

"Yes."

"And then she lost it?"

"Yes."

"That's awfully convenient," I said.

"Sometimes nature needs only a little help."

I trembled and felt the room go cold. A stiff wind blew through the window, rattling the glass, and all I wanted to do was run. Edith had suffered abominably at the hands of men, and more than once. I looked at Laurent, whose eyes turned hard. He stepped forward and reached for me. I stepped back, avoiding his touch.

"You are not to discuss this with anyone," he said. "These events have nothing whatsoever to do with her death."

"Does Vasseur know you arranged this?" I asked.

"No. Only Girard. Everything we did was hidden from Vasseur. It was not his concern."

"How can you believe a man's child is not his concern?"

"When a man is a worthless profligate, nothing is his concern."

"I agree that his behavior was appalling," I said. "But you've told me nothing to suggest he would want to see Edith dead."

"She lost his child. He despised weakness."

"A thin argument at best. Do you know for certain he was aware of the pregnancy?"

"She told him in a letter. I read it before she sent it."

"She shared her correspondence with you?"

"No," he said. "I opened and resealed it. Edith believed he was going to come for her, that they would elope."

"And you wouldn't let that happen."

"She was the dearest part of my heart," he said. "I could not let her come to such inglorious ruin."

"So instead you had her committed and labeled insane? Forgive me if I don't see the kindness in your strategy."

"How could I have known the events would drive her irrevocably mad?"

"Of course. Who would consider that the loss of both the man she wanted to marry and her child would have a deep impact on her mental condition?"

"You need not be sarcastic. I saved her from a worse fate. Girard's asylum is no Bedlam. I intended for her to recuperate in comfort and then come home. For her to have kept the child was unthinkable—she would have been ostracized."

"You have no appreciation for the grief you caused her," I said. "You destroyed her. If you hadn't manipulated the situation she'd still be alive."

He took me fiercely by the arm and leaned in close to my face. "I loved my sister like no one else. Our family did not understand her. I alone knew what was best for her, and I saw to it that she got it. Do not dare accuse me of bringing her to harm unless you should like to suffer a worse fate than she did." He pushed me away, and I fell against the wall, my heart pounding, unable to move until the sound of his footsteps disappeared down the stairs. Then, stepping tentatively, I went to my own room and collapsed on my bed, scared and horrified, but unable to cry.

I didn't want to believe what Laurent had told me; it was too awful, unthinkable. I couldn't believe that a man like Dr. Girard would participate in such an odious endeavor. I pressed the heel of my palm against my forehead, felt a rush of sadness tear through me, and lamented that Edith had suffered such a loss in circumstances worse than my own. Or were they? Could one compare grief? Could solace be found in doing so? I raised my head, resting my chin on my left hand, tugging at the duvet with my right, listening to the sounds of Rouen lumber through my open window. It differed little from what one would hear in any city—carriages clattering over cobbled streets, the chatter of business, laughter and gossip, the tinkling bells that announced the opening of shop doors, the thud of them closing.

But something familiar strained to be heard over the clamor: a thin sound, reedy and sharp, growing louder and more rhythmic. I froze and closed my eyes, concentrating, eager to disprove what I suspected. Shaking, I rose from the bed and stepped to the window, leaning out when I reached it. Lost in the din, it was barely discernible, but still recognizable. The voice I'd heard in the country had followed me to Rouen, its lonely weeping twisted by the breeze fluttering the lacy curtains in my room.

Had Edith heard the same thing? The question hung, unanswered, in the damp air. My thoughts turned to Madeline, who'd also suffered the loss of a child. Children, I corrected myself. Would she hear it as well if she were here? Had I tapped into some ethereal spirit, calling on women whose emotions bled raw? Or was I letting my pain get hold of my imagination? Perhaps Colin's concerns possessed more validity than I'd been willing to admit. Maybe I had succumbed to wallowing, had allowed myself to be consumed for too long by the tragedies of the past.

I reached for the tarnished handles on the sashes of the window-panes and pulled them in, locking the sounds away from me. The silence was almost harder to listen to than the crying and I felt as if I might crawl out of my skin. Agitated, I opened the windows again, this time only to close the shutters outside them. But as I started, my eyes caught a flash of blue.

Across the street, falling from above the height of my room, a narrow blue ribbon danced, buoyed by the wind as it drifted to the pavement below. I opened my mouth, certain I would scream, but found myself unable to make even the slightest noise. My breath shallow, my legs heavy and unmovable, I clenched my hands in tight fists. Soon the horror of moving seemed preferable to the horror of remaining where I stood, and I managed to flee the room, rushing down the steps two at a time, nearly losing my balance as the staircase curved at each landing.

Finding Cécile took no effort—I heard her laughter coming from the sitting room, where she and Madame Prier huddled, thick as thieves, gossiping about long-forgotten acquaintances. They didn't notice me at first when I slipped through the door, standing next to it, silent. Only when I caught a lull in their conversation did I step closer to them.

"Mon dieu!" Madame Prier said. "You're a fright!"

"What is it, Kallista?" Cécile asked.

"I—" I stopped. Every word that came to mind fell short of what I needed.

"Heavens, you've that same awful look Edith used to get," Madame Prier said. "Have I cursed you by putting you in her room?"

"Don't be ridiculous," Cécile said, rising and taking me by the arm. "She needs fresh air, that's all. Her health, you know, is not at its finest."

I gripped my friend's hand, wishing I could stop shaking. "I've pushed myself too hard, that's all," I said.

"Come sit outside," Cécile said, her voice firm and unwavering. "Could you send some tea out to us?"

Madame Prier agreed at once, pulling a richly embroidered bell cord. "Would you like me to give you some privacy?" she asked.

"Thank you," I said. "I'd very much appreciate it. Please forgive me if I've alarmed you."

"It's no problem, really," she said. "But you're the image of poor Edith right now."

"I—I'm sorry," I stammered as Cécile steered me to a set of tall French doors that led to the small garden behind the house.

Our hostess waved off my concerns. "Do not let it trouble you," she said. "But you may want to consider leaving for Paris sooner than you'd planned. I don't think Rouen is agreeing with you."

17

"What happened?" Cécile asked, sitting close to me on a wooden bench in the Priers' flower-filled courtyard.

"I hardly know what to say." With a sigh, I let the whole story rattle out.

She shook her head. "I know not where we should start. Ghosts, Kallista?"

"Inconceivable, I know."

She patted my hand. "Too much stress, that's all it is."

"I don't think so." I stood up and walked out of the garden, Cécile close on my heels. I cut through the house and onto the street where in a matter of minutes I'd searched to no avail. There was no ribbon to be found anywhere—instead, I discovered a crumpled piece of pale blue paper. Was my mind playing tricks on me?

"I'm worried about you," Cécile said, as we walked back to the courtyard bench. "Is it a good idea that you return to London on your own? Do you want me to come with you?"

"I don't want to go at all. Not anymore. I feel like I'm coming close to unraveling Edith's story."

"You promised Colin." She brushed a stray hair out of my face. "And it may be best for you to go. This is not a good place for rest and recovery."

"I'm physically recovered."

"But your emotions, Kallista. Your stay here has not helped them."

"What am I to do? Knowing what happened to Edith is important to me."

"We will pursue answers to the questions plaguing you until the moment we must step on the train to Paris. And then we will spend at least a week in my city, shopping and buying art and drinking champagne. And by then, you'll have forgot all about this."

"How could I forget Edith?" I asked.

"Well, perhaps not her," she said. "But the rest of it."

"I want to know what happened to her."

"We will discover what we can. All you must do is tell me where we start."

"With Toinette, before she leaves for Yvetot. And then Dr. Girard. You'll like him."

"You go to the young vixen. I shall organize a carriage to take us to the good doctor first thing tomorrow morning."

"You're good to indulge me, Cécile," I said.

"I've yet to see the time your instinct wasn't worth pursuing," she replied. "Furthermore, I've never before had the opportunity to see a madhouse."

Toinette had retired to her bedroom, on the floor below mine, to pack for her trip. She feigned delight at finding me at her door, and invited me to come inside. "What fun to have someone with me," she said. "You can help me decide which of my gowns will make the best impression when I'm away. Don't you love how wide sleeves are becoming?"

"Actually, no," I said. "I prefer something more discreet."

"You must be getting too old to appreciate fashion."

I swallowed the biting remark that sprung instantly to mind. "I was hoping, Toinette, not to discuss your wardrobe but to have you tell me more about your sister. She must have confided in you from time to time."

Toinette snorted. "Far from it. She treated me like a baby. Hardly talked to me."

"Did you notice changes in her before she was sent away?"

"Do you mean other than her incoherent ramblings?"

"What did she talk about?"

"Nothing that made even a piece of sense. It was boring, really." She held up a bright pink dress. "Do you like this on me?"

"The color brings out the rose in your cheeks," I said. "Did you ever meet Monsieur Vasseur?"

"Not officially. But I saw him once, waiting for her outside."

"Did she sneak away to see him often?"

"Oh yes. It was the only bit of her character that I really liked," she said. "She was so moody and dull—and jealous of my high spirits. Was always tattling on me, getting me in trouble with *Maman*. But I admired her flair for romance."

"Is he handsome, Monsieur Vasseur?"

"Not at all. But he looks strong, and has decent hair, I suppose. Nice blue eyes. He was wounded in some tedious battle and limped in a most embarrassing fashion. Can't imagine he could dance. Probably would be best if he didn't try."

Her complete lack of sympathy grated on my nerves. "Did she plan to run away with him?"

"She absolutely did. I read all the letters planning the elopement."

"You read them?"

"*Maman* keeps all the interesting books away from me. I've grown most proficient in steaming open envelopes."

"What did you learn?"

"She wanted him to take her to Portugal—heaven knows why—and get married. I think she'd got herself in a spot of trouble."

"Did your parents know about this?"

"My mother has perfected the art of ignoring anything unpleasant. My father is confident no one would disobey his orders. So no, they suspected nothing."

"And what did your brother think of all this?"

"Laurent? He wanted to kill Monsieur Vasseur. Especially when he heard the man had left the Foreign Legion."

"And you know this how?" I recalled Laurent's surprise when I told him Vasseur had given up his life in uniform.

"He'd hired a detective to follow Monsieur Vasseur. I read all the reports."

"What else did they say?"

"Unfortunately, not much of interest. He left Indochina or some other dreadful malaria-ridden place and showed up in Marseilles. That was the last dispatch from the detective. Disappointing, I thought."

"Did your sister ever ask for your help?"

"Never. All she did was scold me."

"Tell me about her descent into madness."

"We're a decent family, Lady Emily. We fall apart behind closed doors. When she refused to accept that my father would not let her marry Monsieur Vasseur, she was exiled to her room. She wasn't permitted downstairs even to dine."

"How long did this go on?"

"Several months until she was sent away."

"Do you have any idea if she saw Monsieur Vasseur during this time?"

"Do you really think my dear parents let me interact with her once she'd become so . . . undesirable? I wasn't even allowed to speak to her," she said. "I couldn't go near her room."

"I find it hard to believe that stopped you," I said. "You don't seem a person who's easily daunted."

"The compliment is much appreciated. But the truth is, I had no interest in talking to her. Reading the letters she sent was diverting enough, but Laurent was the only one of us who could tolerate her once she got dotty."

"Tell me about their relationship."

"They were inseparable until Monsieur Vasseur came on the scene. Laurent didn't like losing his dearest friend to a man he viewed as unworthy."

"Did you have any contact with Edith while she was under Dr. Girard's care?"

"None. My father wouldn't have stood for it. I think he was afraid her condition might be contagious, spread even through letters."

"Did this trouble you?"

"As I said, we were never close, Lady Emily. I can't say that I missed her at all. And frankly it was a relief to not have to hear her ramblings. Does that sound cruel?"

"Perhaps, but it's honest."

"Madness is at first tragic for those who love the victim, but it soon turns into a burden. My sister was lost to me long before she was sent away. And once she was gone, my life opened up. I wasn't allowed to be out at the same time as her, you see. My parents wanted her married first."

"It must have disappointed you when your father deemed Monsieur Vasseur an unsuitable suitor."

"I wasn't happy about it."

"Did you ever consider helping your sister to be with him?"

"And go against my parents' wishes?" Toinette's expression lacked any hint of being genuine. "I'd never dream of such a thing."

The next morning, Cécile and I skipped breakfast in favor of an early start. The drive to the asylum had been uneventful, and the nurse I'd seen before again greeted us at the door and led us to the office at the end of the corridor.

"I feel no surprise at seeing you again," the doctor said, standing as we entered the room. "I know I did not send you away yesterday satisfied."

I introduced Cécile. "I am most impressed with your facility," she said. "As a dear friend of Madame Prier's, I know it must have given her comfort to know her daughter was so well looked after while she was here."

"I'm only sorry Edith didn't stay with us," he said.

"Did you have any reason to believe she'd try to escape?" I asked.

"I'm not sure 'escape' is even the proper word. She wasn't locked up or restrained. I wouldn't have encouraged her to walk out the front door if I'd seen her try, but it's not as if she was a prisoner."

"Why do you think she wanted to leave?"

"I couldn't possibly say." He didn't look at me as he replied.

"You told us she had a gentleman who visited her regularly. Was she romantically involved with him?"

"I'm terribly sorry, Lady Emily. But unless her family has specifically instructed me to reveal the details of Mademoiselle Prier's case, I cannot tell you anything more."

Cécile and I had come prepared. She passed the doctor a letter from Madame Prier—she'd convinced her to write it while I had talked to Toinette. He read it, folded it, creasing the edges with care, and rubbed his eyes. "I can assure you there was nothing romantic between Edith and the man who called himself Myriel."

"We know Edith was with child," I said, leaning forward.

He sat, motionless.

"Laurent Prier told us the whole story."

No reply.

"Did Edith Prier flee because of what you did to her?" I asked.

Now he moaned. "She ran because of what I did, yes, but it's not what you think. Not if you've talked to Laurent."

"What do you mean?"

"I didn't do what he asked of me. I couldn't bring myself to harm the child. But all of that is irrelevant now. And it doesn't pertain to Edith's case, not so far as her family is concerned. I know what I've done, and it's something from which I won't be able to escape for the rest of my life. But it isn't any concern of yours."

"It is if what you did directly or indirectly led to Edith's murder," I said.

"I'm in the business of saving lives, not ending them, Lady Emily. Understand that and you'll know my guilt, though heavy, is not what Laurent told you."

18

I mulled over Dr. Girard's words as our carriage wound its way back along the river towards the bustle of Rouen. If his business was saving lives, and he hadn't done what Laurent asked, what had become of the child he claimed not to have harmed? My head was throbbing with questions by the time we reached the Priers'. I looked at Cécile and sighed as we alighted from the carriage.

"I'm not looking forward to this evening."

"I could not agree more," she said. "But perhaps tonight will be better than the others we've spent here. We may even be able to convince Toinette to stop talking."

And so laughter flowed from me as we entered the sitting room. Laughter that turned to ebullient joy when I saw my darling husband waiting for me. He rushed over and scooped me up in his arms.

"I came here with Gaudet this morning to follow up on a lead and couldn't resist seeing you before you leave for Paris," he said.

"I'm so pleased," I said, kissing his cheek. Cécile, giving me a knowing look, exited in search of Madame Prier.

"I missed you," he said.

"You shouldn't have sent me away."

"How are you enjoying Rouen?"

"It's been beyond fascinating," I said, and briefed him on all I'd learned about Edith. I did not, however, go into the details of my own ghostly tinglings.

"Girard must have let Edith have the baby and then sent it somewhere. It's no surprise a man of medicine wouldn't want to have *helped things along*, as Laurent told you." Colin tapped his fingers on his knee. "Who would have taken the child?"

"You agree the baby's still alive?"

"I do. Think on it. Edith discovers she's with child. Her brother wants her sent away so the situation can be dealt with, one way or another. The good doctor isn't willing to do what Laurent wants, but knows he can hide the birth—Laurent was the only one visiting—and send the baby somewhere safe."

"Of course." I looked at him. "We have to find the baby."

"It could be anywhere—years have passed."

"Edith escaped because she wanted to find it. She must have got in contact with Vasseur somehow. He left the Foreign Legion, came for her, and they went in search of their child. And the mission led to her brutal death."

"It makes more sense than a random killing," Colin said.

"Does it make more sense than thinking the Ripper's come to France?"

"At the moment I'm inclined to say yes. Random violence is rare, and although the manner of Edith's death is reminiscent of the Whitechapel murders, it may be that whoever killed her was deliberately copying his more famous colleague to set the police on the wrong track."

"A theory not originally your own, if I recall." I smiled. "So what will you do?"

"We can't discount the possibility the murderer has come over from England. But this information of yours makes me want to change tactics."

"New tactics that perhaps don't require shipping me off to London?"

"So long as there's no evidence of a madman marauding through Normandy in search of prey, I think I should be able to keep you safe. But are you sure you wouldn't prefer to go home? Or to Paris with Cécile?"

"It's as if you don't know me at all," I said. "Can you possibly believe I'd rather be anywhere than with you? I'd be so happy I wouldn't even object to you keeping me safe."

"I can't believe it."

"Shall I convince you?" I asked. After a brief and extremely pleasant pause, we returned to the matter at hand. "Do you think Edith knew where the child had been sent?"

"We're going to have to question Girard again. My guess would be that she didn't—there would be too great a risk of her trying to get in contact. But it's possible the baby hadn't been sent far."

"He could have easily sent it out of the country."

"True, but let's suppose someone—perhaps this man who visited her—told Edith where the child was. She escaped and wound up dead within a reasonable drive of Rouen."

"So you draw the conclusion that she'd gone as far as she needed to find the child?" I asked. "She might have only just begun her journey."

He grinned. "You're right. I do adore your mind."

"You're too kind," I said. "But I must ask—have you made any progress with our friend Sebastian?"

"*Your* friend, Sebastian. Let's be clear on that point. He's not shown a single sign of being around. I've been working on the assumption he followed you here."

"I wish I could say I'd seen him and recruited him to the Crown's cause."

"This is one bet, Emily, you're not going to win."

"I'm sure you'd like to believe that. But I've not time to discuss it at the moment. Will you excuse me?" I asked. "I want to speak with Laurent. He may prove himself useful yet."

I applied my usual method for locating Laurent—following the sound of moody Beethoven up the stairs to his room. This time, I didn't bother to knock on the door, opting instead to head straight for the passage between our two chambers.

"You're quite good, you know," I said, coming up behind him as he sat at the piano. "Do you compose as well?"

He grunted in my general direction.

"I've spoken with Dr. Girard again. He didn't do what you asked of him. Edith gave birth to her baby and the child is still alive."

He stopped playing. "Impossible."

"Is it?"

"He—" Laurent looked almost flustered, his eyes darting in all directions, his mouth drawn tight. "He wouldn't have done that. Not without telling me."

"He had to have known you wouldn't approve of the choice."

"He had no right."

"So far as I can tell, Edith is the one who should have had rights," I said. "Can you imagine how it must have tormented her not to be able to raise her own child?"

"Of course I can. Why do you think I asked him to do what I did?"

"Wouldn't what you wanted have been even worse than her simply giving the child to someone else to raise until she was recovered from her illness?"

He didn't reply.

"Regardless," I said. "He couldn't bring himself to go through with it, and now won't tell me what became of the child. We have to find it."

"Vasseur. He must have given it to Vasseur."

"Vasseur was already away in the Legion when the baby would have been born. This might, however, be the time to give me whatever information you can about the man. Where is his family? Where did he live?"

"It is time for me to have a very serious conversation with Girard. You have no reason to be part of this." He rose to his feet and stormed out of the room, not even bothering to slam the door behind him. All in all, a disappointing exit. I'd come to expect more from Laurent. If nothing else, one should be able to count on a gentleman like him to brood masterfully.

I started down the steps (long after having heard the front door bang behind Laurent—I was glad his departure from the house hadn't been completely lackluster) and found Colin and Cécile in the garden with Madame Prier and her husband. The sun still stretched high in the summer sky, the air felt warm, and bees skipped happily from flower to flower in search of sweet nectar. Cécile and Madame Prier sat close together, both shaded by Cécile's lacy parasol. Colin, his long legs stretched in front of him, occupied the wrought-iron chair across from them and was fanning himself with a folded newspaper while Monsieur Prier occupied himself with the inspection of a thread that had come loose from his jacket.

"Come join us, Kallista, and try one of these," Cécile said, picking up a plate of bergamot oranges in honey. "You look far too melancholy for such a beautiful day."

I crossed over to them, rejecting the candied fruit and pulling a chair next to my husband's. "I'm not melancholy, just tired. All this to-ing and fro-ing, and I haven't been sleeping well."

"Oh dear!" Madame Prier lifted her eyes to the sky. "It's the room, isn't it?"

"The room?" I asked.

"Dominique—" Monsieur Prier glared at his wife, but she didn't let him continue.

"I shouldn't have dreamed of putting you in Edith's room," she said. "I never gave much credence to her claims of hearing voices, even when I heard her talking back to them. But since her death, it's all tormenting me. What if there really was something in her room, as she insisted? What if some ghostly girl did speak to her? I suppose I wanted to prove to myself it's not haunted or possessed or I don't know what, and I thought—hoped—your staying in it would put my worries to rest."

"What specifically did she hear?" I asked.

"She was never very lucid about it," Madame Prier said. "But she'd speak to someone, and she claimed it was a girl—she'd talk about tying ribbons in her hair—got upset when I told her I didn't see anything. I don't suppose you've heard anything strange while you've been up there?"

I steeled myself, hoping to disguise the anxiety tingling through me at her description of the child that so well matched what I myself had experienced. "Only Laurent's musical efforts."

"He's a dreadful boy, isn't he?" she asked.

"Worthless," Monsieur Prier said.

"He's feeling the loss of his sister keenly," Colin said.

"He's a fine one to talk now," Madame Prier said. "But it was he who first noticed her health deteriorating. He's the one who told us she was talking to people who weren't there. He recognized her delusions before any of us."

"What exactly happened to Edith?" I asked. "Forgive me if it's too painful a question."

She sighed. "I know I ought to be keening and lamenting and mourning," she said. "But Toinette's right. At the moment I'm suffering more from guilt than grief."

"That's not uncommon when one has had to deal with a chronically ill family member," Colin said.

"You're far too reasonable, Monsieur Hargreaves. Edith was difficult from the time she was a little girl. Headstrong and determined. Always getting into trouble. And always with her brother. That's the way with twins, I'm told. They even had a private language when they were small."

"It was ridiculous," Monsieur Prier said. "I wouldn't tolerate such a thing, of course, and forbade them to use it. But as they grew older, and it was time for Laurent to go to school, Edith grew more and more obstinate. She didn't want him to go away from home."

"Did he?" Colin asked.

"Of course he did," he said. "He studied in Paris and then returned to Rouen. We hoped he would marry, but he never showed even the slightest interest in any eligible girls."

"What about the ineligible ones?" Cécile asked.

"You are too bad, my friend," Madame Prier said, laughing.

Monsieur Prier did not share his wife's amusement. "He has had his share of romantic attachments, but none of them have held his interest for more than a few months. I think there was someone in Paris about whom he was serious, but nothing came of it."

"She must have left him," Madame Prier said. "A well and truly broken heart is the only reasonable explanation for him clinging so assiduously to bachelorhood."

"And what about Edith? Did she want to marry?" I asked.

"No doubt by now you've heard all the sordid dealings she had with Jules Vasseur," Monsieur Prier said. "Terrible man."

"I have heard a little about him," I said. "What specifically made him so undesirable?"

"He came from no family—his father was a tradesman." Madame Prier's voice slipped to a coarse whisper. "His mother's people were farmers. Can you imagine? The father was successful enough to send him to school, where he did well, and he eventually managed to become an officer in the Foreign Legion."

"Admirable enough," Monsieur Prier said. "But hardly what one wishes for one's daughter."

"Admirable how, my dear?" Madame Prier asked. "The Legion is full of thieves and vagabonds. An utter disgrace."

Monsieur Prier did not respond to his wife.

"Did Vasseur court Edith openly?" Colin asked.

"He did, until I told him in no uncertain terms that he was not welcome in the house." His voice had taken on a pointed edge, a hint that a nasty temper lurked not far beneath the surface.

"And then?" I asked.

"Then he showed his true colors," Monsieur Prier said. "He crept around here at night, trying to lure Edith to meet him. He followed her when she went out—she couldn't call on a friend without him pursuing her."

"Did she view it that way?" Colin asked.

"At first I think she found it romantic and took it as a sign of his love and devotion, but eventually it became a burden."

"She was extremely upset," Madame Prier said. "As you might well imagine."

"Was she speaking to him through all this?" I asked.

"Absolutely not," Monsieur Prier said. "We'd told her to ignore him."

"But she did love him, didn't she?" I tried to imagine how difficult it must have been for Edith to muddle through such a mess. "Didn't she want to see him?"

"Her pleasant disposition towards him ended when he accosted her at a ball," Monsieur Prier said.

His wife continued. "She'd been dancing all evening—she was beautiful and high-spirited and much in demand. Vasseur was lurking in the background, watching her, growing more and more jealous as she spun around the dance floor with partner after partner. He cornered her when she'd stepped onto a balcony to get some air. She would never tell us what he said, but she ran inside, crying, begging to be taken home. After that, they never spoke again."

"Could she have written to him after that?" I asked.

"I suppose it's possible," she said. "But she never received any letters from him."

"How can you be sure?" Cécile asked.

"He wrote four times a week. We burned everything he sent."

"Did you read the letters?" I asked.

"No," Madame Prier said. "We didn't have any interest in what the worthless profligate might say." I didn't believe her; surely simple curiosity would have demanded otherwise. Who could have resisted opening them? If nothing else, I thought she would have wanted to ensure Edith wasn't writing to him—a question answered in an instant if his words were clear responses to her. I could not rely on the veracity of anyone in the Prier family.

"At what point did you notice Edith's health deteriorating?" Colin asked.

"Soon thereafter. She started sleepwalking—we actually had to lock her in her room," Monsieur Prier said. "She talked to herself. Or rather, she talked to people who weren't there—the little girl more often than not."

"It was beyond alarming," Madame Prier said. "Before long, her personality was lost entirely, and she shouted at me as if she didn't know who I was. She'd beg and plead for us to let her out so she could go home. As if she had no idea she was already there."

"It must have been awful," Cécile said. "You are strong to have soldiered through so difficult a time."

"After she fell down the stairs in the middle of the night, Laurent convinced us she was endangering herself," she said.

"It didn't require convincing," Monsieur Prier said. "We couldn't even determine how she got out of her room."

"I'm not sure about that," his wife said. "But at any rate, Laurent had read about Dr. Girard, and contacted him to see if he felt he could help her. He was willing, so my husband took her to him."

"And you were pleased with the treatment?" Colin asked.

Monsieur Prier shrugged. "You see the outcome was not so great."

"Were you happy with the conditions in the asylum?" I asked, knowing full well Dr. Girard had said neither of them had visited her there. "Did you feel your daughter was being properly looked after?"

"It was clean and bright and she seemed safe there," Madame Prier said. "At that point, what more could I hope for?"

"Did you see her often?" Colin asked.

"We went every week at first, then every other week. She wouldn't talk to us, only sat and looked vacant. So we stopped going more than once a month."

"When did you last see her?" I asked, wondering who was telling the truth: the doctor or the parents? It seemed unlikely Dr. Girard would lie about such a thing. More reasonable, I thought, to believe the Priers preferred to hide their sins of omission when it came to Edith.

"Two days before she vanished," Monsieur Prier said.

"What was her mental state?" Colin asked, his voice calm in the extreme.

"Unchanged."

Madame Prier smiled fetchingly. "This must all be such a bore for you. Please don't feel that you have to ask questions to make us feel better. We'll manage. As I said, we've already grieved the loss. Edith was never herself after she left this house. I do hope, Monsieur Hargreaves, that you haven't come here to collect your charming wife and run away again. It's so nice to have friends around. We must have a party for you."

17 July 1892

Oh the excitement I'm missing! The election is in full swing, and I'm desperate to be in the middle of it. It looks as if the Conservatives shall gain far too many seats—but I cling to the hope they will fall short of an overall majority and the Liberals will be returned to power. If nothing else, we should be able to count on those who support Irish Nationalism, an issue that has been consuming Gladstone for years now, particularly after the defeat of his Home Rule bill . . . a topic on which I would happily speak for days if allowed. Much as I admire the man, to have undertaken the writing of such a piece of legislation essentially without the input of anyone else was a grand mistake. Let us hope, now, he will have the chance to remedy the errors of the past and put an end to all these Irish troubles.

How I miss the days when Nicholas and I hosted political dinners, subtly (and not-so subtly) influencing the views of those around us. Choosing to bury myself deep in the country—exiling myself from England—was not, perhaps, the wisest decision. I've mourned all these years, and will continue to miss the dear man for the rest of my days. But it's time to reengage.

I shall contact my solicitor and instruct him to find a home for me in town. Maybe one in Park Lane, near Colin.

He left for me some of his wife's work. Apparently she is translating Homer's Odyssey *from the original Greek. This evening I shall read what she's done. Is it hubris that enables someone like her to take on such a project?*

19

"We're not staying here," Colin said, tightening my corset before I slipped into a luscious dark red velvet gown for dinner. Madame Prier had promised *sole meunière,* the delicate fish drenched in brown butter and lemon, and I found myself looking forward to the meal more than I'd anticipated. My husband did not share my enthusiasm, but it was not the food that caused him grievance. "I'd rather sleep in rooms over a tavern than in this house."

"They are an interesting lot, aren't they, the Priers?"

"If by 'interesting' you mean 'slightly deranged', yes, I suppose." He fastened his cuff links. "I lunched with Monsieur Prier before you returned this afternoon. He didn't speak to any of us. Read a book through the entire meal."

"Could you see the title?"

"Les Miserables."

"Quite a choice," I said. "According to Toinette he keeps out of the house as much as possible, but she doesn't know where he goes."

"He has my sympathies. I'm ready to flee after less than a day."

"I think there's something to these visions Edith had," I said. "The description of the child matches that of the girl I saw at the Markhams'."

"Insofar as they were both wearing ribbons." He put his hands on my shoulders. "Don't let your mind trick you, my dear. All little girls wear ribbons."

"But pale blue—"

"Madame Prier said nothing about color. You're molding the situation to what you saw."

"I feel like we're missing something. Toinette said Laurent deliberately drove Edith to insanity."

"Do you think he's trying to do the same to you?" Colin asked. The lack of skepticism in his voice took me aback.

"I'm not sure why he would."

"What if he killed his sister? What if he's afraid you'll find him out?"

"Heavens, what's become of you?" I closed the clasp on a delicate gold and ruby necklace. "That sounds more like my wild speculation than the solid sort of theory you'd present."

"Nothing in this case makes sense in an ordinary way. I don't really subscribe to all this nonsense of hauntings and driving people mad. Edith came unhinged—I believe that. There's a history of insanity in the family, and that's the most likely explanation for her illness. Her brother may have exploited that with ghost stories, but I don't believe it's possible he literally made her come undone."

"All right," I said. "So she's been forced to throw over the man she loves. She realizes she's with child, and she's terrified of what her parents will do—her mother's beyond eccentric and it's easy to believe she had cause to be scared of her father's reaction. That sort of stress could put an otherwise stable mind close to the precipice."

"So Laurent plays with her—"

"According to him because he was worried and wanted to get her help."

"And she's sent to Girard, who hides the pregnancy, delivers the baby, and sorts out a caregiver for the abandoned infant."

"Which must have hurt Edith all the more," I said. "To have her child taken from her like that—" I bit my lip and tried not to cry. Colin took my hand in both of his.

"I'm so sorry, my love. This must be incredibly difficult for you."

"I thought you'd decided it was time for me to be over it."

"There are ways in which it is time, but this case seems to be digging it all back up again." Deep furrows appeared in his brow. He dropped my hand and started to pace. "Am I doing the right thing letting you pursue this?"

"*Letting me?*" I asked. "That's not a term of which I'm particularly fond."

"I realize that, but it's also the truth. I say this not to irritate you but to try to make you understand that I'm carrying the burden of your well-being. I'm your husband, Emily. If I allow you to do things that cause you harm, is the end result not, in fact, my fault?"

I could feel myself getting caught up in his use of the word *allow,* but was sensible enough to see the reason—and the fear, and the guilt, and the love—in his words. "What happened in Constantinople was not your fault," I said.

"If I'd been taking proper care of you, it never would have happened."

"We've talked about this a hundred times—you agreed that we both did what we had to, given the circumstances."

"I know that's the case. Intellectually, at least. But emotionally I must confess to having more and more sympathy for husbands who appear to be considerably less enlightened than I. Perhaps there is a certain amount of wisdom to their beliefs about what a woman should be allowed to do."

My heart sank hearing him speak like this.

"I know this is upsetting to you," he said. "And I'm not suggesting at this moment that we revamp entirely the understanding we have about each other's work. But I must be honest with you, my dear—this marriage between equals is more difficult than I expected it would be."

I could hardly breathe.

"It's not that I don't adore you. I love you more than anything," he said. "But how can I love you and not take care of you? I'm having trouble reconciling my intellectual beliefs with emotional reality."

"Who's to say the emotions are what's real?" I asked. "Do you not better trust your intellect?"

"I do," he said. "But I'm beginning to wonder if that's always the correct path."

"What would you have me do?"

"Do you want absolute candor?"

"Always," I said, my heart pounding.

"I would have you study Greek and read scandalous literature and host political dinners and torment society ladies. I would see you catalog art and travel the world, but as a well-educated tourist, not in pursuit of this work of ours."

"It's dangerous for you as well. What if I asked you to give it up?"

"I wouldn't." He closed his eyes. "I'm sorry, Emily. I do consider you my equal—absolutely. But we are not the same. We are not capable of handling the same situations in the same ways. Your strengths are not mine and vice versa. I'm qualified for what I do. You're brilliant and insightful and good at it—but the physical requirements are beyond what can reasonably be expected of a lady. And without being able to handle the physicality of it, you would be putting yourself in danger again and again. I know you hate to hear me say it, but how can I allow that?"

"I—I'm stunned," I said. "I love working with you. I thought we were making progress. This conversation, even—we were analyzing the situation. Making reasonable deductions—"

"Yes. But when it comes time to pursue the culprit—to unmask him—that is a task I cannot in good conscience allow you to take part in."

His words hurt like a slap, stinging against my skin. "You didn't say such things to Kristiana," I said. "You believed she could be your equal in all ways."

"I did. And now she's dead. You and I went into our marriage believing we could do everything together—but look what happened when I let you, forgive me, behave like a man. You were nearly killed."

"I don't know what to say." I wanted to cry, but wouldn't let myself, suddenly feeling an overwhelming urge for privacy.

"I'm so sorry." He knelt in front of me and wrapped his arms around my knees. "I'm at a complete loss and don't know what to do. But I couldn't go on any longer without telling you how I feel. If we can't be honest with each other, we have nothing. I know I'm letting you down, disappointing you, proving that all your hesitations about marrying again were reasonable."

"If things hadn't gone so horribly wrong in Constantinople—"

"They would have gone horribly wrong somewhere else. It's inevitable in this line of work."

"So I'm to sit at home waiting for news that you've finally been bested, that I'm widowed again?"

"I don't know, Emily."

"What happened to your easy arrogance?" I asked, my voice growing stronger and loud. "You used to tell me not to worry—that you were trained, that you were invincible. I didn't believe it, but could understand that confidence helped protect you. What am I to think now? That you've lost faith in yourself?"

"There's no one better than me at this job, Emily," he said. "But even I cannot go on forever."

"Then stop."

He looked up at me, his eyes fixed on mine. "I won't."

"And I've no choice but to accept that?"

"I'm sorry."

"Stop saying that." I could no longer stop the tears from pouring down my face. "You are dashing all my happiness."

"I'd rather have you irritated and alive than dead with a smile on your face."

"That's not your choice to make," I said. "Regardless of your status as my husband." Even as I said the words I knew they weren't true. I'd given up everything when I'd married him. If he refused to let me assist his investigations, I would have to stop my work. He was equally aware of this, but had the courtesy—and good sense—not to broach the subject. Instead, he pulled me down on my knees, so that we were facing each other.

"I'm confused, Emily. I don't know what to do. I've not made any decisions, and can't even tell you our options at this point, because I haven't figured them out. I need your mind—your quick, wonderful mind—to help me solve Edith's murder. But there will come a time in the case when you will have to step back. And when that time comes, I can't have you protesting or sneaking around on your own. I have to be able to trust that you'll do as you're told, or I'll be too distracted to do my work well. And then I will be in danger."

"I don't want that," I whispered.

"Can I count on you to stop when I tell you to?"

"Do I have a choice?"

"No, Emily, you don't."

"Then why bother to ask?"

"Because it matters to me that you understand why I'm doing this," he said. "I'm not some unreasonable brute."

"I know." My voice was barely audible.

"I'm sorry."

"Stop saying that," I said.

He looked at the floor, then rose to his feet, lifting me up with him. "So knowing her child was lost to her made Edith's mental state deteriorate more quickly," he said, his voice rough.

"What if a man came to visit her—maybe the man who was looking after the child?—and he agreed to let her meet the little girl?"

"You're sure it's a girl?"

"Absolutely," I said, numb.

"He helped her escape."

"And months passed before she was found murdered. What happened during that time?" There was no joy in this for me now.

"Forgive me. I see how unhappy you are," he said. "It's not that you can't do *anything*, Emily, only that you can't do *everything*."

I did understand. I did see the reason in his arguments. I even could accept that his position was just, even correct. But it made no difference. The only thing that mattered was wondering if I'd ever be able to forgive him.

20

When I woke the next morning, I knew I would forgive him. Anything else was impossible. Still, I was unhappy with what had transpired between us and the cautious and too-tender smile he bestowed upon me as he turned on his pillow to kiss me was like harsh light in delicate eyes. My body responded the way it always did to his touch, but there was a disconnect, and it was as if I watched us from above instead of drowning in pleasure with him the way I used to. As always, he was beyond attentive, deliciously thorough, but I wanted to cry, wanted to erase the hours that had led us to this painful and awkward place.

Painful and awkward for me, at any rate. My husband did not seem troubled in the least. Quite the contrary. He sprung out of bed, bent over to kiss me, and rang for Meg. "Ready for your morning ablutions?" he asked, whistling an obtrusively cheerful tune.

I rolled over and groaned. "I'm going back to sleep."

"Up, lazy girl," he said. "I'm not cutting you out of the fun altogether, so there's no need to mope. What do you think is our best strategy? Talk to the obtuse Monsieur Prier? Grill moody Laurent? Or shall we pester Dr. Girard again?"

I pulled the pillow over my head. "I'll leave it to you to decide."

"Oh no, my dear." He wrenched the pillow from my hand. "I won't have you making my decision into something it's not. You're still involved with this, and I need your opinion."

Need it now, I thought, *but not when things get interesting.* No sooner had this flown through my brain than a wave of guilt followed, hard on its heels. I could choose misery or accept the reality into which I'd freely entered, a reality that somewhere in my soul I knew to be reasonable. I rolled onto my back and stared at the ceiling. "Monsieur Prier is unlikely to know anything about the whereabouts of the child, and I think that's the piece of the puzzle we need to find next. Dr. Girard has told us what he will—unless you've some hidden plan to torture more out of him when I'm not around."

"You're dreadful," he said, bending over to kiss the side of my neck. Once again, my body betrayed me and my skin delighted at the feeling of his lips.

"I doubt very much he's the only person at the asylum who knew about the birth," I said, sitting up. "We need to speak to the nurses, the orderlies, the rest of the staff. Someone may be able to identify Edith's mysterious visitor. I'm confident he could lead us to the child."

"Do you think she's still alive?" he asked.

"The child?" I asked; he nodded. "You agree with me that she's a girl?"

"I've yet to see reason to doubt your intuition," he said.

This brought immediate tears to my eyes.

"It's not that I've lost any measure of faith in you, Emily. But I'm going to better look after you from now on."

I wiped the tears with the back of my hand.

"And I won't have you wallowing," he said, smiling. "I love you."

"I love you," I said, my insides a mass of confusion.

"So?" he asked. "Do *you* think the child is alive?"

"I do. And we should find her as soon as possible."

"He was definitely French." The girl wriggled in her chair, uncomfortable. "I never really talked to him, though. He came every other Friday, I think it was. Or maybe once a month. Can't rightly remember, but I know I thought of him as reliable. You could always depend on him showing up again."

The young nurse's assistant was the eleventh person to whom we'd spoken. Dr. Girard—who assured us he'd not had a recent visit from Laurent—had not objected to us questioning them, even gave us the use of his office, though he made it clear again he had made no progress when searching out the true identity of the man who, according to the nurses, called himself Charles Myriel. Everyone remembered him as kind and constant, and the general consensus was that his presence soothed Edith, even when she was in the midst of a difficult spell. But no one had ever had occasion to extract from him any personal information. He always came on horseback, alone, stayed exactly an hour, and disappeared with no fanfare.

Frustrated, Colin and I called for the doctor to rejoin us.

"Sir," my husband said. "We appreciate the situation in which you now find yourself. You assisted this lady in her time of greatest need— you refused to *help her along*, as her brother requested, when she was with child. And that means you must have sent the baby—whom you must have delivered—somewhere to be cared for. Now is not the time to hide your courageous deeds. Tell us where she is."

"You know she was a girl?" he asked, slumping in his chair.

"Every vision Edith reported to her family was of a little girl," I said.

The doctor shook his head. "That may be so, but she couldn't have known the gender of the child at the time."

"She had a one in two chance of guessing correctly," Colin said.

"And in this case she was correct," Dr. Girard said. "I wish I could give you something to lead you to this man who visited her, but I can assure you he had nothing to do with Lucy—she was called Lucy. Edith asked if she could name the child. How could I deny her when she was suffering such anguish? She knew her parents would never accept the girl, and agreed to let me send Lucy away—far away—with a cousin of mine."

"So your cousin is raising her?" I asked.

"No," he said. "I felt there needed to be a further layer of distance to ensure Edith's identity would remain secret. My cousin took the baby to Gibraltar—he was on his way to Egypt—and delivered her to the care of a Catholic convent there. So far as I know, the nuns are raising her."

"Do you receive any reports from them?" His story seemed about as plausible to me as the queen deciding to remarry.

"I don't," he said. "Monsieur Prier's reaction to his daughter's illness was so . . . violent . . . I feared for what he might do if he learned the truth."

"Violent?" Colin asked.

"Violent?" I echoed him. "Did you not think pointing out to us that her father was violent might have been a pertinent fact given that she was brutally murdered?"

"You're suggesting that he might, somehow, have found out about Lucy and come for Edith, and murdered her?" the doctor asked.

"You just admitted that you were concerned about the possible violence of his reaction," I said.

"I should, perhaps, have chosen my words more carefully. Violent is what I think of it. Monsieur Prier is an extremely forceful man—and his daughter's mental condition disturbed him greatly. According to her brother, when she first exhibited signs of illness at home, he scolded her vehemently, as if she could control her behavior if only she chose to. His yelling and bullying did not have the desired effect, of course. But that doesn't mean he wouldn't have used similar tactics on her again if he disapproved of her . . . condition. Given my own study and beliefs, I thought any such exhibit of temper could cause her a significant setback."

"What did you think of her relationship with her brother?" I asked.

"Laurent Prier presents a fascinating case of his own," Dr. Girard said. "He was obsessively close to his sister, and she to him."

"Is that uncommon with twins?" Colin asked.

"Not entirely," the doctor said. "But these two took it rather to an extreme."

"Toinette, Edith's younger sister, insists that Laurent deliberately drove Edith mad," I said.

Dr. Girard laughed. "It may have seemed like that to Toinette. His compulsive jealousy and desire to protect her at all costs certainly did not improve Edith's nervous state. But I wasn't in the house with them and cannot vouch for what went on there. I only know that Laurent showed deep concern for his sister's health, stability, and reputation."

"Did you consider their relationship inappropriate?" Colin asked.

"I did, but I cannot say precisely why or how. Something in the way they interacted unsettled me. He did once after a visit leave behind a journal he keeps, and I admit—with no pride in my actions—that I read it. There was nothing enlightening, I'm afraid. Myriel was here the next day and offered to leave it at the tavern for him. They used to run into each other on occasion. But I didn't feel comfortable giving it to him."

"What did you do with it?" I asked.

"I left it with Edith, in her room and her brother collected it on his next visit." He pushed his hands against his desk. "I do wish I could be of more use to you. I should, I suppose, have put in place a system for better identifying my patients' visitors, so I might have been better prepared for foiling their murderers."

His comment—an obvious attempt at humor—did not sit well with me.

"We appreciate what help you have given us," Colin said, rising. I didn't feel quite ready to leave, but had no clear idea of what I wanted to do instead. So I stood as well and took my husband's arm. We thanked Dr. Girard and walked down the long, brightly clean corridor in silence. Only when we stepped outside and were once again alone did I turn to Colin and speak.

"We should go to the village," I said. "Any visitor to the asylum would have to pass through and someone there must be interested enough in gossip to have noticed a regular gentleman caller. There's not much else going on around here."

Colin nodded. "An excellent suggestion."

"If you tell me you believe in nuns in Gibraltar happily waiting for abandoned babies, I'm never speaking to you again." I thought carefully about all I knew of Dr. Girard. He seemed a kind man, decent, but had his relationship with Edith grown inappropriate, as her brother's had? What did he stand to lose if the truth about her child ever came to light? Did he have a motive for wanting her dead?

My husband wrapped his arms around me and pulled me close. "I could not love you more." He kissed me and his lips felt warm and safe and tender. I kissed him back and took his hand, wondering if this was what settling into contentment felt like. We stepped into our waiting carriage and in a few short minutes arrived in the village, which consisted of a single road containing a bakery, a butcher shop, and a tavern.

"Tavern," we both said, simultaneously, and laughed.

Settling into contentment, I thought, might not be all bad.

I caught myself before I tripped on the wide, uneven floorboards of Le Clos des Roses, a name I hoped was meant to be ironic. The walls, with patches of crumbling plaster, seemed poised to collapse on the rough tables filling the poorly lit room, and the only decoration to be seen was the stuffed and mounted head of a wild boar. Great chunks of the unfortunate beast's fur had gone missing along with one of the tusks. Hanging from the one that remained was a dingy rag, whipped down by a skeletal serving girl to wipe the table in front of us.

"Would you like the plat du jour?" she asked, scrubbing vigorously, her rough accent making it hard for me to understand her French. "Chicken with tarragon sauce and potatoes."

I wasn't particularly hungry, but Colin instructed her to bring the special to both of us. "Gives an excuse to be here longer," he said after she'd disappeared into the kitchen.

"I fear for our health," I said. "But we are in France, so there's a distinct possibility that rather than poisoning us, this will be the single most spectacular meal we've ever eaten."

"Let's just hope our poor *poulet* was better treated than the boar," he said. He patted my hand. "I'll be right back." He walked up to the bar and spoke to the surly looking man standing behind it. From a distance, their exchange appeared congenial enough, and a few minutes later my husband returned carrying two glasses of tart cider. "I told the bartender that your cousin—your *French* cousin—was engaged to a girl who wound up here, and that he visited her constantly despite his parents forbidding it. When his father, despot that he is, tried to interfere, your cousin left home and disappeared. We, of course, are here in search of him."

"So what did he say?" I asked.

The girl returned with our food before he could answer. She dropped the plates in front of us, uninterested in preserving the cook's unexpectedly beautiful presentation. "You're looking for a man?" she asked.

"We are," I said. "My cousin."

"He told me," she said, tossing her head in the direction of the bar. "We've a gent who used to come in here. Sounds like it could be him, but he ain't been around for the last couple of months. Thing is, he always said he was visiting his mother, not his fiancée."

"He wouldn't have wanted to draw any attention to what he was really doing, lest his family discovered the attachment was still very much alive." Fiction, it seemed, came easily to me. "Can you remember when you last saw him?"

"Springtime, I think. That was the last time he came regular, at least. Seems like he was here once more, just a few weeks ago, but I didn't talk to him and can't be sure."

"Did you usually speak to him?" Colin asked.

"He was very chatty," she said.

"Did he ever say where he lived?" I asked.

"He kept a room at Madame Renaldi's. The house across from the church?"

Colin thanked her and dug into his chicken as soon as she'd left us to our food. "This," he said, "is extraordinary. Have you tasted it?"

The sauce was tangy perfection, the meat moist and flavorful. But I was still unnerved, still unsure as to what to think about this new turn in our relationship. I didn't like being an unequal partner—or equal but different, whatever that meant—and I didn't like the fact that it was distracting me from the work at hand. I took one more bite, but found I could stomach no more. Colin, unperturbed, traded his empty plate for my nearly full one and polished off my meal.

"I know this is hard, Emily," he said. "But it's for the best. I'm not going to keep you from a fulfilling life. I hope you know that. Trust me, my dear. Together, we'll find our way through this." He folded his napkin into a crisp rectangle and placed it on the table. "Are you willing to miss dessert in favor of Madame Renaldi?"

"Mais oui," I said, fixing a smile on my face. I wanted real emotion back, but all I could summon felt false, painted on. "Lead me where you will. I can't think of a worthier person to follow."

21

Bright blue shutters lined the walls of Madame Renaldi's stone house, and matching flowerboxes, overflowing with red and yellow blossoms, hung from each window. The proprietress herself greeted us at the door and ushered us into a comfortable and welcoming sitting room. Colin did a neat job explaining why we'd come, and I managed a few tears to lend verisimilitude of his story of my poor, missing cousin.

"I can assure you Monsieur Myriel was an ideal tenant," she said, as if the words would soothe a grieving relation. "He wasn't here often, and always left his room in good order."

"Did he only stay when he visited the asylum?" Colin asked.

"He did. But he said he wanted to keep the room available in case his mother—he told me he was visiting his mother—took a turn for the worse. He liked the idea that there was a little home waiting for him whenever he needed it. And his own house was so far away—near Marseilles, I think it was—he needed somewhere to sleep when he was here."

"When did you last see him?" I asked.

"It's been several months at least. I received a letter saying his mother had died and that he wouldn't be back. He included a final month's rent. Never collected the things he'd left in the room, though, and didn't give a forwarding address so I could send them. Could I give them to you? I do hate holding on to someone else's possessions."

"Of course," I said, giving her what I hoped was a poignant yet weak smile. "When he resurfaces, we'll be sure he gets them."

Colin carried the wooden crate she gave us to the carriage, slipped it inside, and went to speak to the driver.

I settled into my seat, pulling the box close to me and opening its top. The contents appeared ordinary enough: two clean, white shirts, fresh socks, other assorted items of clothing, a razor, shaving lotion, a pen and ink. A neat pile of books, their spines facing up, was stacked down one side: *L'Année Terrible*, a book of poems about the Franco-Prussian War by Victor Hugo, Thomas Hardy's *Tess of the d'Urbervilles*, Émile Zola's *La Bête Humaine*, and *The Picture of Dorian Gray* by Oscar Wilde. A small, leather-bound notebook and a golden watch missing its chain had been wrapped in a linen handkerchief embroidered with the initials HPC.

The notebook appeared the most promising, until I flipped through the smooth, cream-colored pages and found them all blank. Ragged edges near the binding suggested some sheets had been removed, and not neatly, but as they'd been taken from the back, not the front, I couldn't study later pages in hope of discovering indentations left behind. The watch appeared extremely old—older than the date, 9 November 1870, engraved on the inside. The case showed remnants of ornate decoration, but the detail had been mostly rubbed off, no doubt from frequent use over many years.

"Anything interesting?" Colin asked, as he climbed in next to me.

"Possibly," I said. We lurched forward as the driver urged on the horses.

"Are you all right, Emily?"

"Not entirely. Last night's revelations sent me reeling."

"I appreciate that," he said, his voice grave. "But rather than give too much thought to things you can't do, focus on what you can. Tell me about Myriel's crate."

"Look for yourself," I said, removing the top. "You may notice something I missed."

"Unlikely," he said, leaning forward and examining the contents of the box. He leafed through it all with care, turning the pages of the notebook in much the same manner I had. I watched his hands, strong and competent, as he pulled out the books, checking their endpapers and leafing through the rest. "Did anything strike you about them?" he asked.

"Only that Hugo also wrote *Les Miserables*, which Monsieur Prier is currently reading," I said. "We've not seen any of Edith's writings. Surely Laurent saved any letters she sent him. And she might have kept a diary—not, perhaps, after she got sick, but even her records of the months before that could prove useful." I flashed him what I hoped was a wry look. "I don't suppose you have a strategy in place for investigating convents in Gibraltar?"

"Quite the contrary," he said, a wicked smile spreading across his face. "I've already mobilized a crack convent investigation team. They'll be on-site within forty-eight hours. We can expect answers in fifty. Sarcasm suits you, my dear."

"You're dreadful," I said. "Have I reminded you of that recently?"

"Not recently enough," he said. "Do you think there even *are* convents in Gibraltar?"

"Yes, but it's irrelevant. Girard blurted out the first thing that came to his mind."

Our knees banged into each other as he leaned forward and took my hands in his. "Emily, I—"

"Don't, please," I said. "I shall come to terms with this, but you must give me time."

"Can we talk about it?"

"Not now. First because my thoughts do me no credit, and second because we must not let ourselves get distracted. We need to find Lucy."

Back in Rouen, we excused ourselves from dinner, asking instead for a tray of pâtés and other cold bites we could eat at our leisure. So while the family feasted on pressed duck, Colin and I set to work. He locked the door to our room from the inside and gave me a quick kiss.

"I wish I was locking this for a different reason," he said. While he began methodically searching and analyzing every inch of the room, I crawled through the passage to Laurent's, heading straight for the door, which I locked. A cursory glance around the room showed me he, too, had a copy of *The Picture of Dorian Gray*, a volume that somehow felt more than a little appropriate for him. When I returned to my room, my husband was inspecting the armoire.

"Did you ask Laurent why there is a passage between these two rooms?"

"No," I said. "But he and Edith used it often. A bit of fun when they were young, I imagine."

"The doorway in the armoire is far too sophisticated to have been done by children. And it would have been odd for them to have installed it as adults, don't you think?"

"It could have been included when the house was built five hundred years ago."

He nodded. "Maybe. But the armoire's not that old. It would have had to be fitted later. I wonder if the Prier parents know about it." He knelt down in front of the hulking wooden piece, running his hands along the base, then inside, where he focused on the mechanism of the hidden door. "This is without question modern. Newer than the furniture, in fact."

"There are no other rooms on this floor," I said. "They could easily have visited each other back and forth through their doors—even without anyone else in the house knowing. To have such a thing installed suggests to me that someone—obviously Edith—was locked in her room."

"Which we know was the case."

"But the impression I've been given is that she was locked in only for the last couple months before she was sent away. Would there have been time for Laurent to have had the panel made? And would he have bothered—given that he was the one lobbying for her to be sent to Dr. Girard, he wasn't expecting she'd be locked up in the house for long?"

"What do you suspect?"

"That Edith's life was considerably more complicated than we've been led to believe. I think you ought to speak to her father when he arrives home. And I think we should make our way through Laurent's room as quickly as possible. We can't count on him to sit through a leisurely family meal."

Laurent's possessions were shockingly uninteresting. Music scores covered the top of the piano, and an unsightly array of wine bottles and glasses had taken up residence on every other available surface. Other than the Wilde novel I'd already spotted, there were no books. A crumpled pile of discarded clothes was heaped on the floor next to the bed—but the unworn items in his wardrobe were perfectly pressed, crisp, and neat.

"It appears he doesn't allow the servants to do much to the room," Colin said.

"So what is it he doesn't want them to see?" I asked. "I can't say anything's catching my attention."

"Nor mine. Pity we don't know what we're looking for."

"How about the attic? I'd like to see if Edith kept journals that might have been put up there." I turned Laurent's key so he'd find the door as he'd left it when he returned from dinner. We crossed back through the armoire and into the corridor from Edith's former room.

"A good idea, but I need to speak to Monsieur Prier. I'm more and more curious about what he does when he's not home. And I'm afraid that I'm going to have to do that on my own. Can you explore the attic without me?"

"I've no doubt Cécile can assist me."

Colin, wanting to interview Monsieur Prier, had made a sensible decision to set off without me. He wasn't home, and odds were the gentleman was not spending his evenings somewhere it would be appropriate for me to appear unannounced. As soon as he'd left I dipped into the drawing room where the Priers had retired after dinner and pulled Cécile aside to whisper my plan to her. I needed her to occupy Laurent while I returned to upstairs.

The attic, accessible through a narrow door on the landing by the main staircase, was lit by sunlight streaming through three gabled windows on the front of the house, and dust drifted in the air, making the bright patches look smoky, while the rest of the space was bathed in darkness. I placed the candle I'd brought from my room on the floor next to a pile of dusty trunks and opened the one on top. A mild tinge of guilt crept up on me—I wasn't accustomed to rifling through other people's belongings—but I had few options if we were to discover what happened to Edith. When I'd asked Cécile if she thought the Priers would allow my search, she shook her head and admonished me to proceed quietly. A conversation she'd had with Edith's mother was the basis for her concern. I trusted her judgment and we agreed to reconvene and talk after the household had gone to bed.

My search was not fruitful. But as I opened the seventeenth trunk, one far in the back of the attic, in a dark corner away from the windows, the temperature in the garret dropped; goose bumps covered my arms and I started to shiver. My lungs tightened in my chest. I rifled through the contents, only to find it, like all the others, contained nothing but old clothing. Then, before I could lower the lid, a crash from across the room jolted me into action, and I leapt up, gripping the brass candle-holder. One of the windows had blown open and was banging against its sash.

It was the wind. The wind. I said the words over and over to myself, but couldn't persuade any of my muscles to set into motion so that I might cross the room and refasten the offending panes. Another crash, this one from the trunk as the top lid fell back into place. I wanted very much to believe I'd caused it myself, when I jumped. But the delay between the two sounds was too great. Or was it? My mind didn't seem to be operating in real time, and I felt disjointed and confused as fear robbed all of my focus. My feet still firmly planted on the floor—absolutely unwilling to move—I forced slow, deep breaths. The strategy to control my anxiety might have worked had my candle not blown out in the next instant.

Now I did feel mad, and I wondered if this was how it had begun for Edith—if a series of small coincidences, catalyzed by her brother, had preyed on her mind, bludgeoning her like an implacable rainstorm bent on destroying a fine spring day. Repeat the scenario at frequent enough intervals and the soundest mind would come unhinged.

I pushed a foot forward and began inching my way back to the doorway, trembling. But then came a sound that stopped me altogether: heavy footsteps coming up the stairs. Cécile wouldn't have dreamed of clomping with so absolute a lack of elegance; she prided herself on always moving with lightness and grace. I pressed against the sloping wall formed by the roof, first taking comfort in its strength, then realizing too late I'd left myself vulnerable, with nowhere to escape. Not that my precise location in the attic could have made much difference—either I could reach the exit uninhibited or not. If an interloper was standing at the top of the stairs, I'd have no hope.

And this proved just the case when Laurent appeared before me, his rage apparent in the flash of his eyes.

"What do you think you are doing?" He lunged at me and gripped my wrist. "Who gave you permission to come up here?"

"Your mother," I lied, my voice shaking. She'd not specifically given me permission, but she'd made a point of telling me to treat the house as my own when I'd first arrived. "I'm terribly sorry if I've offended you, but—"

"But what?" He scowled. "Let me guess. You're exceedingly fond of attics and find them dreadfully romantic and you'd hoped your bored husband would come looking for you and rekindle whatever lost emotion there used to be between you. I shouldn't bother if I were you. He's more interested in flirting with my vapid sister."

"How dare you?" Anger flashed hot through me and I balled my hands into hard fists.

"This is not your house, and my family's concerns are none of your business. I suggest—strongly—that you leave before you come to understand too well exactly what this place, what these people can do to someone who's fallen out of their favor. I suspect you're not quite so strong as you'd like everyone to believe. So take your leave before it's too late." He spat the last words as he dragged me by the wrist to the staircase. "It would be best if you were gone before morning."

22

"Mon dieu!" Cécile said as she embraced me and marched into my bedroom, where I'd been waiting for her since returning from the attic. She lowered herself onto a wide chair that stood in the space between two windows. "I do hope your adventure was productive. What an evening! I do not know how much longer we should stay here."

"What happened?" I asked.

"There is so much—I must consider where to start. This visit, Emily, is making me crave your favorite, port. Champagne does not want to be in this house."

I nearly fell out of my seat. "I didn't know such a thing was possible."

"Nor did I and I am filled with dread and horror."

"You must tell me what happened!"

"First, Dominique is exhibiting behavior most alarming. She told me that she's growing concerned about you—that you remind her so much of her daughter in the days before she fell ill."

"There's nothing wrong with me!"

"Bien sûr," Cécile said. "Any fool can see that. But she's decided that your interest in Edith's death is indicative of you losing your mind. She

198

admitted to having tracked your whereabouts in the house these past days, and that she's asked Laurent to spy on you."

"Why on earth would she do such a thing? Even if she did have reason to think I was going mad?"

"It's a ruse, *chérie*. Perhaps there's something in this house she doesn't want you to uncover. I'm not sure, but it's unsettling me. Edith is dead and will stay that way no matter what you learn."

"Madame Prier can't hurt me, even if she'd like Laurent to scare me off." I told her what had happened in the attic.

"Ridiculous," she said. "But you must have been terrified. Don't try to deny it—you're still pale. What do you hope to find here?"

"Anything Edith's written," I said. "Diaries, letters, whatever there is."

"Those won't lead us to the child. I think it's time to enlist the further help of Monsieur Leblanc. He may have journalistic contacts who could offer assistance."

I nodded. "An excellent suggestion, Cécile. But I must ask if you'd be so keen to reconnect with him if he weren't so handsome?"

She shrugged. "I wouldn't say *handsome*. Dashing, perhaps. But he is, without question, far too young to be intriguing."

"I shall get in touch with him first thing tomorrow morning," I said as the door swung open and Colin strode into the room.

"How pleasant to find you both here," he said. He kissed Cécile's hand and my cheek. "Reminds me of long-ago afternoons in your library at Berkeley Square." The house where I'd lived with my first husband proved an excellent place for me in the years following his death, and Colin and I had spent many happy hours in the library there.

"Those were lovely days," I said.

"Idyllic," he said.

"Did you find Monsieur Prier?" I asked.

"I did indeed," Colin said. He pulled a flask of whisky from his jacket and poured a single finger into both of the glasses on the table near our fireplace. Cécile relieved him of one of them at once and he took a swig from the other before handing it to me. "He spends his evenings happily ensconced with his mistress and her daughter. They live not half a mile from this house."

"How old is the daughter?" I asked.

"Just the right age to be the child whose presence has tormented you."

"Did you confront the father?"

"The *doting* father," he said. "I did and he was entirely nonplussed to find me shocked by the situation."

"It is not, Monsieur Hargreaves, uncommon to find men in such situations," Cécile said. "Do tell me you're not naïve enough to believe otherwise."

"No, no," Colin said, sipping quickly from his flask. "It was his brazen attitude that surprised me. His wife knows about the child."

"And what does she think?" I asked.

"She ignores the situation except at Christmas when she sends a heap of presents to the girl."

"Extraordinary behavior for a spurned wife." I drained my whisky, cringing as it stung my throat.

"Not extraordinary in the least for a doting *grand-mère*," Cécile said.

I dropped my head into my hands, almost laughing. "No—"

"It's possible," Colin said.

"*Et tu?*" I asked. "You're supposed to be my pillar of reason!"

"Think on it, Emily—the doctor would have felt no compunction whatsoever at turning the baby over to Prier."

"It's far too convenient," I said.

"Not every question has a complicated, interesting solution," he said.

"Kallista, you're coming over all rational," Cécile said. "I'm not sure I like it."

"I wish I could say I'd always been rational, but you both seem amused enough already. I have, however, learned something in these past years. The answer might not be complicated or interesting or even seemingly significant, but it's almost never so easy. Can we interview the mistress? Her friends? It's a pity there's no way to prove whether she's the baby's mother."

"Diverting though this speculation is, I must confess to having tested Monsieur Prier's knowledge of Edith's condition as obliquely as I could," Colin said. "He didn't say anything extraordinary, and certainly nothing that suggested he was aware of being a grandfather. I think we must assume the mistress's child is, in fact, his."

I couldn't argue, but it felt all wrong. I had to find out what happened to Edith's daughter.

The following morning, long before Cécile was awake, Colin and I set off to see Monsieur Leblanc, who had taken a room at a nearby tavern. Cécile, perhaps bent on proving she had no interest in the writer, had decided the night before not to join us. The tavern was a lively place, crowded from the moment it opened, its patrons friendly and open, engaged in each other's lives. We inquired after our friend, and were directed to a pretty serving girl who went upstairs to alert him of our arrival.

"I have been productive, *mes amis*," he said, shaking Colin's hand with youthful vigor as he joined us at our table. "The Priers are a bizarre family whose reach goes beyond Rouen. Lesser branches inhabit nearly every corner of Normandy and half of Brittany. Their poorest relations, however, are our own friends—your mother's neighbors."

"The Markhams?" I asked; he nodded and sat next to my husband.

"Madame Prier is of the same generation as Madeline's mother," he said. "They're faraway cousins."

"Which makes Madeline and Edith . . ." I stumbled over the genealogy.

"Some manner of relative not quite distant enough for Madame Prier," he said. "It's not entirely shocking when you consider the madness that plagues both branches of the family."

"But the Markhams aren't poor," I said.

"The money is all George's. Madeline's great-great-grandfather was worse than a prodigal child. Gambled away what little money he had, but married decently because of his parents' reputation. Eventually, his antics became notorious—illegitimate children, unpaid debts, a spectacularly undistinguished career in the army that resulted in him accidentally killing one of his friends. At last his father had enough and disowned him. Without the allowance to which he'd become accustomed, the château gradually fell into disrepair."

"So how did Madeline's mother come to be in the family seat?" I asked.

"No one else wanted it after two more generations of neglect. When she married Breton, a complete reprobate, they needed somewhere to live and had little choice but the old house. He treated her abominably until he was killed in a duel two months before their daughter was born. It's not surprising the woman's unbalanced," he said.

"It's more than that," I said. "It's hereditary—Madeline's showing symptoms as well. And if Madame Prier knew of the family history—which, according to Dr. Girard, she did—she would have been horrified to see signs of the disease in Edith."

"Do the families know of the connection?" Colin asked.

"Madame Prier didn't admit to the relation when Cécile and I spoke to her about the Markhams. All she did was make it clear she disliked Madeline's mother."

"So far as I can tell, there's been no interaction between them at all," Monsieur Leblanc said.

"That's not necessarily unusual," Colin said. "Relatives are not obligated to like each other."

"*Bien sûr,*" he said.

"But the murder," I said. "Edith. Neither Madeline nor George showed any signs of recognition at her name."

"It's entirely possible they never knew her," Monsieur Leblanc said. "Madame Prier, certainly, had no interest in pursuing any sort of acquaintance. I found the obituary written when her father died. It includes an exhaustive list of surviving family members—more cousins than I could count—but there's no mention of Madeline's mother."

"Have you had any thoughts as to Monsieur Myriel's identity?" I asked.

"Unfortunately not," he said. "You did an excellent job querying the villagers. I don't see what more we can do. Myriel is a dead end." This struck me as an odd comment from a journalist—surely he would have faced equally difficult searches before and not backed down so quickly. "I don't mean to frustrate you, of course, but it might be more profitable to try to locate Vasseur."

"An excellent suggestion," Colin said. "You will, of course, make us aware of anything you learn?"

"Of course," Monsieur Leblanc said.

"I don't think it's wise to entirely abandon our search for Myriel," I said. "But I do want to learn more about the familial connection between the Markhams and the Priers. Brace yourself, my dear husband. I've a sudden and mad desire to return to your mother's house."

18 July 1892

Colin left for Rouen with Inspector Gaudet on business, and subsequently wired to say he was staying over with his wife who is no longer being shipped back to England. Well done, Emily, I say. I can't say I approve of the idea of husbands packing their wives off whenever situations grow difficult.

She's sharper than I thought. I'm duly impressed with this Greek work of hers and would like to assist in furthering her intellectual development. There's a flair to her translation—she clearly has an ear for poetry and storytelling. I wonder if she would be suitable for introduction to my friends in the Women's Liberal Federation. We've never discussed politics.

Heaven help me if she turns out to be a Tory.

23

Colin and I took the earliest possible train back to Yvetot. Cécile, who needed additional time to pack and organize her affairs, planned to join us as soon as she could in the next day or so. When we appeared on her doorstep, Mrs. Hargreaves's face betrayed little emotion. She gave her son a perfunctory embrace and nodded at me before continuing on her way into the garden, where, judging from the basket she held, she planned to pick raspberries or whatever other fruit she might find her bushes laden with. Undaunted, I pressed my reticule into Colin's hand.

"Take this upstairs for me, would you?" I asked. "I've some questions for your mother."

"Would you like me to come with you?"

"No," I said. "But thank you. It's time I faced her on my own. I can't let her run roughshod over me forever."

"I love you," he said and gave me a kiss before sending me off in the direction of a brambly sort of patch where the lady of the house was hard at work. She snapped to attention as I stepped near her, and scowled as I began picking the swollen raspberries and depositing them in her ready basket. I said nothing for several minutes, occasionally popping a berry into my mouth and delighting in its sweetness.

"Are they always this good?" I asked.

"I would tolerate nothing less," she said.

"I'm sorry you find me so disappointing," I said. "But at the moment, I must beg you to put aside your disdain and help me."

She didn't look at me, only continued her work. "You should finish your translation of *The Odyssey*."

This stopped me dead.

"Homer?"

"Don't be daft," she said. "Of course Homer."

"Homer?"

"How long do you plan to stand there repeating yourself?" She pulled the fruit too forcefully from a branch, and, seeing it was smashed, flung it to the ground. "Colin gave me what you've done so far thinking I might want to read it, and I was impressed—although I will admit my Greek is not what it should be."

"You read the bits I've translated?" My mouth hung open stupidly.

"You've a decent mind, Emily, and you're wasting it playing detective."

"But I like it," I said before I could stop myself.

"The pursuit of relentless hedonism rarely leads to anything good," she said. I dropped another handful of raspberries into her basket. "My son does tell me you're good at it. Detecting, that is, not hedonism."

"He's far too generous with his praise—"

"Don't play with me, child. I've no interest in false modesty. I holed myself up here because I couldn't cope with my husband's death. It was inevitable, I knew, from the day I met him. Until we married, I lived as you do—following whatever interested me at the moment. It becomes more difficult when you're a wife, harder still when the children start coming."

I swallowed, bracing myself for what I knew must come next, but she shook her head.

"There's a way in which I'm jealous of you, Emily. Your tragedy has given you time," she said. "Time with my son, time for your intellectual pursuits. I was perhaps too quick to dismiss your accomplishments. Your first husband raved to me about your incomparable beauty, and I confess I had not expected to find much in you beyond that, whatever Colin said."

"Philip barely knew me," I said.

"And here you have another chance . . ." her voice trailed. "I cannot imagine such a thing. Do not squander it by running about in search of mystery. Study Greek. Write. Read poetry."

"Those are all things you could do, too," I said. "I cannot imagine how much you miss your—"

"That's correct, you can't," she said, her voice momentarily sharp. "Don't bother to try."

I bit my tongue, sorry to have upset her, and redirected the conversation. "You said your Greek's not what it could be. Let me help you— I'm no expert, but I know enough to guide us through. We could study together."

"Together?"

"I'll give you a passage to work on tonight."

"Tonight?" She paused for a moment, looking at me quizzically. "I'm not sure about this, but I'm willing to try."

"I'm glad," I said. "You don't have to like me, Mrs. Hargreaves, but we do need to at least come to a point where we can tolerate each other."

"Tolerate?" She laughed. "We'll see about that. But I do find your idea worth some consideration. Get me a passage, and we'll see where it takes us." She stood, quiet and still, until a stiff breeze blew the ribbons fastening her bonnet up to her face. "I don't think you followed me out here to clasp my hand in friendship. What brings you back to me?"

"Given the terror I've typically felt in your presence, you know it must be important."

"Excellent," she said. "Impress me."

"Madeline Markham is related to Edith Prier. Did you know that?"

"No, although I had heard rumors that Madeline's mother wasn't the only one in the family to lose her mind."

"How much do you know of Madeline's madness?"

"Only what I've observed and what Colin's told me. He and I frequently discuss his work. He misses obvious clues sometimes, you know."

"Does he?" I blinked. "Do tell."

"You'll have to discover his flaws on your own," she said.

"Fair enough," I said, smiling. "But have you heard any further rumors about the family? About Madeline's . . . inability to have a child?"

"Ah, she told you, did she? Terrible for George, of course. No doubt he wishes he'd made a better choice of bride, though he does love her, heaven help him."

"What do people say about them?" I strained to ignore my own feelings of inadequacy.

"The whole village knows her mother's feebleminded," she said. "And it's no secret that Madeline can't produce an heir—and that this failing of hers has taken its toll on her soul. She ran off one of their gardeners because she couldn't stand the sight of his daughter."

"I've heard the story," I said. "What can you tell me about the girl? Did you ever see her?"

"Oh yes. She was a beautiful child. Long silvery hair, the color of moonlight, always with a ribbon in it."

"Blue?" I asked.

"Blue? I suppose sometimes. I can't say I paid much attention. I used to see her when I drove through the village. She liked to play near the *boulangerie*."

"Where is she now?"

"I think she fell ill. Her father passes through once in a while—has an aunt in service at another house in the neighborhood. But he never brings the child."

"Were there ever any stories that she'd died?"

"Died?" Her basket was nearly full. She stopped picking and sat on a stone bench a few feet from the berry patch. "I don't think so. It's possible, of course. You know how delicate children can be. But other than Madeline wanting desperately for the girl to be gone, there wasn't any interesting gossip wafting about. At least not that I've heard."

"How well do you know Madeline?"

"She's charming when she's herself. A predictable sort, but affable enough. When she's in the midst of one of her spells . . . well. It's disconcerting."

"How desperate is she to have a child? Did she ever speak to you about it?"

"People don't discuss such things."

"They do when they're lonely and afraid and have no one but a kind neighbor in whom they can confide."

"Not here, they don't. Nor anywhere I've ever lived. There's no question Madeline was crushed after all her disappointments. Who wouldn't be? There were times I feared she would succumb to a more rapid decline than her mother's journey into illness."

"Don't you think she has?"

"Sometimes," she said. "But her periods of lucidity are still sharp and frequent enough for me to hope she'll have a better outcome."

"Please tell me the truth."

My mother-in-law shrugged. "She's not as mad as her mother, but I can't say much else. Do you not think, Emily, that it gives me concern to see a woman just your age, unable to have children, slowing driving herself mad? And here you are, in a similar situation, still smarting with grief, relentlessly pursuing a subject that can bring you nothing but further pain?"

"Our situations are entirely different."

"Simply because you've only suffered one loss to date." The sun was high and hot, the air heavy with humidity. She pulled a linen handkerchief from the lacy cuff at her wrist and dabbed her glistening brow with it, unwilling, it seemed, to wait for the next obliging breeze. "Such things can plague a mind when they're repeated ad nauseum."

I winced at her words, but her tone lacked any criticism, as if she'd exchanged chagrin for compassion. "We can hope that won't happen."

"Sometimes I forget how young you are," she said.

"How did Madeline's mother handle her daughter's difficulties?" I asked, not quite ready to continue the conversation she'd begun.

"Better than I would have thought," she said. "But of course, she's had more trouble with her nerves than Madeline."

"How many siblings does Madeline have?"

"None who survived to adulthood," Mrs. Hargreaves said.

"Like me," I said.

"The two of you have more in common than I'm comfortable admitting."

"I need to talk to her." Earnest with enthusiasm, I sat next to her. "Will you come with me?"

"Absolutely not," she said, although the color in her cheeks hinted at her being less horrified at the prospect than she wanted me to think. "I don't like prying into my neighbor's private tragedies."

"But you help your son?"

"He's exceptionally persuasive," she said. "And trying to beat you at your own game. How could I deny him assistance? You and I shall read Greek together. We shall discuss poetry. Someday, perhaps, we shall travel to Egypt with each other. But I will never, ever help you emerge victorious over my darling boy."

"Did you know Toinette will be descending upon us soon?" I asked my husband that afternoon as we crossed on to the main road from the house's drive on our way to visit the Markhams. Patches of dense forest divided the lush pastures and fragrant orchards surrounding us, and in the midst of the tall trees with their dappled light and cool, sweet shade, I felt homesick, reminded of England.

"She told me no fewer than twenty-seven times," he said. "A sweet enough girl. I must tell you, though, she has suddenly changed her plans. It seems you terribly disappointed her by deciding to come back with me."

"She has a crush on you."

"Girls like Toinette don't have crushes," he said. "They have designs."

"So she has designs on you?"

"It would seem so," he said, grinning.

"You shouldn't encourage her. You're so handsome you'll ruin her for other gentlemen. Her expectations will never be met."

"I would never encourage her."

"But you do enjoy her attentions," I said.

"They're mildly amusing. She's entertaining and pretty and foolish."

"I didn't think you liked foolish," I said.

"I don't, Emily. But that doesn't mean I can't be occasionally diverted by it."

"Diverted?" My hands, starting to sweat, slipped along my reins.

"Nothing more than that. And certainly nothing alarming."

"I wasn't aware that you required—" I stopped, unsure of myself. "I thought we—"

"Don't go looking for trouble, my dear. You'll never find any. I'm more devoted than any other husband in England."

"We're in France, Colin."

"I didn't think you'd be impressed by claims of fidelity in relation to that of the average French husband."

"You'd better not let Cécile hear you talk like that."

"She'd be the first to approve," he said. I laughed and shook my head, knowing he was undoubtedly correct. He leaned towards me and put a steady hand on my arm. "You've no need to doubt me on that or any other count. I hope you know that."

"I do," I said. "You know I'd trust you to the ends of the earth. But does that mean I'm not allowed to dislike Toinette?"

He laughed. "Of course not."

We were approaching the château, and I could hear Madeline arguing with a gardener as we crossed the bridge to the main drive. She was begging him to see the merits of keeping bees; he was making no effort even to appear interested in dealing with any stinging insects. I slid down from my horse and handed him off to a waiting groom as Colin did the same. Together we followed Madeline's voice to a small, informal garden a short distance from the dovecote. I did not let myself look at the looming building.

"Ce n'est pas possible!" The gardener's voice grew louder. Madeline saw us and waved.

"We'll discuss it after the bees arrive," she said. "Leave me to my guests." She rushed over and embraced us both with genuine warmth. "It is so good to see you again—your absence was felt keenly. Did you enjoy Zurich?"

"We were in Rouen," I said, hesitation in my voice.

"Rouen?" She tilted her head and frowned. "But you promised to bring me chocolate."

"I—" I looked at Colin, unsure what to say.

"There was none even half good enough for you," he said, stepping forward and kissing her hand. "I fear the Swiss have lowered their standards."

"I suspected as much," she said, laughter returning to her voice. "And am glad, then, that you won't present me with something bound to disappoint."

"We'd never dream of it," I said, going along with Colin's story. "But we do have some news I wanted to discuss with you and George. Is he here?"

"He is. I'll summon him and we can have tea. You've time for a nice long visit, don't you?"

"We're in no hurry," I said.

Colin shot a telling glance at me. "I suppose as long as we're home in time for dinner."

"I'm more interested in what will happen after dinner," I whispered as we started for the house. He drew a sharp breath and nearly lost his footing. He recovered elegantly, though, just as George called out from behind us.

"Ho! Can you wait for me?" he asked, whipping the straw boater from his head and sprinting towards us.

"Don't make it easy for him," Madeline cried, giggling. She grabbed Colin's arm and set off at a fierce pace, pulling him with her while she held onto the brim of her black straw hat to keep it from flying away. Having no desire to run, I waited for the master of the house.

"She's a beast, that wife of mine," George said, out of breath when he reached me. "But bloody good fun. Apart from this new obsession of hers, beekeeping."

"You'll have excellent honey," I said.

He laughed. "I suppose so. Have you come about the robbery?"

"Robbery?"

"Have you not heard? We were burgled two nights ago—the Monet is gone."

"No! Dare I ask if Inspector Gaudet is on the case?"

"He is, my friend, he is. And eager as ever to fight for justice. Unless, of course, it interferes with a meal. Or a party. Or a walk on the beach."

"Are there any leads?"

"I'm afraid only one that points to your old friend, Sebastian."

My heart sank. "Why would he take the painting back after having gone to such lengths to get it to you in the first place?" Much though I would have liked to believe Sebastian would stand by the promise he made to Monet about not taking any more of his paintings, I knew him too well to think he'd be true to his word.

"We found another note—this one questioning our taste. Further analysis must have suggested to him our unworthiness as collectors."

I would need to see the letter, but couldn't imagine who, other than Sebastian, would pen such a thing. "I'm so sorry. He can be such a troublemaker."

"It wouldn't bother me so much if I hadn't become particularly attached to that painting. A fine specimen." His gaze softened. "I'll miss it."

"We will recover it, one way or another."

"I do admire your spirit, Emily," he said. "But tell me now. If you knew nothing of the robbery, what brought you to us?"

"Edith Prier," I said. "There's more to the story of her death than we'd anticipated, and we wanted to ask you a few questions."

"You don't think the murderer still poses a threat?" he asked, blanching. "I admit I've been uncomfortable about letting Madeline out of the house alone. We've someone looking out for her all the time."

"Which is wise," I said. "Although it does seem there's no specific threat at the moment."

"So tell me what more you've learned."

"Did you know Edith is related to your wife?"

"To Madeline?" he asked. "The Priers? That can't be."

"From what I understand it's a distant connection. They're cousins of some sort."

"I'm shocked." He stopped walking and searched my face, confusion written all over his.

"Obviously there was no reason for you to have known this," I said. "But because Edith suffered from a condition similar to that plaguing your mother-in-law, I thought you should know. Particularly as your wife . . ." My words trailed.

"Yes, of course you've noticed." He closed his eyes. "I fear what will happen to her. It's beyond devastating."

"Edith's family put her in an asylum not far from Rouen because of her illness."

He cringed. "I can't do that to my wife."

"I'm not suggesting you should," I said. "Although it might not be a terrible idea to speak with the doctor there—he's more enlightened than I would have expected. It's possible he would have some ideas about treatments—something that might help—"

"Of course. I'm sorry if I reacted badly. It's just that when I think of what my darling girl faces—what I shall be forced to face eventually . . ." He sighed. "It shatters me."

"It's I who should apologize. I sprung this on you with no preamble."

"No, it's an excellent suggestion." He shook his head. "I can't believe Edith and Madeline . . . related. It's stunning news."

"There's one more thing. I tell you this in confidence and must ask for your absolute discretion. Edith had a child—a girl—who went missing sometime before her mother's death. The story's bound to get out eventually, and I thought it might upset Madeline given her experience with children. Hearing it through gossip might prove painful."

"You're very kind to think of her, and absolutely right. She doesn't do well with children. There've been none here since our long-ago unfortunate gardener left. Terrible story, you know. I still can't stand to go in the dovecote," he said. "The little girl died there, you see. She fell down the steps. Madeline had been in there playing with her. She doted on the child. Can't bear to talk about it now, of course."

"How awful," I said, a dull pain in my chest.

"Madeline blamed herself. It was a bad choice of a place to play, and she shouldn't have let her run on the stairs. There wasn't a thing anyone could say to ease her guilt. Her mind was not the same afterwards."

"Poor Madeline," I said. "Why did you not tell me this before?"

"It's not the sort of thing one likes to share with the neighbors. We kept things as quiet as possible and let everyone assume the gardener was sent away because Madeline couldn't bear to have the girl around. I don't think she could have survived gossip on the subject."

"Of course not." I hesitated. "She told me a somewhat different version of the story."

"Yes, I'm afraid her brain morphed it into another miscarriage," he said. "It's as if she forgot about the actual child altogether."

"I'm sorry to have brought up such a painful topic."

"You couldn't have known," he said. "And I'm glad to learn of the familial relation. No doubt Madeline will want to call on the family to pay her respects."

"Have you met any of the Priers?"

"I spoke to the son once at the opera in Paris, years ago. Laurent, if I remember correctly?"

"Yes."

"Bit of a cad, I thought. Not sure I particularly like my wife being related to him," he said. We'd reached the house, where I could hear Madeline's laughter bouncing through the corridors. He stopped walking and turned to me, his expression measured and serious. "I am interested in speaking to this Girard. Could your husband introduce me?"

24

The next day, I was happily settled in the library next to my mother-in-law, working on our Greek. But I was unable to purge George's story from my head. It made the shadowy figure of the girl I'd seen there all the more frightening. I closed my eyes, not moving until Mrs. Hargreaves's voice pulled me back to the present moment.

"*There is a time for many words, and there is also a time for sleep,*" she said. "Is this meant to be a commentary on my company?"

"Not at all," I said, laughter on my lips. "It's just a sentence from Homer I've always liked. Are you ready for more?"

"No time for that, I'm afraid," Colin said, entering the room. "If we're to see Girard before lunch we need to leave now."

The previous day, Madeline had reacted with almost no visible emotion to being told about Edith's child. This didn't surprise me—she would be upset, of that there was no doubt. Most likely, though, the story would affect her most when she was alone, and had the privacy to react in whatever way she wanted to. Hearing Edith was a relative, however, inspired in her nothing but a sigh. "This branch of the family has no interest in the Priers, I can assure you," she had said. George, however, still wanted to call on them, and suggested doing so after we were to see Dr. Girard. He discussed neither plan in front of his wife.

"I feel almost as if I'm betraying her," he said, as our carriage clattered along the road towards Radepont and the asylum. "Her mind can be so fragile—if I tell her I'm consulting with yet another physician it might send her reeling again. And odds are despite having treated Edith, he'll have little to suggest that we've not already tried."

"If Edith's condition was more advanced than Madeline's, it's conceivable he'll know more about the later stages of the disease."

"I've done all I can for Madeline's mother, and she's bound, given her age, to be worse off than Edith ever was." He closed his eyes and let his head fall back. "Apologies. I don't mean to deflate every possibility. But I feel I must prepare myself for disappointment. I've been let down more times than I can count."

I leaned forward and patted his hand. "Absolutely understandable."

"Girard's innovative and sharp," Colin said. "I have faith he will be able to offer you something." We passed the ruined abbey and continued along the Seine to the hospital, serene in its setting, silent except for the sound of the river. Everything was as it had been on my previous visits except that no nurse immediately greeted us at the door. Colin banged the heavy knocker against the hard wood, and we waited. After a few minutes passed, he knocked again, still soliciting no response.

He walked to the edge of the stairs and tipped his head to try to look into the window. "Can't see anything," he said, and set off to investigate the other windows on the front of the building while George took over knocking duties. When at last the door swung open, we saw a disheveled woman, tears staining her face, a crushed nurse's cap in her hand. I barely recognized her as the same person who'd welcomed me on my previous visits. In a few long strides, Colin was back with us, stepping in front of George.

"How can I help?" he asked, pulling out papers that identified him as an agent of the British Crown. Not something I should have thought would inspire confidence in the French, but clearly enough to satisfy the sad figure before us that it would be all right to usher us inside.

"I remember you from before," she said to me, her voice shaking. "Dr. Girard liked you." She looked at George. "Have we met?"

"Unfortunately not," he said, his voice grave. "I've come to speak to the doctor about my wife. Is this not a good time?"

She didn't reply, or say anything as we followed her inside. The corridor looked no different from when I'd seen it last, but everything felt off-kilter. The nurse's uniform was a mess, full of wrinkles, and large rust-colored stains covered her apron.

"What has happened here?" I asked, alarm in my voice.

"Dr. Girard is dead," she said, more tears streaming down her cheeks. "In his office . . ."

Colin waited for nothing further. He raced towards the closed door at the end of the hallway. I started to follow, but he motioned for me to stop. I sat down on a long wooden bench next to George, feeling frustrated, then bit my lip and turned to the nurse.

"Is that blood on your apron?" I asked.

She nodded.

"His?"

Another nod.

"What happened?" I asked. "Has there been an accident?"

"No," she said. "There was a knife . . ." Her tears morphed into consuming sobs.

"Who was with him?" I asked.

"No one, not at the end. I found him there this morning when I arrived."

"Who on the staff was here last night? Did anyone hear anything?"

"Nothing out of the ordinary."

"Where was he stabbed?" I asked.

George shot me a stern look. "Is this necessary? The poor woman's upset. Can we not comfort her now and leave questioning to the police?"

"Oh we won't need police, sir," she said. "He did it to himself. The blade was in his hand." Her face was gray, her skin cold. I looked around for something to wrap around her, and found a blanket in a cupboard partway down the corridor. Colin stepped out of the office and looked at me.

"Would you come take a look at this?" he asked.

"Do you need a second set of eyes?" I liked that he was seeking my help. Maybe this new arrangement wasn't so abysmal as I'd originally feared.

"We're going to need more than that. But you're an excellent observer, Emily. If you can stand the sight, I'd like your thoughts."

I took the blanket to George, who had the nurse well in hand and had summoned an orderly to bring her tea. Colin stopped me as I was about to enter Dr. Girard's office.

"You're sure?" he asked. "It's gruesome."

"Of course I am," I said. "It can't be worse than Edith."

Worse was perhaps not the best choice of word. The doctor sat, sprawled in his desk chair, one arm dangling at his side, the other resting in his lap, a sharp surgeon's scalpel in his hand. Blood had pooled below each wrist, leaving a shiny, coagulating puddle on the floor and a dark, viscous stain on his shirt and waistcoat. I tasted bile and held my breath, unsure if I wanted to see more.

"Why would he do this?" I asked.

"He didn't," Colin said. "There are scratches on his hands. He was fighting with someone. I've no doubt the coroner will find more signs of a struggle. And there's blood on the windowsill."

I crossed to the window, not seeing anything at first. But then, as I scrutinized every inch of the wood, I spotted it—a small speck of dark red smeared on the edge of the sill. "He couldn't have got that here without bleeding everywhere else in between," I said.

"Precisely," Colin said.

"Is there a suicide note? Or something purporting to be one?"

"I've not found it yet. Care to help?"

"Of course," I said. "If I'm allowed."

"Don't tease now. I need to summon the police. Will you be all right in here alone if I leave the door open? I'm only going to call to George and ask for his assistance."

I nodded and could hear him speaking to George as I began my search of the room. Surely a suicide note would be left someplace obvious, but the surface of the desk, the bookshelves, and the tables revealed nothing. Someone had closed the doctor's eyes, and for this I was grateful. I was uncomfortable enough rooting through a dead man's belongings. Feeling his vacant stare following me would not improve things. I circled the space again, and this time opened the desk drawers, but to no avail. Their contents were perfectly ordinary.

Turning, I looked at the poor doctor's body. And then I saw it—a corner of folded paper tucked into his jacket pocket. Delicately, so as not to disturb the body, I pulled it out and opened it. The page had been torn from a lined notebook.

He that is not guilty of his own death shortens not his own life.

Below that, a line had been drawn, with another sentence following:

I should never have let her go.

It gave me chills to read it. Chills made worse as I studied the blood that had soaked through Dr. Girard's clothing and stained the note. The handwriting was familiar, but I couldn't be sure, and thought about how I could get back into Laurent Prier's room to check my suspicions. All of a sudden, Colin touched my shoulder, and I jumped; I'd not heard him reenter the room.

"Success?" he asked. I handed the sheet to him.

"*Hamlet*, I believe," I said. "With the addition of a more personal sentiment. I found it in his pocket."

"You're quick and efficient," he said, flashing me a smile before looking over the words.

"I don't believe for a second he wrote it."

"Why is that?"

"Who puts a suicide note in his pocket?" I asked. "I realize I have limited experience—but I do have some." Less than a year before, I'd found the body of the person who'd murdered Lord Basil Fortescue—the crime for which my friend's husband had been accused. The true culprit, after being found out, committed suicide. "Suicides want their final words to be seen. They don't hide them. And they don't forget to take them out of their pocket."

"Possibly," he said. "But what if this wasn't intended for others? What if this was simply for himself?"

"You don't believe he killed himself—you already said so."

"Quite right. But he might have been murdered and still written these words."

"He feels guilty about Edith," I said. "Or do you think he's referring to the child?"

"The child. He didn't *let* Edith go. She escaped."

"He didn't *let* Lucy go either—he sent her away."

"Is it a significant difference?" Colin asked.

"I'm not sure."

"Well it's worth considering," he said. "I'm finished in here. Shall we interview as much of the staff as possible before the police arrive and take over?"

As we both expected, there was little information to be had from the staff. Colin surmised the doctor had been dead since the middle of the night, when it would have been unlikely anyone would have heard a disturbance. His office stood far from the patient wards, and the orderly who made rounds at night admitted to having fallen asleep around three in the morning, only to wake up after six o'clock. Dr. Girard frequently worked late, so to see his office light on wouldn't have been unusual.

George had remained on the bench near the main entrance to the building, waiting for us to finish. He'd done an excellent job comforting the nurse who'd found the body, and, explaining that he'd trained as a physician, offered to check on any patients who seemed in need of immediate medical attention. In the end his services weren't required, as Dr. Girard's partner arrived soon after the police, ready to take over for his colleague.

"Why don't you sit with George while I handle the police?" Colin said, placing a gentle hand on my arm.

"How exactly are you planning to handle them?" I asked.

"I want to witness their interrogations, to see their assessment of the crime scene."

"Can I join you?"

"It will be difficult enough to persuade them to allow me to accompany them, even with my credentials," he said. "Both of us would be too much to hope for."

Resigned, I took the place next to George. "I imagine this is not how you expected to spend your day," he said.

"Far from it. And while I realize this may sound slightly inappropriate, I'm more than sorry you didn't get to speak to Dr. Girard. I so wanted him to be able to help stave off Madeline's condition."

He shook his head. "That was unlikely regardless. I was foolish to even let myself hope. I should know better." He fumbled through his pockets and pulled out a slim silver case. "What was it like in there? A nightmare?"

"Yes," I said.

He lit a cigarette, drew deep, and blew a thin stream of smoke into the air. "I don't think I could bear to see it. If he was wounded, fine. I spent enough time in the military to handle that—but when a situation's hopeless, when it's nothing but gore . . . I can't stand that kind of brutality. Even sifting through a battlefield you've got a chance of finding someone you can save. Do you think if we'd arrived earlier . . ."

"No," I said. "He's been dead since the middle of the night."

"Would you object to continuing on to Rouen after this? I'd like to call on the Priers unless, of course, you're too upset after what you've seen."

"I find soldiering on preferable to wallowing." My statement was true, but wanting to see the reactions of the Priers to the news of the doctor's death also motivated me.

"I want to express my condolences, of course," he said. "But if you don't think it's too crass, I'd like to ask them about Edith's treatment, see if they think it helped her. If they did, it might be worth going back to the asylum and talking to anyone else who worked on her case."

"If she were my daughter, it would give me comfort if anything gleaned from her condition could stop someone else's suffering."

"Another reason to like you," he said. "You've a wonderful spirit, Emily. Reminds me of my darling Madeline."

"I'm flattered," I said, not sure what else to say. "I know how you adore her."

"She centers me. Accepts me. Doesn't pressure me to devote my life to only one pursuit. I don't think many women would tolerate the way I change my passions like overcoats."

"But not when it comes to her, I hope."

"Absolutely not. There could never be another woman for me. I was designed for Madeline. I think you feel similarly about your husband?"

"I do," I said, blushing.

"Excellent." He puffed on his cigarette. "Makes for a much happier existence if you can be married to someone you actually like."

The sentiment seemed obvious, but I knew how frequently it was disregarded. "I couldn't agree more," I said. We sat in companionable silence for some time. "What will you do if she does succumb to her mother's condition?"

"I shall treat her as I always have and take care of her for the rest of her life. And when she's gone . . ." He shook his head. "I'll live alone, regretting every moment that I'm not with her."

25

Within an hour, Colin had finished with the police, and felt he'd seen all the evidence likely to be gathered from the hospital. The murderer had entered and exited through the office window. A struggle had ensued, and it was unclear whether the vicious criminal had come upon Dr. Girard already in his chair and subdued him there, or if they'd fought and he'd forced him into the seat. If it was the latter, the intruder had tidied up all signs of the altercation before leaving the scene. The doctor had suffered a blow to the head that had likely knocked him unconscious, after which his murderer slit his wrists, planted the suicide note, and made his escape.

"Cretinous," George said as we settled back into our carriage. "What sort of person does such a thing?"

"The patients are the most obvious place to start," Colin said. "But none of them has any marks that suggest having been involved."

"I'm glad," I said. "It's hideous to think someone he was trying to help would lash out at him in such violent fashion."

"But isn't it more frightening to think it's someone of sound mind?" George asked. "Someone who's not confined to an asylum?"

"Are any murderers of sound mind?" I asked.

"No excellent soul is exempt from a mixture of madness," Colin said. "Aristotle, I believe."

"It all comes back to the Greeks, doesn't it, my dear?" I asked. In a short while, we'd entered the city of Rouen and were settled in the Priers' sitting room, I next to Cécile, who rejoiced at seeing us. Madame Prier greeted us alone, and put on a good show, welcoming us as if our presence ranked somewhere near the second coming of Christ. Until, that is, we introduced George.

"Oh dear," she said, giving him her one hand to kiss while she flung the other over her forehead. "Monsieur Markham, do forgive me, but I wish I could have saved you from this association with my dreadful relatives."

"I can assure you, madame, that Madeline is all delightful charm. There's not a lady on earth with qualities superior to hers, and should you have the pleasure of making her acquaintance you would never again consider her branch of the family dreadful."

"I'd expect no other opinion from such a clearly devoted husband," she said. "But the madness that consumes them is not to be taken lightly—it is that I consider dreadful. Apologies if my meaning wasn't clear. I shall pray your wife escapes even a touch of it."

"I understand your side of the family, revered though it may be, suffers from the same affliction," George said, his voice affable, his smile wide.

"So you know our secret, of course you do," Madame Prier said.

"I hope I haven't offended you," George said. "I had hoped you could perhaps offer me some insight into your daughter's treatment— tell me if anything in particular helped her."

"I wish I could, but unfortunately nothing seemed to make a difference." Her face was hard as she talked about Edith, but softened as she turned to Colin. "Monsieur Hargreaves, Toinette will be beyond disappointed to have missed you. She's calling on a friend."

"It's such a shame she didn't come to the country," I said, my smile a masterpiece of the disingenuous. Cécile, who was sitting next to me on the horsehair settee stifled ironic laughter. "I could have thrown a little party for her."

"That would have been lovely," Madame Prier said. "You're so kind to think of her."

"You know how fond we are of her," Colin said. I resisted the urge to kick him. "I'm afraid, however, we've come bearing no glad tidings. Dr. Girard was murdered last night."

"Dr. Girard?" Confusion filled her wide eyes. "Are we acquainted with him?"

"He's the one who treated Edith, *Maman*." Whether Laurent had been lurking in the background from the time we had arrived or whether he'd snuck in, all stealth and quiet, was unclear. But when he stepped out from the shadows, his voice bellowing, it was as if all the heat had been sucked from the room. "How could you forget such a thing?"

"Why would you expect me to remember the horrid man's name?" Madame Prier said. "He did nothing useful for her."

"He did more than you."

"Laurent, have you not yet grown tired of embarrassing yourself in front of guests?"

"Not in the slightest. I take after my dear mother."

I sighed with an almost romantic delight as he stalked across the room and slammed the door. Laurent half terrified, half amused me. I appreciated the drama he could lend to a situation; it reminded me of a sensational novel. As the conversation restarted around me, I wondered what, exactly, he thought of Dr. Girard, and whom he blamed for Edith's escape from the hospital. Most of all, I wanted to see his handwriting. "Can we follow him?" I whispered to Cécile.

Cécile paused for a moment, clasped her hands together, and tapped one thumb against the other. She looked at Madame Prier, then at the door, and then slumped against me.

"*Mon dieu!*" she said. "I've come over all dizzy. Kallista, will you take me to my room?"

Her ploy, while perhaps inelegant for her self-imposed standards, served its purpose. Colin clearly saw through it at once—he watched as I guided her to the stairs, any hint of concern absent from his face. He could not, however, hide his amusement from me.

"I'm impressed with your instant reaction," I said, as we climbed the stairs. "You hardly hesitated at all."

"I don't like to waste time," Cécile said. "And the conversation was putting a terrible strain on my ability to feign attentiveness. It's a shame I'm not in the room you had—we could descend on Laurent unannounced."

As it was, we made our way to the top floor of the house and knocked on Laurent's closed door, which he opened without making us wait. Then, leaving it open, he turned around and walked back to his piano.

"You were quite right, Kallista," Cécile said, following him in and gingerly stepping around piles of sheet music. "He has the cluttered mind of a genius. Or at least the cluttered room."

"Why are you here?" he asked, crossing his arms and scowling at Cécile.

"Your sister's doctor is dead. Murder made to look like suicide. Badly done, wouldn't have fooled anyone. Not a professional," I said.

"A professional murderer?" Laurent laughed. "I can't decide whether to despise you or pity you, Lady Emily."

"We've no time at present for you to do either," Cécile said. "Where were you last night?"

"Me? Are you suggesting I killed Dr. Girard?"

She shrugged. "It's possible, is it not?"

"Aside from the fact I had no reason to want him dead, it's not possible. I was here all night."

"Alone?" I asked.

"Of course alone. Do you think I bring lovers to my mother's house?"

"You like to think you shock me, don't you?" I asked.

"Don't be tiresome, Laurent. Can your family verify you were here?" Cécile asked, then turned to me. "I think, Kallista, that I would perhaps make an exceedingly fine detective. I rather excel at questioning *persons of interest*. Do you think there's a special sort of gown I should adopt for the profession?"

Laurent sighed as if he was irritated, but his eyes betrayed him. Laughter danced in them. "Much as I'd like to see the result of you imposing haute couture on the art of investigation, I'm afraid I've not time for any of this nonsense."

"Are you not interested in what happened to Dr. Girard?" I asked. "His killer might lead us to your sister's."

"That's fascinating, I'm sure, but what have I to do with any of it? I was here last night and certainly wouldn't have killed my own sister."

"Who would have wanted him dead?" I asked. "Does anyone in your family blame him for what happened to Edith?"

"By the time Edith escaped from the asylum, no one in this house—myself excluded—had the slightest concern for what she was going through. You've spoken to my mother. She's relieved her daughter is dead. It's a wonder Edith didn't take her own life the way she was treated."

"I can't imagine your mother killed Dr. Girard," Cécile said. "It would have taken too much effort in directions she would not find interesting."

"You do know her well, don't you?" Laurent asked.

"Well enough."

"What about your father?" I asked. "Was he happy with Edith's progress? With her doctor?"

"He was pleased at having her out of the house."

"Laurent, I think it's desperately important that we try to locate your sister's child. Whom, you should remember, is your niece," I said. "Chances are Edith tried to find her, and this poor little girl is still with the man who killed her mother. Surely you're not willing to let such a situation go unchecked?"

"What do you want from me?" he asked.

"Did you really know nothing about Lucy?"

"Not a thing. If I had, I would have put her somewhere safe myself. And now this useless doctor is dead, I've less of a chance than ever of finding the child—who should, I must point out, be raised by me."

"You?" Cécile was all skepticism. "A bachelor? Living with his parents? You are fit for raising a little girl? Who, for all you know, is already happily settled in a comfortable home? Hubris, my dear Laurent. Hubris."

He replied to her, but I did not hear the words. My attention was focused on the pile of manuscripts nearest to me, on the words scrawled at the tops of the pages and the marginalia on the sides. All written in the same handwriting I'd seen only hours before on Dr. Girard's supposed suicide note. My heart thumping in my chest, I bent down and picked up the sheet.

"Written any suicide notes lately, Laurent?" I asked.

"How dare you?" He grabbed the paper from my hand.

"I thought I recognized the handwriting from when I was last in your room. So why did you kill him? Did he keep Edith's baby? Did she fall in love with him? Were you jealous?"

He slapped me, hard, right across the mouth.

I stumbled as Cécile gasped and stepped towards him. Without hesitating, I stopped her, came forward myself, smacked him back, and watched a deep red mark develop on his cheek. He said nothing, but raised his hand to the spot. I resisted the urge to touch what I knew must be its twin on my own face.

"The paper was ripped out of a notebook, like the one lying there," I said, pointing to a slim volume resting on top of the piano.

"Don't touch that." He stepped in front of me, blocking any progress I might try to make in pursuit of the object in question.

"Why are you so concerned if you've nothing to hide?" I asked.

"What did the note say?"

"It was a quotation from *Hamlet*. And a comment."

He shrugged. "I wasn't near the asylum last night."

"Did you write the note?" I asked.

"I'm not in the habit of depositing my writing with the possessions of dead men."

"Then explain to me how Dr. Girard got it?"

"There's nothing to explain. You can't prove I wrote it—you don't have it in your possession. If the police care to query me on the matter, I shall welcome them with open arms. They'll find nothing."

Something in his tone indicated with supreme strength the truth of his final statement. The police would find nothing, but only because Laurent would destroy anything that might be of use before they even thought to contact him. I was desperate to look in his notebook, but knew he wouldn't let me. His handwriting could be identified by the police in any number of ways—but I didn't need anything further to convince me *who* wrote the false suicide note. I wanted to read more, to find out *why* someone would do such a thing.

And why, after we'd learned the truth about Edith's baby, her doctor—quite possibly the only person who knew the story in its entirety—had been killed. Had our investigation catalyzed more violence?

"Lucy is all that matters, Laurent," I said. "We have to find her."

"I've done nothing but try since you told me she's alive," he said, his voice low and rumbling. "All I know is that there was a man called Myriel who visited her."

"What did you find out about him?" I asked.

"What do you know?" His eyes narrowed and darkened.

"We're in possession of the belongings he left in his rooms near the asylum," I said. "They're remarkably interesting."

"I need to speak to my father," he said. "Forgive me for walking out on such an invigorating conversation, but I've nothing further to say to either of you."

Cécile, intent on liberating Laurent's notebook from its rightful owner, refused to return to the country with us. Colin forbade her to touch the book, but agreed that keeping her in the Priers' house was a rational decision—she might observe something significant in the family's behavior. He knew perfectly well, however, that she would be in possession of the journal the next time we saw her. George had managed to forge some sort of connection to Madame Prier by the time we left the house—she implored him to return for tea, but did not include Madeline in the invitation.

"She's so like Madeline's mother," he said as we drove away from Rouen. "At least the way she was before we were married. Eccentric, yes, but charming all the same. How fortunate that she escaped my mother-in-law's fate."

"Was she able to offer you any useful insight?" I asked.

"Not a shred," he said. "I do wish I could have met Monsieur Prier. He must be a character of his own. Where does he keep himself hidden?"

"Cozied up with his mistress much of the time," Colin said.

"And their daughter."

"Another daughter?" George asked.

"This one much younger than Edith and Toinette," I said. Colin subtly jabbed my side. "Not that it's any of our business, of course."

"No, of course not," George said, laughing softly as he turned to look out the window. "Must be something to have so many children."

Discomfort prickled in the air, as each of us looked away from the rest. Each of us childless. Each of us carrying the small heartbreak of tiny losses.

None of us spoke again for the duration of the journey.

21 July 1892

Emily's questions about the daughter of the Markhams' gardener spurned me to inquire about the matter. The servants wouldn't tell me a thing—no surprise there—but a visit to the boulangerie *in Fréville resulted not only in a spectacular baguette stuffed with ham and Gru-yère cheese, but also the story that circulated at the time. The child, it seems, did die on the property, and the good citizens of our village are convinced she haunts the area.*

Ridiculous, of course. I've no time for wailing cries and misty appari-tions. And ribbons, according to the story. The ghost, you see, has a pro-pensity for dropping them wherever she goes. No doubt they're supplied by every bored adolescent in the area.

Now that I think on it, I saw a ribbon crumpled on the ground when I was out riding some days ago. Blue, though I'm not sure the color is of any significance. I have a vague memory of Emily asking about ribbons in conjunction with the child. I do hope no one has polluted her mind with such nonsense. My opinion of her is much improved, but she's still more vulnerable than I would like.

No one, however, could argue she is not a good teacher.

26

I was pleased, when we returned to Mrs. Hargreaves's house, to find a letter waiting from Monsieur Leblanc. His update primarily served to inform me he'd learned nothing new, but he also asked if he could call soon, saying that he needed my assistance on a matter, but that it could wait until after the questions of Edith Prier's death had been answered. The thought of someone needing me was more than a little flattering. Colin allowed me to assist him on occasion, but would have had no trouble carrying on in my absence.

Allowed. How I hated that word.

A hot fire burned in the sitting room's enormous stone fireplace, the three of us snugly fortified against the damp, each hard at work. Normandy was giving us days that felt more like autumn than summer, but the cool weather wasn't oppressive, not given the bright sun that managed to cut through the clouds often enough to remind us it was July. Mrs. Hargreaves and I had spent no small amount of time on Homer after dinner, and I was more enamored by the poet's work than ever. I'd never before filled the role of teacher, and found that I learned as much while assisting my mother-in-law as I did studying on my own. More, perhaps, as the understanding it took to explain to her the rules of Greek grammar or to help her analyze of passages of the poem required more active and thorough thought than it took to study by myself. I adored every minute of it.

"Ah!" Mrs. Hargreaves said. "I have it now—'The wine urges me on, the bewitching wine, which sets even a wise man to singing and to laughing gently and rouses him up to dance and bring forth words which were better unspoken.' I do like this, Emily."

"I'm glad," I said.

"What we need, Mother, is port," Colin said. "It's appropriate to what you've just read, and it's Emily's favorite."

"I'm afraid I have none," she said. "You'll have to settle for cognac." This may have been the first time a lady had not balked at my preference for drinking port, traditionally considered a gentleman's beverage. My respect for my mother-in-law was increasing exponentially.

"I'll expect you to have filled the hole in your cellar before our next visit," Colin said, filling glasses for each of us as our conversation returned to the Priers.

"Laurent's feelings for his sister go deeper than perhaps they ought," I said. "Could he have crossed an unspeakable line? Could he have been jealous of Vasseur, and furious when he found out Edith had given birth to the child?"

"And killed her?" Colin asked. I nodded. "How would he have found out about the baby? Girard didn't tell him."

"He did seem surprised when we told him Lucy was alive," I said. "But he may very well be an excellent actor. As soon as Edith went missing, he would have started to search for her. And that search may have uncovered the truth about the girl."

"Wouldn't it also have uncovered the girl?" Mrs. Hargreaves asked.

"Possibly," Colin said. "But not necessarily."

"Would he have been so angry that he'd actually kill the sister he loved? And in such violent fashion?" I frowned.

"He's the only one in the family who kept visiting her," Colin said. "He might have felt doubly betrayed—first that she took a lover, second, that she lied to him about the baby."

"Did he not see her during her confinement?" Mrs. Hargreaves asked. "Surely even an ignorant man would take note of her condition."

"It wouldn't have been too difficult to hide," Colin said. "She was in bed, and could have had a mountain of blankets over her. Laurent might have never noticed."

"Which would have angered him all the more once he realized the doctor's real game," I said. "The note in Dr. Girard's pocket is in Laurent's handwriting. That's solid evidence."

"It *may* be in his handwriting," Colin said.

"Yes," I said. "But I'd stake my life on it. The police will confirm it."

"We need more proof than just the note," Colin said. "Even if Laurent did write it, someone else could have slipped it in the doctor's pocket."

"There's also Vasseur," I said. "We must find him."

"I've persuaded the office of the Foreign Legion to give me the two addresses he'd given them," Colin said. "But my subsequent inquiries turned up nothing, so it's time for a personal visit."

"Why don't we go there tomorrow?" I asked.

"That won't be necessary. You stay here and deal with Sebastian. We do have a bet, you know."

"A murder is more significant," I said.

"I'm not trying to give you useless tasks," he said. "You know me better than to think that. I'm convinced your old friend has more of a connection to all this than we've figured out so far. He took Monet's painting to and from the Markhams'—good fun for Sebastian, but I'm beginning to suspect he wasn't in the neighborhood simply to follow you."

"I wonder—" I stopped. I didn't want to say more out loud. I wondered if Sebastian had Lucy. I wondered if he were Jules Vasseur. "How long do you think you can pacify me in this way?"

"Undoubtedly not long enough," he said. The teasing rhythm of his words combined with the warm intensity in his eyes tugged at me deep inside. I wanted to lean forward and kiss him, to feel his arms around me, to hear him murmur soft words against my neck.

"I shouldn't be gone more than a few days," he continued.

"Perhaps when you come home you can buy me a pony if I've been a good girl," I said, teasing him back.

"Don't forget, Emily, I know you're intellectually at least as capable as I am. I'm protecting you from nothing but physical weakness."

His mother coughed. "'It is tedious to tell again tales already plainly told,'" she read. "Simple sentence. Obvious truth. I'm glad you've brought me back to Homer, Emily."

"So I'm to contact Sebastian?" I asked Colin after we'd retired to our room and he was helping me undo the long row of tiny buttons down the back of my dress, slipping them through their silk loops.

"I'm confident you'll find him easily enough." He kissed the back of my neck. "Buy something you think he'd like to steal."

"It won't be that difficult. I had the foresight to set up a method of contacting him," I said, and explained to him how he'd given me his cravat to hang from the window. "It almost seems a pity, though. Tricking him into stealing something would have been much more fun. I could have had a day or two in Paris, shopping for just the right priceless item, irresistible to our favorite thief. You do realize if I did such a thing he would be eternally indebted to me. And that I would then call in the favor and have him join forces with the Crown—and you'd lose our bet."

"A risk that would be worth taking," he said. "Fortunately, however, your foresight has protected me from having to do so. But no more of this right now. If I'm to be away from you for days, my darling wife, I don't want to spend our last hours together discussing the multitudinous charms of Sebastian Capet."

"You don't?" I asked. He was loosening my corset now. "Whatever else did you have in mind?"

"I thought perhaps we could play chess," he said.

"What a pity there are no pieces in our room." Free from my stays, I turned to face him and traced his lips with my finger. "And no board. You'll have to find another way to amuse yourself."

"Have you any suggestions?"

"None that do me credit," I said.

"My favorite kind." He pulled pins from my hair until it hung down my back. I kissed him.

"You're a corrupting influence," I said.

"Would you want any other sort of husband?"

And then, in an instant, every confused and conflicted complicated feeling I'd had for him over the past days vanished. I loved him, even when he wanted to protect me. Even when protection meant curbing my freedom. It wasn't society or some set of arbitrary rules that drove him to hold me back—it was pure and simple love. Tenderness and care. A desire to not lose me before he had to. I melted into his arms and let him carry me to our bed.

It was perfect. Except for the tiniest, darkest part of my soul that was crying out, wishing I could protect him, too.

27

Rain started to fall at half eleven, so I bundled into a thick cloak and slipped into my sturdiest shoes before going to meet Sebastian at midnight. Before he'd left, I'd told Colin what I planned to do—I wasn't about to hide anything from him—and now I made my way quietly though the house, stopping twice when I thought I heard footsteps, then starting again towards the door, opening it silently, and breathing a sigh of relief when I felt the sweet, wet air outside. I pulled up my hood in what, given the force with which the water was hitting the ground, was doomed to be a vain effort. A cloudy sky meant no moon, so I stepped carefully into the dark, not so much because I worried I would fall on the slick pavement in front of the house, but because everything around me made me want to jump.

The cool raindrops turned steamy as they hit the ground, releasing a disheartening mist to meander through the trees on the estate. Thunder rolled in the distance, and the only relief from the black night came from intermittent flashes of lightning. I'd considered bringing a lamp, but didn't want to draw any unnecessary attention to myself. The sound of the storm and its accompanying wind made it difficult to listen for footsteps, and this put my nerves further on edge. I knew Sebastian would come. But I should have liked to be able to listen for any further—and unwelcome—additions to our party.

I remembered times when I'd been afraid in London, when I feared the man who'd murdered my first husband might try to attack me next. As frightening as a city could be, with its narrow streets and darting shadows, the country scared me more. In town, a person was never truly alone. There were always servants or cab drivers or pedestrians on the street within shouting distance. Here, however, if I ventured far from the house, no one would hear me should I cry for help. Just as no one had heard Edith Prier's screams when her murderer attacked her.

Which was why I had no intention of taking a single step beyond Mrs. Hargreaves's gate. But even that felt too far from the warm comfort of her sprawling house. I shivered, wet from the downpour that only grew harder the longer I waited for Sebastian. Clinging to the iron railing posts in an attempt to stop my hands from shaking, I watched for my friend on the road, periodically turning around in case he was approaching me from behind, as he had previously.

"Kallista!" His whisper was harsh, and came from behind a tree a few paces from me. "Come here, quickly."

Without hesitating, I obeyed.

"Someone followed me here," he said. "We need to get you back inside."

"What about you?" I asked.

"I'm afraid I may need to join you. Could your mother-in-law spare a room for me?"

This was hardly a question I wanted to pose to Mrs. Hargreaves so soon after relations between us had begun to thaw, but I saw no other option. "How did you get into the grounds?" I asked.

"Over the west wall," he said. "I heard someone drop behind me less than a minute later."

My heart was pounding. The house felt a million miles away. "Will we be safe inside? Or will he pursue us there?"

"I've not the slightest idea—but it can't be more dangerous inside than out."

I looked around as thoroughly as I could, watching for any signs of unusual movement, and strained my ears to hear beyond the rain. Satisfied there was no visible danger—the best I could manage—I grabbed Sebastian by the hand and ran as fast as I could to the front door. We flew through it, slamming into my mother-in-law, who was standing on the other side.

"There is, I assume, a reasonable explanation?" she asked, looking Sebastian up and down.

He gave his most elegant bow, even as water trickled off the top hat he'd removed the instant he saw her. "I am delighted to see you again," he said. "It's far too long that I've been deprived of your excellent company."

"You waste your time trying to charm me," she said. Quickly assessing the situation as I told her what had happened, she pulled a heavily embroidered bell cord. "You, Emily, need to get into dry clothes at once. You, Mr. Capet, must do the same. Stay here, I don't need you dripping everywhere."

A footman, disheveled, his white wig not quite straight, appeared, out of breath, undoubtedly from running up the stairs. "Madame?"

"Watch this man. He's a thief. I shall return momentarily with clothing for him. Do not let him out of your sight and do not be taken in by his ridiculous manners."

She led me upstairs, but said not another word until we'd reached the bedroom I shared with her son. "What is the meaning of this running about in the middle of a stormy night?"

I explained to her that Colin had wanted me to talk to Sebastian. And then I explained the method Sebastian had given me to contact him. She stepped into our dressing room and began making her way through Colin's clothes, looking for something her unexpected guest could wear.

"Do you think he will be useful?" she asked.

"I hope so."

"Let's find out," she said. "Change your clothes and come downstairs. I'll have the footman continue to keep an eye on Mr. Capet while he dresses. We can't take any risks with that one. Let's hope Colin won't mind lending him a suitable outfit. We can have his own clothes ready for him tomorrow."

She started out of the room, but I stopped her. "Mrs. Hargreaves . . ." I couldn't keep my voice from trembling. "Would you wait for me? I'm afraid I've frightened myself. And Sebastian heard someone following him outside. I—"

"Say not another word," she said, and rested the full weight of her body against the closed bedroom door. "No one is getting through here. Now. Dry clothes. And give me the wet ones." There was a calm to her tone that reminded me of Colin in stressful situations. He was a master at being soothing in the midst of madness.

In short order we'd made our way back downstairs, and soon a blushing Sebastian, his hair wet and unruly, sat across from us in a smallish study dominated by an enormous brass globe. Tall, elegant chairs surrounded the ebony table dividing us from him as he leaned forward, clasping his hands.

"I do apologize for intruding on your hospitality," he said.

"My daughter-in-law has told me everything. Who is following you?"

"I'm afraid I've no idea," he said.

"What did you want to discuss with this man, Emily?"

"Edith Prier's child," I said, staring evenly at Sebastian. "The little girl you were with the last time I saw you outside in the middle of the night?"

"What on earth can you possibly mean? I was alone," he said.

"I heard her crying. It's what brought me outside. And I saw her ribbon in the road—the same one you picked up and took with you after you left me."

"Kallista—Emily—I don't have her," he said. "I don't know what you're talking about. As I told you that night, you're seeing things, no doubt due to the grief caused by your own loss."

"Mr. Capet." Mrs. Hargreaves pulled herself up straight. "You will not torment a member of my family."

"I assure you I've no intention of doing any such thing," he said. "But she's confusing two things here—the neighborhood ghost and a missing child."

"Neighborhood ghost?" I asked.

"Don't play dumb," he said. "Markham told you about the girl who fell down the stairs. What do you think about the supernatural, Mrs. Hargreaves? Are you a believer?"

"I've not given the subject much thought," she said. "I never found it interesting."

"But you can't deny there are strange things afoot here—and that not all of them have simple, or even human, explanations," Sebastian said.

"Of course I can," Mrs. Hargreaves said. "I've seen nothing to make me believe otherwise."

Sebastian turned to me. "Don't you think, Kallista, that the spirit of a lost little girl might seek out a woman who's missing a child?"

I could hardly breathe, had to force words from my throat. "If that's the case, she'd stay close to Madeline," I said.

"Not if Madeline pushed her down the stairs."

We stayed awake half the night, but I had trouble focusing on the conversation. I hoped Sebastian's words weren't true. Surely Madeline could never have done such a thing. I shook off the horror of the possibility, reminding myself we lacked any evidence and were speculating only because we'd been scared. Sebastian continued to insist he'd been followed, but none of us was about to go outside and search for the intruder—we would have needed Colin for that—and in the end decided sleep would be best.

The rain was still falling when Meg brought my tea in the morning. "Are there adventures afoot in the house, madame?" she asked, setting the tray down next to me on the bed.

"Not of the good kind," I said. "Have you heard any gossip about Edith Prier's murder, Meg?"

"Not really," she said. "Everyone's talking, of course, but there's not much to say, you know. Nobody's got a clue who did it and we all—all of us below stairs, that is—is convinced as it's the Ripper, madam, no matter what the police is saying now. I told them all how I was in London when he was doing his evil work there."

The glint in Meg's eyes told me she was thoroughly enjoying getting to be the neighborhood's resident Ripper expert. "Have you heard any other stories of violent death?" I asked.

"Oh, you mean the little girl? Whose father worked for the Markhams?"

"Yes, her." My heartbeat quickened.

"No one talks about that anymore," she said. "I asked on account of knowing you'd want to know about any other *suspicious deaths.*" She emphasized the words with such careful effort I had to bite back my amusement. "There's nothing interesting to report. She's buried at the château, you know."

"The Markhams' château?" I asked.

Meg nodded. "Unmarked grave. So as not to trouble the lady of the house. Who, if you'll forgive my impertinence, hasn't been able to, well . . ."

"Have children?"

"Yes, madam, thank you. I don't like to say it, you know. Specially after . . ."

"That's all right, Meg. I do appreciate it."

I guzzled my tea and dressed as quickly as possible, eager to set out on the day's mission. Mrs. Hargreaves agreed we should try to locate Lucy, and felt Sebastian a worthy companion for me while conducting my investigation. She, of course, didn't want me doing anything dangerous, but did not object to my plan to return to the asylum and search Edith's room again.

"You're a terrible rogue," Sebastian said as we climbed into the carriage and waved to her as it pulled away. "She wouldn't approve of you looking for Girard's house. Or doing any of the other things we're bound to do once you start getting carried away."

I raised an eyebrow. "Do not, Sebastian, make me regret bringing you," I said.

"You can't regret bringing me. You wouldn't have been allowed out of the house on your own."

Allowed. Again. He was perfectly correct, however, and given what had transpired the night before, I wouldn't have dreamed of going off on my own. Colin's mother had sent word to Inspector Gaudet first thing in the morning, asking him to come round and search for evidence of whomever had followed Sebastian. None of us expected him to unearth even a shred of something useful.

I don't approve of lying, and it's certainly not a habit into which I'd like to fall. Sebastian and I were, in fact, going to the asylum. It was theoretically possible we—and the police—had missed something in Edith's room, and it wouldn't hurt to make another pass through it. But I also knew someone amongst the staff would be able to direct me to Dr. Girard's house, and I had great hopes for finding a clue there that would point the way to Lucy's guardian.

Order had been restored at the asylum, though the previously disheveled nurse was nowhere to be found. Another one, whom I'd met only in passing the day Dr. Girard died, greeted me warmly, and was quick to show us Edith's room.

"They've all been through here more times than I can count, you know," she said.

"The police?" I asked.

"And the doctor, of course, as soon as she'd disappeared. And then the police again after they found her body." She covered her mouth. "Oh, you're the one, aren't you madame?"

"I am."

"I do hope you can forgive me," she said.

"Don't think on it," I said. "There's nothing more to be said on the topic. Did anyone else look through her room?"

"Let's see . . . there was her friend, Monsieur Myriel."

"When was he here?"

"Right after Mademoiselle Prier's death," she said.

"Do you know where he went when he left?" I asked, excitement building in me.

"Oh, no," she said. "He didn't talk much. He was awfully upset about Mademoiselle Prier."

Sebastian stood absolutely still in the corner of the room, not appearing to have paid the slightest attention to the conversation. "Did Edith's family collect her belongings?" he asked.

"No one came immediately after we heard of her murder. Her brother did eventually, though." She turned back to me. "He's the other one who came and searched her room. Him and that writer fellow."

"Monsieur Leblanc?" I asked, surprised.

"Yes. Monsieur Leblanc. Wasn't sure I could remember his name. But it's hard to forget his moustache."

"When was he here?" I asked.

"The day after Dr. Girard died."

"Did he find anything?" I was surprised Monsieur Leblanc hadn't told me of his visit.

"I don't think so. The thing is, madame, we'd cleaned out the room real good after she left. And again after we got word she'd died. There wasn't anything left."

"Not unless you're clever enough to know where to look. I have a great breadth of knowledge when it comes to furniture construction—people think they're awfully clever when they hide valuables in pieces that don't have drawers," Sebastian said. He walked slowly through the room, examining every object it contained. Then, his brow furrowed, he crossed to the bed and began to unscrew one of the finials on the metal headboard. Once he'd removed it, he put two slim fingers into the post before returning the finial back to its place and repeating the procedure on the other side. This time, he pulled out a tightly rolled bundle of papers. "Sometimes, my dear girl, you need a gentleman who can think beyond the ordinary constraints of decency."

28

"Love letters," I said, smoothing the pages on my lap. We were all sitting on what had been Edith's bed in the small, spare hospital room, reading words so tender and sweet and true they brought tears to my eyes. Sebastian, however, was unmoved.

"He's a maudlin sense about him," he said. "Not nearly romantic enough. I did much better by you."

I shot him what I hoped he would recognize as a disapproving glare. "Jules. That's Vasseur," I said. "So he knew she was here. But no one called that ever visited her?"

The nurse shook her head. "You saw me check the records again just a minute ago. No one admitting to be him was ever here."

Sebastian sighed. "Isn't it obvious he's your mysterious Monsieur Myriel?"

"It doesn't fit with the time he was away in the Foreign Legion," I said. "And furthermore, if he was so close, wouldn't he have spirited her away soon after she . . ." I didn't want to mention the baby in front of the nurse. "As soon as he realized she was here? Why would he have left her here?"

"She needed treatment, madame," the nurse said. "There was no question. Some days she hardly knew where she was."

"So he took rooms nearby, under an assumed name, so he could visit without drawing her family's attention. It became clear to him the doctor was at least trying to help her, so he didn't press her to leave immediately," Sebastian suggested.

"Did her condition improve at all during her stay here?" I asked.

"I can't rightly say," the nurse said. "Mademoiselle Prier was one of those patients whose condition changed constantly. Some days she was as normal as you, the next she was seeing ghosts. She couldn't have gone home."

"But Monsieur Vasseur—Monsieur Myriel—might have thought otherwise," I said. "Or perhaps . . ." Again I stopped myself and reset my focus. "Do you know where Dr. Girard lived? I'm wondering if he had any personal correspondence with Monsieur Myriel."

"Wouldn't the police have found it?" she asked.

"Only if they knew to look," I said. "Surely it would be all right for you to help us find the house? It's not as if we'd be disturbing him."

"I suppose not," she said, twisting the ends of her apron in her hand. "He can't be hurt any more than he's already been."

Soon, we were banging on the door of a quaint single floor cottage, a quarter of an hour's drive down a narrow, unpaved road from Dr. Girard's asylum. Shoots of green peeked from the top of the thatched roof, and the half-timbered walls gleamed from recent whitewashing. A neat pavement of smooth, round stones led the way from the road, and as with nearly every country house I'd seen in Normandy, hydrangeas filled the garden to bursting.

As we expected, no one answered our knocks. I looked to Sebastian, confident there was not a door in the Western Hemisphere that would not bend to his will.

"You wouldn't rather wriggle through a window, then?" he asked.

"No," I said.

"Such a shame," he said. With a sigh, he pulled something out of his jacket—a thin metal strip—and within seconds the door flung open. He gestured flamboyantly, waving his arm with the grace of a courtier, and bowed. "After you, dear lady."

Nerves filled me as I stepped into the house. What we were doing wasn't strictly unethical—although Sebastian had picked the lock, I rationalized our actions, telling myself looking for clues to find Lucy was working for the greater good. A small entryway opened into a comfortable sitting room filled with books and papers and watercolors of the Norman countryside. I started for the desk in the far left corner, but Sebastian grabbed my arm.

"Allow me, Kallista," he said. "This is my territory." Moving silently, he glided through the room, examining every object, every paper, every square inch of the floor, walls, and ceiling. But when I followed him as he moved into the doctor's bedroom, he stopped me.

"No," he said. "I will help you, Kallista, but you can't expect access to the secret methods of my success. You might decide to turn to a life of crime and steal everything good that I want."

"Sebastian—"

"No." He silenced me with a firm hand over my mouth. "I will not have it. You're welcome to search after I'm done, but I'd be more than surprised if you turned up anything the police didn't."

"The police weren't looking for information about Lucy."

"Be my guest," he said, taking an extravagant bow. "But if you do make a mess, I'm not going to follow and correct your mistakes."

"There's no arguing with you, is there?" I asked.

"You can argue for days if you'd like," he said. "But it will get you exactly nowhere. I'm implacable."

"And proud of it."

"Absolutely."

"Fine," I said. "I'll wait for you here."

He closed the bedroom door behind him while I managed to stifle a sigh. Sebastian was a handful, but an amusing handful, and not without his charms. While I waited for him, I perused Dr. Girard's books. Most of them pertained to medicine. There was also a copy of John James Audubon's *Birds of America*, a Bible in Latin, and a small collection of fiction. Nearly all the novels were French. I glanced through the titles and pulled down one of the few in English, Charles Dickens' *Great Expectations*. I selected it not because it was in my native tongue, but for another reason altogether: it was the story of a young orphan with a mysterious benefactor.

A perfect place to hide information about Lucy's guardian.

By the time Sebastian came out of the bedroom, I'd read nearly three chapters of the book.

"I'm glad you're amusing yourself," he said. "There's nothing of particular interest here. Not, that is, anything that would interest you."

"What did you take?"

"*Moi?*"

"Sebastian." I gave him a severe look.

"Some cuff links. No one will miss them."

I closed the book and crossed my arms. "And?"

"You can't possibly think his paintings are worth my notice. They're pedestrian."

"What else?"

"He has some fantastic eighteenth-century brass buttons."

"Put them back," I said.

"For what? So they can be sold to some unappreciative fool who's as likely to put them on doll's clothing as to use them for something reasonable?"

"It's not for you to decide, Sebastian."

"And why is that? I have a good eye. I love the objects I liberate and I make sure they have good homes. What's wrong with me correcting small injustices?"

"I'd hardly call buttons falling into the wrong hands an injustice," I said.

"I shall remember your insensitivity, Kallista, and will strike you at once from the list of people to whom I would give such exquisite objects."

"Put them back." I glowered at him. "And then we can go speak to Lucy's guardian."

"If we can find him. I'll need to search the rest of the house," he said. "And can't do that until I have some time to mourn the loss of these buttons."

"Return the cuff links as well."

"You're a disappointment."

"Your kind words mean the world to me," I said. "But you don't need to continue the search. I've found everything we need."

"No," he said, badly feigning breathlessness.

"Go," I said. "And don't forget the cuff links."

"You are so horrible to me," he said. "Yet I adore you still. And if you have indeed found what you say, I may have to recruit you to my nefarious lair of criminals." He disappeared into the bedroom, where I doubted he was returning anything. Still, I had to at least try to make him do the proper thing.

I flipped through *Great Expectations*, pausing again at the pages in the part of the book where Pip learns the identity of his benefactor. There, in the margins, someone had scrawled a name and address— Marie Sapin in a not too faraway town called Barentin—and it had to be that of Lucy's guardian. The context was too perfect for it to be anything else.

My deduction did not completely convince Sebastian upon his return from the bedroom, but he could not argue we had anything better to try, and agreed we should go investigate.

"It will, however, be a fruitless expedition," he said, clearly irritated to be without the buttons. I couldn't decide whether his mood was for show, to make me believe he'd put them back, or whether his frustration was genuine.

"Why else would Dr. Girard write such a thing in that precise spot in that precise book?" I asked as our carriage sped towards Barentin.

"There are countless answers to that question, Emily," he said. "Perhaps this Marie Sapin is a beautiful woman the doctor met while on holiday, when he was reading *Great Expectations*."

"Perhaps Marie Sapin is a patient he had to collect from her home," I said. "Perhaps she is a nurse he wanted to interview. Or the woman he hired to look after his elderly mother—that's the sort of name a person would certainly want to bury in a novel."

"I'm glad to see you're getting into the spirit of things," he said, tugging at his spotless gloves.

"But you may find, Sebastian, that I'm right. My reasoning is not without logic. That does not prove it's without flaw, but it's a lead worth pursuing. And in this line of work, not every lead pans out."

"Don't you find that tedious? You'd be much happier treasure hunting through Europe with me. I could get the Trojan gold for you— Priam's treasure, the jewelry that cad Schleimann excavated and draped over his horrible wife. It would look far better on you. And you know, Kallista, *my* leads never fail to pan out."

It felt as if the drive to Barentin spanned centuries. The roads were bumpy, and we were jostled so hard I feared my teeth would fall out. But it was not all unpleasant. Sebastian regaled me with some excessively diverting stories about the perils and pitfalls of being a Thief of Refined Taste, and by the time we reached Madame Sapin's modest but well cared for house, I was laughing so hard I couldn't immediately step out of the carriage.

Once I'd returned to a state of calm, we approached the door. We'd debated the best approach to convincing Madame Sapin that Dr. Girard condoned our expedition. Sebastian persuaded me to come around to his way of thinking which, at the time, seemed a decent option. Now that the moment was nearly upon us, my heart was pounding and our plan seemed a dismal one.

A cheerful maid opened the door, told us her mistress was home, and led us into a small room in the front of the house. The wide planks of the wooden floor had not a speck of dust on them, and the furniture was simple and spare. I looked around, hoping to see evidence of a child's presence, but there was none. In a matter of moments, a tall, sturdy woman came in, her broad face friendly, her cheeks bright pink.

"How can I help you?" she asked. "The girl says Dr. Girard sent you."

"He did, Madame Sapin," I said, my hand shaking as I gave her the letter Sebastian had forged before we left the doctor's house. "He's concerned about Lucy, you see."

She shook her head and crinkled her nose. "I'm afraid I can't read."

"I—I can read it for you if you'd like," I said.

"If you don't mind," she said.

I cleared my throat, nervous:

Dear Madame Sapin,

I hope this letter finds you well. As I'm sure you're aware, the recent murder of our poor Lucy's mother has put my mind in a state of great unease. As a result, I've asked two friends of mine to assist you with the child: Lady Emily Hargreaves, a friend of the Prier family, and Sir Bradley Soane, a gentleman of both impeccable taste and absolute dependability. Please do not hesitate to allow them to assist you in any way possible.

I am, as always, grateful for the kind service you've done
for the child.

Girard

"But he knows she's not here," Madame Sapin said. "I don't under-stand."

"Well of course," Sebastian said, rising and crossing to her. "But he's well aware of the bond between you and Lucy, and knows that if anyone could—" He stopped. "It's all been so difficult, hasn't it?"

"Oh, sir, it has," she said. She dropped her head as her eyes showed the faintest signs of tears.

"Shall I call for some tea?" he asked. "You're upset."

"No, I'll be able to carry on," she said. "I thought it was the right thing to let Lucy go to her mother. Near broke my heart, it did, but how could I deny Madame Vasseur?"

Vasseur? Had Edith married her lover?

"I'm afraid we've more bad news," I said. "Dr. Girard has been murdered as well, and there's speculation the killer might be looking for Lucy."

"Oh this is too, too awful," she said, tears welling in her eyes. "I've never known such a kind man."

"Could you tell me—" I took her hands. "—I know it's difficult. But the more you can tell me about Lucy and the doctor and Madame Vasseur, the more likely it is that we can help the child."

"Dr. Girard never mentioned either of you," she said. "I don't know—"

"Have you other letters from him?" Sebastian asked. "Did he write to you?"

"He knew I couldn't read."

"But he must have occasionally sent you instructions, or informa-tion?" I asked.

"He did."

"Who read it for you?"

"My girl. She's educated, you see. Her mother's blind and likes to hear stories. And the doctor didn't want anyone out of the household to know the truth about Lucy's parentage. You know how these aristocratic types are. My apologies, madame."

"Not at all," I said. "Where are the letters now? Did you keep them?"

"Dr. Girard told me to burn them all once they'd been read."

"And did you?" Sebastian asked.

"Of course," she said. "Shouldn't I have?"

"I just thought that if you had one, you could look at it next to the one we've brought and see the handwriting's the same," he said. "So that you'd feel more at ease with us."

"I suppose I could have my girl look at them," she said, her voice hesitant.

"That's an excellent idea," I said, worried that I was forcing too much enthusiasm into my voice.

The maid was produced, and her reaction reassured me. She nodded her head vigorously as soon as she saw the letter. "Oh yes, madame, this is from the doctor. I'd recognize his hand anywhere. Would you like me to read it?"

Sebastian could not have been more pleased with her reaction to his forgery.

"Yes, I would," Madame Sapin said, kicking my nerves up again. She must not have trusted me to read it accurately. But when the servant spoke the words precisely as I had (she was in possession of a beautiful reading voice), our hostess let her shoulders drop and visibly relaxed, returning to the open, friendly mode in which she'd greeted us. She sent the maid away.

"Please excuse my uncertainty," she said. "Dr. Girard told me discretion was absolutely necessary in this situation, and I have grave worries about dear Lucy. I've heard nothing of her since her parents took her away."

"When was that?" I asked.

"Six months ago, I suppose."

"Did you speak to her mother?"

"No, only her father. He was on his way to collect his wife from the hospital and wanted to bring their daughter to surprise her."

"Had he any proof of his identity?" I asked.

"Oh yes. Army papers or something of the sort," she said. "Foreign Legion. Yes, that's what it was. My girl read them to me. He looked all shaken up—couldn't believe how big Lucy was. She's a beautiful girl, you know. The image of her mother, Dr. Girard always said."

"Did you not expect the doctor to have alerted you to Lucy's mother's release?" I asked.

"He sent a letter, just as he did with you," she said.

And I knew it must have been just as authentic as ours.

"Do you have any idea where they went?" I asked.

"They were setting up house near the sea. Lucy clapped her little hands when her father told her. She's always wanted to build sand castles."

"Was she afraid to leave with him? He was a stranger to her," I said.

"Not at first. I don't think she realized she was really going away. But I heard her crying in the carriage. And she clung to me something fierce when I put her in it."

"It must have been dreadful."

"It was," she said, her face turning ruddier. "But it's the right thing, isn't it, for a child to be with her parents?"

"Of course," I said, hoping the girl was all right. "Have you any idea where on the seaside they were headed?"

"Étretat," she said. "But I don't know more than that."

"Thank you," I said. "You've been more than helpful."

"You will let me know if you find Lucy?"

"Of course."

"I can still look after her, you know. She was happy here."

"I don't doubt that," I said. "This is an extremely welcoming and warm home. A perfect place for a child to feel loved. I'll keep you informed of all developments."

We thanked her again and she showed us to the door. Before we'd reached our carriage, I turned to Sebastian. "Don't even think about it," I said. "Put it back."

"What?" he asked.

"The book," I said. "Go take it back. Now."

"She can't read," he said, his voice teeming with indignation. "And it's *Les Trois Mousquetaires*. A prime first edition. One of my favorite books."

"I'm not arguing about this, Sebastian."

Resigned, he went back to the house while I discussed with our driver the possibility of heading straight for Étretat, the town where, I remembered, Monsieur Leblanc resided.

29

Étretat lay too far from Barentin for us to comfortably reach that day, so we returned to Mrs. Hargreaves's house, where a telegram from my husband waited for me.

"In youth and beauty, wisdom is but rare." How glad I am to have a wife of such rare variety. Homer would sing your praises.

This set what felt like a permanent grin on my face, and I was ready to find Lucy, vanquish the killer, and recruit Sebastian to the service of the Crown. Woe be to the person who tried to stop me!

We'd managed, over crêpes topped with apples, butter, crème fraîche, and sugar, then doused with calvados—Normandy's famous apple brandy—and flamed, to do a decent job recounting the day's events to my mother-in-law, so that she was excited rather than horrified by our exploits. I should have expected nothing less from her, but the experience of my own mother's reactions to my work had taught me to brace myself for constant censure. But instead of criticizing, Mrs. Hargreaves offered to accompany us to Étretat.

"I'm not sure it would do, Emily, for you to go so far away without me. Mr. Capet is an unmarried man of dubious character. It might harm your reputation. If I come, his presence will seem unremarkable."

"You're very kind," I said. "Thank you."

"Who is going where?" Cécile burst into the room. I leaped up and embraced her, delighted to see her.

"Do you have the notebook?" I asked.

"Did you doubt for a moment I would?" She kissed my cheeks. "I am disappointed in you, Kallista." Frantic yipping in the hallway announced the return of Caesar and Brutus.

"Notebook?" Mrs. Hargreaves asked, greeting Cécile in turn.

"You two have made peace," Cécile said, watching the dynamic between my mother-in-law and myself. "And you've collected my favorite criminal mind. I should never have stayed in Rouen for so long."

"My dear Madame du Lac," Sebastian said, rising to kiss her hand. "Your charms are so great you ought never to leave my presence."

"You do have a flair for the dramatic, Monsieur Capet," Cécile said. "I should like to have a lengthy discussion with you on the topic of my country's revolution. Not today, however. There's too much else to talk about now."

It took nearly an hour for us all to catch up on each other's stories, the deliciously nervous energy in the room quickly approaching a feverish frenzy.

"Do you think Lucy's safe?" Cécile asked. "And what happened to Vasseur? Why has he disappeared? And what more of this Myriel? Have you learned anything?"

"Myriel?" Mrs. Hargreaves asked. "The bishop in *Les Misérables*?"

"*Les Misérables*? The book was in Myriel's room," I said.

"Should I care?" Sebastian asked. "It's a painfully unoriginal way to come up with a nom de plume."

"That's true," I said. "But there could be a significance to it. Let's not forget it's what Monsieur Prier has been reading. As for Lucy, Cécile, I've no idea. I pray she's come to no harm."

"We can only hope her father has spirited her away somewhere safe," Mrs. Hargreaves said.

I retired to my room relatively early, wanting to read every word of Laurent's notebook before we boarded the train the next morning. I was missing Colin keenly, and wished he'd given me some indication of whether his own work was proving productive. I pulled his pillow on top of mine, fluffed them both, and settled into bed.

Laurent's writing was devoid of the self-indulgent angst-filled ramblings I'd come to expect from him. Some pages contained sketches, and he wasn't a bad artist. His occasional forays into poetry impressed me, and the bars of music in the volume proved him a competent composer. A Renaissance man. The book did not, however, contain any references to his sister. The only potential clue lay close to the volume's binding: a page had been cut, probably with a razor, in as straight a line as possible. There could be no doubt the edges would match perfectly with the purported suicide note I'd found in Dr. Girard's pocket.

I scrutinized the pages that preceded and followed the missing one. Before it was music. After, a sketch of a bridge that reminded me of the Pont de la Concorde in Paris. Nothing to suggest a connection to Lucy, the doctor, or Edith. Still, I felt as if we were making progress—that Étretat would prove a turning point in the case. But as I pulled the blankets to my neck in defense against the damp night air, anxiety began to tug at me, anxiety with no discernible source. Sleep seemed impossible, and the room grew colder. The sounds of the house assaulted my ears as I listened for anything of significance.

There was nothing. Nothing, that is, until I heard a thin wail below my window, a sound all too familiar. Terror seized me, killing even my curiosity. I didn't get out of bed, didn't look to see who stood in the garden beneath me. I knew exactly what I'd find, and was unequal to the task of facing it. The hideous sound grew louder and sadder until I could no longer hide from it. But as soon as I'd risen to seek the source of the cries, they stopped as suddenly as they'd started.

The next morning, when I opened my shutters, I looked for a blue ribbon, but saw nothing. Perhaps my mind was tricking me. Perhaps my imagination had got the better of me. I'd begun to feel silly, and was in high spirits by breakfast. Less so, however, after we'd piled into the carriage and were en route to the train station. Sebastian leaned close to me and whispered while Cécile and Mrs. Hargreaves were engrossed in conversation.

"I must speak to you, Kallista," he said. "I heard crying last night. By your window. And when I went outside to investigate, I saw nothing, but the sound didn't stop. Something evil is lurking here, and the sooner we're done with this nasty business the better."

We reached Étretat before lunchtime, and the charming seaside town was teeming with visitors. Half-timbered buildings lined streets leading to the water, edged by a pebble-strewn beach. Most impressive, however, were the towering cliffs on either side of the town's cove. Tall and dramatic, their white rock reminded me of Dover, with vast green fields covering the land above them. Unlike Dover, there were dramatic stone arches here, dominating the view, stretching out over the churning water, their jagged tops slicing up into the sky.

I'd sent a wire to Monsieur Leblanc, alerting him to our arrival, and he was waiting for us, as I suggested, in front of the seaside boardwalk. Gathering our forces, we began our search in the *Marie*—the Town Hall—where we pored over marriage records, but found none pertinent. The clerks to whom we spoke did not recognize our description of the couple, nor of Lucy, and had no recollection of the name Vasseur. From there, we went to the police, who were more than a little ambivalent about giving us any information.

I wished I had Colin's identification papers.

"If your friend is missing, madame," said the officer condescending to speak to us, "you may file a report."

"You know of the murder of Edith Prier, I'm sure," I said. "This is her . . . her lover, or possibly her husband—"

"You were her friend yet you don't know if she was married? I'm afraid I cannot help you."

Sebastian stood back, rigid and quiet. I don't think he enjoyed being in a police station.

"I'm disappointed in you," I said, as we left the building. "I thought you'd be able to brilliantly manipulate the men who uphold the law."

"I don't like to draw attention to myself," he said. "I prefer to go completely unnoticed."

"I'd do the opposite," I said. "I'd befriend them. Maybe join them. Know thy enemy, Sebastian. Keep them close and they'll never suspect you."

"I'm impressed, Kallista."

"It's an excellent idea," Monsieur Leblanc said. "Imagine a master criminal who, while in disguise, convinces the police to hire him to search for himself. You should write fiction, Lady Emily."

"I'm sure I couldn't carry it off," I said.

"I believe you could," Cécile said. "But what is our plan now? Shall we go door to door in search of Vasseur?"

"That would take too long," Mrs. Hargreaves said. "Let's think about what he would have needed when they came—somewhere to stay—we can check the hotels—"

"Have you any idea how many there are in a resort like this?" Sebastian said.

"It's not a large town," I said, refusing to be daunted. "And we can see if there are any houses for rent, or houses that have recently been rented. And we can talk to the physician in town, who might have been aware of the child."

"Shall we divide and conquer?" Monsieur Leblanc asked.

"No," I said. "Whoever murdered Edith and Dr. Girard wouldn't hesitate to put a stop to what we're doing. We'll be safer together."

"Have you any suggestions, Monsieur Leblanc?" Mrs. Hargreaves asked. "You do, after all, live here. To whom would you refer friends in search of lodgings?"

"It's difficult to say. Holidaymakers are one thing—there are plenty of hotels for them," he said. "But if Vasseur was looking for a home, he could have wound up anywhere."

"So you've no way to narrow the field?" she asked, looking at him with a critical eye.

He could not, he apologized, offer any further ideas. So we set off, ready to interview the entire town if necessary. In the course of the afternoon, we spoke to more people than I could count, most of them friendly and helpful, but all, sadly, without information that aided our search. One woman did remember seeing a girl of Lucy's description, walking on the cliff path with her mother, but her recollection was not clear, and she never saw the child again.

After several hours of this, Cécile demanded a break, and we stopped at a café housed in a rambling fifteenth-century mass of timber and plaster, full of elaborate wooden carvings of animals and figures and ordered cold glasses of good Norman cider. Mrs. Hargreaves was particularly taken with the image of a salamander, while Cécile preferred some sort of bird. As Sebastian and Monsieur Leblanc started to add their opinions, frustration filled me.

"Maybe coming here was a mistake," I said.

"Étretat is never a mistake," Mrs. Hargreaves said. "We can walk on the cliff path."

"I need to find Lucy," I said. "We don't have time to play tourist. I'm sorry—I don't mean to sound snappish, but I'm deeply concerned about her."

"Of course you are," she said. "But think on it. A child who'd been brought here would want to play on the beach. Perhaps some of the vendors on the boardwalk will remember her."

"An excellent idea," I said. We set off as soon as we'd paid the bill. The day was a brilliant one, the sunlight scattering over the choppy waves of the sea, the sky crisp, the air warm. The beach was only a few blocks from the café, and Mrs. Hargreaves's suggestion was an excellent one—lines of carts and stands filled the area nearby, their owners hawking ices, crêpes, creamy caramels, and every other sort of sweet imaginable.

Lucy, it seemed, had little interest in ice cream. Or caramels. But when we reached our fifth crêpe stand, operated by a short gentleman in a striped sailor-type shirt and a jaunty beret, hope filled my heart.

"A girl you say?" he asked.

"Yes, about six years old. Her mother's about my size and build, with similar hair? Lucy's blond. Her father used to be in the Foreign Legion and has bright blue eyes."

"The Legion? Yes, I think I remember them. He was in Indochina, wasn't he? New to the area, renting a ramshackle house on the hill." He gestured at the cliff behind us. "Don't remember anything striking about his eyes, though. The little girl had ones like that, bluer than anything I'd ever seen. She liked lemon on her crêpes, with butter and sugar."

"Do you know which house?" I asked.

"Not sure, madame, sorry," he said. "Talk to the owner of the Hôtel La Résidence. He assists nearly everyone in town looking for a long-term stay."

We thanked him and darted to the Hôtel, where we quickly found the proprietor.

"Oh, yes, the Myriels, *bien sûr*," he said. "They were in the Guerlot Cottage. I can give you directions if you wish, but I've not seen them for months. Madame's health was not so good and her husband wanted to take her back to Paris."

His map, though hastily drawn, proved easy to follow, and soon we stood in front of the small house in which Edith and Jules had tried to make a home with their daughter. I knocked on the door, but no one answered. Not wasting any time, Sebastian started to work on the lock, and it clicked open almost at once.

"The place has undoubtedly been rented to someone else," Monsieur Leblanc said. "So let's proceed with caution. We could be discovered at any moment."

He was correct. The rooms were full of evidence that the cottage was occupied by a family visiting the seaside: postcards strewn on a table waited to be addressed, the kitchen was stocked with food, and the bedroom wardrobes were full of clothing.

Sebastian darted through the rooms, his eyes sharp and bright. Mrs. Hargreaves and Cécile, both uneasy at the thought of being discovered, stayed near the front door, watching as the rest of us searched, not knowing what to look for. I started to move more methodically than I had done on first entering the place, carefully looking over every inch of the rooms. Then, in the corridor between the bedrooms, something struck me, and I called for Sebastian.

"Something's wrong here," I said.

He pressed his hands along the plaster, which I'd noticed was a slightly different color from that in the rest of the hallway. "It's newer," he said. "Shall we look inside?"

I hesitated, unsure if destroying the wall was a good idea. Monsieur Leblanc arrived on the scene, quickly followed by Mrs. Hargreaves and Cécile. My mother-in-law, her eyes narrowed and focused analyzed the situation in an instant.

"Take it down," she said.

Sebastian did not require further encouragement. He removed from his jacket a metal blade that he used to cut through the plaster, tracing the line of the lighter color. When he reached the end, he pushed it in farther, jiggled the blade, and started to pull out a bit of the now crumbling wall. It came down in easy pieces, and as he removed them, a smell of decay—not overwhelming, but not insignificant—assaulted our senses.

Behind the wall was a body, badly decayed, certainly beyond the point where anyone could recognize him, but I could not doubt it was Monsieur Vasseur. None of us was prepared for the sight of sinewy bones and missing flesh. I ran into the garden where Cécile held my hair back while I was sick. My mother-in-law, however, stayed with Sebastian and Monsieur Leblanc, helping him to lay out the body on the floor, while I, having pulled myself together, summoned the police. Mrs. Hargreaves didn't fall apart until we reached home, where we found Colin waiting, ready to shoulder the burden for all of us.

22 July 1892

Never again do I want to see what I did today. I'm writing on the train, as it seems the only way to escape the insanity of what we witnessed, of the horror one man will inflict upon another.

I'd not given it much consideration before—and was, no doubt, far too harsh in my judgment of Emily after she'd found poor Edith Prier. The fresh wounds must have been even worse.

Monsieur Vasseur reminded me more of the mummies in the British Museum than of a man recently dead. The police said he'd been stabbed. I've not the slightest idea how they could tell, but certainly didn't want any further detail on the subject.

Emily was sick. I did the only thing possible for me: assist Mr. Capet in taking down the body. Being useful and facing the reality of what we'd found seemed preferable to standing outside and wondering how bad it was. The imagination, I always find, often weaves a more frightening picture than the truth.

Colin will not be pleased with what we've done.

30

Calm and focused as always, Colin paced the room, listening to our story when he returned the next day, deep lines across his forehead. His reaction appeared consistent with the myriad other times I'd seen him faced with grim news and difficult work, but something beneath the surface was different this time. His eyes did not linger on mine quite as long as they used to, and the concern with which he was treating me was identical to that he extended to his mother and Cécile—kind and compassionate, sensitive and understanding—but lacking the emotionally intimate connection we'd always shared. My stomach churned, more upset by this than the sight of poor Monsieur Vasseur's body.

"You've done good work," he said, directing the comment to Sebastian. Monsieur Leblanc had remained behind to liaise with the police. "And accomplished more than I. We need to find the child, that's paramount now, as it's evident she's in a fair amount of danger."

"I asked the police to send you a full report," I said.

"Good girl," he said, still hardly meeting my eyes. "It was a brutal day for all of you, and I think it's best we have an early night. I'll set off tomorrow for Rouen as early as possible."

"I'm coming with you," I said.

"We'll discuss that later," he said. "Capet, your particular expertise may come in handy. Can I count on you?"

Sebastian rolled his head back and forth. "So long as what you'd have me do is adequately amusing I have no objection."

"Are you going to talk to Laurent?" I asked.

"Yes," Colin said. "And Monsieur Prier."

"If Monsieur Myriel visited Edith regularly during the entire duration of her commitment, he can't have been Jules Vasseur," I said. "He was in the Foreign Legion some of that time. What if Myriel had been hired to keep an eye on Edith? Her father may have wanted to ensure she wasn't in contact with Vasseur."

"An interesting theory," Colin said. "I'll pursue it. Now, if you ladies will excuse us, I need to speak to Mr. Capet. Emily, I'll join you upstairs shortly."

Hoping for a private chat, Cécile and I had gone to my bedroom after the gentlemen left us. "It's not like him at all. He's kind, but so impersonal. I know he's furious with me." I kept my voice low, not wanting even a hint of what I was saying to carry into the corridor. Cécile, holding her little dogs in her lap, shrugged.

"He is under great duress, Kallista, and has seen you nearly killed. Can you blame him for stepping up and taking care of you?"

"No, I can't. But it feels like more than that."

"He's in a difficult position. Can you imagine the censure he'll face upon your return to England? The gossip that will follow him? People will say his carelessness nearly cost you your life."

"But he did nothing wrong! I put myself in danger. He wasn't even in Constantinople at the time."

"A husband is supposed to keep a firm hand on his wife," she said, pulling her finger away from Brutus, who was bound and determined to bite it. "It is disgusting, of course, but can you see how him not doing that makes him appear less of a man to certain people?"

"I'd not thought of that," I said. "But it should be the opposite—he's man enough, enlightened enough, to value my strengths, even those deemed unacceptable to society. He encourages me, spurs me on, wants me to thrive. He's not threatened by a lady's quest for independence. If anything, he's ten times the man who has to play lord and master over his wife."

"You're right. But that's not how society views the matter. Like it or not, you can't escape the fact." She gave a fierce glare to the still-unruly Brutus, and petted Caesar.

"Society is infuriating."

"That may be," she said. "Yet it's inescapable." Brutus yipped, and I picked him up from her lap, stroking his silky fur, his tiny body warm and soft. He quieted at once. "I'm afraid he likes you, Kallista. Dreadful animal."

"He's very sweet really," I said.

"Don't say that within his earshot. He'll become unbearable."

"I adore Colin," I said, keeping hold of the little dog. "I've not meant to cause him trouble with society. But he did know when he married me I was not going to be an ordinary wife—and he swore he wouldn't want one."

"And I'm sure that was the truth. He hadn't, however, anticipated the extent to which the situation could be complicated by including you in his work. You should think hard on it—is there a way you can satisfy your needs for intellectual stimulation and adventure without compromising his reputation?"

"His reputation shouldn't be compromised!"

"*Shouldn't* is irrelevant," she said. "We are sadly forced to deal with the reality of the shortcomings of the fools who surround us. Unless, of course, you want to go completely eccentric and reject all of them. I'm afraid that would end up tedious. More trouble than it's probably worth."

"Trouble?" Colin peeked through the door and then entered the room. "What sort?"

"Only the best kind, my dear Monsieur Hargreaves," she said. "Nothing to give you the slightest concern." She took Brutus from me, and he immediately began snapping at Caesar in her other hand. "I'll be off with these wretched creatures and shall see you both at breakfast."

After he closed the door behind her, Colin leaned against it and crossed his arms close across his chest. "What were you thinking going to Étretat?"

"I thought Lucy might be there and couldn't let her—"

"She wasn't there, Emily, and you might have stumbled upon something far worse than another dead body. Where is the regard for your safety?"

"Sebastian was with me—"

"Yes, Sebastian. Just the sort of man I'd choose to protect you."

"Monsieur Leblanc was there as well."

"What a comfort. He might have been able to write you out of any predicament."

"I wasn't in need of protection, Colin."

"You couldn't possibly have known that before you knocked on Vasseur's door."

"We'd been told he was living there with his family!"

"Yes, but then his lover was murdered and his daughter abducted. And you choose to go recklessly to the scene of another crime."

"There was nothing reckless in my behavior." Anger welled up inside me. He was not being reasonable—I'd taken precautions, I'd not gone alone. I'd involved the police.

"What you believe about the situation is irrelevant. I shan't have it repeated. From now on, your involvement in this investigation is to be limited to the discussion of evidence. No more gallivanting about."

I was so stunned I couldn't speak, couldn't cry, couldn't even tremble. How could he speak to me like this?

"Do you understand?" he asked, after I'd sat in silence for some minutes.

"How dare you question me as if you were my father—"

"I am your husband, Emily. And I will be obeyed."

Nothing could have wounded me more deeply than his words.

"I'm sorry to upset you, my dear," he said, coming to me and sitting on the bed. "I love you and I'm doing my best to reconcile the conflicting emotions racing through my brain. I realize I had not expressly told you not to follow any leads you uncovered. But I'd hoped that our previous conversation would have made you give more careful consideration to what you were doing. It's not fair, perhaps, to have expected such a thing. So I shall make an effort to be more clear in the future. For now, though, we must get to the end of this case. I'm going to Rouen, and you are going to the Markhams'. They're expecting Cécile as well, if she'd like to come."

"The Markhams'? Why on earth would you send me there?"

"I need Capet with me and I want you to have some sort of protection."

"I'm sure your mother's house is perfectly safe."

"Capet told me he was followed here the night he arrived to meet you. We've no idea who was pursuing him or why. And no idea, in fact, if he was the person's target. You may be, my dear. Can I risk that?"

I swallowed and shook my head.

"I do understand," I said, my voice weak. "But it feels as if you are crushing my spirit, rejecting the very essence of me."

"I'm not, Emily, I swear to you. I love the woman you are. We will figure our way through this, but we need to do it in circumstances less heated than those in which we're presently embroiled. When we're back in England—and we will go there, together, the instant this business is finished—we'll talk it all through, and I promise you will not be forced into a position where your talents will go unused."

He lifted my chin so that I was looking at him.

"Truly, no woman has ever been loved as I love you," he said. "There's nothing I wouldn't give up for you. Please trust me."

"Of course," I said, tears spilling down my cheeks. He kissed me, gently at first, then with an increasing urgency and heat that was irresistible. I put my arms around him and pulled him closer. His embrace enveloped me.

"Do not lose faith in me," he whispered. "I could not bear it."

I woke alone the next morning. Colin had slipped out, not wanting to disturb my sleep, leaving me with two lines of poetry on a sheet of paper placed on his pillow:

I love thee to the depth and breadth and height / My soul can reach . . .

Despite the difficulties of the night, he'd managed to make me smile. I rang for Meg and directed her to begin packing my belongings as soon as she'd helped me dress. Cécile and Mrs. Hargreaves were already seated at the breakfast table when I arrived downstairs. I sank into a chair, accepted a cup of steaming tea, and put a still-warm croissant on my plate.

"I confess, Emily, to feeling a certain sadness that my household is being so disrupted by all this tragedy," Mrs. Hargreaves said. "It's a dreadful thing not to feel one's own home offers adequate protection for guests."

"It's no fault of yours," I said. "There's nothing more to be done. What of you, Cécile? Will you join me in exile?"

"Much as I hate to abandon you, Anne," Cécile said. "I don't want to leave Emily with only Madeline for company."

My mother-in-law nodded. "She's a dear girl, but not, perhaps, the best of companions given all that you've recently suffered." I did like Madeline, but Sebastian's suggestion that she'd pushed the gardener's daughter to her death still haunted me, and I wondered if it could be true. I hated the thought of returning to the place where I'd seen the eerie specter in the dovecote, but preferred that to being shipped home by myself in what might be viewed by society as disgrace. "And at any rate," Mrs. Hargreaves continued. "You shan't be abandoning me. I'm to come with you as well. Colin doesn't want any of us unprotected in this house."

It was nearly four o'clock before we set off for our friends' estate, where we were greeted with great exuberance from George and Madeline. I was happy to find Madeline in a lucid state of mind, free from any hint of madness, and wished there were some way to keep her from slipping again into its bonds.

"It's a bloody disaster what's going on," George said, crossing to us and leaving his wife to direct the servants' handling of our luggage. "But we're so pleased to have you all here. It will be an unending party. I've set up Japanese lanterns in the garden and thought we could have midnight wanderings through the maze if it's not too chilly."

"An excellent plan," I said. I was torn. On the one hand, I hated being cut out of the remainder of Colin's investigation. On the other, so long as I was cut out, I felt tempted to throw myself with wild abandon into vacuous pleasures. If I couldn't be useful, I might as well take full advantage of the entertainments presented to me.

"I think we should make this as extravagant as Carnival in Venice," Cécile said. "The sooner we can push the hideous events of the past weeks from our minds the better. How much champagne do you have on hand, sir? And where is your butler? I would have him send a telegram to Moët for me."

Before long we were all settled in pleasantly decorated bedrooms in the renovated section of the château. Cécile's and mine were adjoining, which would make for excellent late-night consultation. Mrs. Hargreaves's stood across the corridor, two doors down from that occupied by George and Madeline. Despite the size of the house, we were nestled in a cozy and friendly group.

Madeline had planned an exquisite menu for dinner, and when we were all stuffed with *côtes de veau vallée d'Auge*—the most tender veal cutlets I'd ever tasted, cooked in sweet Norman butter and doused with a creamy cider sauce—we retired to the sitting room where there was still a space on the wall for the missing Monet.

"Can't you persuade Sebastian to bring it back?" George asked. "I can't bear the room without it."

"And I'm affronted that he no longer appreciates our taste," Madeline said. She was happy and well-balanced, no signs of her illness tainting any facet of her personality. Her mother, however, had not joined us. She, George had told me, was in the midst of a bad spell, and was keeping to her room, where a nurse tried to calm her by reading aloud.

"I promise I shall ask him about it when next I see him," I said. "He's off with Colin now."

"Saving the world," George said. "And thank heavens someone will do it. I'm not capable, but I am tired of feeling as if our little slice of paradise is tainted by these murders."

"It's deeply unsettling," Mrs. Hargreaves said.

"But we're not going to think about it tonight!" Madeline said. "Let's play cards until it's dark enough to light the lanterns. I've had enough of worry and misery, and now want only to enjoy the company of good friends. Do you like bezique?"

"Only two can play that," George said. "You ladies divide up and I'll float between tables giving bad advice to everyone."

I was not familiar with the game, but Cécile was a huge proponent, and soon she'd taught me the rules. We took one table and Mrs. Hargreaves and Madeline the other, laughter erupting with great frequency as George bounced between us, stealing cards and generally making mischief. Some time after we'd switched partners and I was paired with Madeline, a footman came into the room with a telegram.

George glanced at the envelope and handed it to me. I tore it open. "It's from Colin," I said. "He's well. They're close, he says, to having the final bit of evidence they need. He doesn't think it will take more than three days and he'll be back with us. And he says we're safe where we are, that there's no need for any worry."

"This could not be better news," George said and turned to the waiting footman. "Take Lady Emily's reply, my good man, and then bring us a bottle of champagne."

"You don't think to celebrate now is premature, my dear?" Madeline asked, concern tugging at her pretty face.

"Only if you object to celebrating again once the madman has been apprehended and jailed," George said.

"I do not understand, monsieur," Cécile said. "Objecting to celebration? Is such a thing possible?"

We all toasted and drank to Colin's efficient success, giddy with relief that the end was all but in sight. I was proud of my husband, delighted with the speed of his success, and eager to return to London. George was about to open a third bottle of champagne when Madeline stopped him.

"Look," she said, pointing out the window. "They've lit the lanterns. Let's go outside."

Glasses still in our hands, we stepped into the garden, brilliantly bathed in dancing light, and made our way to the maze. George raised his hands to silence our chattering when we reached the entrance.

"Madeline and I have a tradition of racing each other through the maze," he said. "Which does, of course, mean we're starting on unequal footing here, but there it is. I say we all set off at once. And I warn you, I may lead you astray should you try to follow me. First one to the center and back wins. There are five scrolls in the center—pick one up and bring it back with you. I've written poems on each and when we're done we'll read them aloud."

It was an excellent idea for an entertainment. We quickly split up after entering the labyrinth hedge, none of us at first wanting the others too close by. Laughter drifted through the night air, Madeline's louder than the rest. I'd never been particularly good at mazes—I'd forget which direction I'd taken when and found the only way I could make my way through was by not paying too close attention to the fact that I would have to encounter every dead end on my way to the solution.

After more than a quarter of an hour I still hadn't found the center. As I reached yet another stopping point, a feeling of panic filled my chest, and it seemed as if the dark hedgerows were closing in on me. I slowed my breathing and turned around, continuing on. When I again dead-ended, I retreated back to the last junction I'd been at and tried to remember which way I'd gone before. Making the best guess I could, I marched on, finding myself in the same dark spot I'd been in only moments before. Back at the junction, I turned what I thought was the other way, but wound up yet again in the place I'd started.

Unless it was an identical dead end. I felt trapped, more scared than frustrated, my breath coming faster and my heart rate increasing. Surely I couldn't have been going back and forth to the same place over and over again all this time? I dropped my handkerchief to the ground and returned to the junction, where I closed my eyes, concentrated, and went in the direction opposite from whence I'd come.

The white linen of my handkerchief struck my eyes like a blow. This time, I marched back to the junction and kept going, but the path only returned me to where I'd been. I'd somehow become trapped in a portion of the maze that went nowhere. I stopped, the feeling of claustrophobia pressing in harder now, and fear gripped me. I couldn't get out. Couldn't find my way. Couldn't even backtrack. I was about to shout for help when I heard Cécile and Mrs. Hargreaves chatting in the distance. Reassured, I reminded myself this could not be so difficult, and set off for another try.

Only to find, once again, my handkerchief.

I could no longer hear my friends, but far away in the distance rose the sound of a thin wail, growing louder and louder as it came closer to where I stood. Shaking, I reached into the bushes, wanting to push my way through them and force my way out, but they were too thick. Running now, I retraced my steps, determined to escape.

This time, I didn't find my handkerchief. Instead, crumpled on the ground in front of me, I saw a blue satin ribbon. The keening sound had followed me, weak and sad, and I felt as if it was nearly upon me, its eerie moan a plea for help or release.

Against all my principles and everything I believed in, I did something I abhorred with a passion.

I fainted.

31

I woke up to the sensation of someone tenderly rubbing my forehead. I opened my eyes, expecting to see Colin, surprised to find George instead. I parted my lips to speak but he covered my mouth, gently, with his hand.

"Don't exhaust yourself, Emily. You need your rest now."

"Rest? I only fainted," I said, groggy and confused. "I'm fine." I tried to sit up and realized that I'd been bound to the bed on which I lay. Leather straps at my ankles and wrists secured me, and instinctively I pulled against them. "George! What is this?"

"Just one more, my friend," he said, and tightened something around my forehead. What a mistake to have thought I'd been awakened by sweet ministrations.

"Where are we?"

"In the tower I've convinced Madeline is unsafe. It's the only way I could ensure privacy for my work."

"Work? What work?"

"There's no need to worry about that now, dear." He stroked my cheek. I flinched.

"Where are the others?"

"At the house, resting happily after drinking the laudanum-laced brandy I poured for them after we came inside. There's no danger any of them will wake up until morning."

"What do they think became of me?"

"You, my friend, succumbed to a fit of the vapors after getting lost in the maze. I found you and carried you to your room, where everyone believes you are sleeping peacefully. Cécile herself tucked you into bed. I didn't move you here until they were all asleep."

"Our rooms are adjoining. She'll check on me."

"She won't wake up."

"Why would you do such a thing?" I asked, my heart racing.

"I need your help, Emily. Madeline needs it. Edith was taken away from me too soon—I couldn't finish the work. But you're the right size, and I was close, so very close to solving the problem. You must understand, though, that I can't test it on her. The risks are too great."

"I don't know what you're talking about." I struggled to release my hands.

"Don't," he said, gripping my wrists. "You'll only hurt yourself. Edith had terrible sores from trying to escape. I didn't want to hurt her, you know. I was trying to help her, too."

I looked around, desperate to find a way to escape. The architecture matched the oldest parts of the château, but there were no windows that I could see in the room, only unbroken stone walls. There was nothing else to do. I screamed for help.

"You really shouldn't do that," he said, forcing a dirty rag into my mouth. "I don't want to make you uncomfortable, but I can't have anyone finding you here. Not right now."

I strained against the leather straps.

"This may hurt some, but it won't kill you, and you're doing so much good, so much for my Madeline."

On a table next to me I saw a strange object: a metal cylinder with a crank and a jar full of clear liquid attached to it. A long wire, of which George held the terminus, extended from the end of the tube.

"It is through this the electricity flows," he said, explaining as if I were his pupil. "A fascinating machine, elegant in design, simple to operate. We attach the wire here—" He put it on my temple, something sticky catching on my skin to hold it in place. I was struggling to pay attention to everything he said, to remain focused, as it occurred to me my only hope for survival was to understand this contrivance. "And then I turn it on. First, though, I'll adjust the current." He spun a knob on the base of the platform. I heard a whirring sound, a sudden pop, and my muscles convulsed as pain shot through me. Tears poured from my eyes. George wiped them with his handkerchief and removed the rag from my mouth, covering it once again with his hand.

"You mustn't scream again, do you understand?" he asked. "Or I shall have to put a real gag on you."

"What are you doing?"

"I'm making it so you can help your friend," he said. "That's all you need know."

"No, George, tell me what this is. I'm scared." Whatever he was up to, there seemed to be some small measure of compassion still present in him, and at the moment, appealing to it seemed all I could do.

"This is a treatment—medical electricity—that can be used for nervous disorders, but it's not been much studied, and as you see, it's painful. I think it may help Madeline, but I must be sure before I try it on her."

"I don't have a mental disorder, George. You can't learn anything from doing this to me."

"You're just her size," he said. "I didn't notice it until you wore her clothes after you both got soaked in the rain. I have to figure out how much current is required—and how much is too much—so I can try to stop the progression of the hideous disease that's destroying my dear girl."

"But you won't know the effect on her brain," I said, hoping to keep him talking until I could make an escape from the leather straps. They weren't terribly tight, but tight enough. I might be able to wriggle my way out of them if given enough time. I rolled my ankles, not wanting to draw his attention to my hands. "What you're doing to me is futile."

"No, no, you're wrong," he said. "Edith started to respond to the treatment and as the results got better and better I escalated too quickly, although I wasn't giving her even half what this machine can generate. When the volts went too high, she fell into a coma. It was a horrible sight. She foamed at the mouth and twitched violently. She recovered in less than half an hour, but I could see that she was no longer herself. She was more crazed, and she broke free and lashed out at me. Knocked me against the wall and I lost consciousness for a brief moment. When I woke, she was gone."

"You killed her."

"I had no choice, Emily. If she'd made it to the village, she would have told them, she would have brought the police, and all my work would have been for naught. Would you have me let my wife slip into the irrevocable bonds of madness?"

"You can't save her by killing others," I said.

"Edith shouldn't have died. I admit, it's my fault for escalating the experiment at the wrong pace. But she left me no option once she'd fled. I found her easily enough—she was crying, couldn't stop from the sound of it. All I had to do was follow the sound."

"But the manner in which you killed her. It was so brutal, George . . . how could you?" The horror of being trapped so near a person capable of such crimes was beyond any words. I was sweating, my stomach churned, my muscles clenched. My very bones ached with pain as my entire body revolted at his proximity.

"I did it quickly. The knife was sharp. The rest . . ." He covered his eyes. "It was terrible for me, too, you know. But I thought if I made it look like something it wasn't—if I mimicked a crime more famous . . . perhaps I would avoid all scrutiny."

"You have to let me go, George."

"Oh, Emily, I should like nothing better. But you know I can't do that, especially now. I've always liked you, and Madeline adores you, so I can promise to be as kind as the situation allows. I have to figure out how much current you can take before the seizure, and that I will do slowly. But in the end . . ." He choked on the words. "I will do it when you're unconscious. You will feel neither pain nor fear. And you can die knowing you're giving back to me the woman I adore more than anything."

I couldn't speak, could hardly think. No terror could be compared to this, no dread, no hideous imagining. I let my eyes meet his, wanting to see if madness was visible on his face. His pupils were dilated, his skin flushed, but he looked otherwise like a perfectly ordinary man. To have found otherwise might have provided a slim parcel of comfort.

"Where's Lucy?" I asked, desperate to distract him from the course of action on which he was bent.

"Don't worry about the child," he said. "She will come to no harm. I'm taking care of her and soon will introduce her to Madeline, who I know will be an excellent mother to her."

"Why did you take her? Would it not have been better to leave her where she was safe and well cared for?"

"She may show signs of the illness, too. I might need her."

"You can't do this, George. The poor child! What must she think? Surely she knows something is dreadfully wrong."

"No, I've taken exquisite care of her, even if I have had to hide her away. Sometimes she gets upset in the night and cries for her mother— which is to be expected, I suppose. I take her for long walks in the countryside until she falls back asleep. She's come to quite depend on me. She knows that her mother's illness was fatal, and all orphans, you know, long for a real home. I've told her she's to have one."

I shuddered, realizing the eerie keening I'd heard had been the child—a real one—weeping over the loss of her mother. The reality of this all-too-human pain, hopeless and devastating, felt far more frightening than any ghostly apparition could have.

"And what will you tell everyone else?" I asked. "You can't just magically have a child appear in your household."

"Lucy believes that her father, Vasseur, had an accident on his way home from the Foreign Legion, and asked me, as he lay dying, to look after her. She thinks her mother had to spend time away from her because she was ill, and that Madame Sapin was taking care of her only until I came for her."

"What really happened to Monsieur Vasseur?"

"I served in the Foreign Legion with him—did a stint after serving in the British Army as a physician. We traded stories of the girls we loved. When he confessed to me his amour had been sent away in hopes of having her progressive madness cured—the symptoms of which I recognized all to well as those beginning to plague my own dear wife—I told him of Madeline's troubles. In short order, he realized she was Edith's distant cousin, a revelation that made me all the more interested in her treatment. If something worked for her, it would almost certainly help Madeline. I made note of the location of the asylum to which she'd been sent by her family, and when I returned to France, I visited her, telling her Vasseur had sent me."

"Did she believe you?"

"Why wouldn't she?" he asked. "We bonded almost at once, both of us knowing the pain of having the one you love taken away from you. She trusted me."

"And Vasseur? Did he trust you?"

"We lost all contact after I left the Legion. He did, however, keep in touch with Edith. I read all of his letters while she slept—she hid them in her headboard. Eventually, I decided I could use him to lure her away from the asylum."

"Why did you want to remove her from Dr. Girard's care?"

"Girard was making no progress with her, so I talked to him, asked him to consider more radical treatments. But it was to no avail. I'd studied enough to have learned of the potential benefits of medical electricity, and the fact that Madeline and Edith were nearly the same age and build . . ."

"You befriended Edith so that you might use her to test treatments for Madeline?"

"Can you fault me for it? Would you not do the same for your own husband?" he asked.

"How did you convince her to leave?"

"I told her Vasseur and I had arranged to bring her to live with him in Étretat. I thought it would be dead easy, but she refused to go unless Lucy was with her. She'd told me about the girl early on in our friendship. I would have preferred not to be saddled with her, but Edith grew quite hysterical on the subject, and I knew that Lucy might prove useful herself, so I found her and brought her to Edith's window on the night we fled. She did not hesitate for an instant once she saw her child."

"Did Vasseur know what you were doing?" I asked.

"Not at first," he said. "But Edith managed to send him a letter begging him to meet her in Étretat. He realized her parents didn't know where she was going, and I suppose felt it would be safe, at last, for him to try to be with her. A terrible misjudgment on his part."

"You killed him."

"I tried not to. I explained to him that I wanted to help Edith—to find a treatment that would cure her. But he wouldn't agree to let me try even one course of electricity on her. He left me no choice, Emily."

"Please tell me where Lucy is, George."

"She's here and safe. I tried to place her at a school in Rouen not long ago, but she cried so much on the way we never even made it to speak to the headmistress. Once things have calmed down here, I shall try again. Madeline and I will visit her, but Lucy will not come here until enough time has passed for this scandal to be forgot."

"Murder goes beyond scandal."

"No one will ever connect me with murder."

The irrationality of this statement pushed indignation ahead of fear in me. "My husband will notice I'm missing, George."

"Not quite, Emily. He'll notice you're dead. When you're unconscious, I will drop you off this tower, and he will believe you could no longer bear the pain of the loss of your child."

"He'll never believe that."

"Of course he will. You left a note." He waved a page taken from the diary I'd brought with me to the house and left in my bedroom—I could not read the words, but could guess it was something I'd written in the dark haze of mourning that paralyzed me after my days in Constantinople.

"It won't work. He'll recognize it as being from my journal."

"He'll be consumed with grief and more malleable than you can imagine."

"That's a risky assumption," I said.

"I'm confident," he said. "He's got nothing but a clear mind now and is convinced Laurent Prier killed Edith. If he does decide you were murdered, Laurent will be found guilty of that as well."

I needed time. Time to get away, time to find Lucy, time to get Cécile and Mrs. Hargreaves away from this house. "We've had a raucous, celebratory evening," I said. "No one would believe I'd kill myself after such a night."

"You collapsed in the maze," he said. "You were frightened and overwrought and slipping into madness. Everyone knows you've been seeing ghosts, that your grasp on reality has become more and more elusive over these last weeks."

My situation was beyond dire. "When are you going to do this?" I asked, not bothering to fight back my tears. "Can I at least have time in private to make peace with myself?"

"I'm not a monster, Emily," he said. "Of course you can. I'm going to check on the others and make sure they're sleeping soundly—though I can't imagine laudanum would let me down. I shall return in less than a quarter of an hour and we shall begin. I know it's hard to accept such a fate, but I beg you to focus on the good that will come from it."

"Do you have a Bible?" I asked. "It would give me comfort to read."

"I'm afraid I can't unfasten your hands so that you might hold a book. I understand all too well how strong the instinct to survive is— you forget I saw how Edith fought. Pray, cry, do what you must. I will return shortly, and promise to be as kind and gentle as possible."

32

I heard the lock snap into place as he turned the key after closing the door behind him. Knowing I had extremely limited time, I forced all fear, all thoughts of what might lie ahead of me from my head and focused on the only task that mattered: freeing my hands. I twisted and wriggled against the leather straps, but to no avail. They weren't tight enough to cut off my circulation, but they were too tight to allow for escape. Tears stung in my eyes, but I ignored them, working harder on the leather.

Stretching it seemed the only hope, so I mustered all my strength and pulled as hard as I could, over and over until I could feel the slightest hint of a gap forming between the straps and my wrists. It wasn't enough, though. Now, instead of trying to free both hands, I expended my energy all on the right, using the whole of my body to tug against the rails on the side of the bed to which I was attached. The leather was bending to my will, but not quickly enough.

And then I heard it. The wailing. The sad sobs, the small voice. Was Lucy up here with me? I was not going to see her lost to the clutches of a maniac like George Markham. I would find her, I would save her, I would return her to Madame Sapin, the only mother she'd known. I felt as if something primal in me had kicked in, enabling me unlimited strength to defend this child.

Only my strength fell somewhat short of unlimited. Nonetheless, with repeated, brutal tugs, I finally managed to slip my right wrist, bloodied and battered, through the binding strap. With a shaking hand, I unbuckled the cuffs on my other hand, ankles, and forehead. Lucy's cries were fading again, and I rushed in the direction of them, pausing when I realized that if I did not first stop George, there would be no escape for either of us.

I assessed the space around me. There was little furniture, and no hope I could block him out of the room for long. The door opened inward, so I dragged the bed in front of it, figuring its presence might buy me at least a few extra seconds. Then I turned my attention to George's strange machine.

I'd heard of the use of electricity in medicine, but never paid much attention to the topic. My mother had once mentioned that a long-ago Duchess of Devonshire had been a proponent of it. That, unfortunately, was my entire knowledge of the subject. The device looked simple enough—turning the crank had to provide the power, so I began working on it at once, figuring I would need as much stored up as possible— and I knew George hadn't been turning it when he shocked me. I then moved the contraption to the bed. Electricity needed metal, so I wrapped the wire George had used to shock me around the tarnished doorknob.

And then I had to figure out how to turn up the current. I played with the dial on the flat surface of the machine's base, carefully touching the wire. Nothing happened. Frantic, I studied the object before me again, finally seeing a small switch. I threw it, touched the wire, and recoiled at the shock. I then turned the dial farther to the right and touched the wire again. A harder shock.

I spun the dial as far to the right as it would go, made sure the switch was still on, and was careful to touch neither the wire, nor the doorknob. I stepped away from the bed and steeled myself for George's return, hoping the shock he got would knock him out, even if only momentarily. He'd said he'd not gone even halfway up with Edith, so surely full strength would have a diabolical effect on him.

The thin wail of Lucy's cry filled the room again. Startled and on edge, I spun around, taking better stock of my surroundings. Where could she be? There were no windows in the room, so the sound could not have been coming from outside—it wouldn't have been able to penetrate the thick stone walls—and there was no visible door except the one through which George had exited. There had to be another one— hidden—that I hoped would lead to the child.

A cold chill shot through me. Scared out of my wits, I shuffled back to the door, my legs so feeble I could hardly support myself. I felt a presence—someone had to be here, but it didn't seem possible. The crying ceased and was replaced by the sound of heavy footsteps just outside.

My heart pounded. I pressed my lips together and closed my eyes, knowing I had only one chance at survival. I could hear him on the other side of the door. He'd stopped walking but hadn't yet touched the door.

I heard him sigh, fumble with a key. I held my breath waiting for it to slip into the lock, then turn. The instant the lock clicked, I turned on the machine.

And then, a buzz, a hum, and a shriek—a hideous shriek of pain— followed by a thump. More scared than ever, and trembling uncontrollably, I closed the switch on the machine, hesitating to touch the wire even though I knew it should be off. Then, afraid he might return to his senses quickly, I took a deep breath, steadied myself, and reached for the wire.

Nothing happened.

I ripped it from the knob, pushed the bed away from the door, and opened it. George lay before me on the floor, twitching, foam bubbling from between his lips. My stomach turned and I felt sick, but there was no time for contemplation, guilt, or compassion. I raced down the stone spiral stairs to the bottom of the tower, then stopped.

Lucy had to be somewhere near, and I couldn't leave her here in case George should wake up before I could return with help. I forced myself back up the steps, took the key from the door, and locked myself into the room from which I'd only just escaped. Unable to stop shaking, I made my way around the perimeter, steadying myself against the stone wall, feeling for any imperfection that might unlatch the hidden door I was convinced had to exist. Weren't castles full of passages through which escape would be possible should the inhabitants have fallen under siege?

The silence around me was oppressive, broken only by the sound of my heart thumping and the blood beating its way through my ears. I circled the room for a fifth time, with each rotation scrutinizing another swathe of the wall. Finally I found a place where the smoothness of the stone gave way to a rough patch, a spot where the mortar had crumbled. I thrust my fingers into it, and felt a cold, hard switch. It took all the strength left in my already injured hands to pull it, and as I did, a rectangular piece of the floor swung down like a trapdoor to reveal a narrow staircase.

I grabbed a lamp from the table on which George had placed his machine. Pausing, I considered checking to make sure he was still unconscious, but it didn't seem wise to waste any precious time. I placed a foot carefully on the first step and made my way to the bottom, where I found a tight passageway, too short for me to stand up straight. Another switch was here, on the wall, a twin to the one I'd found in the tower. Holding my breath, I flipped it, knowing it would close the way from which I'd come. Another layer of protection should George wake up.

Frightening, though, if it wouldn't reopen should I need it to. I could not, however, imagine the point in building a secret passage that led to nowhere.

I continued on as quickly as I could, my feet slipping on the mossy pavement, until I heard Lucy's cries, and the sound of small footsteps. In an instant, the child was in front of me, tears streaming down her pale, dirt-streaked face, a blue satin ribbon crumpled in her little hand. I scooped her into my arms and held her close, then shot the rest of the way down the tunnel to where it hit another set of steps.

At the top of which was a door that led to the dovecote.

Above it, a key hung on a high hook. I jumped up and grabbed it, unlocked the door, burst through it, and didn't stop running until I'd reached Mrs. Hargreaves's house.

27 July 1892

At last it's all over, thank heavens. If I never am subjected to such drama again, it will be too soon. It's impossible to reconcile the neighbor and friend I'd known for years with the brutal killer for which he's now been exposed.

Emily's strength shows through better now than ever before. The servants say she appeared here with the child, breathless and exhausted, surely terrified out of her mind, but she was calm, direct, and put them all at ease as she told them what to do.

The police came in short order and it's all settled now. No more murderous neighbors to contend with, no more ghost stories or strange cries in the night.

I have, without question, been in the country too long.

Gladstone's won. It's time I return to London.

33

"I think perhaps I ought to be slightly affronted you didn't come res-
cue us before sending for help," Cécile said as we all sat at a rough-
hewn table under the shade of a magnificent tree in the garden at Mrs.
Hargreaves's house the next afternoon. None of us had touched the
spread of cakes on pretty silver platters, but the scalding hot tea
proved a panacea for all, and we consumed pot after pot at an alarming rate.

"I was afraid if he woke up he'd catch me again before I could sound
an alarm," I said. In fact, he hadn't regained consciousness until after
Inspector Gaudet and his men arrived, having been summoned by Mrs.
Hargreaves's servants the instant I'd told them what happened. His
physical condition was not great—I'd injured him severely—but his
mind was intact, and the police physician who examined him predicted
what he called a *full-enough recovery.*

"It's terrifying to think—" my mother-in-law started, but stopped
at a fierce glare from Colin. We all fell into a tense silence. Madeline
was still with us, shaken and devastated, incoherent. I wished Dr.
Girard could look after her. We'd arranged for his partner to come for
both her and her mother, and I had no doubt they'd be well taken care

of in the asylum, although seeing them committed felt something like a failure. George, for all his evilness, had started with a noble motive—trying to cure his wife's illness so that she would never be relegated to hospital. His ill-formed plan had in the end served to do nothing but guarantee she would spend the rest of her life in one. And he would certainly be executed.

"Adèle!"

The sound of Madeline's voice startled me. Cécile dropped her fan and Mrs. Hargreaves poured tea onto the table instead of into her son's cup. Madeline had been only short of catatonic all day, but now her face was bright, her eyes eager.

"Adèle!" she said again. "What do you think? Should we go to Paris? It's been too long since we've been to a real ball, and I'm desperate to see Mr. Worth about new dresses."

"Oh, Madeline," I said, sitting next to her and taking her hand. "Of course we'll go to Paris."

"I've met the most handsome gentleman and I'm certain he's going to propose to me. He's English—but I suppose I can learn to tolerate that. He's called George, and I absolutely adore him."

Mrs. Hargreaves rose from her seat and bent over Madeline's shoulder. "Do come inside with me dearest," she said. "I want to hear all about George and to ask your advice on my dinner menu. You will help me, won't you?" She led her towards the house. I felt sick, unable to determine which was worse—that she believed she'd only just met George and was hoping to marry him or the fact that she'd never see him again. Would she even know?

"That's a relief," Sebastian said as soon as they were gone. I glared at him. "Don't even think about scolding me, Kallista. It's beyond awkward having her around here now in that state of mind. There's nothing more any of us can do for her. No point in suffering with her."

"You are so heartless," Monsieur Leblanc said, tugging at his moustache. "It's inspiring."

"Why, thank you," Sebastian said, puffing himself up. "It is a delight to be appreciated."

"You've put me on a new track," Monsieur Leblanc said. "I want to abandon journalism altogether—can't be any more difficult than abandoning the law, wouldn't you say?—and turn instead to fiction. I'm going to chronicle the adventures of a gentleman thief."

"And base him, *naturellement*, on *moi*," Sebastian said.

"Does your ego know no bounds?" I asked.

"I certainly hope not," Cécile said. "That would be a grand disappointment."

"I shall call him Arsène Lupin," Monsieur Leblanc said. "And I will, perhaps, let it be known—or at least rumored—that he's not altogether an invention."

"I shall come to you at Étretat twice a year and update you on my exploits," Sebastian said. "And I may even adopt the name Vasseur as a nom de plume, seeing as how it goes with eyes of a certain shade of blue. Might be useful if people thought I'd been in the Foreign Legion."

"Capet!" Colin's eyes gave a stern warning, then he looked away, his attention diverted by a bright flutter at the garden gate.

"We set off the moment we got your telegram," Madame Prier said, Toinette trailing behind her in a yellow dress. "You have saved us all from the distress of never having justice done for our dearest girl!" She pulled me out of my chair and embraced me, not balking at my expression of disbelief. Toinette, however, was not yet so practiced in the art of selective notice.

"She doesn't believe you for an instant, *Maman*," she said, and took the seat closest to Colin, who immediately rose and crossed to me, standing behind my chair and putting a hand on my shoulder.

"You should treat your mother with more respect, Toinette," he said. "Impertinence is not an attractive trait in a young lady. Not, that is, when it is full of malice."

Toinette opened her mouth and closed it again without speaking. Her mother lowered herself onto a chair and accepted a cup of tea from Cécile.

"My husband apologizes for not coming with us," Madame Prier said. "He is much engaged in business at the moment. But his relief at what you have done is palpable."

Toinette snorted.

We all ignored her.

"Have you learned anything else from that horrible man?" Madame Prier asked. "I can't believe I received him at my house. It makes me want to move. I can hardly bear to go into the sitting room anymore."

"He admitted to having stolen the page from Laurent's notebook after he found it in Edith's room at the asylum during one of his visits to her," Colin said. "He was already planning to kidnap your daughter, and considered Laurent's words a sort of insurance should anything go wrong. Planted correctly, he thought it would implicate Laurent in his sister's disappearance."

"Despicable beast," she said. "And he was calling himself Myriel?"

"Yes," I said. "And disguised himself with a moustache and spectacles. Told her he'd been paying for Lucy's care."

"I always knew one couldn't trust any member of the Foreign Legion. Mercenaries, all of them," Madame Prier said.

"Did it ever occur to you, *Maman*, that had you actually visited Edith instead of pretending to she might not have accepted Myriel's false friendship?" Toinette asked. "And hence you might have averted this entire situation?"

"There's no point thinking that way," I said. "George was fixed on his purpose. He would have got to Edith one way or another. No one could have prevented it." I didn't entirely believe my words, but saying them seemed the right thing to do.

Madame Prier leaned forward. "May we see Lucy now?"

My heart clenched. I hated the thought of the little girl in the hands of the Priers, even if they were her closest relatives. "She's resting now," I said. "But you'll meet her soon."

Toinette rolled her eyes. "And that will be a delight, I'm sure."

Cécile cleared her throat, no more eager to see Lucy handed over to her grandmother than I. "I haven't figured out all the details of this horrendous crime. Why did George take Edith away from Étretat?"

"He knew all along it wouldn't be practical to stay there indefinitely, but it made for an excellent starting point—a perfect place to hide where there was no connection to him. He'd used Vasseur's name to take the house, so if Edith ever were traced there, everyone would believe she'd gone with her lover."

"As soon as her illness grew worse, he sedated her," Colin said. "He told Lucy her mother was ill, and that he was taking her to hospital. Instead, they went to the château, where he'd set up a makeshift laboratory—"

"With which Emily is all too familiar," Cécile said.

"Quite," Colin continued. "He stashed Lucy away in a hidden room in the dovecote—one connected by secret passageway to his laboratory—and started to work on her mother. He was convinced it would lead him to a way to help his wife—something that until that point had seemed to him utterly hopeless."

Already, Gaudet had found two physicians with whom George had consulted, asking them to do more aggressive electrical treatment on Madeline than either of them thought responsible. There hadn't been enough research, they said, so he pursued it on his own, even building his own machine. And in the months that followed, he tortured Edith with his experimental treatment, until the fatal day when he turned the current too high.

"Why did he kill Dr. Girard?" Monsieur Leblanc asked, looking up from the notebook into which he had furiously been scribbling notes.

"First, he was afraid Girard might recognize him as Myriel. Second, because he got nervous, and thought—erroneously—that another death so far removed from his life with Madeline would protect him from being considered a possible suspect," Colin said. "He still had the page from the diary, and knew that we were suspicious of Laurent."

"A dreadful business, all of it," Cécile said. "Thank goodness it's over."

"All that concerns Markham," Colin said, turning to Sebastian. "There is one further thing to consider: the matter of the stolen Monet. I know you, Capet, swear you had nothing to do with it."

"I promised the artist himself I would never touch another of his paintings!" Sebastian said.

"Let me see . . ." I closed my eyes as if deep in thought. "You might not have actually *touched* the painting, correct? You could have used gloves, had an accomplice lift it for you. Or perhaps you get around your promise by claiming that you have not, in fact, touched *another* painting. You've merely re-stolen what you'd already taken once."

"You wound me, Kallista," Sebastian said, rising from the table and leaning against a nearby tree. "How could you think so ill of me?"

"All this crime!" Madame Prier said, fanning herself. "It's beyond anything a decent person could tolerate."

"Let's hope we've reached the end of it," I said. "As for the painting, I shall never change my mind about what happened to it."

"I suppose it couldn't have been Monet who took it," Cécile said. "Although I half wish is was. It would make for a good story, an artist stealing his own work, don't you think? Perhaps you should write it, Monsieur Leblanc."

"An interesting suggestion," Monsieur Leblanc said. "But somehow I don't think Monet has much of the criminal element in him."

"Fictionalize it, dear man!" Cécile cried. "Replace him with Manet if you must."

All save Toinette laughed. She, instead, practiced what I could only imagine was an expression she thought made her appear particularly fetching: lips in a half-open pout, eyes wide. She looked as if she was about to speak and, I assumed, change the subject.

I wasn't about to let her. Not when I had the opportunity to coax a confession from Sebastian, whom, there could be no doubt, was one hundred percent culpable for the missing Monet.

"Mr. Capet—" I began but stopped as I turned to the tree against which he had only just been leaning. Now he was nowhere in sight. I met Colin's eyes and he leapt up at once, with me following as close behind as my impractical shoes (silk, lovely, heel far too high for running) would allow. He sprinted away from the others towards a forested section of the garden.

I did not make it far into the woods before I felt a rough hand on my arm as my husband disappeared from sight in the distance ahead of me.

"I owe you an apology." Laurent's face was dark, only half-visible in the shadows of the towering trees. "You did find justice for Edith, and for that I am grateful."

A tingling warmth rushed through me. I'd not thought it possible to impress Laurent in any way under any circumstances. "You're welcome," I said. "I only wish she hadn't found herself in need of justice."

He scowled. "Don't bother to congratulate yourself too much. If you think you've made things better, you haven't. All you've done is delivered another child into the hands of my parents. Do you think Edith would have wanted that for her daughter?"

"I—"

"Though I'm not sure in the end I care. I'll help Lucy as I see fit, but the truth is, I want to see the monster who killed my sister punished even if it does mean her child will wind up in a situation as bad as the one from which Edith escaped." He stepped closer to me and I could feel his breath hot on my face. "It's what makes us different, you and I, Lady Emily. You care for the living, and I for the dead."

Footsteps approached, and Laurent started. He grabbed my hand, kissed it, and took his leave moments before Colin arrived on the scene.

"Interesting conversation?" he asked.

"Yes," I said. "Do you think Laurent capable of anything else?"

"He elevates brooding to the level of art."

"Did you find Sebastian?" I asked. My husband shook his head.

"No one—and I know that you, Emily, of all people, will be delighted to hear me admit this—can escape like Capet. Our elusive friend is long gone."

I sighed, not entirely displeased to see him make another successful escape. "I'd wager anything that if I were to wire Davis right now, our indomitable butler would tell me a package of just the right dimensions to match the missing Monet had arrived at Park Lane only last week."

"That's a bet I am *not* willing to take," he said, taking my hand as we dropped, short of breath, onto a little bench far from the picnic grove where our friends, who had not joined the chase, waited for our return. "However, I must inform you that *you* have lost the wager we *did* make. Sebastian has agreed to work with me."

"Oh, heavens!" I said. "I'm beyond disappointed. Not, my dear, because I hate to lose to you, but because there's something painfully tragic about Sebastian taking up an honest occupation."

"He won't be abandoning his other work altogether. On that you may depend. What convinced him in the end were some dubious statements I made implying he might receive immunity from other indiscretions if he helped me on occasion."

"And will he?"

"Possibly," he said.

I sighed. "Well, I suppose it's time I journey to Épernay, to Moët et Chandon, so I might collect your case of champagne. It's a pity they've no special vintage or extravagant batch designed for only the most extraordinary of celebrations. Because I do hope you know, my darling husband, this is the last time I'll lose a bet to you."

"Perhaps you can convince them to pursue such a thing—a special-label vintage. Name it after that blind monk—what was his name?"

"Dom Pérignon, who said drinking champagne is like tasting the stars."

"I'm sure he didn't put it quite so elegantly," he said, slipping his arm around my waist and pulling me closer to him. "But then, I've yet to meet anyone, man or woman, who could call himself your true equal when it comes to turn of phrase or anything else."

"Are you trying to flatter me?" I leaned close to him, so that my lips nearly brushed his.

"Precisely," he said. "I've learned my lesson, Emily. Trying to protect you backfired horrendously and I can hardly breathe when I think of how close I came once again to losing you. If I'd only left you to your own devices, you'd have been safe in Rouen with me."

"And Lucy wouldn't have been found, and George wouldn't have been caught."

"We'd have solved it eventually, and together," he said. "A much better prospect than what in fact transpired. Can you forgive me?"

"I do seem to recall, from the days of our courtship, that you're particularly gifted when it comes to persuasion. I must warn you, however, of the possibility I may have grown immune to some of the maneuvers you've already used on me."

"Then I shall have to search the recesses of my soul for new ways to impress you. If I'm clever enough, will I be able to convince you to trade investigation for a more thorough pursuit of classical knowledge? Perhaps a term at Oxford?"

I laughed. "No, Colin, you'll never dissuade me from wanting to pursue those things at which I excel, investigations included."

"You'll be the death of me, you know," he said.

"Would you have it any other way?" I asked. The only reply he gave was a kiss, deeper and more passionate than any in my memory. It might have been he was avoiding the question, but I preferred to consider it his answer, and that I could live with for all the rest of time.

1. What did you know about the treatment of madness in the nineteenth century before you started to read *Dangerous to Know*?

2. How does insanity affect families? Do they still deal with a sense of shame because of madness?

3. Are we, as a society, more enlightened today when it comes to how we judge individuals with mental disorders?

4. Are there some forms of madness that are more socially acceptable than others? If so, why is this?

5. Is there a touch of madness in everyone?

6. Mrs. Hargreaves's journal entries mark the first time in the series when we see someone else's view of Emily. Did her observations about her daughter-in-law change your view of Emily?

7. Do you believe it's possible to drive someone mad?

8. Who was your favorite character in the book, and why?

9. How is Lady Emily different from other woman of her era? Do you think she was "ahead of her time?" What do you see as her most and least admirable qualities? Take a moment to talk about women and their place in Victorian society.

10. How do women, in the past and today, find ways to be independent in restrictive societies?

11. To what extent do you think Tasha Alexander took artistic liberties with this work? What does it take for a novelist to bring a "real" period to life?

For more reading group suggestions, visit
www.readinggroupgold.com.

A
Reading
Group
Guide

St. Martin's
Griffin

Turn the page for a sneak peek at
Tasha Alexander's new novel

A Crimson Warning

Available November 2011

I was dancing while he burned, but I had no way of knowing that, not then, while spinning on the tips of my toes, my husband's grip firm around my waist as he led me around the ballroom again and again, glistening beads of sweat forming on his forehead. My heart was light, my head full of joy, my only complaint the temperature of the room. Its warmth was oppressive, humid, and thick; the air heavy with the oil of too many perfumes. Looking back, I realize I had not even the beginning of an understanding of real heat, or of the pain of fire with its indiscriminate implacability. How could I? I was in Mayfair at a ball. The man meeting his fiery end might as well have been on the opposite side of the earth.

That evening, my side of the earth was Lady Londonderry's ballroom, one of London's finest, where I stood surrounded by friends and acquaintances, happy and safe, with bubbles of political gossip and society rumors floating around me. The ornately decorated room, with its columns and gilded surfaces, took up nearly the entire first floor, and was rumored to have been modeled after the site of the Congress of Vienna. Lord Londonderry displayed his collection of paintings on the walls. Marble statues, in the Greco-Roman tradition, stood in regularly spaced nooks. The house seemed to pulse as the orchestra began a waltz, my favorite dance.

"Shall we continue?" Colin asked.

I shook my head, out of breath. "It's too hot, even for a waltz."

Colin Hargreaves, a man always capable of anticipating a lady's every need, whim, and—sometimes more importantly—desire, steered me through the crowds in both the main room and its antechamber until we'd reached the landing of the grand staircase. Here, leaning against the gilded railing, I was considerably less cramped. I could almost breathe.

"Better?" Colin asked, removing two champagne flutes from the tray held by a waiter who disappeared with swift precision before we could thank him.

"Much." I lowered my fan—cerise silk to match my dress—and gulped the cool drink.

Colin touched my cheek. "Easy, my dear, or I'll have to carry you home in disgrace."

"The thought of you throwing me over your shoulder is hardly a disincentive." I titled the glass again and drained it, marveling at how handsome my husband was. His neat black jacket was perfectly tailored, his crisp shirt and narrow tie both spotless white, his skin tanned from the summer sun and flushed from dancing.

"I should hope not," he said, his dark eyes full of the sort of heat to which, unlike that caused by extremes of weather, I would not object.

"If anything, it encourages me to overindulge. I may need quite a bit more champagne."

"Champagne or not, I've plans for you when we get home," he said. "Dancing with you always has a profound effect on me." In the early days of our acquaintance, after the death of my first husband, Colin had inquired whether the conventions of mourning helped me manage my grief. I'd told him no, and admitted to keenly missing dancing. He'd taken me in his arms at once, there in my drawing room, and the waltz we shared left me breathless, tingling, and more than a little confused.

All these years later, the memory of that evening never failed to make me tremble with desire. My eyes met his and I felt the delicious anticipation that comes with waiting for a kiss.

The kiss did not come. The pleasant sounds that had surrounded us—the Highland Schottische, laughter, and the rustle of silk skirts—faded to nothing as a voice boomed below us.

"I'll kill you!" The speaker was standing at the bottom of the stairs, talking so loudly no one in the immediate vicinity need strain to decipher every syllable of the conversation. "She's innocent in all this. I will not stand by and see her ruined."

He looked like every other man at the ball, elegant in his evening kit. But the strain on his face—bulging eyes, cherry red splashed across his cheeks—came from anger, not from the exertion of dancing. The gentleman across from him stepped back, raising his hands as if to push away his companion.

"It's not any business of mine," he said. "I was only trying to warn you. To keep you from making an enormous mistake."

"Speak of this to anyone else and you are a dead man. I'll not have Polly's reputation destroyed."

He was already too late to save it.

"Emily!" Ivy Brandon, my dearest childhood friend and quite possibly the sweetest woman in England, tugged at my arm. "Have you heard? Polly Sanders, who's to marry—"

"Shhh, listen," I said and motioned to the gentlemen below.

"Oh. Oh, I say." Ivy's eyes widened and she lifted her hand to her mouth as she watched Thomas Lacey punch the other man square in the jaw. "It appears he already knows."

Colin broke away from us and rushed down the steps, forcing himself between the fighters, ducking to avoid a blow.

"That's enough," he said. "Whatever it is, you're causing more of a scene than it sounds like you want, Lacey. Walk with me and tell me what's going on." They hadn't taken more than five steps when the

Londonderrys' butler approached and pulled my husband aside. Their heads bent together for only an instant as the servant handed Colin an envelope. He bowed to my husband and retreated but not before shooting a disparaging look at his mistress' recently fighting guests.

"Sort this out amongst yourselves in private if you must," Colin said to the gentlemen, folding the note when he'd finished reading. "I've no more time for your antics." He turned on his heel and took the stairs two at a time, reaching Ivy and me in a matter of seconds.

"Urgent business, I'm afraid. There's been a fire in Southwark. Forgive me? I know I can rely on the Brandons to see you home," he said, giving me a quick kiss on the cheek. "I'll meet you there as soon as I can."

One might have thought the ball would fall to pieces after such a scandalous interruption, but this was not the case. The orchestra continued to play, couples turned around the dance floor, and the guests consumed a steady stream of champagne. But Ivy and I had lost our taste for frivolity so we asked her husband to call for the carriage and take us to my house in Park Lane.

At the end of festive evenings, my friends and I often retired to my library, with its tall windows, wide fireplace, and cherry bookcases that went all the way to the ceiling. I displayed my collection of ancient Greek vases here, and felt more sentimental about them than I did any of the other objects in the house. It was a Greek vase owned by my first husband that had sparked my interest in antiquities. As for the room itself, it had been my preferred gathering spot from the moment Colin and I were married. Tonight, however, it felt too hot and close. The night had cooled, but the air inside was still cloying, so we sat in the garden, Ivy and I perched on wrought-iron chairs while her husband, Robert, leaned against a large tree near one of the Japanese lanterns lighting the space around us. Behind him rose a sculpture of Artemis, her graceful arm steady as she pulled back an arrow in her strong bow. An old friend of mine had made the piece, a modern copy of a Roman copy of the long-lost Greek original, fashioned by my favorite ancient sculptor, Praxiteles.

"I still hold out hope for Polly," Ivy said. "Thomas Lacey is a younger son. It's entirely possible his mother will let him go through with the marriage. It's not as if it would make any real difference to the family."

"There is no possibility that Polly Sanders is going to marry any son of Earl Lacey. The countess is far too proud," Robert said. Robert Brandon was a man of principle who had once been a great political hope for the Conservative party. A staunch traditionalist, he had seemed on a fast path to greatness until he was charged with murdering his mentor, a man universally despised throughout Britain. Desperate and abandoned by all his former supporters, he'd summoned me to his cell in Newgate and asked me to help clear his name. I was more than glad to assist. The fact he was with us now was a testament to the success of my subsequent investigation.

I pressed my hands against my temples. "Let me understand. A woman of ill repute steps forward to claim she is Polly Sanders's mother, and that Lord Sanders persuaded his wife to raise the child as her own?"

"It wouldn't be the first time such a thing has happened," Ivy said. "Georgiana, Duchess of Devonshire, raised her husband's illegitimate daughter."

"Ivy." Robert shot her a sharp glare.

"It's true," Ivy said. The beadwork on her gown, made from Nile-green embroidered silk, sparkled as she moved to reach for her husband's hand. "Even if it was a hundred years ago."

"Why are we to believe this woman?" I asked. "What has Lord Sanders to say about the matter?"

"Unfortunately, he's chosen to remain silent on the subject," Robert said. "He left the ball without uttering a word. Which, naturally, leads those around him to assume the veracity of the woman's story."

"She decided to confront him in the Londonderrys' ballroom?" I asked. "She couldn't possibly have thought she'd gain admission."

"She didn't need to. She did a masterful job of causing a scene outside. More effective than if every guest in the house had seen her, I'd say," Robert said. "Far better to let the story make its way through the crowd on its own."

"Our old friend gossip," I said.

"It was hideous," Ivy said. "Half the room knew what had happened before the countess—and they were all breathless waiting to see what she would do. I was standing not three feet from her when she turned on poor Polly. The girl withered in an instant."

"Lord Thomas seems more concerned with defending his fiancée's honor than in throwing her over," I said.

"That will change as soon as his father's through with him," Robert said. "The family will not allow him to marry the daughter of a housemaid."

"I'd imagine not," I said. "Of course, if her mother had been a mistress of higher class, we'd all turn a blind eye, wouldn't we?"

"We would not!" Ivy said.

"No," I said. "You're correct. Because a mistress of higher class would have raised the child herself and everyone would have pretended to believe it to be her husband's, not her lover's. Society prefers a fine, well-bred deception."

"Emily!" Ivy's smooth brow furrowed. "You know perfectly well that sort of thing hardly ever happens."

"I won't argue with you, Ivy. It's too hot."

The sound of crunching gravel announced the approach of my incomparable butler, Davis, who arrived carrying a tray heavy with a large pitcher of cold lemonade.

"Madam?" he asked.

"Please pour for us, Davis," I said. "I'm exhausted and can hardly move. Too much dancing in the heat."

He did as I asked, then bowed and turned to leave, stopping before he'd taken more than half a step. Looking back at me, he raised his eyebrows and his lips quivered ever so slightly.

"Yes?" I asked.

"I left Mr. Hargreaves's cigars inside, madam, as the combination with lemonade would be rather atrocious."

"You're very bad, Davis," I said. "I'll expect an entirely different outcome the next time I call for port rather than lemonade." With another bow, he left us. "He knows Colin doesn't mind when I smoke, but dear Davis refuses to be an accessory to what he views as my ruin."

"A good man, your butler," Robert said.

"I won't take any nonsense from you, sir." I smiled. Robert had long ago given up on trying to influence me. He had come to tenuous terms with his wife's own small rebellions (drinking port with me, for example), so long as she restricted them to private situations. Decorous behavior, however, he required in public.

It was I who had corrupted Ivy, just as I'd corrupted myself. While locked up in mourning after the death of my first husband, I'd undergone an intellectual awakening and taken up the study of Greek. I'd learned to read the ancient language, reveled in the poetry of Homer, and become a respected collector of classical antiquities. As I became more enlightened, I'd also come to despise the restrictions of society, and in the course of rejecting them, had come to discover the simple pleasure one could afford from a glass of port, a drink ordinarily forbidden to ladies. Now, at the prodding of another dear friend, I'd expanded my studies to include Latin, and had convinced Ivy to learn it as well. She might not have been quite so enthusiastic a student as I, but she had a sharp mind and was learning quickly.

The lemonade cooled us and we sank into more relaxed postures as the blue light of dawn reached for the dark sky. I wondered how much longer Colin would be. His work as one of the most trusted and discreet agents of the Crown took him from me at odd times of the day and night, and I had come, after more than a year of marriage, to trust his competence absolutely. His missions might be dangerous, but no one was better suited than he to handle them. When he at last staggered into our garden that night, his evening clothes were tattered, his face black, and the bitter smell of smoke heavy on him.

"Colin!" I cried, jumping out of my seat. He raised a bandaged hand to my cheek, a crooked smile on his face.

"Don't be alarmed, my dear, I'm perfectly fine." He dropped onto a chair and Robert poured a tall glass of the now lukewarm lemonade for him, emptying the pitcher. "But I'm afraid I do come with terrible news. Mr. Michael Dillman is dead, burned to death in his warehouse south of the river." He swallowed hard and ground his teeth.

I hadn't known Mr. Dillman well, but there was no one in London unfamiliar with his stellar reputation. He ran a successful export business and treated the men who worked in his warehouses more decently than was the current custom. He paid them generously and ensured his personal physician was on hand whenever their family members fell ill. Several charities depended on his generosity, and he was a great supporter of the arts. Yet, despite all this and a not insignificant fortune, he wasn't much of a fixture in society. He could be socially awkward, not because he was unkind or disinterested, but because his personality tended to a quiet shyness rather than the buoyant joviality required during the season. I regretted that I had not taken the time to know him better.

"What happened?" I asked.

"Someone chained him to the bars on the office window and set the building on fire. I'm sorry, Robert, to speak of such horrors in front of your wife, but I see no point in disguising the truth. The newsmen were there almost as soon as I was. There will be no hiding from the story."

"He . . . he was to be married next week," Ivy said, her voice thin. "Cordelia showed me her wedding dress not two days ago."

"Cordelia Dalton?" I asked. Ivy nodded. Cordelia was a quiet, thoughtful girl who'd made her debut the previous season. She'd not made much of a splash amongst the fashionable set, but that was likely due to a failing on their part rather than hers. We'd discussed novels when our paths crossed at parties, and she always seemed more interested in reading and sketching than in dancing. I was quite fond of her.

"I'm more than sorry, Ivy," Colin said. "Your friend will need your comfort now."

I did not listen to the rest of the conversation; the words no longer made sense to me. I could not stop imagining the hideous scene, the terror the poor man must have felt when he realized what was happening, the pain he must have endured before succumbing to death.

I shuddered. And remembered that only a few hours earlier, I'd had the audacity to complain about the heat in a ballroom.

6 June 1893
Belgrave Square, London

How quickly things change! I was pleased when Colin asked Robert and me to bring Emily home from the Londonderrys' ball. Not because Colin had been called away for work, but because I was looking forward to quiet time with my dearest friend and discussing all the gossip of the night. Polly Sanders has all my sympathy, and I do wish there was something I could do to secure her happiness. But the moment Colin arrived with his dreadful news, Polly's plight seemed utterly insignificant.

I felt almost paralyzed when he told us Mr. Dillman had been murdered. Emily was equally affected, though she retained her composure better than I. She's more experienced in such matters. But I know she gets little crinkles that creep around her eyes when she's upset, and I saw enough of them tonight to tell me I was not alone in my reaction. I hope I never see enough of this sort of brutality to control my emotional response. To acquire such strength would swallow who I am.

Poor, poor Cordelia. When I think of what she must be feeling I can't help but cry. Robert says it's unbecoming to take on someone else's misery, and I'm certain he's right, yet I can't find a way to stop. I remember the joy that consumed me as I became a wife. Cordelia will never feel that. Even if, years from now, she finds affection somewhere else, how could she ever escape a constant dread that her happiness is about to be ripped away from her?

I suppose it can happen to any of us, at anytime. I feel so fortunate to have escaped a similar fate. My husband languished in prison, but only for a relatively short period of time (although at the time it did not seem so). He wasn't taken from me forever, he was returned to me, and now I've the sweetest daughter on earth. What does one do to deserve such luck?

I'm off to see Emily now. She's persuaded me—much against my will—to accompany her to some dreadful meeting. I never could refuse her anything. I have two hopes: one, that it won't last too long; two, that it is more interesting than Latin. Surely the latter is a certitude.